"Too Good to Be True"

"TOO GOOD TO BE TRUE"

THE LIFE AND WORK OF LESLIE FIEDLER

Mark Royden Winchell

UNIVERSITY OF MISSOURI PRESS COLUMBIA AND LONDON

Library of Congress Cataloging-in-Publication Data

Winchell, Mark Royden, 1948–
    "Too good to be true" : the life and work of Leslie Fiedler / Mark Royden Winchell.
        p. cm.
    Includes bibliographical references and index.
    ISBN 0-8262-1389-8 (alk. paper)
    1. Fiedler, Leslie A. 2. Criticism—United States—History—20th century.   3. Authors,
American—20th century—Biography.   4. Critics—United States—Biography. I. Title.
PS3556.I34 Z944 2002
810.9—dc21
[B]   2002024564

♾™This paper meets the requirements of the
American National Standard for Permanence of Paper
for Printed Library Materials, Z39.48, 1984.

Designer: Stephanie Foley
Typesetter: Bookcomp, Inc.
Printer and binder: Thomson-Shore, Inc.
Typefaces: Gill Sans and Granjon

Frontispiece: Leslie in Kyoto, Japan, in the late 1980s

FOR MATTHEW ROYDEN WINCHELL

CONTENTS

THIS BOOK is written in response to the conundrum suggested by the epigraphs with which it begins. The contributions of Leslie Fiedler should command considerable space in any objective history of American criticism during the second half of the twentieth century. In a sense, Fiedler has had four overlapping careers. He first came to prominence as one of the premier Jewish intellectuals of the postwar era—writing on literature, culture, and politics in such magazines as *Partisan Review* and *Commentary*. At approximately the same time, he was helping to lead the attack that myth criticism was mounting on the hegemony of the New Criticism (often, as it turns out, in the presumed house journals of the New Critics themselves). Although Northrop Frye has constructed a more comprehensive *system* of myth criticism, Fiedler has made more practical use of this approach in judging particular texts and in explaining the importance of song and story in human experience. Had he stopped writing entirely in 1960, Fiedler would still be remembered as an important cultural critic of the fifties.

With his brash and groundbreaking magnum opus, *Love and Death in the American Novel* (1960, rev. 1966), Fiedler established himself as a revolutionary interpreter of our native literary tradition. Subsequent critics of American literature have either had to adopt or attack his positions (sometimes doing both at the same time). Simply to ignore them has been nearly impossible. In this third (and most significant) of his careers, Fiedler changed the terms in which we discuss the American novel to a greater extent than anyone writing before or since.

Not content with reinterpreting the past and analyzing the present, Fiedler has tried to chart the future of our culture. He was one of the first critics to proclaim the death of modernism and to suggest some of the directions that literature might take in its aftermath. (The *Oxford English Dictionary* credits him with being the first individual to apply the term *postmodernism* to literature.) This fact alone was enough to earn him the enmity of many who had built their careers on the assumption that modernism would last forever or at least outlive them.

Although his admirers have always appreciated the breadth of Fiedler's achievement, the academic clerisy has frequently seen him as a gadfly and dilettante. His lack of solemnity and his wild flights of imagination have made him seem like an amateur among professionals (a charge to which he gladly pleads "guilty"). No one who enjoys himself that much could possibly be taken seriously. To compound matters, he is one of the favorite critics of young people and non-English majors. Also, unlike more conventional revolutionaries, he has managed to remain disreputable, even as his once controversial views have become received wisdom. Like Huck, returned to the raft from the fog, he often seems too good to be true.

I first became acquainted with Fiedler's achievement in an undergraduate course in literary criticism, which I took in the spring of 1970. Then, in 1985, I published a brief introduction to his writing in Twayne's United States Authors Series. It became apparent to me at the time that a much fuller treatment of his life and work was needed. The present volume is based on extensive interviews and other research conducted well after my earlier book went out of print. The primary connection between the two studies is my abiding interest in Leslie Fiedler as an influential and provocative critic, who has made a profound difference in American literary studies.

As with any prolific writer, Fiedler's performance has been uneven. I have not sought to write a hagiography. Nevertheless, the opportunity to return to his work is a pleasure for all who enjoy the life of the mind. Fiedler, even when he seems to be in the wrong, is more engaging than most critics when they seem to be in the right. Perhaps because he is someone to whom literature has actually happened, readers of Fiedler are particularly curious to know something about the man behind the words. In thinking of Leslie Fiedler, I am reminded of Holden Caulfield's assertion: "What really knocks me out is a book that, when you're all done reading it, you wish the author who wrote it was a terrific friend of yours and you could call him up whenever you felt like it." Fiedler is one of the few academics who has that kind of effect on readers. In lieu of his phone number, I offer this account of his remarkable life.

ACKNOWLEDGMENTS

THIS BOOK would not have been possible without the assistance of many generous people. Leslie Fiedler's secretary, Joyce Troy, provided many helpful documents and consented to a personal interview. In addition to granting an interview, Bruce Jackson and Diane Christian also supplied several photographs that are used with permission and gratitude. James M. Cox read and commented on this book in manuscript, and William Empson's biographer, John Haffenden, supplied valuable information concerning Empson's life. David Ritter devoted many hours to proofreading the text, and he and Cari Carter assisted in preparing the index. As always, I received encouragement and support from my wife, Donna, and my sons, Jonathan and Matthew.

Thanks are also due to University of Missouri Press director Beverly Jarrett and her staff. Beverly believed in this project when it was no more than a proposal and saw it through to fruition. The book is also better for the perceptive suggestions and infinite patience of copy editor Sara Davis. Among university presses, Missouri is fast becoming the publisher of record for politically incorrect scholars.

Grateful acknowledgment is also made to the following for permission to quote from protected material: Valerie Eliot for portions of a letter from T. S. Eliot to Leslie Fiedler; Helen Ransom Forman for portions of John Crowe Ransom's correspondence; Jacobus Empson for portions of Sir William Empson's correspondence; the Richard Nixon Library and Birthplace for portions of a letter from Richard Nixon to Leslie Fiedler; and *Partisan Review* for portions of William Phillips's correspondence.

My largest debt is to Leslie and Sally Fiedler, who sat for interviews, provided access to their personal archives (including priceless photographs damaged in a catastrophic house fire), and granted permission to quote from both published and unpublished material far beyond the accepted bounds of fair use. Although Leslie Fiedler placed no restrictions on what I had to say or how I said it, I hope that his influence can be detected in the following pages.

"Too Good to Be True"

It's too good for true, Honey.
... It's too good for true.

—NIGGER JIM UPON HUCK'S
RETURN TO THE RAFT

The typical pattern with one
of my books is that when it
comes out everybody abuses it.
Ten years later they're still
abusing it, but they've begun to
steal ideas from it. Twenty years
go by, and they decide it's a
classic, although nobody's ever
said anything good about it.

—LESLIE FIEDLER
TO DAVID GATES, 1984

PART ONE

FLIGHT FROM THE EAST (1917–1955)

CHAPTER ONE

Newark Jew

LEIB ROSENSTRAUCH was born some time around the middle of the nineteenth century. The region of his birth, traditionally known as Galizia, has been claimed at various times by Russia, Poland, the Ukraine, and the Austro-Hungarian Empire. Although apprenticed to a cabinetmaker at age thirteen, Leib had other aspirations in life. He soon ran away and wandered through Europe, finally arriving in Hamburg, Germany. There, he earned enough money to finance passage to America. With no formal schooling, Leib (who had now anglicized his name to Leon) lived as a manual laborer in the New World. Teaching himself to read and write Russian, Yiddish, German, and English, he lived a secret life of the mind. But it was the sweat of his body that put bread on Rosenstrauch's table.

After working all over the East, Leon finally settled as a leather worker in Newark, New Jersey. As times got worse, he operated as a secret union organizer in an industry that had always resisted the labor movement. (He had long since abandoned his Jewish faith for revolutionary socialism.) Seeking to curry favor with the bosses, a supposed friend named Smitty turned Leon in and cost him his job. Some years later, Leon approached his daughter Matilda: "Tildy, I want you should take me some place." (Despite his many accomplishments, Rosenstrauch never learned how to drive a car.) As they neared their destination, Matilda said, "We're driving in the direction of the house that Smitty lives in." "Yes," Leon replied, "we're going to see Smitty. He's having bad luck, and I know of a job for him." Incredulous, his daughter reminded Leon that Smitty had gotten him fired. "I know," said Leon, "but everybody is human."[1]

Incredibly strong and self-assured, Leon was nevertheless dominated by his four-feet-eleven-inch wife, Perl. Unlike her husband, Perl could neither read

---

1. Leslie Fiedler, interview with Bruce Jackson, Apr. 7, 1989. Unless otherwise indicated, information in this chapter comes from this interview. (All interviews cited took place in Buffalo, New York.)

nor write. (When she had raised her family, she actually enrolled in school but was sent home after a week as a disruptive influence.) At night, she would listen to Leon read the Yiddish folktales later collected by Isaac Bashevis Singer or provide his own interpretations of English and American literature. (In Leon's rendering of *The Merchant of Venice,* Shylock was a sober-sided *Litvak,* who took advantage of the more mystical Galizianers.) In the typical pattern of Jewish assimilation, Leon Rosenstrauch should have had a son through whom he could have vicariously lived his own frustrated dreams of a literary and intellectual existence. Instead, his one son, Charlie, was a philistine, who dreamed of getting rich. Leon had to skip a generation and vest his hopes and ambitions in a talented grandson. The boy was born to Leon's daughter Lillian (originally Leah) and her husband Jack (originally Jacob) Fiedler on March 8, 1917. Although his Hebrew name was Eliezar Aaron, his birth certificate carries the more Anglo-Saxon–sounding name of Leslie.

All his life, Leslie Fiedler has taken a kind of perverse pride in the fact that he was born in the year of the Russian Revolution—the beginning of a social experiment that he has now outlived. On both sides, he is descended from poor Jews who were completely unsuccessful in Europe. (His paternal great-grandfather was a herring peddler who became the first of the Fiedlers to emigrate to America.) These people had no love for the czar and generally saw Communism as a means of social and economic salvation. The Soviet Union might be a world away, but it came to symbolize a glorious future. The only vision that could have competed with such millennialism was the all-American dream of success, first articulated in Franklin's *Autobiography* and later mythologized in the works of Horatio Alger. For Leslie Fiedler and most of his friends, however, the petty bourgeois aspirations of a Ragged Dick seemed neither possible nor desirable. No one Leslie knew subscribed to such a dream—except for his father, Jack.

Strictly speaking, Jack Fiedler harbored no personal illusions about rising in American society. He taught himself pharmacy (a profession he came to loathe) and worked hard all his life to support his family (a second son, Harold, was born in 1919). Nevertheless, he believed in the American system and hoped that one of his sons would enjoy the worldly success that had been denied him, perhaps even gaining admission to West Point. Jack was a fervent anti-Communist with strong Puritan tendencies. He was constantly writing letters to the newspapers decrying the corruption of American youth and castigating the long-haired men and short-haired women who confused liberty with license.

Despite his Rotarian social values, Jack shared the Jewish reverence for literature and philosophy. He read Schopenhauer and Nietzsche and composed poetry in his spare time. He also wrote lyrics for popular songs. He naively sent one, called "Cross Words," off to a music company, only to see it recorded without his receiving attribution or royalties. As his eyesight worsened over the years, Jack needed to read with a magnifying glass in addition to his spectacles. He would read the newspaper from beginning to end, then quiz his sons about the news of the day. A militant atheist, Jack was constantly quoting Bob Ingersoll and Tom Paine. Although Leslie attained the sort of intellectual success his father would have liked to have had, nothing he ever did was good enough to please Jack Fiedler. "You are a constant series of shocks and surprises," Jack would say, his tone making it clear that they were not pleasurable shocks and surprises.

Jack Fiedler grew up in Orange Valley, New Jersey, a tiny town with virtually no Jewish population, where his own father worked in a hat factory. For the first ten years of his life, Jack was known to all his friends as "Sheeny." Although this designation began in malice, it soon became nothing more than the boy's accepted nickname. As an adult, he was a thoroughly assimilated American with no connection to Jewish culture. Often he could be heard shouting, at the top of his voice: "One thing I can't stand about Jews is that they talk *so* damn loud."

Just two generations earlier, Jack's grandfather, the former herring peddler, had been just as totally unassimilated. Throughout his long life, he spoke only Yiddish. Leslie, who was eight or nine when the old man died, remembers his blue, blue eyes and white, white beard. (Many years later, when he was giving a lecture in Florida, a cousin of his father's came up to Leslie and said, "You look just like Grandpa.") His great-grandfather's funeral was one of the most traumatic experiences of Leslie's childhood. A little graveside sermon was delivered by a friend. At one point, all the women who were around the grave began screaming and weeping. The eulogist had said, "This man suffered the worst indignity a human being could suffer. He saw his children die before him. And this is because, in America, those children abandoned their faith."

Jack Fiedler and Lil Rosenstrauch had fallen in love at age fifteen and remained so for the rest of Jack's life. Their infatuation with each other was so total that they had little affection left over for their children. An impatient woman with no talent for mothering, Lil would beat Leslie, her incorrigible child, and seize every opportunity to shift responsibility for his care to others. The first physical affection Leslie ever experienced came from a black girl who was hired to take care of him when he was little more than a year old. His family was so horrified by his caressing and kissing her that the girl was promptly fired.

During Leslie's childhood, Leon and Perl Rosenstrauch were more like parents to Leslie than were his own father and mother. Perl, who rarely had a kind word to say about another person, doted on her grandson—at least after he was out of infancy. Believing Leslie to be unattractive as a baby, Perl had taken him out strolling with the cover over his carriage. In the old country, her family had been so vain that one relative, who was an actor, was said to have thrown himself out a second-story window at his thirtieth birthday party rather than face the inevitable ravages of age.

In contrast to the irascible Jack Fiedler, Leon Rosenstrauch was an infinitely kind and patient male role model. Before Leslie learned to read, he heard fairy tales from his grandfather. They all seemed to begin with the line: "Once there was a young man who got on a white horse and rode out into the world." Many years later, Leslie observed that his grandfather resembled the protagonist of such stories less than he did a peasant, whose youthful companions would jump on a local farmer's horse and ride into nearby orchards to steal fruit. Leon had a mark on his foot, which he claimed came from a horse's hoof, although Leslie believed that the foot was probably just shaped that way. On Jewish high holy days, Leon Rosenstrauch would take his grandson to some storefront synagogue and say, "Not that I believe, but so you should remember."

Although he has never been a member of any Jewish congregation or a particularly observant practitioner of his religion, Leslie Fiedler *has* always remembered. Perhaps for that reason, some of the most traditional Jews continue to count him as one of their own. In the early 1970s, he was summoned to the Crown Heights section of Brooklyn for an audience with Rabbi Menachem Mendel Schneerson, the undisputed leader of the Lubavitch Hasidim, one of the most orthodox and influential forces in world Jewry. The seventh in a line of grand rabbis, or rebbes, of the Lubavitch, Schneerson taught his followers (who numbered 200,000 at the time of his death in 1994) that they could hasten the arrival of the Messiah if they practiced the traditions laid out in the Hebrew Bible. Many of the faithful believed the rebbe himself to be the long-awaited savior and hoped that he would declare himself such before he died.

Leslie remembers that it was 2:00 A.M. before he was finally ushered into Schneerson's presence. The rebbe seemed never to sleep and was constantly meeting with people. Because he was concerned about the plight of America's youth, particularly its Jewish youth, he wanted to speak with the Jewish professor who was said to have a great influence on America's young. When he asked Leslie his name, his visitor replied, "Leslie Fiedler." "No, your real name," Schneerson insisted. Looking into piercing blue eyes that reminded him of his great-grandfather's, Leslie responded, "Eliezar Ben-Leah" (that is, Eliezar, son of Leah). The rebbe nodded his approval and promised to ask a blessing for him under that name when he next talked to his predecessor, who had been dead for twenty years. "The house is burning, Eliezar," he said. "We must save the children."[2]

---

2. Leslie Fiedler, interview with author, June 22, 1997.

I

Although Leslie was born in Newark, the family soon moved to East Orange, New Jersey, where Jack's pharmacy was located. There Leslie began his formal education in a school that consisted almost entirely of Gentile teachers and students. He remembers attending weekly school chapel services and being forced to recite the Lord's Prayer at the beginning of each day. Although these practices made him uncomfortable, Leslie realized that self-preservation required outward compliance, even as he muttered obscenities under his breath. It wasn't until one day in the school yard, when "all hell broke loose," that he and the other children fully realized how much of a stranger he was in their midst. Nearly seventy years later he recalled the incident with particular vividness:

> During recess and after class, when my fellow students gathered together to choose up sides for a game, more often than not they would end with Protestants on one side and Catholics on the other (for me it was a baffling distinction without a difference), then proceed to pummel each other in a mock Holy War. On this occasion, however, for reasons I still don't understand, they noticed me slinking off alone, as I customarily did; and remembering that I was a Jew, which is to say, the legendary enemy of both, joined together to chase me all the way home screaming, "You killed our Christ."

It was at that moment, Leslie observed, that the Ecumenical Movement was born.[3]

The family soon moved back to the south side of Newark, where few white Anglo-Saxons could be found. In fact, throughout childhood and adolescence, Leslie was convinced that his part of the world was populated by only two races—blacks and Jews. Jack Fiedler now ran a drugstore across the street from a General Electric factory, where almost all the employees were black. These men were generally the store's best customers. On payday, they would come in and buy large boxes of candy for their wives, hair straighteners, skin bleach, and little charms to hang around their necks for "the misery." They were the first to be fired when the depression came.

Although none of his best friends was black, Leslie came into daily contact with African Americans. When his family was prosperous enough, they employed part-time domestic help, which meant Negro maids. One such person, who came to work for the Fiedlers during Leslie's adolescence, was an aging woman named Hattie. An ardent disciple of the cult leader Father Divine, she

---

3. Leslie Fiedler, *Fiedler on the Roof: Essays on Literature and Jewish Identity,* 161. Subsequent references will be cited parenthetically in the text as *FOR.*

"would dance abandonedly in one corner of the kitchen when the spirit moved her or preach at us in the name of peace." Hattie enjoyed camping the role of the plantation darky, calling Leslie's mother "Miz Lillie," while clowning and grimacing for all she was worth. While the rest of the family roared with laughter, the earnest young Leslie left the house "equally furious with Hattie for her play-acting and my own family for lapping it up."[4]

While he was growing up, Leslie's closest bond with a black man came when he worked in a shoe store at the age of thirteen or fourteen. More than a little frightened by the "cynicism and worldliness of the other boys (some of whom were as old as sixteen!), much less the salesmen and the hose girls," he began to eat his sack lunch with a colored porter, "while all the others were off at cafeterias or lunch counters." Later, from his perspective as a literary critic, Leslie saw this man as his own approximation of Sam Fathers or Nigger Jim. As he recalls, the porter "would speak to me gravely and without condescension about life—mostly sex, of course, which he thought the salesmen made too much of in their boastful anecdotes and I was overimpressed with in my callow innocence" (*CE*, 1:463). After they finished eating, Leslie "would retouch the crude sketch of a gigantic, naked woman that someone had roughed out on one of the cellar walls." The porter would lean back and criticize his efforts. "Before we went upstairs to work again, he would help me push a pile of empty hose boxes in front of our private mural" (*CE*, 1:464).

One of Leslie's indelible memories of childhood is of walking to high school through a poor black neighborhood. He particularly recalls the disconcerting feeling that he was in hostile territory and that his own belief in racial equality did not render him safe from attack. One day when walking with his mother through this run-down neighborhood, he remembers her pointing to one of the drab, alien houses from which he had shrunk day after day and saying, "I was born there" (*CE*, 1:470). Many years later, Leslie attended an urban affairs conference in Newark, at which he and the black poet Leroi Jones were the only persons who had been born in the town; both performed with their mothers in the audience.

A superhighway now runs through the site of Leslie's old home in Newark. He used to go back and see it because his mother insisted on living in or near Newark until the last few years of her life. When she moved across the city line to Irvington, New Jersey, she could still look back at the wreck of Springfield Avenue, which was burned and pillaged by blacks during riots in the 1960s. "It's never really been repaired," Leslie recalls. "It's just a disaster area, forever. It looks a little like London just after the war."

---

4. Leslie Fiedler, *The Collected Essays of Leslie Fiedler,* 1:465. Subsequent references to both volumes will be cited parenthetically in the text as *CE*.

Leslie has always regarded Newark as the place where he was educated. The influence of the public schools, however, was decidedly mixed; the main thing they did for him was to "educate" him out of his mother tongue. He was taught to speak an artificial standard English, rather than the street language with which he grew up. (The drama of cultural assimilation was a common feature in the lives of urban Jews of his generation.) Although 90 to 95 percent of the students in the schools he attended were Jewish, he did not have a single Jewish teacher prior to high school. The Gentile teachers who were shipped in from the suburbs would keep him after school and teach him how to pronounce certain vowels and get rid of ethnic cadences in his speech. The most severe brainwashing came from the teacher who prepared him to give the eighth-grade commencement address. Because Leslie was the brightest boy in school, he ended up keeping his teachers' grade books for them and helping them administer intelligence tests. By early adolescence, he realized that he was smarter than they were. "Most of them were dumb beyond belief," he later recalled, "besides being goyish beyond belief."

Most of what Leslie learned came from his own independent reading. Since the turn of the century, the Newark public library had been one of the world's best. He recalls going to that library at age sixteen and seeing a long line of books with beautiful red covers on them, which turned out to be a translation of Proust's *Remembrance of Things Past.* When he couldn't make it to the main library, he would go to the branch library in his neighborhood, where he claims to have learned about the world and its relation to books. There, all the books he wanted to read were kept in what was called "the locked room." At age fifteen, he had a battle with the librarian over permission to read Joyce's *A Portrait of the Artist as a Young Man,* which was considered a "locked room" book. Nearly seven decades later, Leslie observed that it was a nice way to come to high literature, as something forbidden. After awhile, however, the librarian let him read anything he wanted. "She was a monstrous woman, with whom I had a strange kind of love-hate relationship," he recalls. In addition to locking away anything that might be too challenging, "she used to get all the photography magazines and find the nude pictures and stamp them three times—left tit, right tit, and crotch—with the library date stamp."

The first book that Leslie ever purchased with his own money was Harriet Beecher Stowe's *Uncle Tom's Cabin.* He was deeply moved and wept shamelessly over this sentimental tearjerker. His subsequent literary education taught him to be embarrassed by this unsophisticated reaction to fiction. In an age when high modernism reigned supreme, irony, paradox, and what Leslie himself would come to call "tragic ambivalence" were the most revered values in literature. Although Stowe's novel had always had its defenders among professional literary folk, it was more often dismissed as noble propaganda. The fact that it was probably the best-known and best-loved American novel ever written simply seemed to confirm its inadequacy as high art. As a young boy, however, Leslie Fiedler had not developed elitist tastes. At the age of ten, he could recite Rudyard Kipling's "Gunga Din" and Robert Service's "The Shooting of Dan McGraw" by heart. The word in his family was, "He may be ugly, but put him on a table and he'll say a poem."

II

As mesmerized as he may have been by imaginative literature, Leslie got his earliest knowledge of the world through real-life experience. Like so many of his fellow Jewish intellectuals, who would later constitute a major force in twentieth-century American criticism, Leslie earned his first paychecks doing nonintellectual work. His Saturdays at the shoe store his uncle managed would begin at eight in the morning and last until he and his fellow workers had cleaned the place at eleven or eleven thirty at night.[5] With the passage of the National Recovery Act, his salary was raised from two dollars to two dollars and fifty cents a day. On occasion he would be sent to New York to pick up or deliver merchandise. He remembers once going down Fifth Avenue, when the Empire State Building was being completed, carrying twenty-four boxes of hosiery. A strong wind came down and scattered the lingerie all over Fifth Avenue. It was one of the great catastrophes of his young life.

At the shoe store, Leslie got his first sexual education—from a man who surreptitiously (and illegally) sold condoms, while entertaining his coworkers with long, thrilling, and largely apocryphal stories about his own sexual exploits. It was also at the shoe store that Leslie first learned to drink. (In part, this was another act of rebellion against Jack Fiedler, who was himself a teetotaler and the son of a teetotaler.) At a Christmas party when he was fifteen, everyone seemed to want to pour the kid one more shot. As a consequence, he experienced the pleasures of intoxication and the pains of the morning after. Later, one of his coworkers, an aspiring songwriter named Eddie Seiler, persuaded Leslie to go with him to little local nightclubs. (Prior to his death, which occurred before the age of forty, Seiler wrote two hit songs, "Red Roses for a Blue Lady" and "I Don't Want to Set the World on Fire.") On one occasion, Leslie nearly lost his job for trying to organize the shoe salesmen. Eventually, the owner of the company summoned him to the main office in New York and admonished him for getting mixed up in politics. "Play ball with us," he said, "and we'll take care of you. We'll help you through college."

---

5. For Fiedler's recollections about the shoe store, see Bruce Jackson's interview of Aug. 20, 1989.

From a literary standpoint, the greatest advantage of Leslie's experience in the shoe store was the introduction it afforded him to the infinite variety of human nature. The most fascinating personality he encountered there was Moie Backer, an eccentric salesman and bizarre human being, who shows up as the character Abie Peckelis in Leslie's story "Nobody Ever Died from It" (1956). Backer used to astound his fellow workers by shouting at the top of his voice the foulest obscenities to the women who were his customers. He would get away with this outrageous behavior because no one could really believe what he was doing. He would take a brush for cleaning suede and say, "Lady, this is also good for the hair around the hole." Another of his favorite routines was to take a shoe, put it in a stretcher, and scream at the top of his voice: "Take it out, Daddy, it hurts." Then, he would pull the stretcher out and let the shoe relax. "Put it back in, Daddy," he would say. "I love it." Leslie's uncle believed that Backer was such a good salesman because his extreme homosexuality (his gay pseudonym was "Florence") gave him a special insight into female psychology. "But he was a tragic figure, too," Leslie recalls. "He would walk out and say as he was going home, 'Four walls. Diamonds isn't everything,' returning to an obviously lonely life. His sister was a prostitute. His brother was a small-time gangster."

In "Nobody Ever Died from It," the narrator, Hyman Brandler, gives us a grossly vivid physical image of Backer's alter ego:

> I begin always by describing Peckelis: the identical oily ridges of his marcelled hair, and sullen droop of his fat lips, the eyelids as heavy as if hewn in stone. I think of his face in profile—despite the blueness of his beard, the face of a wicked queen in an Assyrian bas-relief; a face ravaged by passions it does not understand—and set anomalously on the flabby body in the draped jacket, the peg-top pants. It is an ugly body, uglier because borne with such outrageous assurance of its allure: the swollen female breasts visible beneath the sag of the coat from the padded shoulders, the movement of the hips a parody, savage and tender, of womanly charm.[6]

One afternoon, the hose girls give Peckelis a gift-wrapped package, containing two round, red Christmas tree ornaments attached to a limp hot dog.

Throughout the story, the flamingly effeminate Peckelis (as in peckerless?) takes young Brandler into his confidence, assuming that the boy's intellectual pretensions make him more sensitive and sympathetic than the ordinary working stiffs at the shoe store have proved to be. And yet, at the end of an abbreviated and booze-soaked Christmas Eve, Brandler betrays Abie by joining in laughter at his friend's expense. (The catalyst is the obvious delight that

---

6. Leslie Fiedler, *Nude Croquet: The Stories of Leslie A. Fiedler,* 156–57. Subsequent references will be cited parenthetically in the text as *NC.*

Abie shows when being goosed by a policeman's nightstick.) Although the youthful epiphany recollected from the perspective of one's mature years is a familiar theme in literature, Hyman Brandler fails to experience such an epiphany when young, and in his "mature" years compounds his betrayal of Abie by telling his story time and again, whenever there is a lull at a party. Because he makes Brandler a successful storyteller but a failed novelist, Leslie may be suggesting that human understanding is the quality that separates the true artist from the mere raconteur. As if to emphasize Brandler's continuing lack of this quality, the story ends with the narrator remembering (in present tense) the ridiculous and accusing figure of Peckelis: "I smile smugly to myself at the nuttiness of Abie Peckelis—I who at fourteen believe I have never betrayed anything, and know that I never will" (581).

Many years later, Peckelis would make a return appearance in "What Used to Be Called Dead," a story that Leslie published in the winter 1990 issue of the *Kenyon Review*. In this highly surrealistic tale, a dying old man dreams of being holed up in a cave underneath a burning Newark with a bunch of shoe salesmen with whom he used to work. There, Abie Peckelis undresses a display mannequin he has retrieved from the store and stands "before her blank nakedness, his fat hands slapping his plump thighs, and his marcelled head thrown back as if he bellowed in pleasure."[7] Shortly after writing this story, Leslie observed: "I've lived in many places, some of them for a long time. . . . But in my deepest imagination, I'm always in Newark."

III

Although it was his first love and has proved to be the dominant passion of his life, there was a time when Leslie Fiedler found literature to be of less immediate importance than politics. Viewed in purely personal terms, one could interpret his adolescent commitment to Stalinism as a rebellion against his father's social conservatism and a kind of homage to the example of his maternal grandfather. (For all their apparent differences, when Jack Fiedler and Leon Rosenstrauch entered the voting booth, they both habitually pulled the Democratic lever.) Even if his family situation had been different, Leslie probably still would have gravitated toward politics. For Jewish literary intellectuals of his generation and a generation earlier, some form of socialism seemed almost a substitute for religion. For such people, the impending revolution was as much a palpable reality as the Second Coming of Christ for fundamentalist Christians.

---

7. Leslie Fiedler, *A New Fiedler Reader,* 586. Subsequent references will be cited parenthetically in the text as *NFR*.

At South Side High School in Newark, there was a group of fifteen to twenty-five students who simultaneously discovered the revolution and avant-garde literature in the early 1930s. Leslie recalls that, at age thirteen, he read his first copy of *transition* and met his first Communist. At fourteen, he was committed to both modernism and socialism. (Although some hardcore ideologues saw literature as a frivolous pursuit when people were standing in breadlines, Leslie never doubted that books were of central importance to life.) He proudly recalls his entire geometry class being put on two weeks' detention because they were passing under their desks e. e. cummings's translation of Louis Aragon's *The Red Front*.

Leslie's own earliest encounters with the proletariat came after he started working Saturdays in the shoe store. He would eat his lunch across the street in Military Park, where an assortment of hobos and bums could always be found. He acquired a knowledge of the world and considerable "street smarts" from listening to the stories they would tell. He would listen in fascination and disgust when bums, far gone in syphilitic decay, told him about pieces of their scalps falling out when they combed their hair in the morning. It was in Military Park that someone first made a homosexual pass at him. The most literate of the hobos was a fellow named Frenchie, who would sit and read aloud chapter after chapter from Jack London's *The Iron Heel* to the rest of the bums in the park.

Dominated by a huge statue called the *Wars of America,* Military Park was the place where everyone from itinerant preachers to Communist orators would turn up to speak their minds. It was here that Leslie developed his street-corner speaking style. At this time, his audiences were mostly white. Later, however, he would periodically flee his graduate studies at the University of Wisconsin for the more cosmopolitan surroundings of Chicago. There, he spoke in Washington Park to all-black audiences. He would say something, and they would respond, "Now you're preachin', brother." He would say something else, and they would shout, "Go right on preachin'."

As fate would have it, his street preachin' almost got Leslie arrested at age sixteen. It was the summer of 1933 and a hot night on Bergen Street in Newark. A group of adolescents were out ostensibly looking for girls, but willing to settle for whatever relief from boredom they could find. What they found were street-corner orators "on their rickety little wooden stands, with the required American flag drooping beside them in the no-breeze of a Newark June."[8] Pausing beside a soapbox where a speaker from the Socialist Labor Party was giving a largely inaudible speech to a handful of bystanders, Leslie and his

8. Leslie Fiedler, *Being Busted,* 14. Subsequent references will be cited parenthetically in the text as *BB.*

companions began to jeer and heckle. " 'Louder and funnier,' we yelled. . . . 'Can't hear a word you're saying.' " More incensed with these young toughs than with the capitalist system he was denouncing, the speaker suggested that his tormentors get the hell out and start a street meeting of their own. This, they promptly did.

Using a ukelele and their own youthful enthusiasm to draw a crowd, they found the situation to be somehow more real, or at least more alive, than high school debates, "with evidence cards and speech teachers as judges" (*BB,* 15). Leslie was intoxicated by the effect of his presence on the crowd. As he tells it:

> I kept watching all those people who didn't even know my name over-flowing the sidewalk in a growing circle whose center I defined; after a while, they were hunched together, shoulder to shoulder and belly to back, out into the roadway, blocking traffic as baffled drivers tooted their horns and leaned out of open car windows to curse us. And then I stepped down, hearing the crowd, silent until I was through and for a second or two after, really let go: roaring half in approval, half in mockery, glad and embarrassed at the same time, because there was someone dumb enough, young enough, loud enough to stand up and cheer and yell for them. (*BB,* 16)

Just as the next speaker was warming up, someone in the crowd began waving a gun. It was an off-duty Irish cop on his way to a local saloon. Apparently feeling intimidated at the sight of people boisterously exercising their First Amendment rights, he hauled the speaker down from the podium in midsentence. Although the revolutionary youth were frightened enough by this plain-clothes buffoon, the matrons in the crowd verbally abused him as a drunkard and a thug. Leslie theorized that they were able to hate police so wholeheartedly because their own sons were more likely to be outlaws than cops. In fact, the neighborhood hero was a Jewish gangster named Longie Zwillman, who rose all the way to number fourteen on the FBI's Most Wanted List, while making sure that his mother wore mink. Those local youth who were not in the mob were apt to be radicals, who were also in constant trouble with the law. During political riots, their mothers would shove pepper up the nostrils of the police horses.

That long-ago night on Bergen Street, the cop who broke up Leslie's political meeting turned out to be drunk "enough to think he was in some movie about the Royal Mounties. . . . And so waving his gun in ever wider and more wobbly circles, he yelled, 'Stand back, I'm a police officer and I always get my man' " (*BB,* 17). Arguments over constitutional rights quickly dissipated when sirens were heard and a long black touring car appeared, filled with *uniformed* cops packing Thompson submachine guns. Just as Leslie was preparing to heap contempt on the disappearing crowd, he discovered that he was at the far end of a dark alley he didn't remember entering, "my heart pounding and my breath coming short as I stared down at a lidless garbage can and listened to my own voice saying, incredulously, 'You ran, you schmuck. Goddam it, you *ran*'" (*BB,* 17).

For someone who read Thoreau at twelve and Marx at thirteen, running from the forces of oppression seemed the ultimate act of bad faith. What made the situation even more ironic was the fact that Leslie had just finished haranguing the crowd. Had he spoken longer or the off-duty cop arrived sooner, Leslie would have been the one waltzed off to jail. (The actual martyr, Milton Ritz, introduced Leslie to the Communist Party and later ended up a successful stockbroker in Dallas.) It is true that Thoreau let his Aunt Maria bail him out of the slammer, but at least he had spent his symbolic night in jail. Leslie got his friend sprung by ducking into a drugstore near the courthouse and calling the Republican county committeeman from his district, a real estate lawyer who enjoyed beating Leslie at checkers. He and the judge (also a Republican) worked out a deal to give the young revolutionaries a stern reprimand but no sentence. When the judge asked the arresting officer what the boys had actually been talking about, he replied, "About Roosevelt, about the President." "'And were they for him or against him?' the judge asked. And this jerk scratches his head and says, 'I don't know, the words were too big'" (*BB,* 19).

From that point on, Leslie found his encounters with the law to be closer to slapstick comedy than to melodrama, more reminiscent of Groucho Marx than of Karl. In exasperation, he asks, "[H]ow can a man—at sixteen or twenty or forty or fifty or whatever—come on like Thoreau or Dreyfus, Joe Hill or Sacco and Vanzetti or Tom Mooney, when the cops fate has chosen for him are always straight out of some Keystone Comedy? . . . I have continued to feel that I am doomed to be robbed always of the final solace of finding my suffering noble, since what falls on my shoulders is likely to be a rubber truncheon, what hits me in the face a custard pie" (*BB,* 18).

IV

Throughout history writers have immortalized young men of seemingly infinite promise who died before their prime. Milton had Edward King; Dryden, John Oldham; Tennyson, Arthur Hallam. For Leslie Fiedler, the golden friend of his youth was Alfred Eisner. A Newark boy who shared Leslie's background and politics, Al Eisner nevertheless seemed to live a charmed life that set him apart from his contemporaries. He was an Eagle Scout and a great fisherman. At age sixteen, he had such a facility for mocking any writing style that he was publishing in *Field and Stream* and a church journal called *Our Weekly Messenger.* He was also the first of the Newark boys to make it to Europe. He somehow managed to get into the seaman's union and work his way to France. As Leslie recalls, "he was the guy who did everything we all dreamed of doing first."[9]

While most of Leslie's crowd ended up at Dana College in Newark or CCNY or one of the branches of NYU, Al Eisner started at the University of Wisconsin and later transferred to Harvard. Like other members of the Young Communist League at Harvard, Al took a pseudonym—in his case, "Leslie Fiedler." (For many years thereafter, Leslie had a program from a production of Clifford Odets's *Waiting for Lefty* in which Al Eisner appeared under this name.) While at Harvard, Al lived in a suite with two other students— Norman Brisson and an aspiring composer named Lenny Bernstein. (After he became an established force in the musical world, Bernstein included a memorial composition dedicated to his old roommate in his own *Seven Anniversaries*.) Following graduation, Al went to Hollywood, where he worked briefly as a junior screenwriter for MGM. By age twenty-three, he was dead of cancer.

One of the reasons Al Eisner was able to rise so far so fast is that, when he was a senior in high school (no more than sixteen or seventeen), his Latin teacher fell in love with him. Hattie Schenk, who was closer to fifty than to forty, was so smitten with this student a third her age that she gave up everything to be with him and to finance his advancement in the world. After their romance began to breed scandal, she quit her job and took an apartment in Greenwich Village, where she and Al could be together. When Leslie went to visit them, they would take him to eat in restaurants he had never dared to enter and buy him real Havana cigars, which cost a buck a piece. When Al died, the only souvenirs that Leslie had of his friend were a book of Yeats's poems Al had owned and a large selection of letters.

In one such letter (which is undated), Al comments on his relationship with his sponsor:

> Hattie came down to see me yesterday and the day before. . . . I am finally positive that I have nothing to worry about for college. She assured me that I could have all the money I wanted. . . . The woman is in a bad way, Les; there was more than a modicum of truth in all your fanciful gabbings. And none of this thwarted mother-love stuff, either. The last flickerings of the flame are burning high and I had a hell of a time. It was all I could do to get out of her room when I said good night. It was repugnant to me of course, but I pitied her too. She poured out her heart to me, told me just how she felt and asked me over and over again to forgive her and not let it make a difference in our relation. She is deathly afraid of any break on my part. Finally, she begged me to bestow on her such a little thing but

9. Fiedler, interview with Jackson, Aug. 20, 1989.

it meant everything to her: to . . . kiss her. I looked at her a few seconds, shrugged and complied. She sighed like a wounded doe and passed her hands over my face and shoulders and arms. No, not my wang, you shit ass. Hell, the thing means nothing to me and the returns certainly warrent [*sic*] the little I give. . . . Merely looking sympathetic over a dinner table and saying things she would call sweet.[10]

Shortly after Al's death, Leslie went to see Hattie, who was now living alone in her apartment in the Village. She took him aside and explained that Al's ghost still came back to visit her and pointed to the places in the apartment where the ghost appeared. About six months later, the milkman noticed bottles piled up outside of Hattie's door and smelled her decomposing body. When she had taken up with Al, she had left her former life and friends so far behind that there was no one but strangers to discover her death. The whole sad tale affected Leslie to the point that Al Eisner became the subject of the first story he wrote as an adult.

"The Fear of Innocence," published in 1949, features a *wunderkind* named Hal, a middle-aged Latin teacher named Carrie, and an unnamed narrator. Although the story is a work of fiction, it provides insight into the meaning his friend's strange relationship had for Leslie as he was just beginning to pass from adolescence to adulthood. The character of Hal possesses that peculiar vulnerability that disguises itself as cynicism—a fear of innocence. Speaking of his aging mistress, he says: "Oh, I'm sorry for her in a way, but she's a mean and ignorant old bag, and you know it. It's enough I give her something to practice her dammed-up love on before it chokes her. Hell, how many sons love their mothers? Mostly I think she's old and scared, and now at least she won't have to die alone—she thinks" (*NC,* 100).

The issues of innocence and the fall that ends it are raised directly on the final page of "The Fear of Innocence." After leaving the apartment where he has discovered Carrie's rotting body, the narrator encounters a little girl, who is bouncing a rubber ball and chanting, "Bouncey, Bouncey, Ball-ee! I hope my sister fall-ee." In response, the narrator says: " 'I hope she does.' . . . It was as simple as that: the state of evil as the world of love, another innocence" (133). Then, a short paragraph later, the narrator compulsively remembers an unidentified line from Milton: "Home to his Mothers house private return'd." While he thinks it inapt to the present situation, he cannot dispel this line from his mind.

This is the concluding line of *Paradise Regained.* Jarring though the reference might seem, one might make something of the fact that the redemptive figure of Jesus in Milton's poem is not the god who is ritualistically sacrificed

10. This letter is contained in Leslie Fiedler's private papers.

on the cross for the sins of humanity, but a man who faces down temptation. (In this regard, Milton's poem borders on heresy.) As we know from Book Twelve of *Paradise Lost,* the paradise to be regained is not another Eden, but a condition far more glorious. Man is redeemed not by a return to innocence, but by his savior's courage and fortitude (after which that savior returns to his mother's house before being about his father's business). One can imagine the narrator of this story, and Leslie Fiedler himself, agreeing with such a vision, if not with the Christian symbolism in which it is rendered.

Innocence is, of course, the one inescapable theme for American writers. Emerson believed that in his time a war for the national spirit was being waged between the parties of memory and hope. Given the background that Leslie Fiedler and Al Eisner shared, historical memory was short and tenuous. Their immigrant ancestors had cut their ties with the Old World, and the heritage shared by more deeply rooted Americans was not theirs either. They had to create a new tradition. If the prototypical American is constantly reinventing himself, then the seemingly alien and alienated youth culture to which Leslie belonged was authentically American by virtue of its obsessive newness. Nevertheless, American life and literature are also filled with cautionary tales about the dangers of innocence. What "Hal," and perhaps his real-life counterpart, did not fully realize is that innocence can be overcome not by fear disguised as swagger, but by experience redeemed in knowledge.

Although Leslie Fiedler has described Al Eisner as his Edward King or Arthur Hallam (the man who taught him that dreams of fame can be thwarted by early mortality), there are differences as well as similarities to be noted. Eisner's death seems not to have reaffirmed any faith, in the manner of "Lycidas," or challenged one, in the manner of *In Memoriam.* Far from mythologizing his friend in the character of Hal, Leslie presents him as a talented naïf, who dies before he has the chance to grow up. Unlike the Little Evas and Little Nells of nineteenth-century fiction, the innocent Hal (and perhaps Eisner himself) does not die because he is too pure to live in this fallen world. His tragedy is that he dies too young to benefit from the fall into knowledge and experience.

Leslie makes precisely this point in his first published poem, titled (not surprisingly) "O Al!" The second stanza of that poem reads as follows:

> O Al,
> What does the tongue unspell
> Where now,
> Beyond the fear of innocence,
> You stow
> The gab, the mock of eloquence,
> All paid performance of the will?   (*NFR,* 471).

CHAPTER TWO

All the Irvings Did

LESLIE GRADUATED from high school in 1934, in the depth of the Great Depression. Although he had gotten a small college scholarship, his mother and father sat him down and told him that they couldn't afford to make up the difference. Fortunately, after six months of work, he was able to scrape together enough money to do so himself. So, every day, he would commute by bus, ferry, train, and subway from Newark to a school in the Bronx called NYU Heights. He remembers it as the kind of campus one would not have expected to find in what was already a decayed urban neighborhood. In addition to a neoclassical colonnade pretentiously called "The Hall of Fame," it housed an elegant but inefficient round library designed by Stanford White and a small arena called Goldmann Stadium, where concerts were held in the summertime.

There were some fifteen hundred students in the Arts College (about 90 percent of whom were Jewish) and an almost equal number (almost all Gentiles) in the Engineering School. Such de facto segregation existed because it was believed that Jews couldn't make it as engineers, and it was hoped that most who got into college would take pre-med courses. Because his interest was almost exclusively in literature, Leslie felt at home with neither group. Although he would later be better known for his criticism, his first literary passion was for poetry, which probably began when he was in first or second grade and was permitted to read his poem "Mercury and the Invention of the Lyre" to the entire student body. He later wrote his undergraduate honors thesis on Gerard Manley Hopkins, the Victorian poet whose achievement was only then beginning to be recognized. To this day, Leslie possesses a bibliography that Al Eisner compiled of all the volumes by or about Hopkins in the Widener Library at Harvard.

It was during his undergraduate years at the Heights that Leslie had his first direct encounter with a poet he admired. The experience proved disconcerting, as Robert Frost turned out to be anything but the kindly old man

19

Leslie imagined him to be. Frost began his private meeting with Leslie by heaping scorn on everything the aspiring young poet held dear—from his left-wing political allegiances to his fondness for Hopkins. Quite unexpectedly, Frost asked Leslie to define the opposite of a poet. Then he paused and answered his own question by observing that some people would say a grocer or a soldier or a dentist, but that he believed the opposite of a poet was "a poetess, like Gerard Manley Hopkins." As a literary neophyte, Leslie was reluctant to challenge Frost, who was probably, after Hopkins, his favorite poet.[1]

Reflecting back on that moment, Leslie surmised that most writers (Frost included) were sons of bitches. But, even so, he found them preferable to the timid and genteel academics who responded to his writing by giving him an unexplained A or F, the latter often accompanied by the comment "bad taste" written in red ink. Consequently, Leslie had no difficulty deciding whose side he was on when an Italian American boy, who drove a truck all night, stormed out of class one day, declaring that he could not abide being taught about the nature of humanity by a scared virgin.

The one teacher from whom Leslie believed he actually learned something was an English professor named Mallory, who had gone to Oxford on a Rhodes Scholarship from New Mexico. Although far from brilliant, Mallory had mastered the Oxford tutorial system. During his junior and senior years, Leslie was released from half his regular courses so that he could pursue a reading program under Mallory's direction. After two years, they had made it all the way from the beginning of English literature to the end of the seventeenth century. At the same time, Leslie introduced Mallory to more recent writers, such as Hopkins and Kafka. The relationship proved intellectually stimulating for both men.

Leslie would devote much of the time he spent commuting on the subway to writing. One day, when his class was allowed to write a story rather than an "essay describing a process," he wrote a tale about a woman who had an orgasm every time she passed through a turnstile on the subway. The story ends with her being picked up in the subway station, where she has fainted away in the midst of a crowd of indifferent onlookers. As she is dying in a Catholic hospital, she looks up and sees the crucifix on the wall going round and round like a turnstile. In another classic example of "bad taste," he wrote about a man who married a seal but could never find a way to consummate their union. (Both the man and his bride eventually perished of frustration.) This story was originally written in uncertain French, after Leslie discovered that the French word for seal was *phoque*.

---

1. Leslie Fiedler, interview with author, Nov. 5, 1998.

I

For all its surface conventionality, NYU Heights was a politically active campus. At that time, one of the advantages of being a Communist was that it served as a means of upward social mobility for young Jews from working-class neighborhoods. It enabled Leslie and his friends to meet rich people who gave parties on Park Avenue. (Radical chic was rampant in those days.) One could also meet girls from Vassar and Sarah Lawrence who believed in free love. In fact, the first time Leslie ever saw Vassar was at a huge anti-Japanese rally sponsored by the Communists. It was there that he got a cheap erotic thrill from seeing girls tear off their silk underpants and throw them in the fire in protest of the Japanese silk trade.

When he first entered college, Leslie was still committed to the Soviet Union and its leader. He even joined the Young Communist League at the bidding of a man whom he now believes to have been a double agent. He remembers devoting much time and effort to raising money for the Spanish Loyalists, even as he felt guilty for not going to Spain to fight himself. (One of his fellow students did go and was killed.) During his brief career as an active Stalinist, Leslie took on several pseudonyms. One was "John Simon." Although he has since come to know three or four people by that name, he was thinking of himself only as "Simple Simon."

After six months as a Communist, Leslie dropped out of the league and became a follower of Leon Trotsky. (Upon joining the Trotskyite cause, he took the name of Dexter Fellows, in honor of the man who was in charge of public relations for the Barnum and Bailey Circus.) This was the sort of conversion experienced throughout the intellectual community in the 1930s. Although Marx, Engels, and Lenin were men of considerable learning, Stalin was an uncultured peasant. As Soviet ruler, he turned art into a blatant instrument of propaganda, calling writers the "engineers of the human soul." That might have been tolerable as long as one was able to see the Soviet experiment as a grand utopia or perhaps as only the least imperfect society in the world. Unfortunately, by the end of the 1930s, such a delusion had become difficult for intelligent people to maintain.

Upon witnessing the brutality and cynicism of the Stalinist-backed Republican forces in Spain, John Dos Passos and George Orwell turned against the Soviet Union. (Dos Passos ended his life as a Goldwater Republican, while Orwell wrote two of the most powerful anti-Communist novels imaginable: *1984* and *Animal Farm*.) Stalin's ruthless consolidation of power, which resulted in the infamous Moscow show trials, alienated thousands of others who could not reconcile their humanist sensibilities with what amounted to a totalitarian purge. For others, the final betrayal was the nonaggression pact that Stalin signed with Hitler in 1939. If the socialist ideal was not to be abandoned altogether, one needed to find a different standard-bearer. For a brief but crucial period in the intellectual history of the Left, the man who called himself Leon Trotsky became that standard-bearer.

Born Lev Davidovich Bronstein, Trotsky was a genuine hero of the Russian Revolution. He was first arrested in 1898 for his insurrectionist activities and imprisoned in Siberia. He escaped, using the surname of his jailer, Trotsky, which he retained as his official name for the rest of his life. After his escape, Trotsky traveled to England, where he worked with another revolutionary exile, V. I. Lenin. A return to Russia in 1905 led to more revolutionary activity, a second imprisonment in Siberia, and a second escape. Trotsky spent the next twelve years in Europe and America. When Czar Nicholas II was toppled in 1917, Trotsky helped lead a successful Bolshevik takeover of the government. He was a man of both revolutionary zeal and great physical courage. Also, unlike Stalin, he was an intellectual in the tradition of Marx and Engels. No less a critic than Edmund Wilson believes that Trotsky's books *1905, The History of the Russian Revolution,* and *Literature and Revolution,* along with his own autobiography and his life of Lenin "are probably a part of our permanent literature."[2] Becoming a Trotskyite allowed one to despise Stalin and all his many sins without renouncing the ideal of socialism.

Even when the United States was allied with the Soviet Union during World War II, American Trotskyites maintained their animus toward Stalin. Not only was he the persecutor of their hero, he also harbored a view of socialism very different from Trotsky's. While Stalin was primarily interested in maintaining his own power in the Soviet Union and building a model Communist state there, Trotsky believed that the revolution must be worldwide. American Stalinists had to be content with showing unblinking loyalty to a government on the other side of the world, while Trotskyites could believe that they were fomenting revolution in their own backyard. When a Stalinist operative murdered the exiled Trotsky in Mexico in 1940, he transformed a nuisance into a martyr.

Since his death, Trotsky's legacy has been claimed by a variety of political factions, which seem more intent on excommunicating each other than on transforming society. The common denominator that unites them is hostility to the Soviet government. The dwindling number of latter-day Trotskyites have been far more sympathetic to Mao's China and Castro's Cuba than to the Russia of Stalin's successors. Some New Leftists of the 1960s invoked the image of Trotsky as a symbol of revolutionary purity. But Trotsky is far more often remembered as yet another god that failed. Many of those who moved beyond the Trotskyism of their youth eventually came to realize that Trotsky himself had more in common with Stalin than they had wanted to believe.

2. Edmund Wilson, *To the Finland Station: A Study in the Writing and Acting of History,* 436.

Both in theory and in practice, Trotsky was a proponent of revolutionary terrorism. Once the revolutionaries were in power, however, this meant government suppression of dissent. Particularly damaging to Trotsky's reputation among idealistic leftists was a series of revelations about his role in crushing the Kronstadt rebellion in 1921. When a group of sailors from the Kronstadt soviet announced the liberation of their workers' council from the dictatorship of the Communist Party, the rebellion was crushed by Bolshevik troops, and the sailors were executed on Trotsky's orders. After the grisly details of this episode became known in 1937, a wide range of independent American leftists denounced Trotsky. "For many," writes Gary Dorrien, "the recent revelations about Trotsky's past suggested that the essential difference between Trotsky and Stalin was that Trotsky lost."[3]

In the last analysis, Trotskyism is probably less important as a political movement than as an interlude in the intellectual development of some of the most seminal minds of the twentieth century. For Jewish literary critics of Leslie Fiedler's generation, this interlude is forever identified with New York in the late 1930s. In a memoir of his own days as a Trotskyite at City College, Irving Kristol recalls that the college lunchroom was the center of political and intellectual activity on campus. The various alcoves in the lunchroom were populated by different groups of students (Catholics, Zionists, Orthodox Jews, athletes, and blacks among them). But for Kristol, the only alcoves that mattered were those that housed the Stalinist and anti-Stalinist Left. Because the Stalinist group (whose most notorious member was Julius Rosenberg) refused to debate with any other group, the only political dialogue on campus emerged from the anti-Stalinists in Alcove Number One. "I have no regret about that episode in my life," Kristol writes. "Joining a radical movement when young is very much like falling in love when one is young. The girl may turn out to be rotten, but the experience of love is so valuable it can never be entirely undone by the ultimate disenchantment." When I expressed surprise that such a staunch neoconservative as Irving Kristol had started out as a Trotskyite, Leslie replied, "All the Irvings did."[4]

Beginning in the 1930s, the one magazine that all the Irvings read (and eventually contributed to) was *Partisan Review.* The sophisticated upper class might have considered the *New Yorker* to be the best magazine in the world, but for the earnest, young intellectuals who were committed to Marxism in politics and modernism in literature, *PR* (as it was affectionately known) was the only game in town. As Irving Kristol recalls, "*Partisan Review,* the journal of the anti-Stalinist, left-wing, cultural avant-garde, was an intimidating presence

3. Gary Dorrien, *The Neoconservative Mind: Politics, Culture, and the War of Ideology,* 26.
4. Irving Kristol, *Neoconservatism: The Autobiography of an Idea: Selected Essays 1949–1995,* 470. Leslie Fiedler, interview with author, June 23, 1997.

in Alcove No. 1. Even simply to understand it seemed a goal beyond reach. I would read each article at least twice, in a state of awe and exasperation—excited to see such elegance of style and profundity of mind, depressed at the realization that a commoner like myself could never expect to rise into that intellectual aristocracy."[5]

While rejecting the ideological tunnel vision of more orthodox Marxist publications, *Partisan Review* always tried to remain politically engaged in a fiercely independent, often idiosyncratic manner. Because of their aversion to the vice now known as political correctness, the editors of *PR* often seemed to go to the other extreme—publishing the work of such unapologetically reactionary writers as Allen Tate and T. S. Eliot (becoming, for a while, Eliot's chief American outlet). In contemplating this phenomenon, Fiedler would later argue that "*PR* has been obsessed with the notion of a two-fold avant garde, political and artistic, both segments regarded as a threat by middle-class philistines." Perhaps because the magazine came into being at "the moment when experimentalism in art was being consolidated and academicized all over the world, the concept that serious art is, per se, as revolutionary as Marxism has been difficult to maintain" (*CE,* 2:46).[6]

If *Partisan Review* came along too late to help midwife the birth of modernism, it was instrumental in creating another phenomenon that would be of immense significance for twentieth-century criticism—the major literary quarterly. Such magazines fall somewhere between the extremes defined by the experimental "little magazines," which flourished in the 1920s, and the strictly academic literary journals, which seem always to have been with us. According to Monroe K. Spears, "The literary quarterly or critical review is a noncommercial magazine, uncompromisingly highbrow in character, which publishes criticism of literature and to some extent the other arts in the form of essays, book reviews, and chronicles, together with fiction and poetry selected according to the kind of high standards defined and employed in the criticism."[7] For most of its existence, *Partisan Review* has been one of the most impressive examples of such a magazine.

II

As an undergraduate, Leslie made a point of not saluting the flag when the ROTC parade went by and everybody else stood at attention. (Years later,

---

5. Kristol, *Neoconservatism,* 478.

6. For a time, that concept got an inadvertent boost from democratic nativists such as Archibald MacLeish and Van Wyck Brooks, who began launching jingoistic attacks on modernism in their zeal to promote bourgeois American values at the dawn of World War II.

7. Monroe K. Spears, *American Ambitions: Selected Essays on Literary and Cultural Themes,* 110.

when he refused to stand for the IRA anthem in a bar in Dublin, he informed the outraged Irishmen that he stood only for "the Lord God Jehovah.") This apparent lack of patriotism resulted in his initially being barred from Phi Beta Kappa, although he was later admitted when a civil libertarian rose to his defense. The university officials, many of whom wore sunflowers to indicate their support for Alf Landon, tried vainly to civilize Leslie. When they held afternoon teas to try to teach the students how to act in polite company, Leslie would simply show up wearing a button that said "Vote for Foster and Ford" (the Communist candidates for president and vice president). Although he had the grades to get into a first-class eastern graduate school, the same bluenosed professors who had tried to take away his undergraduate scholarship refused to recommend him. A particularly indignant teacher of Italian had placed a note in his file that saying that, despite his brilliant mind, "Mr. Fiedler will never be a gentleman or a scholar."

Although the elite Eastern schools closed their doors to this notorious troublemaker, Leslie secured a scholarship from the proudly liberal University of Wisconsin. For him, leaving the familiar environs of Newark and the Bronx for America's Heartland was like moving to another country. It was not the rural life that was new to him. After all, New Jersey called itself the Garden State, and one of his mother's brothers had actually married a farm girl, who had survived her childhood on a diet of rotten potatoes and sour milk her father couldn't sell. Getting used to the sights of the Midwest was easy compared to adjusting oneself to its idiom. The first time someone responded to his "thank you" with "you bet," Leslie felt as if he were hearing a foreign language. Moreover, lighting out for Wisconsin was itself an adventure. Sometimes he would take the interminable trip by Greyhound bus. More often, he would hitchhike. Occasionally, he and several other guys would pool their money to buy a junker car, hoping that they would all arrive in one piece.

Part of the strangeness of living in Wisconsin was relieved by the fact that a Newark friend named Mel Tumin was also enrolled in the university. When he and Leslie arrived in 1938, they roomed together in a house owned by a slow-witted local family. Referring to her husband, the wife warned her two boarders, "When you talk to Louie, speak slow and use small words; he don't understand so good." The daughter was an aspiring pianist, who practiced at all hours of the day and night. Although the boarders did not enjoy kitchen privileges, Leslie would periodically raid the refrigerator. Because of his cherubic appearance, the family never suspected him but cast all the blame on Mel. The accommodations were so sparse that the roommates had to share a bed. Some nights, Leslie would awake to find Mel's leg cast over his body and his friend mumbling "Jane, Jane" in his sleep.

If times had frequently been hard in Jack Fiedler's house, the living was more spartan away from home. Even with his scholarship, Leslie had to survive on forty cents a day. He would roam the cafeteria, looking for empty coffee cups he could take back for free refills. He soon learned that he could get free buttermilk at the ag school and that there were always plenty of cookies at sorority parties. Also, selling hotdogs at home football games entitled him to free admission to the game and all the hotdogs he could eat. It was a hard life but not an uncommon one during the depression.

It wasn't long before Leslie became the unofficial leader of a group of ne'er-do-wells, who hung out in a slum that was alternately called the Goat's Nest and the State Street Soviet. The group itself was simply known as Fiedler's Dead-End Kids. One of the kids carried a straight razor with him at all times. Another sprouted what looked like pubic hair on all parts of his body. A third would roam the Goat's Nest with a ribbon tied around his perpetually erect penis. But perhaps the most interesting one of the entire crew was an Arab Christian named Freddie Camper.

Freddie, a native of Green Bay, hung out at the docks when he was supposed to be attending classes. He had committed large portions of Eliot's poetry and six books of *Paradise Lost* to memory. On occasion, he and Leslie would get drunk and run past the Jewish fraternity houses screaming, "Kill! Slay! Slay! in the name of Allah!" One night, shortly after Leslie and Freddie had picked up a couple of girls in Green Bay, they found themselves lost in a political argument. Having had enough of being ignored, one of the girls ordered them to stop the car. When she got out, she turned around and said, "Shit on you, Karl Marx." Freddie's one near brush with fame occurred when a novel he had written about the Devil coming to Green Bay was accepted for publication by Random House. Unfortunately, when Freddie stopped by the Random House offices to discuss the project with the legendary editor Albert Erskine, he was put off by all the symbolism Erskine claimed to see in the book. In a huff, Freddie walked out, vowing to peddle his novel elsewhere. It never found a home, and Freddie spent his own final days driving a taxicab in Madison.

Throughout his time in Wisconsin, Leslie remained a committed Trotskyite. The political activities that had caused him so much trouble as an undergraduate in the Bronx were benignly tolerated in Madison. The university prided itself on its broadmindedness and would certainly not have extended Leslie a scholarship had it intended to persecute him for his beliefs. The strongest opposition that he and his comrades encountered came not from Republicans or Democrats but from Stalinists. With all the high spirits of rival fraternities, the Stalinists and the Trotskyites tried to take control of various student organizations. It was considered a coup for one group to steal a member from the other. Leslie's most significant conquest in this competition was a young Stalinist named Margaret Shipley.

When Margaret came by at a friend's suggestion to talk to Leslie, he was laid up with a cold and barely able to speak. (As it turns out, it was also Leslie's twenty-second birthday.) Over a period of a few weeks, however, he had converted her—if not to Trotsky, at least to himself. She remained for a while as a double agent in the Stalinist camp but found it increasingly difficult to maintain her cover while being the girlfriend of one of the leading Trotskyites on campus. Whatever her political effectiveness might have been, Margaret was the first serious love interest in Leslie's life. Also, as a girl of some financial means, she was able to alleviate his penury. When Margaret walked into his life, living on forty cents a day and fraudulent coffee refills came to an end.[8]

Strange as it may seem, Leslie had known Margaret's father before she had. Joseph ("Bud") Shipley was a charmer, who found it difficult to stay married to any woman for very long. He walked out on Margaret's mother when Margaret was four and enjoyed short-term liaisons with several women thereafter. (The woman with whom he remained the longest, his literary agent, was one he never bothered to marry.) He taught English for much of his life at New York's famed Stuyvesant High School, where his most famous student was James Cagney. Bud Shipley also edited various reference books, including the *Dictionary of World Literature,* where Leslie landed his first three professional publications—definitions of "Courtly Love," "Saga," and "Surrealism."

Because of Bud Shipley's desertion of his family, Margaret never knew what to call herself when she was growing up. Should she use her birth name "Margaret Shipley," or should she call herself "Margaret Shaffner" in deference to her stepfather, Buck Shaffner? Certainly, Margaret could not have found men more different than the two her mother married. Whereas Bud Shipley was a poet and intellectual, Buck Shaffner was a gambler with ties to the underworld. He managed the Mounds Club, a large, elegant gambling establishment outside Cleveland. Featuring free food and entertainment, the club made its profit at the gambling tables. One of the great thrills of Leslie's life came when Buck let him shill at the crap table one night when business was slow.

Leslie remembers Buck Shaffner as one of the calmest, mildest, and sweetest men he ever knew. Although Buck probably never laid hands on an instrument of death himself, the owner of the Mounds Club was Cleveland's leading gangster, Tommy McGinty, and his associates seemed to have stepped right out of a Damon Runyon story. (Buck was the first person Leslie had ever heard use the word "fuzz" in referring to the police—"fuzz on the Erie" being the signal he and his friends had used as boys to warn each other that the cops were coming.) One night Buck and the treasurer of the Mounds Club, a man named Rubber Goldberg, were walking down the street side by side, when Goldberg was gunned down in his tracks. It was a clean professional killing, in which no innocent bystander was harmed. When Buck's career in Cleveland

---

8. Leslie Fiedler, interview with author, Nov. 7, 1998.

came to an end, he moved to Las Vegas. One of his greatest pleasures as an old man was to regale kids with stories about the Purple Gang and memories of a yellow Studs Bearcat that was the first car he ever stole.[9]

When Leslie and Margaret decided to marry, after having known each other for only a few months, they did so against the opposition of nearly everyone they knew. Leslie's family thought that, at twenty-two and with no job, he was ill prepared to take on the responsibilities of marriage. Margaret's mother, still traumatized by her experience with Bud Shipley, believed that all literary intellectuals were bastards. Finally, the young couple's radical friends regarded marriage as a hopelessly bourgeois institution. (Leslie and Margaret knew a couple who kept the fact of their marriage secret for over a year for that very reason.) When they finally did exchange vows, it was before a justice of the peace who had been one of the leaders of the Farm Moratorium Movement. As a youth, he "had been captured shotgun in hand when his ammunition ran out, and had become heavyweight wrestling champion of the Wisconsin State Reformatory." Leslie will never forget this man's one piece of premarital advice. " 'Be intimate with your wife,' he admonished me, 'but not familiar. When you have to fart in bed, lean your ass over the edge" (*BB,* 33).

The first piece of furniture that Leslie and Margaret bought was a mimeograph machine so that they could turn out leaflets denouncing their professors as social fascists. Their honeymoon was spent at a Trotskyite convention in Cleveland. This was a time when the entire international socialist movement was coming apart. Although the Socialist Workers Party, to which the Fiedlers belonged, championed Trotsky over Stalin, some of its members were beginning to find fault with Trotsky himself. The Old Man, as he was affectionately known, remained at odds with Stalin but could not entirely disabuse himself of the notion that the Soviet Union remained a socialist state. Consequently, he demanded unconditional support for the Soviet invasions of Poland and Finland. In his column for the Trotskyite *Socialist Appeal,* the independent radical Dwight Macdonald argued that Trotsky himself was advocating a Stalinist position. When the Old Man unleashed a torrent of personal abuse at Dwight and all "Macdonaldists" for their deviationism, a schism within the American branch of the Socialist Workers Party seemed inevitable.

That schism officially occurred at the party's national convention held in Manhattan in April of 1940. A minority faction led by Max Shachtman split off to form the American Workers Party. Dwight Macdonald assumed editorship of the new party's official magazine, *Labor Action,* and did a considerable amount of writing and technical work for a second magazine called the *New International.* Although he was gradually withdrawing from all involvement

9. Leslie Fiedler, interview with Bruce Jackson, June 10, 1989.

with Trotskyite politics, the philosophical godfather of this new faction was James Burnham, whose highly sophisticated concept of the managerial revolution challenged some of the simplistic doctrines of orthodox Marxism. As a part of this group, Leslie Fiedler was committed to a political movement that traced the ills of the Soviet Union all the way back to Lenin and which dared to doubt the infallibility of Marx himself. He had come a long way from the hardcore Stalinism of his adolescence in Newark.

Leslie recalls being in an elevator somewhere in Madison in August 1940 when he heard the news that a Stalinist agent had killed Trotsky with an ice pick to the head. What most impressed him about this news was the realization that he had once met the assassin, Ramon Mercader, at a party in New York. Mercader hung around Trotskyite circles and became the boyfriend of an unattractive young woman who was close to Trotsky. Even then, he must have been working for Stalin with his ultimate objective in mind.

When Leslie and Margaret first announced their engagement, some of Leslie's more worldly friends said, "The girl is pregnant, I assume." In fact, she was not. The Fiedlers delayed starting a family for over a year; however, by late 1940, Margaret was with child. One afternoon in February 1941, Leslie was sitting in a class in Old Provencal when a friend summoned him to the door to tell him that Margaret had just given birth two months early because of a ruptured appendix. When Leslie arrived at the hospital, an officious young intern told him to prepare himself for the prospect that both mother and child would die. As it turned out, Margaret had been taking an antibiotic for an unrelated ailment and managed to recover fairly soon. Young Kurt, however, was kept in the hospital for several weeks—until he weighed five pounds. The first time his proud parents risked taking him out of the house was in May, when Leslie received the diploma officially awarding him a doctorate of philosophy in English literature.

III

Given his choice, Leslie would not have gone to graduate school at the University of Wisconsin. The faculty in Madison was certainly superior to that of his undergraduate school in the Bronx; however, the literary attitudes that prevailed in Wisconsin seemed to belong more to the nineteenth than the twentieth century. The old-line philological scholarship remained largely unchallenged by even the most conservative variety of literary criticism. (In one break with tradition, two of the most distinguished scholars in the department were women—Helen White and Ruth Wallerstein.) Marxism might be tolerated as a political faith, if only to preserve the legendary reputation for liberal tolerance enjoyed by the state and university, but no serious scholar at Wisconsin would apply Marxist ideas to literature. The professors with "advanced" ideas were conspicuous by their scarcity.

One professor whom Leslie remembers with fondness was Miles Handley, a pioneer in comparative linguistics. His classes were enjoyable and enlightening but also potentially dangerous. The man was an epileptic who would sometimes go into seizure in the middle of a lecture. (Students in the first row would stay on guard against his flailing convulsions.) Handley's wife sat in the back of the class in case her assistance was needed. Another original thinker on the faculty was the director of freshman English, a young semanticist named S. I. Hayakawa. Leslie remembers him as a congenial colleague with an interesting perspective on how language should be taught. (All of the instructors under Hayakawa's charge used his book *Language in Action*.) Of Japanese ancestry, Sam Hayakawa was particularly intent on being seen as 110 percent American.

Above everyone else on the Wisconsin faculty, Leslie revered the eccentric poet and intellectual polymath William Ellery Leonard. Born in 1876, Leonard was already in his sixties when Leslie first arrived in Madison. Although he is largely forgotten today, there was a time when Leonard was regarded as one of the most important American poets to write between the end of the Civil War and the rise of modernism. A native of Plainfield, New Jersey, Leonard was the son of a Unitarian clergyman and the namesake of the great American Unitarian William Ellery Channing. (As a child, he had told his mother: "I cannot be as good as Jesus but I can be as good as Dr. Channing."[10]) When Leslie was still an adolescent in Newark, he had actually written a paper on Leonard under the direction of Ephraim Eisenberg, the only male Jewish teacher on the faculty of South Side High School.

As a scholar-poet, Leonard was a throwback to Longfellow. His academic credentials were equal to those of any of his colleagues, but he refused to fit the normal academic mold. In an age of increasing specialization, Leonard taught whatever interested him—from Old Icelandic to Chaucer and Burns. With his long flowing white hair (Leslie calls him the last of the old longhairs) and his Windsor tie, Leonard was an unmistakable presence on campus. Nevertheless, Leonard's life was plagued by unhappiness that would have destroyed a lesser man. When he was unfairly blamed for his first wife's suicide, he weathered the storm and wrote a sonnet sequence called *Two Lives*. (Stephen Vincent Benét once declared this work to be the greatest poem written by an American in the twentieth century.[11]) Leonard also suffered severe agoraphobia as a result of a childhood encounter with a train. This experience inspired his

10. William Ellery Leonard, *The Locomotive God*, 39.
11. See Chester E. Jorgenson, "William Ellery Leonard: An Appraisal," 258.

extraordinary autobiography, *The Locomotive God*. Leonard's condition worsened as he aged until he could not travel more than a short distance from his home. Toward the end of his life, he held class in his house. His popularity was such that students didn't mind making allowances so that they could sit at his feet. For Leslie Fiedler, William Ellery Leonard represented everything that a professor of literature ought to be.

Leonard directed Leslie's thesis in 1939 and his dissertation in 1941. These two extended works of scholarship reflect the range of Leslie's literary interests and critical opinions at the time. The earlier work was a Marxist interpretation of Chaucer's *Troilus and Criseyde,* while the later one sought to place John Donne's love poetry in the context of medieval thought. If the study of Chaucer was a kind of bravura performance designed to irritate some of the more traditional scholars in the department, the work on Donne showed that Leslie was perfectly capable of shining at the traditionalist's own game.

In a long chapter on courtly love (which owes much to C. S. Lewis's *The Allegory of Love*), Fiedler shows how certain poetic conventions regarding romantic love arose in reaction to the medieval Catholic view that all sexual activity was fundamentally evil. Poets who accepted this view naturally saw the intractable reality of sexual desire as the source of much suffering. For all its elegance, there is something inherently sadomasochistic about courtly love. Donne cannot reconcile the conflict between the flesh and the spirit as readily as Shakespeare does in his romantic comedies or as Spenser does in his hymns to married love. And he certainly does not anticipate the twentieth-century view that salvation can be achieved through erotic ecstasy.

If Donne's views were greatly influenced by medieval Catholicism, the world in which he lived was neither medieval nor Catholic. The conflict between his actual and his ideal world created a tension that can be seen in both the ideas and techniques of his poetry. Fiedler believes that this tension lies behind the *discordia concors* Samuel Johnson identified as the defining characteristic of the metaphysical conceit. The dissertation goes on to make a telling point:

> It is sometimes remarked in nostalgic tones that the metaphysical poets possessed the ability of living in divided worlds. Those who pity our time for having lost that amphibian secret forget that the faculty arose only because these poets possessed in the first place a divided world, and that the awareness of that fact was by no means pleasant to some of the artists of the time, Donne, for instance, who, unaware of the virtue the twentieth century would make of his necessity, was busily engaged in an attempt to re-achieve the single world of the Middle Ages.[12]

12. Leslie Fiedler, "John Donne's *Songs and Sonnets:* A Reinterpretation in Light of Their Traditional Backgrounds," 153. Subsequent references will be cited parenthetically in the text.

At the heart of Donne's *Songs and Sonnets,* we find a fundamental conflict between the pleasant lies designed to regulate sexual ardor and the actual experience of one who tries to believe those lies. If the virtue of romantic faithfulness is seen as giving order to an otherwise divided universe, the speaker in Donne's poetry has had too much experience with infidelity to find much comfort there. Moreover, any attempt to sanctify human love must somehow explain away the biological desire that it shares with the coupling of beasts. Finally, if the mythos of love requires the veneration of women, "men have always found it impossible to ignore the fact of woman's spiritual and intellectual inferiority, as a thousand myths, including that of the Fall, testify" (156). This note of misogyny is sounded again and again in Donne's love poetry. As Fiedler asserts: "His verse is the flesh and blood of the awareness, skeletal for most of us, that woman is ethically different from man, forever betrayed by her need for the very emotional stimulus which is her only path to an integrated life. He speaks of our need for that weak and uncertain creature, our strange desire to find her worthy of adoration. He tells us of the paradox of her completing us by a feeling that is greater than herself" (158).

If Donne's uncertainties concerning love make him seem almost a part of our world, the philosophical assumptions that give rise to those uncertainties belong to a world that is decidedly premodern. What connects his world and ours involves more than the universal incidence of human lust and is finally more profound than the various strategies we devise for ennobling that lust. "The brief collision of the bodies we can take for granted," Fiedler writes; "the intricate systems by which we rationalize and adorn our feelings shift with the tides of social change; the world between, where we are eternally aware of the ineluctable gap between our flesh and our fictions of love, has been and will remain the common possession of mankind. It is that world which John Donne has sung" (158).

IV

Although Leslie's nominal residence from 1938 to 1941 was Madison, Wisconsin, he spent as much time as possible in Chicago. He, Margaret, and Mel Tumin would often hitchhike the 150 miles separating the two cities to visit one of Leslie's childhood friends from Newark, Harold Kaplan. Although he wrote under the name H. J. Kaplan, this remarkable man was always known to his friends as Kappy. By the late 1930s a formidable group of young anti-Stalinist intellectuals had gathered around him. In a sense, they constituted a midwestern outpost of *Partisan Review.* These ambitious young men, who were generally supported by hardworking wives, were all convinced that they would one day win the Nobel Prize. One of the group, a young novelist named Saul Bellow, actually did.

Not only was Kappy Leslie's oldest friend among the Chicagoans, he also remained closest to him longest. (The name "Leslie Fiedler" first appeared in print as the name of a character in a story Kappy published in a *New Directions* anthology.) On nights when the conversation lasted so late that an immediate return to Madison seemed impractical, Leslie and Margaret would make a crib for Kurt in Saul Bellow's bathtub and sleep four in a bed with Kappy and Kappy's wife. After publishing some early fiction in *Partisan Review* and two novels, including a Jamesean tale called *The Plenipotentiaries,* H. J. Kaplan abandoned literature. His facility with language enabled him to enjoy a successful international career in both business and government service. He was the main translator at the Paris peace conference that finally brought an end to the Vietnam War. Also, for years, he wrote a "Letter from Paris" for *Partisan Review.* His daughter Leslie, who is more French than American, is Leslie Fiedler's goddaughter and namesake and now a well-respected European novelist.

One of the most argumentative members of the group was Lionel Abel. Although he probably had some fixed political and cultural beliefs (of the Trotskyite/*Partisan Review* variety), Abel was always willing to alter them to assure a lively discussion. (He was particularly adept at arguing about the merits of books he had never read.) Like so many of the anti-Stalinist crowd, Abel eventually drifted far to the political right; however, his basic personality and zest for argument remained unchanged. In 1976, Alfred Kazin remarked that "nowadays I meet Lionel Abel on Fifth Avenue, and he opens up by explaining how proletarianized America is becoming. . . . [He] seems much exercised about intellectuals who unlike himself have not gone from Sartre to Reagan."[13]

Of all the Chicagoans, none showed greater literary promise than Isaac Rosenfeld. He had grown up with Saul Bellow in Chicago, and early on it seemed that one of the two was destined to become the first great Jewish American novelist. When he won the first *Partisan Review* prize for fiction in 1946, Rosenfeld appeared to be well on his way to stardom. But, like so many gifted young people, his actual production never equaled his promise. Alfred Kazin has observed that, "unlike Bellow, who could use every morsel of his experience, Isaac lived his fantasies, and in company."[14]

As Bellow continued to produce highly regarded novels, Rosenfeld became less a writer than a literary personality. He was a charming dinner guest and drinking companion until even his old mentors, principally Philip Rahv at

13. Alexander Bloom, *Prodigal Sons: The New York Intellectuals and Their World,* 425 n.12.
14. Ibid., 296

Partisan Review, began to consider him a loser. Isaac Rosenfeld died in a furnished room in Chicago, in 1956. A decade later, Leslie wrote: "I . . . find myself thinking often these days of Rosenfeld, who might well (it once seemed) have been our own Franz Kafka and who perhaps *was* (in a handful of stories like 'The Pyramids' and 'The Party,' dreams of parables or parables of dreams), all the Kafka we shall ever have" (*CE,* 2:186).

Perhaps the strangest member of the Chicago circle was neither a literary man nor a left-winger. Born in 1909 in Konawa, Oklahoma, Willmoore Kendall seemed to do just about everything at a younger age than anyone else. He learned to read at the age of two by playing with a typewriter. While still a child, he was driving his father, a blind Southern Methodist minister, around the state. He graduated from high school at age thirteen and had a B.A. from the University of Oklahoma by the time he was eighteen. In 1935, with an M.A. from Oxford in hand, Kendall left for Spain as a correspondent for United Press. A champion of the Loyalist government, he was soon disillusioned with their brutal tactics and Stalinist politics. In later years, he became one of the most important intellectuals in the postwar conservative movement and, as William Buckley's professor at Yale, a guru to the neo-populist Right.

During his time in Chicago, Leslie enjoyed his first experience living in an intellectual community. Although Newark was not far from New York, he had never spent much time among the New York intellectuals. (There were certainly none to be found on the Bronx campus of NYU.) With a few notable exceptions, his faculty and classmates in Madison did not seem to live for ideas. They were competent, at times masterful, at what they did, but the sense of originality and excitement that characterizes a truly *engaged* community of minds was largely missing. He hoped that, with his Ph.D. in hand, he could secure a job in such a community. But the prospects were not great; teaching positions in college English departments were few and far between. Wisconsin was even keeping many of its own graduates in low-paying temporary instructorships as they sought tenure-track appointments wherever they could find them.

Late in the summer of 1941, Leslie was finally offered a job at Montana State University in Missoula. Over four decades later, Hugh Kenner imagined the situation in the following terms: "In '41, straitjacketed in his new doctorate, the burly Fiedler was bundled by implacable Fate into the train that would haul him off kicking and fuming to the academic Gulag in Montana. Folklore has cherished and doubtless improved the scene at his departure: the sighs of commiseration on the platform, the indomitable leonine head at the coach window, its defiant shout through roars of escaping steam: 'I'll publish my way out in five years!' "[15]

---

15. Hugh Kenner, "Who Was Leslie Fiedler?" 69.

CHAPTER THREE

Those Beautiful Chinese Nights

IF MADISON, WISCONSIN, was 150 miles from Chicago, Missoula, Montana, was 150 miles from nowhere. One had to drive seven hundred miles to the east just to get to North Dakota. Idaho was to the west, Alberta to the north, and Wyoming to the south. For such a vast expanse of land, Montana was sparsely settled. One could travel for hundreds of miles without seeing another human being. It was possible to live as a virtual hermit in Montana. By the same token, a truly gregarious person could know almost everyone in the state. Missoula turned out to be the end of Leslie's journey to the West, which can be more properly understood as his inadvertent flight from the East. If it took him much longer than five years to "publish his way out," it was because he soon developed a love-hate relationship with his adopted state, which made it very easy for him to be away for extended periods of time but very hard to leave permanently.

Although he had taught as a graduate assistant at Wisconsin, Leslie's career as a teacher actually began in Missoula. He recalls his eagerness to establish his symbolic role as professor—perching safely behind the teacher's desk, scrawling his name in a bold, illegible hand on the blackboard, half fearing that someone would "slap me on the back and ask me to my beardless face . . . if I'd met the new Professor from the East" (*BB,* 32). In Montana, the term *professor* was less likely to call to mind a politically engaged intellectual than the piano player in a whorehouse.

Leslie soon discovered that, politically speaking, Montana was a state without a middle. Still a leftist of sorts, he found himself "dashing about to White Fish and Butte and God knows what other Montana places whose very names I could scarcely believe—organizing for the Teachers Union and talking to old-timers, pleased to have found a new ear, about the Wobblies and the Western Miners Union, and especially about 'the Company' that controlled then not only the copper but all the radio and press in the state" (*BB,* 33).

At the university, Leslie would occasionally find a fellow misfit. The library subscribed to most of the internal journals of the Communist Party because the librarian for many years was a Communist. Montanans tended to elect conservative politicians to statewide office but send liberals to Washington. Their legendary senator Burton K. Wheeler was Bob La Follette's running mate on the Progressive Party ticket in 1924. Another progressive political figure from Montana was a native of Missoula named Jeanette Rankin. The sister of Wellington Rankin, the largest landholder in the state (and the man who taught his ranch hand Gary Cooper how to box), Jeanette was an early crusader for woman suffrage. She was also the first woman ever to sit in Congress and a lifelong pacifist. Long after suffering a serious political setback by voting against American involvement in World War I, she returned to Congress in time to vote against entering World War II.

During Leslie's first year at the university, he had an office next to a young history professor named Mike Mansfield. Even then, Mansfield seemed to have the ideal credentials for political success in Montana. He was a Roman Catholic in a state with a large Catholic population. Montanans revered the military, and Mansfield had been a marine. He was also a trade union member in a highly unionized state. He never forgot a name or a face and seemed to have memorized the family relations of every person he ever met. He was elected to Congress in 1942 and won a seat in the Senate ten years later. When Lyndon Johnson left the Senate to become vice president in 1961, Mansfield was elected that body's majority leader. In true Western fashion, he was a progressive on domestic issues and an isolationist on foreign policy. The Mansfield Amendment, which was never passed into law, would have drastically reduced the American military presence in Europe.

The head of the English department in Missoula was a teacher of creative writing named H. G. Merriam. He had come up the hard way, peddling papers as a boy in front of the Brown Hotel in Denver. After being among the first batch of Rhodes Scholars from the United States, Merriam returned to his native West, where he founded *Frontier and Midland,* the first respectable magazine to take Western literature seriously. Although he scared his faculty to death (they thought the H. G. in his name stood for "Holy God"), he could never bring himself to fire anyone. Merriam would tell incoming faculty: "You come into this school, any course you teach is your course; you can do anything you want in it. Just don't let me ever catch you sitting down when you teach."[1] He would walk around and peer through classroom windows to make sure that his order was being followed.

1. Fiedler, interview with author, Nov. 5, 1998.

Leslie had been in Missoula for only a few months when the Japanese bombed Pearl Harbor, Hawaii. As a husband and father, he could have gotten a deferment from military service. Instead, Leslie sensed that the war would become the one great communal experience of his generation. His students were leaving in great numbers to fight. If he were left behind, he would miss out on his last chance for adventure. Perhaps his parents had been right in sensing that he was too young to settle down with a family. World War II offered a return to prolonged adolescence. So, during a period when he and Margaret had not been speaking for several days, Leslie impulsively joined the navy. It was a decision that helped define what would be one of the central roles of his life.

Shortly after his induction into the navy, Leslie gained admission to the Japanese Language School in Boulder, Colorado, where he was able to learn his first non-Indo-European language. As a married man with a child, he was allowed the privilege of living off base with his family. When the government discovered how few Americans knew the language of their enemy, it became imperative to find the brightest young men in America and subject them to intensive training in Japanese. Of necessity, the faculty consisted of "an odd assortment of Japanese-American greengrocers, gardeners, optometrists, typists, and car salesmen, plus a handful of pale-face missionaries from the East, temporarily out of work" (*BB,* 47). As it turned out, many of the more intellectually gifted students in the language school were also security risks, because of either their past political affiliations or their sexual predilections. Leslie remembers walking past the commanding officer's headquarters one day and hearing one of the dismissed students protesting, "But, goddamn it, *everybody was a Communist in those days.*"

Finally, everyone in Leslie's group had either been sent home or duly commissioned—except for him. It was unclear what would happen. One guy who had appeared at a Quaker symposium against the war was dismissed, while an organizer for the Communist Party was allowed to slip through. (The situation was complicated by the fact that America and Stalinist Russia were now allies.) Assuming that he would probably be rejected, Leslie told Margaret to pack their bags for the return trip to Missoula. The next day, his commission was officially approved.

Leslie later learned that the investigator assigned to Newark had stopped a girl in his old neighborhood to enquire about him. Leslie remembers her as "the sister of a childhood friend: a hysterical girl . . . given to throwing kitchen utensils at both of us in her inscrutable rages, but who, confronted by a nosey outsider, drew back the lid of the pram in which her firstborn lay and screamed so all could hear, 'You see this kid here. If he grows up to be one-half, one-tenth the man Leslie Fiedler is, I'll die happy.' " Meanwhile, the investigator assigned to Missoula asked one of Leslie's colleagues, Baxter Hathaway, whether "Mr. Fiedler was ever a Marxist." Responding, in widely spaced and barely audible words, Baxter replied: "Well, I couldn't rightly say, not knowing much about Marxism myself. But it seems to me that Mr. Fiedler may have been, just may, understand, I wouldn't want to commit myself, some sort of Lovestoneite" (*BB,* 40). Apparently having never encountered Lovestoneism in his official glossary of left-wing splinter groups, the investigator probably figured that he could clear Leslie with impunity.

Having been elevated from yeoman second class to lieutenant junior grade, Leslie was finally a naval officer, although he felt no more comfortable as such than in the role of college professor. (By the end of the war, there had been surprisingly few casualties among the graduates of the language school—only "a suicide or two out of loneliness or despair, plus a couple of dishonorable discharges for incidents involving indiscreet newspaper boys" [*BB,* 38].) After fourteen months in the language school, he was now deemed qualified to go overseas and interrogate Japanese prisoners. If he was uneasy wearing the mantle of an authority figure, the idea of being an interpreter or translator intrigued him. During his subsequent career as teacher and critic, Leslie has found himself mediating among various groups who might not otherwise have been able to communicate with one another.

The students in the language school had been divided into smaller classes. The group of five to which Leslie belonged included Reed Irvine, a serious young Mormon with a Japanese wife. He and Leslie were later together at Pearl Harbor and Iwo Jima, parting only when Reed decided to go into the marine corps and Leslie stayed in the navy. After a separation of more than forty years, Reed stopped by to see Leslie in the late 1980s. By that time, Leslie had gained a reputation as a guru of the counterculture, while Reed was the right-wing operative behind Accuracy in Media. The cohorts of both men found them to be an unlikely pair; however, they enjoyed a pleasant evening talking about nothing but the good old days.

Even as he was preparing to be separated indefinitely from his family, Leslie welcomed his second son. Eric Ellery Fiedler (who was named for the explorer Leif Erickson and for William Ellery Leonard) arrived in the world on New Year's Day 1943. There had been great difficulty finding a naval doctor who had not been partying the night before. Nevertheless, the circumstances of Eric's birth had not been nearly as traumatic as those of his brother, Kurt. A few Saturdays later, when Leslie went to pay the medical bills at the Seventh Day Adventist hospital where his son had been born, he was told, "We can't take your money today. It's the Sabbath, you know."[2]

2. Ibid.

I

By the time Leslie arrived at Pearl Harbor in 1943, little visible evidence was left of the bombing that had taken place in December 1941. With the illusion of invulnerability forever shattered, the naval base was now functioning as an integral part of the war machine. The various units doing translation all had strange names. One was called "JIC POA: Joint Intelligence Center, Pacific Ocean Area." Another, which was charged with breaking the Japanese code, was "FRUPAC: Fleet Radio Unit, Pacific Area" (or "Fruit Pac," as it was irreverently known). "[M]ost of the codographers were fruits, in fact," Leslie recalls; "it seemed to go with the profession." Other than the translators, very few people remained on the island. Leslie remembers it as a good life, where he stood watch from three in the afternoon until midnight. After midnight, he could do pretty much what he wanted, so he usually got a little sleep and then spent the middle part of the day on the beach. He also got to know some of the local Japanese residents. The one he knew best was a farmer from whom he learned to milk goats. Another acquaintance was the mother-in-law of the secretary of the territory, a formidable lady with a formidable moustache, who would engage Leslie in long discussions of Jane Austen. Because Japanese citizens were so integral to the Hawaiian economy, they were not rounded up and placed in internment camps, as those on the American mainland had been.

When the drudgery of translating documents got to be a bit too much for him, Leslie volunteered to do virtually anything else, and so he was assigned to the command ship for the fleet preparing to leave for Iwo Jima. Somewhat apprehensive, he said to the commanding officer: "Look, I don't know what to do. I never had any combat training. I don't even know how to scramble over the side of a ship." The commander's first response to this and all other questions was "Go shit up a rope." His second response was "Do whatever the guy in front of you does." The commanding admiral was an extremely vain man named Hill, who fancied himself a writer. When he heard that Leslie was a man of letters, the admiral invited him up to his cabin and pulled out a book he had written and had privately printed. It was called *Maryland's Charm as Shown in Her Silver.* "I must have betrayed somehow that I was more amused than impressed," Leslie recalls, "because he shooed me out quickly and never spoke to me again— perhaps forgot that I existed."[3]

All told, Leslie was on board ship for sixty days, enough time to play endless card games (some poker and more cribbage) and make it all the way through *Finnegans Wake.*[4] The ship sailed evasive maneuvers, heading for various

3. Leslie Fiedler, "Remembering Iwo Jima: A Trip through Time," 4. Subsequent references will be cited parenthetically in the text.
4. Leslie Fiedler, interview with Bruce Jackson, May 7, 1989.

places, but putting ashore for only a few hours at a time. They seemed to have everything aboard, including three-color printing presses. Consequently, the crew was able to turn out leaflets containing information from the latest intelligence reports. Aboard ship, Leslie's job was to interrogate prisoners. At first, they were brought to the ship as it lay fifteen hundred yards offshore. Leslie saw the Battle of Iwo Jima being fought in the distance as if he were sitting in a theater watching a newsreel. On the third day, he went ashore to pick up more prisoners.

Leslie remembers with particular vividness the night he heard wailing sirens, warning "us that we were the target of a Japanese bombing plane." "Even after . . . two bombs . . . had just missed us, fore and aft," he continues, "I felt alive but somehow guilty—and eager to put the blame on someone else." His shipmates, who shared this feeling, agreed that the culprit was Admiral Hill. " 'Too damn proud,' I heard a voice behind me say. 'That's why he kept his two star [admiral's] flag flying day and night—and almost killed us all' " ("Remembering," 3).

The only prisoners Leslie encountered on the ship were those who were too traumatically wounded to commit suicide. The marines who were guarding them would swat each of them with a baseball bat, first on one side of the head and then on the other, just to make their point. Because they assumed that they would never be taken alive, the prisoners did not know how to behave after being captured. Many of them compulsively confessed. All of them had to be shaved for body lice. When they saw the razors coming out, they were certain that they were going to be castrated. In fact, one guy got so scared when the razor came close that he ended up pissing all over Leslie. This so shamed the man that he tried to commit suicide, first grabbing someone's knife and then trying to jump overboard. Afterward, he and Leslie looked at pictures of the man's wife and kids. In a classic example of the Stockholm syndrome, the prisoner said, "I love you," and begged Leslie to take him home with him.

So much of the interrogation went on in sick bay that Leslie felt a shock of recognition when he first saw the movie *M*A*S*H*. He remembers that one prisoner whose legs were blown off insisted on climbing the ladder to the ship on his stumps. He would have lost face had he allowed himself to be hauled aboard. The only time Leslie was in actual danger came when he and a doctor unwrapped a carefully bandaged patient. Inside, after they had touched him, they noticed a little sign someone had written: "gangrene." The doctor immediately shot himself and Leslie up with an antidote. Although the doctor took ill for a time, Leslie came away unharmed. At that point, he resolved to wear rubber gloves when handling anyone who might be infectious.

Leslie was present when the American flag was raised over the island. Because the wind was wrong the first time, the entire ritual had to be photographed a second time. He saw "the photographer (dreaming no doubt of a Pulitzer Prize) gesticulating frantically as he urged his weary amateur cast to act once more—and this time get it *right*—themselves in their historical roles." ("Remembering," 3). Not until years later was it discovered that an unarmed stretcher-bearer had provided the flag for this second photograph before being pushed off the knoll by one of the six immortal "flag raisers." "[T]o be authentically American," Leslie writes, "an icon had to be at least partially fake."

Trying to get ashore, Leslie swam toward the black lava beach. The only problem was that he "could not take two successive strokes without crashing into a splintered spar, a spent shell, a twisted hunk of plastic or metal—even something that looked enough like a severed human arm that [he] did not examine it too closely." As he approached the shore again, he could see a marine crawling over the ridge on his belly, clutching an unidentified object. "As he came nearer," Leslie recalls, "I could make out that he was saying, 'It's real—a real Jap helmet—a genuine souvenir.' Then thrusting it almost into my face, he turned it over so I could see it was indeed a *real* helmet, holding half of a *real* Japanese skull in a *real* puddle of blood."

> "Get the hell out of here, or I'll . . . I'll," I yelled, not really knowing what I could or would do next. Meanwhile, he was still trying to make a sale. "Just make me an offer," he pleaded. "What do you think it's worth?" And then, seeing he would get no answer, he shrugged, grinned and muttering, "Some days you just can't make a dollar," turned around and started to climb back to where he had come from. At the crest of the ridge, he paused and called out, " . . . Have a good day . . ." Then as if noticing my stripes for the first time added, " . . . sir . . . have a good day, *sir.*"[5]

Leslie was on the island of Guam when he heard that the atomic bomb had been dropped on Hiroshima. He was listening to Radio Tokyo, which seemed greatly confused about what had actually happened. The first stories were that a whole fleet of planes had flown over and done a heavy bombing. Then, it was only one plane but with a new kind of weapon. Although he had the highest possible security clearance, Leslie had no idea that the war would come to such a quick and decisive end. Had there been an invasion of the Japanese mainland, he would have been assigned to interrogate kamikaze pilots who had accidentally survived. He was not looking forward to what promised to be a protracted ordeal. (Perhaps for that reason, he stayed drunk most of the time he was on Guam.) His immediate reaction to the bombing of Hiroshima was one of spontaneous celebration for all the lives (American and Japanese) that had been saved by the end of the war.[6]

5. Leslie Fiedler, "Getting It Right: The Flag Raisings at Iwo Jima."
6. Fiedler, interview with author, Nov. 5, 1998.

II

Throughout the war, Leslie wrote letters to Margaret and his two sons. For many years, he toyed with the idea of using these letters as the basis for a book on his wartime experiences. Unfortunately, before he ever got around to the project, many of these letters were badly burned in a house fire that destroyed a significant number of books and valuable papers. Although few bear a legible date, most of the surviving fragments seem to be from February 1945, the magical month when Leslie celebrated Valentine's Day twice by crossing the international date line.

An intact six-page letter he wrote from somewhere in the South Pacific on February 6, 1945, contains an evocative description of a ship being refueled at sea. "To see a ship oiled at sea," he writes, "is a strange experience; the craft to be replenished nuzzles up the long flat ugly oiler, sometimes two at a time[,] tugging at its either tit, but ungainly large children they are, ill proportioned to the metaphor as they lean their larger shadows over their mother. One thinks absurdly of the monstrous Tom Wolfe of two (someone told me once, a North Carolina [man], this story as a revelation) still suckling."[7]

The next day, Leslie wrote again, noting all of the men he served with who cherished literary ambitions. One, in particular, had known Al Eisner both at Harvard and in Hollywood. It was more than a little strange for Leslie to see someone so familiar to him through another person's eyes. He describes his fellow officer to Margaret as follows:

> He is Harvard '40, was a junior script writer, too; he knew Al not very well, but has been deeply touched by his death. It is odd for me to talk to [him]—for he looks at Al backwards from my point of view, as a hero, an object of emulation, unreservedly the Golden Boy, talented, bright and poised. (He would not like the word, but quite like Kappy's Angel.) He had crept often to the room of Al and Leonard Bernstein to hear Stravinsky (L. B. sounds like a shit: he used to say that the *Sacre de printemps* gave him an orgasm). [He] love[d] in Al beyond what he had written the promise—"oh he was much better than any of us—" And he told me about finding a girl in Hollywood who had known him, and their sharing grief together. His version of his death (and of the rest of the legend: Hatty, his origins) was garbled: an infection of the testicles that had spread to the brain he had it—all done up with apocryphal tales of how bad Al felt being told on going to Hollywood that he would have to fly away from tail.

Leslie then reflects on the irony that, "after all his small successes," it was Al's fate "to be remembered so tenderly as legend." "Perhaps this is, after all, the

---

7. These letters are contained in Leslie Fiedler's private papers.

glorious consequence for which he was all along so visibly intended," the letter continues. "He could never have lived up to the glow he created, this way
he lives by it." "I am scared sometimes," Leslie concludes, "at being the last
alive of us three to carry the burden of the silly Hattie adventure as if it entails
some obligation of which I have not yet become aware. I am moved all out of
proportion as I always am by mentions of Al."

The letters are filled with references to Leslie's two sons, and some passages are addressed directly to them. In a letter dated February 10, 1945, Leslie
writes, "I have been thinking of Eric with a large, gruff voice—I'm glad at any
rate he can bellow (cartoon in our paper today—a timid 2nd Lt, sticking his
head into the general's room, 'Did you bellow, sir?' What if Eric should become a general: stuff for nightmares) like a true son of mine; his special charm
comes thru so amazingly in the letters—caught in a paragraph, I am always
left moved to wonder when I realize that the texture I touch is flat paper, not
the warm flesh with its pad of fat."

Sometimes references to the boys would bring back recollections of Leslie's
own childhood and the close relationship he had once enjoyed with his brother,
Harold. A letter written when Leslie was off the coast of Saipan (probably in
February of 1945) reads in part:

> Your little sketch of the boys in the barber shop pleases me; I want them
> very much to delight each other, to be together redolent of cheap scent
> and shaved behind the ears. I have no comparable memories of Harold &
> I seated next to each other; he always squalled like mad at a barber chair,
> was taken specially by himself, on one dread occasion by my *Father,* when
> my mother had twice failed to drag him there. I was brave but uneasy—
> and we discovered at last an amiable brusque barber who kept us both in
> line by threatening to "dust our pants" (the phrase sticks) if we squirmed
> or protested. It was all a game, but we were never really *sure,* and used
> to walk past the place fast when on other errands waving gingerly to the
> barber as we speeded by.

Leslie's genuine affection for his wife comes through in burned fragments now
almost totally obliterated. At one place, he writes, "[G]row old with me; I am
just suspended now, shall when the war is over collapse into wrinkles and a
gross belly like the joker in the movies when his supply of monkey glands
fails." Elsewhere, he confesses, "[M]y whole libido . . . is concentrated in you.
I shall not you may be sure learn (or even practice in some inadvertent gesture
of defeat) indifference, try to convince myself that life is in any meaningful
sense significant without you. On the contrary, I practice each day to feel more
specifically precisely what I am losing; I shall by the same token know what I
have recaptured when I return better than I have realized before." Then, with
an oblique reference to his poetic alter ego, A. Lazere, he concludes, "This

is spoken by and for the pristine, original, unadulterate Leslie; Lazere agrees but has nothing to do with formulating these ideas—They exist in a world on which his partial, oblique, witty soul can only make a conversation, with which he can never achieve a real exstasis."

On the next page, Leslie continues in much the same vein: "I should of course not want to swap you for anything; you are my more than habit, grafted to me flesh of my flesh; without you I have never had anything beyond the most generalized animal itch for a woman or a sentimental child's impulse. What there is of me that knows how to love a woman has been created by you— would cease to exist with your removal. Any talk of another woman, mythic or real[,] is purely a metaphor." Perhaps in a further attempt to assure her of his constancy, he writes, "I have in me a strong impulse toward asceticism & particularly I think celibacy. It is a reflex in part of fear—but more, I think, a genuine distrust of the flesh—and a, perhaps irresponsible, love of an ordered life on the easier levels, the uncomplicated chastity of utter denial. But since you that tendency in me is utterly hopeless, fails forever against what you have taught me of a domestic decorum, the chastity of marriage. Oddly, what my exile does is make me more nearly immune to the more generalized temptations of the flesh."

These protestations of love are made within the context of a very traditional understanding of the proper relationship between men and women. On February 3, 1945, Leslie described the situation as follows:

> It is like a man and a dog; it doesn't matter if the man is dull, the dog clever; the former is by definition the head of the latter; or think of it less grossly as child and parent, where so long as the relationship child-parent exists, quite independent of the character of either the child or the adult, the former must yield to, respect, obey the latter. In the same sense a woman is first by nature as she is physically organized, and by function as she is a wife[,] subordinate to the man: she can be other only by usurpation and perversion, a betrayal of her own being and of the pattern of human life. . . . It is still the woman who sold us to evil—still the man who is nearer God.

Periodically, Leslie speaks of the men with whom he serves. (One of his jobs was to censor the mail of enlisted men, a job that gave him a privileged glimpse into their dreams and fantasies.) On April 5, 1945, he writes, "These men and boys regarding their fate a little sadly, a little amusedly—move me, with all their special skills, the smoke expert, the breaker of codes, the naval gun fire man, the student of beaches, some with decoration for assiduity that they dare not think more than a mockery—hemmed in by an aura of comparative safety, and a hundred small comforts and moral indignities from the possibility of heroism." Then, in a fragment now burned beyond dating, he mentions a particular individual. "I spent a couple of hours with Reed Irvine today," he writes; "he is a good kid, was so pleased to see me—it seemed like a very homecoming. . . . [W]e talked of you and the boys . . . and Margaret, his Margaret, who is at the University of Chicago, . . . studying English."

When he was on Saipan in February 1945, Leslie was responsible for interrogating civilians who had held out to the bitter end. From there, he writes of the fierce desperation of the nearly vanquished people:

> This day Reed and I set off for the stockade to, as the Japanese say[,] "play" visit genially with the remnants of the band that on this Island killed their children, cut their stomachs or throats according to their sex and skill or lived on the rocks that rim the sea, drinking sea-water, eating the scraps of food they had preserved, poor peasants from the sugar fields, or soft petty bureaucrats from the offices of the South Sea Exploitation Company, eyeing the grenade—guessing by the sounds at the course of battle. The emperor had asked in a special cablegram to the civilians for a demonstration to the world . . . in this first place largely inhabited by your true Nipponese to fall to the Americans. It is not easy to kill one's children.

With the fighting almost done, the island has returned to a kind of pristine, prehistoric grandeur. It "rises with some beauty out of the sea in three broken merged rings of color. The coral beach is white shading to dun, the green tropical middle ground separates it from the great perpendicular rock walls very grey except where they show black the caves in which the last resistance centered. There is little evidence of destruction; it was too complete." Farther inland, the scene changes. "The stockade is different—a palpably artificial community, its citizens have adapted, but as one adapts to a disaster. I do not know how to begin to describe it. You must imagine some great Hooverville—an incredible aggregation of the sort of shacks that the bums inhabit along the rims of the Jersey meadows, all organized in rows with the suggestion of a pattern of a city, gross and dim."

As the letter progresses, the descriptions become more detailed.

> The smell of excrement and the color of snot set the atmosphere—it was not sad merely dirty. The Buddhist priest alone appeared in a clean T-shirt, over a recently washed pair of jeans; cleanliness was his only insignia. He was a quick little man, with no hint of the ceremonious. We walked with him among the graves of those who had died since the camp was set up (the bones of their other dead are in the mountains; each day they come patiently with the antique plea to be allowed to gather them and are refused). There are too many resisters still left in the hills; the day I was there a plane had spotted 350 of them armed—and one family decided to surrender. The grave markers were bare sticks—and larger versions of

them before which were set withered fruits or scraggly clumps of flowering grass did duty for the unknown, uncounted, unhoused dead.

While on Saipan, Leslie participated in a tea ceremony with a Buddhist priest
and an old lady. (Having no better vessels, they used rusted tin cups.) After
the ceremony was over, the old lady asked Leslie how many women he had
raped in the great war. When he said "none," she replied, "You making the
honorable joke, perhaps."[8]

Amid the horrors of war, there were moments of farce as well. When
Leslie's ship reached the shores of Eniwetok (the date is indecipherable), an
officer's club was set up on the sandy beach. There were beach umbrellas and a
long bar at which one could obtain rum and rye but no mixer other than Coke
or water. The mural behind the bar showed a little rabbity naval officer standing on a tropical island, behind every rock of which there appeared a luscious
girl in a bright bathing suit. "The slot machines down the room's center creak
and bang and rattle (not often)—and there is shade & chairs: all the symbols
of civilization centered here." Drinking frosty cans of beer, the men would
exchange such remarks as, "Jesus, what a place to be stationed"—or "Imagine
fighting for *this*."

Predictably, arrangements for boats back to the ship got fouled up. Not being able to discover the proper boat in the scurry and bustle of the pier, the
men were late in getting off. By the time they finally arrived back at the ship,
the gangway was up, and no one on board seemed even to have noticed their
absence. "We all sat silently suffering from the same urge," Leslie recalls, "for
we had all been drinking beer—until at last one wizened colonel said, 'I don't
know what you gentlemen are going to do—but I'm going to piss!' In five
minutes we were all lined up along the leeward side of the boat, arranged
roughly by rank, making water peacefully into the evening breeze. It seemed
for an instant—the one conclusion to the infamous movie that would never be
filmed: And so we leave Eniwetok as the sun sinks into the west."

III

Although most American military personnel began heading for home
as soon as the war was over, Leslie's role as a translator kept him in China
for three more months, where he helped to repatriate the Japanese population there. When the Americans entered the liberated city of Tientsin, they
were treated like conquering heroes. Although it was too hot to wear a helmet,

8. Fiedler, interview with author, Nov. 5, 1998.

Leslie wore a helmet liner and a uniform he never quite believed in. Most of the Europeans living there were émigrés from Bolshevik Russia. They had come much earlier as far as Manchuria and had eventually made their way down to China. Among them were quite a few Russian Jews, who made their living by changing money, running sleazy nightclubs, or pimping. Going down to the Imperial Hotel on Sunday mornings to have bagels and tea, Leslie would run into one particular money changer. When he gave the man a five- or ten-dollar American bill, he got several thousand units of local Chinese currency in exchange. "Thank you," Leslie said, and the money changer looked up at the heavens in a classic Jewish pose. "Look at him. He gives me good American money, and I give him shit paper, and he says 'thank you.'" It was then that Leslie knew the Jews would never die.

One of the marines stationed with Leslie in China was a fast-talking Texan named Jack Brooks. Known as Babbling Brooks, he was with the signal battalion of the first marines when Leslie was attached to that unit. After being ashore for one day, Brooks had managed to secure complete furnishings, a desk, and a beautiful Eurasian girl. Because he was small for a marine, he never went out without brass knuckles in his pocket. Although military rules insisted that a serviceman traveling the streets carry a gun with him at all times, Jack found that the .45 made too much of a bulge in his tailor-made uniform. So Leslie ended up carrying the gun. ("One more bulge under you won't be noticed," Jack observed.) After the war, Jack Brooks was elected to Congress and later served on the Judiciary Committee that voted articles of impeachment against Richard Nixon.

During the brief interregnum after the Japanese had been driven out and before the Communists had seized control, two young Chinese officers in absolutely immaculate uniforms asked for Leslie's help in arresting a "war criminal." They had learned that a former factory owner was hiding out nearby. He was reported to have once castrated a coolie in a fit of rage. Also (and at this their eyes lit up), he was said to have a buried a large fortune in gold in his backyard. Because he spoke Japanese, Leslie was to serve as interpreter. As he recalls, "the War Criminal turned out to be a plump, scared businessman in padded trousers and a stained skivvy shirt, whose only hoard was an accumulation of canned goods, chiefly fruit." The twelve-year-old girl who was alleged to be his love slave "clung to him not like a prisoner but like a ward, though whether she thought of him as father, uncle, or lover was hard to tell. . . . 'The daughter of an old friend,' he explained hopelessly. 'I promised her mother I would look out for her when the troubles came.'" But when Leslie translated, "The Chinese officers only snickered louder" (*BB*, 42).

Leslie suddenly felt as if he had been turned into a Gestapo agent. He hauled the "war criminal" down the stairs and off to prison. When they dug up his yard the next day and found no gold, Leslie began to doubt the reliability of all the charges against the man. When he went to the prison to talk to the poor wretch, he got the bureaucratic runaround. After an hour and a half of tea and obfuscation, the jailers informed him that no such man had ever been arrested, much less confined to a cell in that prison. Whether the man was guilty or not, Leslie realized that he had unknowingly delivered him to his death.

One day, when he was walking down the street in Tientsin, Leslie was confronted by a Japanese political scientist who seemed to have stepped out of some racist propaganda poster—he had buck teeth and glasses patched with adhesive tape. They went up to the man's room, where he showed Leslie his books—some in English, some in Japanese. "Is there anything I can do for you?" Leslie asked. "Yes," the man replied. "I'd dearly love some coffee." When Leslie got him a pound or two of American coffee, the political scientist said, "In return for this, I would like to give a small party for you and fifty of your closest friends." Although Leslie didn't have fifty close friends, he invited the two that he did have and forty-seven other marines.

In addition to being a political scientist, Leslie's new friend was a powerful figure in the Japanese community. When the Americans arrived at the rented hall where the party was to be held, they found fifty place settings and fifty of the most refined Geisha girls to serve them. There was painted scenery, classical Japanese dances, and elegant food. Everything proceeded with great formality until one of the marines, no longer able to control himself, grabbed the Geisha behind him and yelled, "Let's make the Big Love, baby." As if on cue, everyone leaped, and in five minutes the place was a shambles. Leslie fled. A day later, he returned to apologize to his friend, but before he could haltingly offer amends, his friend said, "This is an occasion we will never forget. You honored us with your presence." And on he went in this vein. "What the hell?" Leslie thought. "I'm a barbarian." And so he said, "You're welcome" and returned to his quarters convinced that he could never defeat the Japanese on the field of courtesy.

By the time Leslie finally got his discharge, he and Margaret had been apart almost as long as they had been together. If he had never quite gotten used to thinking of himself as a naval officer, he had played that role longer than he had that of a college professor. And he would have to learn again what it meant to be a husband and father. "Bringing home Number Two Wife," he wired Margaret from China. "The hell you are," she wired back. His great adventure come to an end, Odysseus was heading home.[9]

9. Fiedler, interview with Jackson, May 7, 1989.

CHAPTER FOUR

Too Good to Be True

WHEN LESLIE finally arrived back in the United States in late 1945, he had been gone from home so long that he initially did not recognize Margaret standing in the airport to greet him. He was, of course, a complete stranger to Kurt and Eric. If his great war adventure had enabled him to flee the mundane responsibilities of family life and civilian work, he was now brought back to those obligations. If anything, his military experience seemed like a dream from which he had awakened to quotidian reality. His certificate of discharge simply read: "The individual was employed in a position of special trust and no further information regarding his duties in the Navy can be disclosed. He is under oath of secrecy, and all concerned are requested to refrain from efforts to extract more information from him" (*BB,* 45).

After Pearl Harbor, Iwo Jima, and China, Leslie's next stop seemed destined to be Missoula. But before he could return there, the Rockefeller Foundation offered him a year's postdoctoral fellowship at Harvard. Returning to school was equivalent to prolonging his adolescence for yet another year, even if he did have to share his prefabricated housing with a wife and two kids. As a child in Newark, Leslie had viewed Harvard as a kind of WASP utopia, reserved for blue bloods and a few golden ethnics such as Al Eisner. (The closest he had previously come to Harvard was the occasion Al had used the name Leslie Fiedler when appearing in the YCL production of *Waiting for Lefty.*) Not only was Leslie now a certified member of the Harvard community, he also enjoyed the privileged position of being neither a student nor a professor. The Harvard Leslie remembers seemed to be "inhabited chiefly by veterans like me and their wives pushing baby carriages: an island of irrelevant grass constantly invaded by whooping kids on tricycles, pursued by whooping parents, who, drunk and after dark, took over those tricycles" (*BB,* 44).

Although Leslie took a wide variety of courses, the center of his life that year was the Harvard Poetry Society. Most of what he wrote and published at that time were poems, and most of the people with whom he associated were aspiring poets. This included the most brilliant graduate student in the English department—a young patrician named Dick Wilbur. At one level, Leslie and Wilbur were close friends, seeing each other nearly every day to discuss their shared interest in poetry. And yet, beneath Wilbur's charm lurked an air of condescension. He seemed like nothing so much as a character out of a short story by F. Scott Fitzgerald. One night, Dick got drunk at a party and proceeded to display his athletic prowess by climbing a tree too fragile to hold him. As everyone predicted, he fell out and broke his arm.

One day in Harvard Yard, Leslie met another poet, who would prove to be an even closer friend. As he recalls: "I saw this apparently spastic or crazy woman criss-crossing her own path as she crossed the yard, and when I asked her what was happening, the young woman . . . answered that she was trying to get from one side to the other . . . without stepping on an ant." The woman was Ruth Stone, wife of a Harvard graduate student named Walter Stone. Over the next half century, Ruth published poetry that would win a small but devoted following. Except for Leslie Fiedler, however, her work might never have seen the light of day. In an essay on Ruth published in 1996, Leslie recalls having "rescued and deciphered a balled-up, scribbled page that she had tossed under the bed in her tiny prefab house just off Harvard Yard." Then later, when Walter and Ruth moved from Harvard to the University of Illinois, where Walter secured his first teaching position, Leslie sent a group of Ruth's poems to Karl Shapiro, editor of *Poetry* magazine. Shapiro immediately took them all.[1]

In addition to writing verse, Ruth Stone adopted the persona of a poet. An unpredictable free spirit, she kept a cluttered and disorganized house. (If you were invited for Thanksgiving dinner at two in the afternoon, you were lucky to be fed by midnight.) At one point after the Stones' move to Illinois, the debris in their house got so bad that the fire marshal heard about it and came by to serve a summons. Undaunted, Ruth greeted him stark naked, screaming at the top of her lungs. Not surprisingly, he never came back.[2]

At Harvard, Leslie also seized the opportunity to study Old Testament Hebrew. (When he was supposed to have done so in preparation for his bar mitzvah in Newark, he had lectured the rabbi on Jewish racism toward blacks, only to be told he read like a Cossack.) He learned enough to make it into a class in exegesis of the prophets and recalls spending what seemed like an entire semester on the fifty-third chapter of Isaiah. The class, which consisted of an interesting mix of believing Jews and believing Christians, was taught by

1. Leslie Fiedler, interview with author, Feb. 25, 1999. Sandra M. Gilbert, "An Interview with Ruth Stone, 1973," 61.
2. Fiedler, interview with author, Feb. 25, 1999.

Robert Pfeiffer, "who believed in nothing but grammar and syntax."[3] Leslie also studied the *Physics* of Aristotle and worked in the library on an international anthology of verse, which he never completed.

In terms of launching his career as a critic, Leslie's most valuable acquaintance during his year at Harvard was with a young writer named Delmore Schwartz. Although Delmore was only four years older than Leslie, he had already established himself as an important critic and short story writer. For a brief period, he was also the most anthologized poet of his generation. He had entered the University of Wisconsin as an undergraduate a decade before Leslie had arrived in Madison. Although Delmore had not been able to get on the tenure track at Harvard, he had been teaching there as an instructor since the early 1930s. A New York Jewish intellectual, he was one of the advisory editors of *Partisan Review*. (Delmore was such a legendary prodigy that Saul Bellow made him the model for the title character of *Humboldt's Gift*.) Leslie remembers Schwartz as being a very insecure young man who carried a hip flask of gin with him at all times.

One of Leslie's other vivid recollections is of a class in modern American poetry taught by F. O. Matthiessen. Occasionally, Matthiessen would let Leslie teach the class, especially when the syllabus dealt with Jewish poets such as Karl Shapiro. Although he was by now an experienced teacher, Leslie had never before had such a distinguished group of students listening to what he had to say. As one might expect, the most charming and articulate student in the class was Dick Wilbur. In the back row sat a sullen undergraduate named Robert Creeley. Meanwhile, literary agents, publisher's representatives, and the editors of little magazines descended on Cambridge, certain that a postwar literary renaissance was in the making.

Leslie recalls Matthiessen himself as being a "little gray professor, . . . making silences into which we rushed, as he curled like a cat in his chair" (*BB*, 47). Although he could sense that this professor was a troubled man, Leslie would not comprehend the extent of his distress until Matthiessen leaped to his death from a twelfth-floor window in Boston's Manger Hotel on March 31, 1950. He had suffered a nervous breakdown in the late 1930s and periodic bouts of depression thereafter. Only the year before Leslie's time at Harvard, Matthiessen's beloved companion, Russell Cheney, had died. Moreover, by the end of the 1940s, Matthiessen's political idealism had been shattered by the increasing hostility of the Cold War. In retrospect, his suicide appears to have been a disaster waiting to happen. In the midst of his unhappiness, however, Francis Otto Matthiessen had done more than any other scholar to establish the legitimacy of American literary studies in the academy.

3. Fiedler, interview with Jackson, Apr. 7, 1989.

When Matthiessen entered Yale as an undergraduate in the fall of 1919, *Moby-Dick* was shelved under "Cetology" in the university library. Any student interested in the literature of his own country had to pursue that passion outside the classroom. In an article on the teaching of American literature published in the March 1928 issue of the *American Mercury,* Ferner Nuhn concluded that our universities considered American literature to be of about equal importance to Scandinavian literature; one-half as important as Italian literature; one-third as important as Spanish or German literature; one-fourth as important as French literature; one-fifth as important as either Latin or Greek literature; and one-tenth as important as English literature.[4] The canon of American writing that existed at that time was largely the creation of genteel New Englanders, who seemed to belong to an earlier age.

The discovery of American literature in the second decade of the twentieth century was in large part an attack on the earlier canon and the earlier sensibility. The new movement probably began with George Santayana's influential lecture "The Genteel Tradition in American Philosophy," in 1911, and was carried forward by the iconoclastic writings of Van Wyck Brooks and H. L. Mencken. In the 1920s, it reached a new level of intensity with Lewis Mumford's *The Golden Day* (1926) and V. L. Parrington's *Main Currents in American Thought* (1927–1930). Some of the greatest American literature was being written in the twenties, even as the previously neglected geniuses Herman Melville and Emily Dickinson were being admitted to the canon. When Matthiessen began work on his critical masterpiece *American Renaissance* in 1930, the scholarly community was ready for a radically new interpretation of the American literary tradition.

By the time *American Renaissance* finally appeared in 1941, the innovations of modernism had inspired a revolution in critical thinking. T. S. Eliot and his admirers had revised the canon of English literature by stressing close textual analysis (an approach that served some writers better than others). Matthiessen had thoroughly mastered the techniques of close reading. At the same time, he was constantly trying to extend questions about form and technique into the realm of moral judgment. A model of the passionately engaged critic, he could not sacrifice the art of literature to a cultural vision, nor could he ignore the needs of culture to make a fetish of art. His most characteristic theoretical essay was called "The Responsibilities of the Critic." If Matthiessen's attempts to combine aesthetic and social impulses were never perfectly realized, any more than was his desire to unite the patrician and frontier strains in American culture, the seriousness of his effort and the extent of his achievement set a standard for all who were to follow. In the late forties, Leslie Fiedler could hardly

4. Ferner Nuhn, "Teaching American Literature in American Colleges," 328.

have imagined that he would become one of the most important inheritors of the Matthiessen legacy.

I

Leslie's debut as a critic of American literature came about almost by accident. Although he had published fiction, poetry, book reviews, and several short articles on contemporary culture, he had not written anything about the American literature of the nineteenth century. (As he was not a professional Americanist, there is no reason why he should have.) Nevertheless, in reading the great American boys' books to his sons Kurt and Eric, Leslie was struck by a motif that no one else seemed to have noticed. When he managed to articulate his reflections in print, he sent the finished product to Delmore Schwartz at *Partisan Review.* In a letter dated May 6, 1948, Delmore replied: "We liked your essay very much and we'll use it as soon as possible."[5] "Come Back to the Raft Ag'in, Huck Honey!" appeared the following month, and American literary studies have never been the same since.

Reading "Come Back to the Raft" over half a century later, one tends to forget that, prior to Fiedler, few critics had discussed classic American literature in terms of race, gender, and sexuality. The fact that Fiedler did so would have been revolutionary enough, had he not compounded the scandal by using such socially charged terms as "homosexuality" and "homoerotic passion." The thesis of his essay (and much of his later writing on American literature) is that we find at the center of our classic novels something very different from the typical European preoccupation with heterosexual love. From Rip Van Winkle on, the typical American hero is likely to be fleeing the constraints of what Washington Irving called "petticoat government." Making this point even more emphatically over three decades later, Fiedler writes: "The uniquely American hero/anti-hero . . . rescues no maiden, like Perseus, kills no dragon, like Saint George, discovers no treasure, like Beowulf or Siegfried; he does not even manage at long last to get back to his wife, like Odysseus. He is, in fact, an anti-Odysseus who finds his identity by *running away from home.*"[6]

Fiedler believes that our great novels (or at least those recognized as such) are boys' books because American men are to a large extent boys at heart. An essential aspect of our sentimental life is "the camaraderie of the locker room and ball park, the good fellowship of the poker game and fishing trip, a kind of passionless passion, at once gross and delicate, homoerotic in the boy's sense,

---

5. This letter and others cited in this chapter are contained in Leslie Fiedler's private papers.
6. *What Was Literature? Class Culture and Mass Society,* 152. Subsequent references will be cited parenthetically in the text as *WWL?*

possessing an innocence above suspicion" (*CE,* 1:143). It is only by decrying overt homosexuality that we can protect this macho utopia and vindicate the mythic chastity of male companionship. To do otherwise would be to "destroy our stubborn belief in a relationship simple, utterly satisfying, yet immune to lust; physical as the handshake is physical, this side of copulation" (143).

Although the refugee from matriarchal civilization is occasionally isolated (as was Thoreau at Walden or Rip in the Catskills), we more often see a wilderness bonding between males. The central enduring relationship in our literature, this bonding is a pure anti-marriage, because it is freed from the complications of sexual passion and the responsibilities of domestic life. In a world without women, it is possible to enjoy both freedom and community—even if it is only the community of a boy and a runaway slave floating downriver on a raft. As the Bible tells us of the bonding of David and Jonathan, it is a love "surpassing the love of women."

What makes the American experience of male bonding more complex (and seemingly at odds with the official mores of American society) is that it frequently joins a white and a colored man. The most famous, though hardly exclusive, examples are to be found in the *Leatherstocking Tales* (Natty Bumppo and Chingachgook), *Moby-Dick* (Ishmael and Queequeg), and *Adventures of Huckleberry Finn* (Huck and Jim). When the white man—or boy— dreams himself a renegade from society, he is symbolically joined to that alien other who has always, as if by definition, been a renegade. It should not be surprising, then, that that dream finds its embodiment in our most mythically resonant literature. Nevertheless, our social taboos are such that it has usually been foreigners—e.g., Lawrence and Lorca—who have guessed the truth. At the very least, it was a breach of etiquette for an insider such as Fiedler to expose this archetype at the heart of the American experience.

When Fiedler uses the word *archetype,* he is suggesting at the very beginning of his career as critic the direction that that career will take. From the time that he composed his first poem, "Mercury and the Invention of the Lyre," at age seven or eight, he assumed an intimate connection between literature and myth. In calling the Huck-Honey paradigm an archetype, he is referring to "a coherent pattern of beliefs and feelings so widely shared at a level beneath consciousness that there exists no abstract vocabulary for representing it, and so 'sacred' that unexamined, irrational restraints inhibit any explicit analysis" (146). If we were to object that Fiedler himself is engaging in explicit analysis, he would reply that his essay is more a meditation, a spontaneous response to reading, than a merciless dissection of the pattern story.

To be sure, the more widely accepted myth of race relations in America is one of heterosexual violation—from antebellum slave uprisings to Willie Horton ads, from Thomas Jefferson mounting Sally Hemmings to redneck boys getting their ashes hauled in a ghetto whorehouse. Thus, the innocent vision of interracial male love is deeply subversive. As Fiedler puts it: "Behind the white American's nightmare that someday, no longer tourist, inheritor, or liberator, he will be rejected, refused, he dreams of his acceptance at the breast he has most utterly offended. It is a dream so sentimental, so outrageous, so desperate, that it redeems our concept of boyhood from nostalgia to tragedy" (151).

What Fiedler did not fully realize in 1948 was the degree to which the Huck-Honey motif would permeate American popular culture. (Even by then, the Lone Ranger and Tonto had become fixtures of American radio drama.) Looking back on the situation in 1982, he notes the pervasiveness of inter-ethnic male bonding "in a score of movies such as *The Defiant Ones, The Fortune Cookie,* and the belated film version of Ken Kesey's *One Flew over the Cuckoo's Nest,* as well as in numerous TV shows, ranging from *I Spy* to *Tenspeed and Brown Shoe, Chips* and *Hill Street Blues*" (*WWL?* 16). Moving beyond 1982, one could cite the TV show *Miami Vice,* and the seemingly endless series of *Lethal Weapon* films. Even the daily comic strip "Jump Start" features what John Gregory Dunne once called a "black and white in a black-and-white."[7]

Strangers are constantly writing Leslie to mention different sightings of the Huck-Honey motif. On October 25, 1967, Geoffrey Williams suggested that someone "write an essay on latent homosexuality in British fiction to be called, 'Elementary, Watson Dear.'" Nearly two decades later, on February 4, 1986, Paul A. Roth of the philosophy department of the University of Missouri at St. Louis, sent Leslie a paper called "Come Back to the Millennium Falcon Ag'in, Han Honey: Sex and Society in *Star Wars.*" (The possibilities for alien male bonding in deep space had already been noted years before when one of the early reviews of the TV series *Star Trek* was titled "Come Back to the Space Ship Ag'in, Spock Honey!") Closer to home, Carol Green suggested that the Eddie Murphy film *Beverly Hills Cop* "may be the first time that Nigger Jim gets to tell *his* side of the story." Responding to her elaborately developed theory of the movie, Leslie notes that "it is always an especial delight to see people working out implications of ideas which I started so long ago."[8]

If ordinary readers have generally responded well to this notorious essay (even if they know it only by reputation and can't quite manage to spell Leslie Fiedler's name correctly), the literary establishment has been more measured in its reaction. Philip Rahv, who was co-editor of *Partisan Review* when "Come Back to the Raft" was published, tried to absolve himself of responsibility by claiming that he thought the essay a put-on. "And in this opinion the writers

7. John Gregory Dunne, *True Confessions,* 4.
8. Although Leslie had not yet seen *Beverly Hills Cop,* he went on to say, "I have a hunch that what is happening in that film is that Jim now thinks he is Huckleberry Finn, too. Everybody thinks he or she is Huckleberry Finn these days."

of the first fan letters it occasioned concurred, referring to it (troubled elitists turning typically to French) as a *boutade,* a *canard,* a *jeu d'espirit*" (*WWL?* 15). The only time Leslie ever met Ernest Hemingway, the ailing novelist greeted him somewhat warily. "Fiedler? Leslie Fiedler," he said. "Do you still believe that st-st-stuff about Huck Finn?" (*CE,* 2:349).

II

"Come Back to the Raft Ag'in, Huck Honey!" has suffered the appropriate fate of truly controversial criticism. It has been attacked from both the left and the right. As one might expect, much of the unease the essay has generated has come from those who disapprove of what they take to be Fiedler's views on homosexuality. Had he used a fashionable euphemism such as "male bonding" instead of "homoerotic passion," he might have avoided confusion, especially on the part of those who knew of his essay only second or third hand. (At one point in *Love and Death in the American Novel,* Fiedler expresses his exasperation with readers who persist in thinking that he was "attributing sodomy to certain literary characters or their authors."[9]) As things turned out, people who knew nothing else about Leslie Fiedler were convinced that he believed Huck and Jim—and a host of other characters in American literature—were "queer as three-dollar bills" (*WWL?* 15). This naturally offended righteous heterosexuals. Somewhat surprisingly, the homosexual lobby itself was less than pleased with Fiedler's position. The queer theorist objection to "Come Back to the Raft" is forcefully presented in Christopher Looby's essay " 'Innocent Homosexuality': The Fiedler Thesis in Retrospect."

Looby renders Fiedler the dubious tribute of taking him quite literally. Refusing to see homoeroticism as some kind of metaphor, he asks: "What's so interesting about claiming that, after all, Huck and Jim are just good pals?"[10] Looby argues that it is anachronistic to try to understand the sort of male relationships that existed on the American frontier in terms that are more appropriate to late-twentieth-century urban life. He goes on to cite anecdotal evidence suggesting that intimate physical contact between males in the early nineteenth century was too common to indicate anything as portentous as sexual orientation. It is only in our own time that we have fallen from the Garden of polymorphous perversity into the wasteland of homophobia. Moreover, Fiedler's constant references to "innocent homosexuality" and "chaste" male

---

9. Leslie Fiedler, *Love and Death in the American Novel,* 349. Subsequent references will be cited parenthetically in the text as *LD*.

10. Christopher Looby, " 'Innocent Homosexuality': The Fiedler Thesis in Retrospect," 538.

love simply mark him as a man of his time—a secret fag hater posing as an enlightened liberal.

Looby's excursions into frontier history might convince us that overt homosexuality was more common in our national past than we had supposed. (Mark Twain's own secretary, Charles Watson Stoddard, was an effeminate homosexual, and one recent Twain biographer has even tried to "out" the laureate of American childhood himself.[11]) It does not follow, however, that homosexual behavior was regarded as normative in the nineteenth century. Most of our anti-sodomy laws originated prior to the twentieth century (that is, before the time when Looby would have us believe that the concept of the homosexual was invented), while almost all efforts to destigmatize sexual preference date from the late 1960s. If anything, Fiedler strikes one as prescient for saying in 1948 that "our laws on homosexuality and the context of prejudice they objectify must apparently be changed to accord with a stubborn social fact" (*CE*, 1:143).

The case that Looby makes for Fiedler's alleged homophobia rests largely on his use of the term "innocent homosexuality." "The implication," Looby writes, "is that there is some other, 'guilty,' form of homosexuality."[12] Anyone possessing even a nodding familiarity with Fiedler's work must realize how tendentious this accusation is. When Fiedler speaks of "innocent" sexuality— homo, hetero, or whatever—he is referring merely to unconsummated desire. Far from rendering a personal moral judgment, he is alluding to that baneful tradition in Western thought that would label *all* sexual activity, including procreative relations within the sacrament of marriage, as evil. It is understood that the saintly young girl of nineteenth-century fiction must be killed off before the onset of puberty. Our male heroes escape the complications of heterosexual domesticity by finding their freedom in the wilderness. Like all myths, this one is immune to the tyranny of both logic and political correctness.

If some in the gay lobby thought Fiedler a closet homophobe, many on the Right thought that he was trying to make buggery seem as American as apple pie. While ostensibly reviewing *What Was Literature?* in the January 1983 issue of *Commentary,* Kenneth S. Lynn comments at length about what he takes to be the sinister subtext of "Come Back to the Raft." Noting that Fiedler's controversial essay was published the same year as Alfred C. Kinsey's *Sexual Behavior in the American Male,* Lynn writes:

> So eager was [Fiedler] to challenge both the folk wisdom of the American people and the clinical wisdom of the psychoanalysts, so fervently was he dreaming of a Kinseyesque America of sexual pluralism and guilt-free

11. Ibid., 545.
12. Ibid., 538.

self-indulgence, that he found it easy to convince himself that every important American writer from Cooper to Faulkner was on his side. The
authors of the Kinsey Report believed in their dubious statistics no more
firmly than Fiedler did in his fraudulent vision of American literature.[13]

The truth of the matter is that right-wing critics did not need the issue of
homosexuality—innocent or otherwise—to find fault with Fiedler's controversial essay. They were sufficiently offended by the notion that Huck—and,
by implication, Mark Twain himself—was pronouncing a wholesale condem-
nation on American society. Although Fiedler might not have said this explicitly, he had come to represent all critics who found Huck's decision to "light
out for the territory" to be a profound act of social criticism. When Kenneth
Lynn attacked this interpretation of *Huckleberry Finn,* half a dozen years before his review of *What Was Literature?* he titled his essay "Welcome Back
from the Raft, Huck Honey!" even though it makes no specific reference to
Fiedler.

In the late 1950s, Lynn reminds us, Henry Nash Smith had tried to counter
the more radical reading of Huck's decision to light out for the Territory by
pointing out that Tom Sawyer had wanted to "go for howling adventures
amongst the Injuns, over in the Territory, for a couple of weeks or two." When
Huck says he means to set out ahead of the others, Smith argues, "there is nothing in the text to indicate that his intention is more serious than Tom's." Putting
the matter bluntly, Lynn concludes: "For decades, students who have finished
reading *Huckleberry Finn* have been encouraged by their teachers to entertain
misleading fantasies about a young boy's continuing search for freedom and
self-realization in the tabula rasa of the Territory. In more properly conducted
classes, they would be encouraged to speculate about what sort of life Huck
will lead when he returns to St. Petersburg."[14]

I suspect that Lynn is more logically correct and Fiedler more mythically
true. Imagining Huck and Jim back in society takes us away from the archetypal heart of the novel. (Their pure anti-marriage can exist only on the raft in
those lyrical moments when reality can be held at bay.) That is perhaps why
Twain himself repeatedly failed to write a convincing sequel to *Huckleberry
Finn.* It is not easy to edit one's dreams, as irresistible as that temptation might
be for a writer who is both a realist and a humorist. As Fiedler reminds us,
there is pathos as well as triumph in Jim's declaration to Huck: "It's too good
for true, Honey. . . . It's too good for true."[15]

13. Kenneth S. Lynn, "Back to the Raft," 68.
14. Kenneth S. Lynn, *The Air-Line to Seattle: Studies in Historical and Literary Writing about
America,* 42.
15. Mark Twain, *Adventures of Huckleberry Finn,* 98.

III

When Leslie finished his year at Harvard, he had a choice of three jobs. He could become a Californian and join the English faculty at either Berkeley or Santa Barbara or he could return to Missoula. His decision to go back to Montana made sense to him if to no one else. He feared that teaching on the Left Coast would be like settling back in the Northeast. In Montana, he would find people who could teach him things that literary intellectuals could not. Also, he wanted to write at his own pace rather than be forced immediately into a publish-or-perish situation, especially if the publication had to be in stuffy academic journals. Finally, in Montana, Leslie had the opportunity to shape and direct an interdisciplinary humanities program, which enrolled approximately half the student body.

While living in Montana, Leslie became acquainted with several western regionalists who had studied under H. G. Merriam.[16] There was also a steady passage of writers from elsewhere coming and going. (When Leslie finally left for good, he was replaced by the poet Richard Hugo.) I. A. Richards and his wife loved Montana so much that they helped map Glacier Park when they were young and continued to return as they grew older. An aging Upton Sinclair gave one of his last talks in Missoula. When the legendary muckraker drifted away from his announced topic, his wife would rise in the audience and remind him: "You already said that Upton." Unfazed, he would smile and ask rhetorically, "Isn't she the most beautiful woman in the world?"[17]

Because he was something of a glorious misfit in the Far West, Leslie naturally gravitated to the company of other misplaced persons. One of these was Joe Kramer, an Eastern European Jew who had never lived in an American city. He was one of a group of Jews who had been brought to this country through Galveston to be settled directly on the land. Joe worked on farms and eventually earned a degree in forest botany. When Leslie arrived in Missoula, Joe was teaching in the forestry school. Although he was an atheist, Joe remembered enough of ancient Jewish custom to preside at Kurt Fiedler's bar mitzvah. "I'm a perfect Jew," he used to say, "except I don't happen to believe in God." To the day of his death, Joe Kramer maintained a comic East European accent. On the first day of registration, he would walk up to the youngest and most naive looking faculty member and say: "Excuse me. Tell me what course I should take to find out what is the good life and how I should lead it?"

Joe liked to chop wood, and one day he got a little careless, chopping off two of his fingers. Nevertheless, he got up early every morning and walked to

---

16. Among those western writers whom Leslie knew in Missoula were A. B. Guthrie, Jr., Dorothy M. Johnson, and Walter Van Tilburg Clark.

17. Leslie Fiedler, interview with Bruce Jackson, Aug. 9, 1989.

the gymnasium, where he shot baskets and ran around the track. He continued doing this even as he began closing in on seventy. The students in Montana had never seen anything like him. In an effort to adopt him as a Westerner, they gave him the nickname of Smokey Joe. The only member of the Communist Party on the faculty at that time, he would take his students up the side of a hill and say: "You see the plant on this side? It's thriving because the wind is right. The plant on the other side is not thriving because the wind is wrong. You don't blame the plant because the wind is wrong!"

Joe's sons disappointed him greatly. One became a reporter and actually got bylines for a while in the *New York Times*. But Joe would only say, "Why can't he do something socially useful?" In general, he despised journalists and other public figures. Joe was a menace at political meetings and lectures because he would get up and ask absolutely endless questions—sometimes philosophical, sometimes just esoteric. The first time an official spokesman from Israel appeared in Missoula, everyone wondered what Joe would do. He got up and said: "Isn't it wonderful we have a country now all Jews. Jewish soldiers, Jewish cops. . . ."[18]

Leslie's own sense of himself as a Jew remained intense, even as he lived in an almost exclusively Gentile region of the country. Perhaps more troubling was what struck him as the pervasive anti-Semitism of the literary canon he revered. In a fit of youthful courage (or brashness), he dealt directly with this matter in a letter to T. S. Eliot, dated December 13, 1948. Although that letter has not been preserved, Eliot's reply of January 14, 1949, is currently housed in Leslie's private files. Essentially, Eliot sees the charges against his own poetry as a matter of geographical and generational sensitivity. Neither the Jews he has known in England nor his older Jewish friends in America have ever mentioned evidence of anti-Semitism in his work. (The poems in which the word *Jew* appears were all published by Jews—in England by Leonard Woolf and in America by Alfred Knopf and Horace Liveright.) In any event, those poems were written many years ago, before racial sensibilities had become as polarized as they are today. Eliot then concludes on a personal note. "Incidentally, and last," he writes, "as you say that you are Jewish: I hope that you will not consider it an impertinence of me to express the hope that you are diligent in attendance at your synagogue (if you are so fortunate as to have one in Missoula), that you observe the Law and read the Scriptures, and that you cherish the faith of your fathers."

Even if he had not been a Jew, Leslie's identity as an Easterner would have eventually posed problems for him, especially since he seemed to have a compulsive urge to publish whatever was on his mind and a more or less regular

18. Leslie Fiedler, interview with Bruce Jackson, June 29, 1989.

forum in *Partisan Review*. During the two decades that he lived in Montana nothing that Leslie wrote stirred more local controversy than "Montana; or the End of Jean-Jacques Rousseau," published in the December 1949 issue of *PR*. Although few of his neighbors read highbrow Marxist literary reviews, those who did quickly spread the word that this Eastern ingrate—in the South he would have been known as a carpetbagger—was biting "the fine, generous Western hand that was feeding him" (*CE*, 2:331).

The passage the locals found most offensive was Leslie's description of the "Montana face": "developed not for sociability or feeling, but for facing into the weather. It said friendly things to be sure, and meant them; but it had no adequate physical expressions even for friendliness, and the muscles around the mouth and eyes were obviously unprepared to cope with the demands of any more complicated emotion. . . . [T]he poverty of experience had left the possibilities of the human face in them incompletely realized" (*CE*, 1:135). The vehement reaction to this passage has never ceased to amuse Leslie. He notes that "some of those most exercised have been quite willing to admit the inarticulateness, the starvation of sensibility and inhibition of expression, of which 'the Face' is an outward symbol. To criticize the soul is one thing, to insult the body quite another!" (*CE*, 1:134).

Leslie begins his notorious essay by identifying three stages in the development of the frontier. In the first stage, the struggle for survival is so intense that the settlers have neither sufficient time nor energy to contemplate the hideous contradiction between their romantic dream of utopia and the barrenness of their present surroundings. However, when the schoolmarm moves out from the East, displaces the whore, and marries the rancher, "the Dream and the fact confront each other openly." This confrontation results in the perceived need "for some kind of art to nurture the myth, to turn a way of life into a culture" (*CE*, 1:133). Consequently, the West is reinvented in terms of a sentimentalized image of the frontier purveyed in pulp novels, Western movies, and fake cowboy songs. At the time that Leslie was writing, Montana was coming to the end of this second phase of frontier development and moving into a third.

The most recent transformation exploits the images of pop art for purely commercial purposes. It brings us the West of the dude ranch and the Chamber of Commerce rodeo. In effect, popular mythology has become so powerful and so pervasive that life not only begins to imitate art, but also to forget that any discrepancy exists between the two: "Certainly for the bystander watching the cowboy, a comic book under his arm, lounging beneath the bright poster of the latest Roy Rogers film, there is the sense of a joke on someone—and no one to laugh. It is nothing less than the total myth of the goodness of man in a state of nature that is at stake every Saturday after the show at the Rialto; and, though there is scarcely anyone who sees the issue clearly or as a whole, most Montanans are driven instinctively to try to close the gap" (136).

The degeneration of the frontier dream was probably unavoidable. In the past, men would simply discard a failed utopia by pushing west in search of a new one. But because of Montana's position on the last frontier, geographical eschatology inevitably gave way to fantasy. The real cowboy imaginatively re-creates himself as Roy Rogers, while the upper-class Montanan identifies himself with even older prototypes of frontier nobility—the pioneer and mountain man (e.g., Jim Bridger or John Colter). Some who are of a liberal or roman-tic sensibility even try to redeem the image of the Indian as Noble Savage, without really coming to terms with the presence of today's Indian, "despised and outcast in his open-air ghettos" (141). Whatever evasion they may have chosen, Leslie urges his fellow Montanans to make the painful but necessary adjustment from myth to reality: "When he admits that the Noble Savage is a lie; when he has learned that his state is where the myth comes to die (it is here, one is reminded, that the original of Huck Finn ended his days, a re-spected citizen), the Montanan may find the possibilities of tragedy and poetry for which he so far has searched his life in vain" (141).

Whenever he found the world of the Missoula PTA and small-minded civic boosterism to be too much to bear, Leslie withdrew to the seedy saloons which for him represented the real Montana. Entering one such dive on a typical Saturday night, he noticed "a 'Western Combo,' complete with tenor, the gui-tars electrified and stepped up so that 'Sixteen Tons' sounds like an artillery barrage and no one is tempted to waste good drinking time by attempting conversation" (*CE*, 2:335–36). On this particular occasion the young bartender, a dropout from journalism school who is "only two years away from the Near North Side of Chicago," is sporting a new pair of cowboy boots:

> "Worth thirty-five bucks," he says proudly, indicating the boots. "I got 'em from a wine-o just off the freights for half a gallon of muscatel. Christ, he needed it bad. Walked next door to drink it (*we* don't let 'em drink from bottles at the tables here, but next door they don't give a damn). Walked out barefoot—*barefoot*—and it was snowing, too. 'Take it or leave it,' I told him, 'half a gallon for the boots.' They were red with yellow threads but I had them dyed black. Look pretty good, don't they? Thirty-five bucks." The band begins to play "You are my Sunshine," good and loud and I can't hear any more, but I get it. I'm home. Montana or the end of you know who. (336)

CHAPTER FIVE

Enfant Terrible

WHEN LESLIE broke with the orthodox Trotskyite movement to join the schism led by Max Shachtman, James Burnham, and Dwight Macdonald, he had, in effect, severed his ties with any form of Communism. Although he might not have fully articulated that position in 1940, he had cast his lot with those who saw the corruption of the Soviet Union as dating all the way back to Lenin. By the postwar period, only a small group of fellow travelers persisted in seeing the USSR as an essentially progressive society that espoused democratic values. (These people found their champion in former vice president Henry Wallace, who mounted a minor party campaign for the presidency in 1948.) Far more influential were the liberal anti-Communists who formed the American Committee for Cultural Freedom, which was itself allied with the (European) Congress for Cultural Freedom.

Those who gathered under the banner of the Committee for Cultural Freedom included New York intellectuals such as Sidney Hook, Daniel Bell, Clement Greenberg, William Phillips, Philip Rahv, Delmore Schwartz, and Lionel and Diana Trilling. They made their case to fellow highbrows in the pages of *Partisan Review* and to intelligent general readers in two other important magazines—the *New Leader,* whose cultural section was presided over by Isaac Rosenfeld, and *Commentary,* which was founded by the American Jewish Committee in 1945. Although the mercurial Elliot Cohen was the nominal editor of *Commentary,* Irving Kristol deserves most credit for keeping the monthly magazine going during those early years. (It was he who solicited and edited almost all of Leslie's contributions to its pages.) After leaving Alcove Number One upon his graduation from City College, Kristol defected to Shachtmanism and later to the Cultural Freedom movement. By 1947, he was assistant editor of *Commentary.* Over half a century later, Leslie still regards Kristol as the best magazine editor he has ever had. Kristol possessed a sure sense of what was missing in the draft of an article, and his patient editorial queries nearly always improved the final product.[1]

In an undated letter that was probably written in the late summer of 1950, Irving suggests that Leslie might want to review Alistair Cooke's latest book, *A Generation on Trial,* which purported to be an objective account of the Hiss case. As urbane as he might be, Cooke simply did not "know the situation from *within,*" at least not to the extent that a former American leftist such as Leslie might. Irving's letter continues, "We have in mind something along the lines of what Diana Trilling did for PR—only less smug, less long-winded, more intelligent; more profound (!) One of the themes that we think ought to be explored is the relation between the American intelligentsia (using this term so as to include Hiss, Chambers, *et al.*) and American society, the relation of this intelligentsia to the secular religion of Communism, the idea of treason, etc."[2] Leslie accepted the assignment, and his essay "Hiss, Chambers, and the Age of Innocence" appeared in the August 1951 issue of *Commentary.*

I

The generation Alistair Cooke believed was on trial consisted of American liberals and fellow travelers who saw in the Soviet Union only an ally against Fascism. Although few such people committed espionage, many who flirted with Communism felt themselves capable of having done so had the opportunity presented itself. They would not have considered such an act treason against their country, but rather loyalty to the more abstract cause of progress and humanity. To proclaim Hiss innocent was to say that, even if he did steal sensitive government documents, his motives were pure, because no deed committed on behalf of the Left could be fundamentally evil.

Leslie Fiedler's article found Hiss to be the epitome of the Popular Front Bolshevik—a Communist whose very usefulness to the party lay in appearing to be everything it theoretically hated. He was an establishment American of impeccable credentials—law clerk to Justice Holmes, aide to President Roosevelt, highly placed State Department official, and later president of the Carnegie Endowment for World Peace. His accuser, on the other hand, was a throwback to an earlier period of party history—the obsessive poet-bum, a Dostoyevskian underground man. Appearances were all on Hiss's side (so much so that Secretary of State Dean Acheson's investigation of rumors about Hiss's Communist ties consisted of asking Alger's brother Donald if the

---

1. Fiedler, interview with author, June 23, 1997.
2. Except where otherwise indicated, the letters cited in this chapter are contained in Leslie Fiedler's private papers.

charges were true; "after all, he had known 'the Hiss boys' since they were children" [*CE,* 1:22].) All that Whittaker Chambers had going for him was the fact that he was telling the truth.

What is most significant about the Hiss case is not the behavior of its principals, as historically revealing and intensely dramatic as that was, nor even the impetus that it gave to the career of Congressman Richard Nixon, who championed Chambers against Hiss. Rather, the Hiss case will be remembered as a watershed in liberalism's long struggle for (or perhaps against) maturity. "American liberalism has been reluctant to leave the garden of its illusion," Fiedler writes, "but it can dally no longer: the age of innocence is dead. The Hiss case marks the death of an era, but it also promises a rebirth if we are willing to learn its lessons." The primary lesson, of course, is that there is evil on the Left as well as on the Right; that "there is no magic in the words 'left' or 'progressive' or 'socialist' that can prevent deceit and the abuse of power." Finally, Fiedler leaves us with a warning: "[W]ithout the understanding of what the Hiss case tries desperately to declare, we will not be able to move forward from a liberalism of innocence to a liberalism of responsibility" (24).

Fiedler's belief that the lessons of the Hiss case could be beneficial to liberalism (a *felix culpa,* if you will) strikes James Seaton as one of the most remarkable characteristics of this essay. He notes that "Fiedler does not use the Hiss case to make a simple about-face to the Right or to withdraw from politics, saying 'a plague on both your houses.'" "Disillusionment is an experience that affects every generation," Seaton continues; "a characteristic American response is simply to give up politics altogether. It is Fiedler's willingness to identify himself with liberalism even as he criticizes liberal culture that infuses the essay with real moral weight and makes it relevant decades later, even for those who might quarrel with its factual assumptions."[3]

Even more spectacular than the Hiss melodrama was the spy case of Julius and Ethel Rosenberg, two American Communists whose activities helped the Soviets construct an atomic bomb. First Julius, then Ethel was executed in the electric chair at Sing Sing, just minutes before the beginning of the Jewish Sabbath on June 19, 1953. For the die-hard Left, the Rosenbergs (or rather a contrived image of them) have always been martyrs to the "witch hunt" mentality of the 1950s. They have also been eulogized in various works of literature, the best known of which are E. L. Doctorow's *The Book of Daniel* and Robert Coover's *The Public Burning.* Leslie Fiedler's more objective assessment of the case, "Afterthoughts on the Rosenbergs," appeared in the inaugural issue of *Encounter* magazine, published in October 1953, less than four months after the Rosenbergs were put to death.

---

3. James Seaton, *Cultural Conservatism, Political Liberalism: From Criticism to Cultural Studies,* 109.

Irving Kristol edited this essay, as well. In 1953, he had just left *Commentary* to found *Encounter* with the British poet Stephen Spender. Published in London under the sponsorship of the Congress for Cultural Freedom, this new magazine sought to become the European counterpart of *Partisan Review, Commentary,* and the *New Leader.* Joining Leslie in the first issue of *Encounter* were such Continental luminaries as Christopher Isherwood, C. Day Lewis, Albert Camus, Denis de Rougement, Spender himself, and (posthumously) Virginia Woolf.

"Afterthoughts on the Rosenbergs" argues that there were really two Rosenberg cases—the actual one tried in a court of law and the symbolic one that continues to be tried in the court of ideology, but because these two very different cases are referred to by the same name, it is difficult to talk sense about them. The legal case against the Rosenbergs is easier to discuss because it is the more tangible of the two. Like Alger Hiss, the Rosenbergs steadfastly maintained their innocence in the face of overwhelming evidence to the contrary. Fiedler suspects that this might have been just a shorthand way of saying that whatever I may have done was justified by a higher loyalty. Just as establishment New Deal types such as Dean Acheson were reluctant to see the truth about Hiss, so too were American radicals and fellow travelers incapable of admitting that the Rosenbergs were guilty. The Communists, who knew the truth, simply exploited the situation and sacrificed the Rosenbergs for their own strategic ends.

By becoming symbols for their attackers and defenders, and ultimately for themselves, the Rosenbergs ceased to exist as human beings. They simply became generic "victims"—and generic Jewish "victims" at that. (If Leslie could feel little cultural affinity for the blueblood Hiss, Julius Rosenberg was the sort of fanatical Jewish leftist he might have grown up with.) If for no other reason than to affirm their individual humanity, Fiedler argues, the Rosenbergs should have been spared. In a desperate effort to demythologize this hapless couple, he describes them in all their vulgar particularity. "Under their legendary role," he writes, "there were, after all, the *real* Rosenbergs, unattractive and vindictive but human; fond of each other and of their two children; concerned with operations for tonsillitis and family wrangles; isolated from each other during three years of not-quite-hope and deferred despair; at the end, prepared scientifically for the execution: Julius' mustache shaved off and the patch of hair from Ethel's dowdy head. . . . This we have forgotten, thinking of the Rosenbergs as merely typical" (*CE,* 1:33).

When the Rosenbergs' humanity was denied by their comrades and by themselves, the burden of its defense was left with us. While it is true that our execution of two guilty people pales when compared with the Soviets' "execution" of millions of innocents, a commutation for the Rosenbergs would have been an even higher road for us to take. "Before the eyes of the world we lost an opportunity concretely to assert what all our abstract declarations can never prove: that for us at least the suffering person is realer than the political moment that produces him or the political philosophy for which he stands" (45).[4]

If the Hiss case raised the specter of Soviet infiltration of the U.S. government, the exposure of the Rosenbergs reminded Americans of what was at stake. As the technological sophistication of warfare increased exponentially with the development of nuclear weapons, the cost of espionage became correspondingly greater. This fact put the Democrats, who had originally protected Hiss, on the defensive and gave the Republicans their first real issue in twenty years. It also stirred a kind of populist resentment among middle Americans who might have liked Roosevelt but who detested the liberal aristocrats and eggheads he brought into government. All that was lacking was a right-wing demagogue opportunistic enough to take advantage of the situation. That vacuum was filled at 8:00 P.M., February 9, 1950, when Senator Joseph McCarthy of Wisconsin told the Republican Women's Club of Wheeling, West Virginia, that he knew of 205 Communists in the State Department.

The "us" whom Fiedler was indicting in his discussion of the Hiss case were naive liberals; in his meditation on the Rosenbergs, self-righteous radicals. When he looks at the McCarthy phenomenon, however, he targets intellectuals who condemned McCarthy without understanding the circumstances that made him an historical inevitability. Fiedler came to this task with several advantages. Because of his years in Wisconsin, he understood the political culture that could produce a progressive populist such as Bob La Follette and a reactionary populist such as Joe McCarthy. (McCarthy had been preceded in the Senate by Bob La Follette, Jr., and followed by the maverick liberal William Proxmire.) Also, as a resident of Montana, Fiedler was better equipped than most northeastern intellectuals to appreciate sentiment in the American Heartland, even if his fellow Montanans insisted on associating him with the northeastern elite and the essay itself was published in the foreign pages of *Encounter.*

Given the enthusiasm (some would say the hysteria) of both the pro- and anti-McCarthy forces, Fiedler was challenging conventional wisdom in suggesting that the senator was neither a knight on a white horse nor a homegrown Hitler, but a depressingly ordinary and venal politician, who was much smaller than the controversies in which he was embroiled. Similarly, those who supported and those who attacked him frequently did so for self-serving reasons—the former out of cultural or partisan animus toward his targets, the

---

4. For a discussion of Fiedler's essay and the reaction to it, see Ronald Radosh and Joyce Milton, *The Rosenberg File,* 554–57.

latter out of a desire to discredit the entire anti-Communist movement. In the end, McCarthy was brought down not because of the harm he was doing to civil liberties or to the fight against Communism but because his idiosyncratic hostility toward the army caused him to attack one of the few institutions in American life about which the general populace was not suspect.

The one thing about which liberal mythology is most certain is that McCarthy and McCarthyism brought a temporary halt to free speech in America. In fact, although some innocent people did suffer during the McCarthy era, the vast majority who attacked the senator and his methods—including, finally, a majority of the United States Senate—did so with impunity. (In intellectual circles, his supporters were more likely to experience ostracism.) Fiedler sets the record straight on this point without arguing—as William Buckley does—that the intemperance of McCarthy's enemies somehow vindicated the senator himself. I suspect that Fiedler's opinion would be closer to that of Peter Viereck—that the Communist cause was served both by fellow travelers such as Owen Lattimore and by McCarthy himself: Lattimore "by the way he defended it," and McCarthy "by the way he attack[ed] it."[5]

At least for a time, Fiedler's political essays—particularly the one on the Rosenbergs—were as widely known and as frequently misread as anything he had published. (In 1963 the British critic Ronald Bryden wrote facetiously: "Leslie Fiedler is probably known to English readers as the man who defended the Rosenbergs' execution, stuck up for McCarthy as the heir to William Jennings Bryan's corncob throne and accused Huckleberry Finn of being a nigger-loving liberal homosexual.") Consequently, those who have written about those essays have been sharply divided in their views. Arguing for the affirmative, James Seaton contends that Fiedler's early cultural criticism "remains important, even after the end of the cold war, while books such as *Being Busted* . . . and *What Was Literature?* seem dated already."[6] What Seaton finds so compelling about the voice that speaks to us here is its willingness to include the speaker himself in the general indictment being made. As Fiedler candidly declares, "I have . . . been pleased to discover how often I have managed to tell what still seems to me the truth about my world and myself as a liberal, intellectual, writer, American, and Jew" (*CE,* 1:xxi).

Expressing a much different view, Alan Wald denounces Fiedler for having written "virulent anticommunist essays . . . full of dubious psychologizing and calls for atonement by the entire left." In a celebration of the cultural innocence of the 1960s (*The Gates of Eden* [1977]), Morris Dickstein fumes, "It would be hard to find more vicious examples of serious political writing. . . . Joseph K.

5. Peter Viereck, *The Shame and Glory of the Intellectuals,* 58.
6. Ronald Bryden, *The Unfinished Hero and Other Essays,* 239. Seaton, *Cultural Conservatism,* 106.

in Kafka's *Trial* is charged with no crime but rather stands 'accused of guilt'; Fiedler is not content to malign the guilty: he indicts a whole generation for its 'innocence.' "[7]

Reactions such as those of Wald and Dickstein suggest that Fiedler's call for "a liberalism of responsibility" was not totally successful. Dickstein, in particular, sees Hiss and the Rosenbergs as victims of Cold War hysteria. He chides Fiedler for not entertaining doubt about the guilt of these individuals but offers no evidence to refute their guilt. It is sufficient merely to dismiss persons concerned with the facts of the case as vicious anti-Communists. (It is revealing that the knee-jerk Left never uses the adjective *vicious* to describe an anti-Fascist or an anti-racist.) Dickstein even rejects Fiedler's plea that the Rosenbergs be granted clemency because: (1) he has used the (vicious?) Christian term *grace;* and (2) such an action would have put America in too favorable a light.[8]

The most sustained contemporaneous attack on Fiedler's position comes from the art critic Harold Rosenberg. In his essay "Couch Liberalism and the Guilty Past" (1960), Rosenberg strains to draw an analogy between the defendants who confessed to misdeeds at the Moscow Show Trials of the 1930s and ex-Communists who confessed their guilty pasts before Congressional investigating committees. Even though he reveals some superficial similarities, Rosenberg glosses over the fundamental differences between these two phenomena. The victims of the show trials were frequently confessing to crimes they had not committed, prior to imprisonment or execution. America's penitent ex-Communists more often told the truth to the applause of a forgiving nation. Although there were real excesses in the anti-Communist crusades of the 1950s, no reasonable person would judge them morally equivalent to the totalitarian purges committed by Stalin.

In contrast to the defenders of Hiss, the historian Allen Weinstein seems to exemplify the liberalism of responsibility Fiedler calls for. Weinstein originally assumed Hiss's innocence but later changed his mind in the face of irrefutable evidence to the contrary. Pondering the significance of the Hiss case for persons of Fiedler's generation and political history, Weinstein notes that "for Fiedler and other liberal intellectuals, the emergence of postwar anti-Communism in American politics coincided dramatically with their own efforts to convince others like themselves of the essential symbolic meaning of Alger Hiss's con-

7. Alan Wald, *The New York Intellectuals: The Rise and Decline of the Anti-Stalinist Left from the 1930s to the 1980s,* 279. Morris Dickstein, *Gates of Eden: American Culture and the Sixties,* 41.

8. Dickstein, *Gates of Eden,* 42. For a discussion of the Rosenbergs quite similar to Fiedler's, see Robert Warshow, "The 'Idealism' of Julius and Ethel Rosenberg," *The Immediate Experience: Movies, Comics, Theatre & Other Aspects of Popular Culture* (New York: Doubleday, 1962), 69–81. This essay was originally published in the November 1953 issue of *Commentary.*

viction: not alone the 'end of innocence' proclaimed in Fiedler's essay, but, in a practically religious sense, the shame of gullibility."[9]

Interestingly, not all of the criticism Fiedler received for his position on the Hiss case came from the Left. Whittaker Chambers, who always seemed to view life's choices in apocalyptic and Manichaean terms, did not feel comfortable being defended by liberals, even anti-Communist ones. After reading Fiedler's article in *Commentary,* he wrote to Ralph De Tolendano to claim that "the piece is dishonest." He goes on to say, "Its purpose is to hose out the Augean stable, the Liberal mind, by getting rid of *both* Hiss and Chambers—the first of whom makes them feel guilty, and the second of whom makes them feel—an even less forgivable sin—small. . . . To achieve their triumph, it has been necessary to denigrate Chambers even more than Hiss."[10]

A far more positive response came in a fan letter Leslie received from another *Commentary* reader. "I wish to take this opportunity to tell you how very impressed I was with your able and searching analysis of one of the most tragic and difficult cases of our time," the reader begins. He goes on to say, "So much has been written and said about this case which has completely missed the real points involved, that it was a pleasure for one who was so close to it, as I was, to read the objective analysis which you presented." The letter was signed "with all good wishes" by the new senator from California, Richard Nixon.

II

While his cultural criticism was appearing in *Encounter, Partisan Review,* and *Commentary,* Leslie also submitted more purely literary work to John Crowe Ransom's *Kenyon Review* throughout the late 1940s and early 1950s. When his early submissions were rejected, Leslie expressed his pique to Ransom in a letter dated October 19, 1947. "It requires a stubborn act of faith to send you more of my stuff," he writes. "Yours is the only publication from which in my year + a half of submitting material I have received nothing but the dumb rebuke of a form rejection slip. In most cases I get at least some acceptance—in all, decent + interested notes of rejection. I should be less than frank, if I did not say that these anonymous pale slips of yours irk, annoy (and even, tho I am a resilient fellow, discourage) me. I like, in general, your taste, but am equally fond of my own pieces. What is it?"[11] This letter produced a detailed reaction to the story submitted with it, along with Ransom's invitation to review for his magazine. Over the next decade, Leslie became a frequent

9. Allen Weinstein, *Perjury: The Hiss-Chambers Case,* 516.
10. Ibid., 518.
11. See Marian Janssen, *The Kenyon Review, 1939–1970: A Critical History,* 185.

contributor to the *Kenyon Review* and was even named a Kenyon Fellow in Criticism for 1956.

Although Leslie grew to admire and respect Ransom as both a person and a man of letters, the difference in generations and cultural background kept them from becoming close friends. (Despite the older man's pleas to "call me John," Leslie was never able to call him anything other than "Mr. Ransom.") "He seemed to be out of a different world which had ceased to exist when I was born," Leslie recalls. "I would send stories to the *Kenyon Review,* and he would say, 'Where did you ever meet people like that.' " Writing to Leslie on May 4, 1951, Ransom says of his latest submission: "It is one of the best pieces of writing that we've had coming over the desk for a long time. The two dreams are grotesque, beautiful, and moving." He nevertheless found the story as a whole to be a less than successful mixture of poetic and prose tendencies. He ends on a conciliatory note: "Trilling once told me I had a blind spot against your fictions. But anyhow, you have got me where I try hard to be receptive. And I'll still be trying if you will give us another chance, other chances."[12]

Two years later, Ransom finally accepted one of Leslie's creative submissions—a verse drama or masque called "The Bearded Virgin and the Blind God." (This and the first half of Robert Penn Warren's *Brother to Dragons* were the only drama Ransom ever published in the *Kenyon Review.*) The play, which is reminiscent of Eliot's *Murder in the Cathedral* and the verse drama of Christopher Frye, concerns a young convert to Christianity, whose pagan father insists on marrying her to a pagan husband. "Praying that her God might forestall so cruel an event by afflicting her with a curse that would make her undesirable in the eyes of all, she was blessed with a thick growth of beard, affliction enough apparently to cool the ardor of her pagan lover. But her enraged father revenged the broken match by brutally crucifying her in the manner of her own Hanged God."[13] In a letter to Leslie, dated July 8, 1953, Ransom writes that this contribution "makes me think of Beggar's Opera; or, as you suggest, of some masks, even Dryden's. . . . The verse is just right. The whole thing as spare as it could be. . . . The general effect is of a strange ancient contretemps of great force, and we are left saying, Where have you been all this time, How did we ever give up this order of verse drama?"

In addition to editing the *Kenyon Review,* Ransom sought to spread the gospel of criticism by sponsoring a series of summer institutes, in which the most distinguished critics writing in English would train the rising generation of literary intellectuals. This enterprise began with the Kenyon School of English in Gambier, Ohio, in the summer of 1948. After three summers at

12. Except where otherwise indicated, letters cited in this chapter are in Leslie Fiedler's private files.

13. Leslie Fiedler, "The Bearded Virgin and the Blind God," 540.

Gambier, the program moved to Indiana University, where it became the Indiana School of Letters. As the *Kenyon Review* itself became more open to differing approaches to criticism, the staff of Ransom's summer institute grew ever more diverse. (At various times, Jacques Barzun, Philip Rahv, Alfred Kazin, Lionel Trilling, and Delmore Schwartz taught with Ransom.) In the summer of 1952, the faculty included R. P. Blackmur, Kenneth Burke, Francis Fergusson, and three younger critics who became known as the "the boys"—Robert Fitzgerald, Randall Jarrell, and Leslie Fiedler.

James M. Cox, who was a student at Bloomington that summer, remembers that the School of Letters met in a hut that had been a U.S. Navy sick bay, which had been moved to the Indiana campus at the end of the war. Not only did it lack air-conditioning, it was situated in a vale where no air could circulate. Because sessions ran six weeks, classes met for two hours, three times a week. "These then were the conditions," Cox recalls, "—as hard and hot and humid as I had then known or have known since. Day after day, it seemed to me, the temperature hovered between ninety and ninety-five outside, and surely over a hundred inside, with the humidity always over eighty." It was in this challenging environment that Jim Cox first encountered Leslie Fiedler.

Remembering the experience four decades later, Cox writes:

> Short in stature but barrel chested, Fiedler faced the class with a compact force. Once he started to speak, his whole presence radiated intensity and energy, all concentrated in his voice. He had notes, written in such a minuscule hand that he could contain a two-hour lecture in remarkably few pages. Though his notes were in front of him, he did not seem to read them, but I felt they were actually manuscript rather than mere headings. His voice had a fierce urgency, often rising in intensity to the threshold of something between a cry of agony and a painful laugh, before descending on a line of measured and periodic finality.

"Even to try to describe his 'delivery,'" Cox concludes, "may make it seem that he was histrionic. He never seemed so to me. Intense, yes; even a performer, yes; but his lectures were never staged or stagy. They were urgent, gripping in their concentration, and explosive in their insights. Their substance for me always outweighed their rhetoric."[14]

When class was not in session, Fitzgerald, Jarrell, and Fiedler would escape the heat and humidity by swimming in an abandoned limestone quarry pool just outside town. To reach it, one had to drive down an old country road and walk a quarter mile or so. This whole enterprise was somewhat daring, in that

14. James M. Cox, "Celebrating Leslie Fiedler," 144.

the quarry was supposed to be off-limits to both those at the university and townspeople. Most often, the boys were accompanied by a couple of female students from the School of Letters. Over a decade later, Fitzgerald would recall his friend Jarrell "coming up for air, his hair plastered over his forehead, his line of mustache dripping, eyes shut tight."[15] What Fitzgerald does not mention is that, for all his love of the water, Randall had never learned how to swim.

Although Randall had taken both his B.A. and M.A. degrees at Vanderbilt and had taught with Ransom at Kenyon, he was neither an orthodox southerner nor an orthodox New Critic. His enthusiasms included the verse of Kipling and children's literature. (Jim Cox remembers Randall "wondering what would become of us if we didn't realize that Beatrix Potter was probably the greatest writer of the twentieth century."[16]) As both poet and critic, he was very much his own man, although his vocabulary was no doubt influenced by his having spent most of his career teaching at schools for women. When he read a poem that particularly impressed him, he might say "Isn't that dovey?" or just "Baby Doll!"

In a letter to his future wife, Mary Von Schrader, some time in June 1952, Randall writes, "I'd have been terribly bored except that Leslie Fiedler was very interesting and amusing. You really would like him—he's awfully nice; very appealing, looks so warm and human when he talks about his children." Later in that same letter, Randall observes, "The heat has moved me to such desperation that I made funny jokes all thru lunch so that everybody laughed and laughed. I can't remember anything now except saying (in a note of despair) when the waitress brought us bread and butter plates with a little shallow circular spot of cherry jelly on each: 'They've shot my plate.' "[17]

Writing to Mary the following month, Randall expresses his full-throttle admiration for Leslie's critical mind:

> Leslie gave the most incredibly wonderful lecture on Criticism last night. It was very like [Jarrell's own] "The Age of Criticism" in some ways (we took exactly the same line, I agreed with *every word* he said) but he made his general and reasoned-out and an explicit, sensible, absolutely convincing Statement, not something so poetic as mine. Everybody, practically, was overwhelmed. And his answers to questions would have done credit to Aristotle, Dr. Johnson, and Lenin rolled into one—never *saw* anybody so good at Reasoning, Convincing, and Stating in Wonderful Form right while standing there thinking about it.[18]

15. Robert Fitzgerald, "A Place of Refreshment," 71.
16. Cox, "Celebrating," 143.
17. Mary Jarrell, ed. *Randall Jarrell's Letters: An Autobiographical and Literary Selection,* 358.
18. Ibid., 360.

The quality of students at the School of Letters was decidedly mixed. Two of the papers written for Leslie's class were immediately published. One became the core of Mark Spilka's book on D. H. Lawrence. Jim Cox's "The Sad Initiation of Huckleberry Finn" was the beginning of its author's career as a distinguished Twain scholar. (Cox's *Mark Twain and the Fate of Humor* [1966] is considered one of the truly indispensable books in the field.) One student who did not fare nearly so well was Hilton Kramer. Considered the star by his fellow students, Kramer went into his oral exam thinking that he would be quizzed primarily on the New Criticism. Immediately, Kenneth Burke asked him to identify two lines of rhymed poetry, which happened to come from Shelley. Kramer identified the passage as an heroic couplet from Pope and proceeded to fail the exam. Nevertheless, he went on to become an art critic for the *New York Times* and the founding editor of the *New Criterion*. He still owes Leslie a paper from that long-ago summer in Bloomington.[19]

When Leslie returned to the School of Letters in the summer of 1954, the British critic William Empson was also on the staff. Although a brilliant reader of poetry, this strange, intense Englishman was not easy to know, even on a superficial level. His close friend Kathleen Raine recalls his being "indifferent to the impression he made to the point of absent-mindedness." Despite that fact, his mere presence proved spellbinding. Raine particularly remembers Empson's shapely head, his fine features and his "full lustrous poet's eyes, . . . shortsighted behind glasses and nervously evading a direct look."[20] (Well before it became fashionable, he grew a long and unkempt beard, which only added to his bohemian appearance.) Leslie recalls that in Empson's flat in Bloomington, one would see nothing but piled-up dishes, stuck together and spilling all over the floor. Empson would feed himself by mixing two cans of anything he picked at random off the shelf. When Leslie first visited this pigsty, Empson said, "You Americans think we Brits are filthy. Well, I *am* filthy."

Empson had entered Cambridge as a mathematics major but switched to literature when he took a course from I. A. Richards in his fourth year of study. One day in class, Empson showed Richards how Robert Graves and Laura Riding in their book *A Survey of Modernist Poetry* analyzed Shakespeare's sonnet "The Expense of Spirit Is a Waste of Shame" much as a jeweler might take a watch apart to see how it worked. He then calmly announced to Richards that he could do the same for any poem written in English. Throughout the 1930s and '40s, Empson established himself as a fine minor poet and an even more important critic. (*Seven Types of Ambiguity* [1930] and *Some Versions of Pastoral* [1935] are classics of New Criticism.) During much of that time, he

19. Fiedler, interview with author, June 23, 1997.
20. Kathleen Raine, "Extracts from Unpublished Memoirs," 15.

taught English in the Far East, his career as a fellow at Magdalene College, Cambridge, having been derailed when a porter discovered a packet of condoms in his belongings. Empson would occasionally come to Ransom's summer institutes directly from his professorship at the University of Peking.

Leslie recalls one evening in Bloomington when Empson was scheduled to deliver a lecture on the general topic of "poetry and criticism." Instead of speaking on the assigned topic, he appeared in a Chinese Communist military uniform, so drunk that he could barely stand up. As he spilled his drink on his notes and teetered on the edge of the platform, Empson delivered an impassioned attack on United States foreign policy and a defense of the Maoist regime. On another evening Empson and Leslie got into a lively argument over the charge that America had used germ warfare in Korea. Their dialogue began at 7:30 or 8:00 in the evening and didn't conclude until 4:00 in the morning, when the police appeared. Margaret had summoned them, certain that there had been a terrible accident. Such was the life of the mind at the Indiana School of Letters.

III

The summer of 1952 inspired one of Leslie's best short stories, a roman à clef titled "Pull down Vanity!" The protagonist of the story is a poet named Milton Amsterdam, who is something of a composite of Randall Jarrell and Leslie himself. During a summer writer's conference at a midwestern university, Amsterdam jousts with an old critical nemesis (based loosely on Richard Blackmur) and allows himself to be seduced by a nubile young secretary, long before the days of sexual harassment suits. The secretary, Judith Somers, is married to an aspiring young working-class poet, who has been rendered temporarily impotent by his inability to publish his verse. Convinced that her husband's confidence and sexual prowess will be restored if someone praises his poetry, Judith pursues an affair with Amsterdam. Victimized by the lies he has told about his own potency (he boasts of having fathered seven children), Milton cannot perform with Judith when she finally gets him in the sack. At the end of a wild and boozy party, Amsterdam confesses his earlier lies, tells some new ones, and leaves in the dawn, as Judith and her husband are reunited.

In dealing with an environment he knows intimately, Fiedler sounds authentic. He is at his best when he is wittiest. Consider, for example, the titles of some of the critical essays he mentions. Amsterdam has written, though not yet published, a definitive discussion of the Blackmur character (Edward Fenton), which he calls "Edward Lear as T. S. Eliot." Fenton himself is the author of "Ronald Firbank, a Female Jane Austen" and "Tennyson after Dachau." For negative blurbs, one could hardly do better than Amsterdam's description of a fellow poet's work (published in an omnibus review in the *Kenyon Review*) as being "the sort of verse which might have been composed by a retarded but diligent child of eleven whose only model was a parody of Keats by Louis Untermeyer." (Although the poet in question oversees the writer's conference, he bears no resemblance to John Ransom.) Among creative works, Amsterdam's own estranged wife has written a best-seller called *Love among the Cactus.* The scene in the novel in which the wife of an English instructor and her fifteen-year-old lover "tenderly pick cactus spines out of each other's rear ends has by this time become a standard item in the repertory of radio comedians and night-club entertainers" (*NC*, 177).

The character of Milton Amsterdam is far from impressive. If he is not nearly so much of a wretch as Hyman Brandler, who narrates Fiedler's "Nobody Ever Died from It," he is even less close to being a true composite of Randall Jarrell and Leslie Fiedler. (One almost suspects the author of suffering from a reverse Walter Mitty complex.) This point becomes even more striking when one recalls the passage from Pound's *Cantos* that provides the title for the story:

> Thou art a beaten dog beneath the hail,
> A swollen magpie in a fitful sun,
> Half black half white
> Nor knowst your wing from tail
> Pull down thy vanity. . . .

If Amsterdam is an obtuse narrator, then his story can be read as an extended dramatic monologue in prose, which inadvertently exposes his own inadequacies. The closest he comes to encountering a true antagonist is in the person of Judith's husband, the working-class poet Hank Somers. When Amsterdam accuses Hank's idol Carl Sandburg of not being a real poet, Hank replies, "He's *real,* for God's sake! It's you fellows who are word merchants, aesthetes—Raw experience! that's why you don't understand him" (194). Such opinions are, of course, aesthetically incorrect (especially for the elitist that Leslie Fiedler was in the mid-1950s). Even more shocking is the political incorrectness of Hank's anti-Semitism and his brutality toward his wife (both of which become more pronounced when he is drunk). Nevertheless, Hank possesses a passion for both life and literature that the professors at the writers' conference conspicuously lack. That might not make him a particularly admirable character, but it at least makes him a useful foil to the Milton Amsterdams of this world.

In some ways, Judith Somers is the least objectionable character in this story. Even when she is dallying with Milton, she remains in love with her husband and totally committed to his vocation as a poet. (She carries a folder of his poems to her tryst with Amsterdam.) Handled differently, she might have seemed a whorish manipulator, using her erotic favors to promote her husband's career. But she finally comes off as too ingenuous to be suspected of ulterior motives, and Amsterdam seems anything but a lovesick dupe. Because we never see Hank's poetry, we have no way of knowing whether it is any good. We have only Judith's word, but that may be the point. When one strips away all of its theoretical underpinnings, literary criticism is finally a matter of subjective response. Rather than forcing us to choose between populist and elitist standards of judgment, Fiedler leaves us with the ethos of Judith Somers as critic and as wife.

As fine a story as "Pull down Vanity!" undoubtedly is, it does not seem to do justice to the summer of 1952 as it was remembered by Randall Jarrell and Jim Cox. But a story that was truer to life might have exposed Leslie himself to charges of vanity—especially if he had come across as a combination of Aristotle, Dr. Johnson, and Lenin or as a teacher who could make you sit spellbound for two hours in stifling heat and humidity. Leslie had turned thirty-five in March of 1952. He had reached the halfway point in his journey to the biblical allotment of threescore years and ten. Because he never thought that he would live to middle age, he was unprepared to do so. Like Milton Amsterdam, he was beginning to experience a midlife crisis in the privacy of his soul. It was a condition that would only grow worse as he approached his fortieth birthday.

CHAPTER SIX

A Newer Criticism

WHEN LESLIE Fiedler began making a name for himself as a literary critic, the dominant approach to reading fiction and poetry (and, to a lesser extent, drama) was a version of aesthetic formalism associated in the public mind with John Crowe Ransom and the *Kenyon Review.* The term *New Criticism* (with its built-in obsolescence) was inadvertently coined by Ransom when he used it as the title of a book he published in 1941. Although he might just as well have called the book "Some Recent Trends in Criticism," because the figures he discussed were espousing different critical methods, the term *New Criticism* stuck and has since become a fixture in the literary history of the twentieth century.

While encouraging the search for new exegetical techniques, the first generation of New Critics was generally undogmatic about the ways in which one might read the difficult texts of modernism. Unfortunately, a later generation threatened to turn what had once been an innovative approach to reading into a stale orthodoxy. As Christopher Clausen has noted: "A bright student who knew little history, no philosophy, and no foreign languages could learn to analyze literary structures in terms of a small number of technical concepts. After that, nothing more was needed than a good anthology . . . , a supply of paperbacks, and perhaps, for the adventurous, a subscription to the *Kenyon Review.*"[1]

It would be wrong to link Leslie with this lockstep formalism simply because of his relationship with Ransom and his journal. Although Ransom is popularly regarded as the godfather of the American version of New Criticism and his magazine as its unofficial house organ, the truth is actually more complicated. The *Kenyon Review,* like the original series of the *Southern Review* before it, was a remarkably eclectic journal, equally hospitable to contributions

---

1. Christopher Clausen, "Reading Closely Again," 55.

from southern Agrarians and New York intellectuals. Moreover, as Marian Janssen argues persuasively in her history of the *Kenyon Review,* Ransom himself had begun moving away from the New Criticism by the early 1940s and had effectively ceased to publish a New Critical journal by the time Leslie was contributing to the *Kenyon Review.* In addition to Leslie, such varied and heterodox individuals as Irving Howe, R. W. B. Lewis, Richard Ellmann, and Howard Nemerov received Kenyon fellowships in criticism in the 1950s, while the thoroughly conventional New Critic Robert Wooster Stallman found his application repeatedly turned down.[2]

It is clear in Leslie's essays from the early 1950s that he found New Criticism to be a useful, perhaps even necessary, touchstone against which to measure his own evolving view of literature. We see this process at work in "Toward an Amateur Criticism," his contribution to a symposium the *Kenyon Review* ran in 1950–1951 under the heading "My Credo." By endorsing an "amateur" criticism, this essay rejects not only the New Criticism but all systematic approaches to reading literature.

Although he is reluctant to call himself a romantic, Fiedler believes that doctrinaire antiromanticism can lead to a fatal contempt for the imagination. Making a point with which Ransom certainly would have agreed, he argues that the chief enemy of literature in our day is the " 'liberal' or scientific mind, with its opposition to the frivolous and the tragic, its distrust of such concepts as God, the Devil, Genius and Taste, and its conviction that it is impertinent to ask just how many children Lady Macbeth *did* have."[3] By definition, the amateur critic would be one who loved literature and conveyed a sense of pleasure in writing about it. In two important respects, his vocation is similar to that of the poet: "First, he must join in irony and love what others are willing to leave disjoined, and second, he must be willing to extend awareness beyond the point where the lay reader instinctively finds that quality profitable or even possible" (562). The critic also bears a third responsibility—which is only an option for the poet—to be comprehensible.

If this warning against critical jargon was useful in 1950, it sounds downright prophetic over half a century later. In an age when readers of *professional* criticism are all too often mesmerized by the glossolalia of poststructuralist theory, it is easy to forget that the purpose of criticism is to clarify not to obscure. "In *intent,*" Fiedler reminds us, "the good critic addresses the common reader, not the initiate, and that intent is declared in his language. That in fact there are in our own time few general readers in the Johnsonian sense, is completely irrelevant. The primary act of faith which makes criticism possible compels

---

2. See Janssen, *Kenyon Review,* 173.
3. Leslie Fiedler, "Toward an Amateur Criticism," 562. Subsequent references will be cited parenthetically in the text.

the critic under any circumstances to speak *as if* to men and not to specialists. The compulsory comprehensibility of the critic is not a matter of pandering to indolence, prejudice or ignorance, but of resisting the impulse to talk to himself or a congeries of reasonable facsimiles of himself" (563).

Fiedler next attacks one of the cardinal tenets of New Criticism—the notion that literary evaluation must always be intrinsic to the work itself. Not only does this belief contribute to the further atomization of modern life, but it is also a canard that is honored more in the breach than in the observance. As he correctly notes, "even the terms of 'aesthetic' criticism, complexity, irony, simplicity, concreteness, betray themselves as metaphors, one element of which rests on ethical preconceptions" (566).

Although Fiedler does not develop this point, it is interesting to note how the technical judgments of the New Critics often presuppose a particular view of reality. When Cleanth Brooks is analyzing particular poems in *The Well Wrought Urn,* he uses such intrinsic aesthetic terms as wit, irony, and paradox; however, his more general theoretical comments later in that same book hold that a poem is to be judged by its "coherence, sensitivity, depth, richness, and tough-mindedness."[4] As sound as this position may be, it represents a moral rather than a merely literary point of view. Different aesthetic judgments would certainly be rendered by someone who preferred an incoherent, insensitive, shallow, superficial, and sentimental interpretation of reality. Fiedler thinks it proper that the critic's view of literature be influenced by his moral and religious beliefs and regards talk about intrinsic criticism as disingenuous nonsense.

Fiedler is not rejecting the value, only the sufficiency, of close reading. He believes that "the point is not to choose between the complementary blindness of the 'formalists' and the 'historians,' but to be more aware than either: to know, if possible, when one is making aesthetic judgments and when philosophical or ethical ones, or, at least, to realize when one is confused" (564). In other words, because there are pitfalls in every known system of criticism, it is best to avoid all systems and rely on one's own intuition and tact to make literary judgments. The most obvious objection to this position is that we are left with no standards by which to criticize the critic. The one advantage shared by critical systems, whether aesthetic or ideological, is that they give us some basis for judging whether or not the critic is a competent practitioner of his own craft. Unfortunately, Fiedler's "amateur" criticism can easily lead to relativism and subjectivism. The only way to escape this dilemma is to validate one's judgments by appeal to some external source of authority, which can range from popular opinion to elitist taste.

4. Cleanth Brooks, *The Well Wrought Urn: Studies in the Structure of Poetry,* 229.

Because Fiedler's position since the 1960s has become increasingly populist, it is surprising to discover that his earliest critical writings were distrustful of the vox populi. In the *Kenyon* symposium, he argues that even the amateur critic must oppose those who consider Carl Sandburg superior to Wallace Stevens simply because Sandburg "is much admired by high school students and the teachers of high school students" (569). Fiedler believes that criticism should not be "a rival to the attempt to achieve final hierarchies, but rather a handmaiden. The only way to find out if a poet is immortal is to kill him; Milton and Wordsworth slain have risen; Cowley and Shelley are rotting in their tombs" (570).

Fiedler contends that voice is more important for a critic than method. The polemical article (more often a book review than a full-length critical thesis) is the perfect vehicle for criticism. "The occasional piece discourages the framing of elaborate vocabularies, and encourages a tone committed to communication and sociability" (571). Such an article avoids the opposite extremes of technical jargon (here typified by Kenneth Burke) and the "grey, standard, glutinous prose" of reference books such as *The Literary History of the United States* or middlebrow journals such as the *Saturday Review of Literature* (571–72). "The true language of criticism," Fiedler writes, "is the language of conversation— the voice of the dilettante at home. Its proper materials are what the civilized, outrageous mind remembers and chooses to connect, not what the three by five cards scrupulously preserve or the printed glossary defines" (572). One hears this conversational voice in critics as diverse as "Longinus," Nietzsche, Coleridge, and D. H. Lawrence. "One feels in their tone and texture an assurance that the works of art being discussed have really *happened* to the men that discuss them, and have been ingested into the totality of their experiences" (572).

After spending more than a dozen pages condemning critical systems and methodologies, Fiedler confesses that he finds himself "more and more drawn" to myth criticism. Unlike more scientific and rationalist approaches, myth criticism expresses a proper reverence for the mysteries of artistic creation and offers an intriguing standard for evaluation in the concept of "mythoplastic power, that goes beyond the merely formal without falling into the doctrinal and the dogmatic." An additional advantage is that "writers like Dickens and R. L. Stevenson, who have fared ill at the hands of the historical and formalist critics alike, reveal the source of their persistent power over our imaginations in the light of myth doctrine" (574). Whereas a criticism based on aesthetics or ideology tends to be divisive and reductive, myth criticism offers the possibility of cultural synthesis. It enables the critic "to speak of the profound interconnections of the art work and other areas of human experience, without translating the work of art into unsatisfactory equivalents of 'ideas' or 'tendencies' " (574).

I

As the fifties wore on, Leslie's fascination with the possibilities of myth was serving him as a critic in several ways. First, it enabled him to move beyond the "close reading" of the New Critics without retreating to the old historicism or getting mired in the sort of ideological warfare that had damaged both criticism and literature itself in the 1930s. Second, it offered a way of explaining the primordial and universal appeal of song and story. If literary creation consisted of nothing more than solving a series of technical problems, it is doubtful that literature would have moved the mass of humanity the way it has over the course of recorded history. Finally, myth criticism seemed to offer the most plausible means of determining why even sophisticated readers are reluctant to banish certain writers who lack the ironic and paradoxical sensibility so prized by modernism. The daunting task that Leslie Fiedler faced was to turn these potential advantages into a coherent theory of criticism, which could be usefully applied to specific texts both past and present.

As his critical stance has grown more aggressively antielitist over the years, Fiedler has begun to feel profoundly uneasy with the scholarly attention devoted to his early theoretical forays into myth criticism. He would much prefer to be known as the iconoclastic author of "Come Back to the Raft Ag'in, Huck Honey!" than as a pontifical Jungian. When he published his second collection of essays, *No! In Thunder,* in 1960, he included "In the Beginning Was the Word: *Logos* or *Mythos*" and "Archetype and Signature: The Relationship of Poet and Poem," but added the disclaimer that "they are examples of the kind of theorizing which threatens to leave literature and its appropriate delights for the sake of amateur philosophizing" (*CE,* 1:513). Nevertheless, these early manifestos are essential to defining Fiedler's role in the backlash that was already forming against the hegemony of New Criticism.

One of the stated goals of New Criticism was to free poetry from the confining notion that there was such a thing as inherently poetic subject matter. I. A. Richards and Cleanth Brooks both argued for what they called a poetry of inclusion. They were reacting against what T. S. Eliot believed was the dissociation of sensibility that entered English poetry at the end of the seventeenth century. According to received New Critical doctrine, this development purged wit and intellect from poetry and led to an undue emphasis on inspiration and emotion in the romantic period as well as to the celebrated "high seriousness" of the Victorian era. Fortunately, things got back on track when modernist poets (and their New Critical interpreters) rediscovered the lost virtues of the metaphysical school.

By restoring irony, paradox, and extended metaphor to respectability, the New Critics expanded the range of acceptable poetic content but narrowed the range of acceptable poetic technique. In *Modern Poetry and the Tradition* (1939),

Brooks tends to underrate the verse of the eighteenth and nineteenth centuries. In *The Well Wrought Urn* (1947), he tries (some would say too ingeniously) to redeem the best of that verse by finding in it the qualities he most admires in the poetry of the seventeenth and twentieth centuries. Still, by virtually defining poetry in terms of its inclusiveness of texture and ambiguity, the New Critics couldn't help excluding from the canon much literature that has moved people over the ages. Thus, Fiedler's more recent efforts to "open up the canon" may actually be prefigured in his early attacks on the formalist orthodoxies of New Criticism.

In emphasizing close reading of the text (what both Fiedler and the old historicist Douglas Bush too readily dismiss as remedial reading), New Criticism helps us see literature as an aesthetic mechanism. It shows us, in the words of John Ciardi, "how a poem means." As a result, it is less concerned with what "literature" is—or was—than with what specific texts ought to be. In contrast, Fiedler's two seminal exercises in theory approach the task of criticism from the opposite perspective. Something of a mystic at heart, he sees the artist as neither copyist nor maker, but as priest—the shaman who sacramentalizes in song and story pure essences, which—be they Platonic forms or Jungian archetypes—exist prior to experience.

Although "In the Beginning Was the Word" (1958) was originally published six years after "Archetype and Signature," Fiedler placed them in reverse chronological order in both *No! In Thunder* and his *Collected Essays.* This revised order makes sense because "In the Beginning" provides a theoretical justification for the importance Fiedler assigns to the central concepts of his earlier, more famous essay. The distinction between mythos and logos posits the ontological roots of poetry, while the interaction of archetype and signature accounts for the existence of actual poems.

In opposing mythos and logos, Fiedler is sounding the same lament that one hears in the work of most myth critics. According to Vincent B. Leitch: "More or less self-consciously, Myth Critics reacted against the aridities of formalism and antiquarianism and against the emptiness and absurdities of a godless scientific world." This latter note was sounded with particular urgency by Nietzsche, when he wrote in *The Birth of Tragedy* (1872) that "man today, stripped of myth, stands famished among all his pasts and must dig frantically for roots." Myth critics have little question what has caused this lamentable state of affairs. Giambattista Vico speaks for the whole tribe when he says that science has "destroyed myth and, by the same token, displaced poetry from its native soil and rendered it homeless."[4]

Of course, myth critics were not alone in rendering such a critique of modern society. John Crowe Ransom devoted *God without Thunder* (1930) to be-

4. Vincent B. Leitch, *American Literary Criticism from the Thirties to the Eighties,* 116.

moaning the decline of supernatural belief wrought by our scientific age. (Ransom was himself too much of a positivist to believe in the dogma of religion, but he felt that the absence of religious ritual in the modern world impoverished man's aesthetic and spiritual life.) In opposing logos and mythos to each other, Fiedler shares Ransom's belief that poetry and science constitute antithetical modes of knowledge. Fiedler, however, defines the salient epistemological distinction as actually being between poetry and philosophy, "understanding philosophy in the older inclusive sense." Mythos is the source of poetry, and logos the language of philosophy. Put another way, "[P]hilosophy invented *logos,* but *mythos* created poetry." Moreover, Fiedler observes, "poetry is historically the mediator between *logos* and *mythos,* the attempt to find a rationale of the pre-rational (which is to say, form)—and if philosophy quarrels with poetry, it is not because it considers its own mode of perception superior to the mythic way, but because it considers that there is *no* mode except its own; that mediation is therefore a betrayal of the truth" (*CE,* 1:518).

Where Fiedler parts company with Ransom and other New Critics is in his metaphysics. The New Critics value poetry over science because of its superior concreteness. Fiedler's preference for poetry is due to its superior universality. It is the means by which we intuit "those archaic and persisting clusters of image and emotion which at once define and attempt to solve what is most permanent in the human predicament" (519). Whether we refer to these "archaic and persisting clusters" as archetypes, mythos, or simply myth, they are—in Fiedler's judgment—the very essence of poetry. That is because they are the very essence of reality.

In attempting to place his critical insights into a metaphysical context, Fiedler is forced to make distinctions between the way things are and how they are understood (i.e., between ontology and epistemology). Borrowing Jacopo Mazzoni's notion that poetry is the "credible marvelous," he elaborates a series of conceptual categories: "The Marvelous as Marvelous is *mythos;* the Marvelous as Credible, Poetry; the Credible as Credible, philosophy and science; the Credible as Marvelous, the ersatz of Poetry which appears in ages oppressed by philosophy or science: rhetoric, journalism, *kitsch*" (521). Thus conceived, the marvelous is not simply an adornment—or, worse yet, a distortion—of the rational but a reality in its own right. Furthermore, if we regard Fiedler's series as an ontological hierarchy (a chain of being, if you will), then mythos is not only different from but superior to logos. As Fiedler once told a Communist guide in the Soviet Museum of Atheism, Michelangelo is closer to the truth than Darwin.[5]

5. Fiedler made this comment to William F. Buckley, Jr., in an appearance on *Firing Line,* Nov. 15, 1974.

II

Fiedler's controversial and frequently anthologized essay "Archetype and Signature" is an attempt to construct a theory of literature and to suggest the appropriate critical approach to that literature. Before he can even begin that undertaking, however, he must demonstrate the inadequacies of prevailing critical dogma. Although he never mentions New Criticism by name, that is clearly his target. The pejorative term that he uses is "anti-biographist," by which he means those critics who try to rip literature out of its human context and reduce it to mere words on a page. Fiedler notes that when I. A. Richards defines a poem as an "experience," he is rejecting the notion that it might also be an "imitation," an "expression," or a "communication." If, as Richards strongly implies, literary language is nonreferential, then it is divorced from the rest of human experience. Although no one could have foreseen it at the time, later observers have argued that it was precisely this notion that eventually enabled deconstructionists to dismiss all language as simply an arbitrary system of linguistic signs with no objective meaning.[6]

Fiedler believes that extreme literary formalism is based on the nominalist assumption that we can speak of individual poetic texts but not of something so general as poetry itself. Such a position, he argues, is "metaphysically reprehensible" (*CE*, 1:529). Nominalism was one of the traditional responses to the epistemological dilemma of the one and the many. Simply put, nominalism holds that only individual entities exist. Universal concepts are nothing more than the *names* we devise for groups of objects. Although he does not explicitly attribute this position to the major New Critics, Fiedler does ridicule Wright Thomas and Stuart Gerry Brown's *Reading Poems,* an anthology that seems like nothing so much as an unintentional spoof of the intrinsic approach to literary analysis. This book presents a selection of poems "printed out of chronological order and without the names of the authors attached, lest the young reader be led astray by what (necessarily irrelevant) information he may have concerning the biography or social background of any of the poets" (534).

One suspects that this textbook is a variation on the far more famous experiment that I. A. Richards conducted in the 1920s. Richards gave a total of thirteen unidentified poems to his students at Cambridge and asked for critical responses. Confronting the text without the benefit of history or biography, the

---

6. A connection between New Criticism and deconstruction has been alleged by Gerald Graff in "Fear and Trembling at Yale" (*American Scholar* 6 [autumn 1977]: 467–78); and Christopher Clausen in "Reading Closely Again." In point of fact, Richards's argument that literary language is nonreferential has long bothered other New Critics because of its radical implications. In *Literary Criticism: A Short History,* Cleanth Brooks worries that Richards "seemed to be arguing that poetry was literally nonsense, though, for reasons bound up with his psychologistic theory, a peculiarly valuable nonsense" (626).

students not only varied widely in their judgments, but also committed what Richards regarded as egregious misreadings.[7] However valuable such an experiment might have been as a *diagnostic* exercise, it was not meant to exclude context from the teaching of literature. The first generation of New Critics understood the value of context. It was only their second-rate imitators (e.g., Thomas and Brown) who reduced the movement to self-parody.

The more seminal New Critics were not averse to devising a general theory of poetry. They simply approached the task inductively. In *The Well Wrought Urn*, for example, Cleanth Brooks examines ten highly respected poems from different periods of British literature, identifies their common virtues, and postulates an aesthetic that transcends the particularities of time and place. Although Fiedler does not mention them by name, and may not even have had them in mind, the formalists who were nominalists and proud of it were the Chicago neo-Aristotelians. In a protracted essay published in the spring 1948 issue of *Modern Philology,* neo-Aristotelian godfather R. S. Crane castigated Cleanth Brooks for the "bankruptcy of 'critical monism.' "[8] What Crane regarded as Brooks's cardinal sin Fiedler would have seen as one of the defining roles of the critic—to make of the many one.

In leveling his criticisms at the "anti-biographists," Fiedler is gracious (or devious) enough to make some strategically insignificant concessions. He admits, for example, that a poem cannot be regarded as the sum total of its author's intentions. What the intrinsic readers have done is to distort that valid insight into the rather extravagant contention that "nothing the poet can tell us about his own work is of any *decisive* importance" (533). Even though a poem may contain more or less than what its author intended, Fiedler argues, we must speak of what it obviously aims at to judge what it actually achieves. (By such a standard, intentional farce would be good art, whereas unintentional camp would not be.) This position sounds so sensible that one could hardly imagine anyone disagreeing. Fiedler, however, finds two such culprits among the big guns of New Criticism. He declares that "the notion of 'intention' implies the belief that there is a somehow existent something against which the achieved work of art can be measured; and although this has been for all recorded time the point of view of the practicing writer, every graduate student who has read Wimsatt and Beardsley's ponderous tract on the Inten-

7. An even more radical experiment was conducted decades later by Stanley Fish. Coming into his class at Johns Hopkins one morning, Fish failed to erase the names of several prominent linguists that had been written on the blackboard in a previous class in linguistic theory. Instead, he drew a line around this list of six proper names and wrote at the top of the frame "p. 43." By convincing his class in seventeenth-century religious poetry that this list of names constituted a poem of the type they had been studying, Fish carried the denial of context and reference to ludicrous extremes.

8. R. S. Crane, "The Critical Monism of Cleanth Brooks."

tional Fallacy knows that we are all now to believe that there is no poem except the poem of 'words' " (533).

The only problem with Fiedler's argument is that it distorts the position of W. K. Wimsatt and Monroe C. Beardsley. If one reads their "ponderous tract" (which, like "Archetype and Signature" itself, was originally published in the *Sewanee Review*), it becomes clear that they are making the more limited and sensible point that a writer is not always the best *judge* of his own work and that sincerity is no excuse for ineptitude. Fiedler is also guilty of caricature when he suggests that Wimsatt and Beardsley believe "that there is no poem except the poem of 'words.' " However much W. K. Wimsatt may have distrusted archetypal criticism, he was just as skeptical of the sort of infantile formalism that would treat a work of literature as something palpable and mute. When the Chicago critics tried to make a fetish of the poem as artifact, Wimsatt rebuked them in terms Fiedler himself might use. "[I]f anything about poetry is clear at all," Wimsatt writes, "it is that a poem is not really a thing, like a horse or a house, but only *analogically* so. . . . [A] poem is, if it is anything at all, a verbal discourse; . . . hence it is a human act, physical and mental. The only 'thing' is the poet speaking."[9]

Like early Christian heretics, the anti-biographists were dangerous not because they were totally wrong (for then they could be dismissed as harmless cranks), but because they were partially right. The genteel formulation is to say that they provided a needed corrective to past excesses. In Fiedler's judgment, these excesses include two grotesque misuses of biography by supposed literary critics: the extreme subjectivism of latter-day romantics and the arid pedantry of what Gore Vidal calls "scholar-squirrels." (Of the latter, Fiedler writes, "[S]o long as notes proving that Milton was born in one house rather than another continue to be printed in magazines devoted to the study of literature, people will be tempted into opposite though equal idiocies, which have at least not been for so long proved utterly bankrupt" [534].) In an attempt to redeem poetry from the nominalism of the close reader and the "opposite though equal idiocies" of the romantic and the pedant, Fiedler asks that we think of the poem as "Archetype" and "Signature."

He tells us that he is not using the word *archetype* in a narrow Jungian sense (what he speaks of may reside in the Jungian collective unconscious or in the Platonic world of ideas). Instead, he means what in his later essay he will call mythos—"the immemorial patterns of response to the human situation in its most permanent aspects: death, love, the biological family, the relationship with the Unknown, etc." By signature, he means "the sum total of individuating factors in a work, the sign of the Persona or Personality through which

9. W. K. Wimsatt, *The Verbal Icon: Studies in the Meaning of Poetry,* 50.

an Archetype is rendered, and which itself tends to become a subject as well as a means of the poem." Consequently, literature "can be said to come into existence at the moment a Signature is imposed upon the Archetype" (537). Because of their nominalist predilections, formalist zealots would disavow the archetype; because of their anti-biographical prejudices, they would disregard the signature.

And yet, as Fiedler amply demonstrates, even the most orthodox intrinsic reader is sometimes forced to violate in practice what he asserts in theory. By expressing a willingness to study an author's "idiosyncratic use of words," even the most adamantine anti-biographist admits that information outside the *text* of the poem can occasionally be necessary to an understanding of the poem. If that is so, Fiedler asserts, then such information must also be useful for purposes of evaluation. For a proper appreciation of John Donne's poem "Loves Alchymie," one must determine whether the line "they'are by *Mummy,* possest" contains a deliberate pun. "Can we read the line as having the two meanings: women, so fair in the desiring, turn out to be only dried-out corpses after the having; and women, once possessed, turn out to be substitutes for the Mother, who is the real end of our desiring?" (540). Linguistic research renders such an interpretation possible, but we need some knowledge of Donne's relationship with his own mother to realize that the pun, with all its rich associations, was probably intended. The error of the intrinsicist is that he views the literary text as if it were "a tight little island instead of a focus opening on an inexhaustible totality" (541).

Fiedler concludes his essay with a discussion of the archetype that makes all of literature possible—that of the poet. In an age when myth is first becoming literature (i.e., when the archetype is "reaching tentatively toward a Signature"), the poet is regarded as a passive conduit through which the Muse speaks. When the communal system of belief breaks down, the poet is perceived as more signature than archetype (the alienated egoist) and, consequently, is stigmatized by society. We currently live in such a fragmented age, deprived of "Greek myths, the fairy tales and *novelle* of the Elizabethans, the Christian body of legend available to Dante" (545).

Fiedler discerns three separate strategies that contemporary writers have devised for confronting this dilemma. Artists such as Graham Greene and Robert Penn Warren have sought to elevate the formulaic narratives of "popular art" ("the thriller, the detective story, the Western or science fiction") to the level of high literature. Poets can also "ironically manipulate the shreds and patches of outlived mythologies" (546); this has essentially been the approach of T. S. Eliot, James Joyce, Ezra Pound, and Thomas Mann. Then, there is the extreme expedient—employed by William Blake, W. B. Yeats, and Hart Crane—of devising one's own private myth system.

Rejecting all three of these approaches, Fiedler suggests that, in our atomized culture, the poet cannot redeem, create, or reconstitute a common body of stories; he is left only with himself as archetype—with the archetype of the poet. By plumbing the depths of his own psyche, he can transcend the eccentricities of signature and return "to his unconscious core, where he becomes one with us all in the presence of our ancient Gods, the protagonists of fables we think we no longer believe" (547). Thus, by Fiedler's reckoning, the poet becomes something akin to Emerson's representative man or Whitman's national bard. He speaks for his society not as propagandist but as seer. "In the Mask of his life and the manifold masks of his work, the poet expresses for a whole society the ritual meaning of its inarticulate selves; the artist goes forth not to 're-create the conscience of his race,' but to redeem its unconscious. We cannot get back into the primal Garden of the unfallen Archetypes, but we can yield ourselves to the dreams and images that mean paradise regained" (547).

Even though Fiedler may have been reticent in naming names, the New Critics were never in doubt that he had them in mind when he attacked the "anti-biographists" in "Archetype and Signature." In *Literary Criticism: A Short History* (1957), which he wrote in collaboration with W. K. Wimsatt, Cleanth Brooks devotes more than a page to critiquing Fiedler's essay. He charges that the notion of an archetype is really a disguised attempt to define "a privileged poetic subject matter . . . [because] any great poem must be an acceptable rendition of this special poetic content." The problem with this objection is that Fiedler has not catalogued a limited number of archetypes from which a great poem must be written. It is clear from his essay that his notion of the archetype is expansive enough to admit virtually any subject matter that can be rendered in song and story. A more plausible charge is that Fiedler's understanding of myth is too broad rather than too narrow.[10]

If Brooks has difficulty with Fiedler's notion of the archetype, the signature gives him problems as well. He argues that "in Fiedler's conception, a poem is not an object to be known; it is rather a clue to an event in the poet's psyche." This characterization would cast Fiedler in the straw man role of psychobiographer. In fact, he most assuredly does regard the poem as "an object to be known." He simply believes that a familiarity with the poet's life can aid in the act of knowing. If he sees the poem as a clue to anything beyond itself, it is to the collective dreams of a people. He uses literature not so much for psychoanalysis as for spiritual anthropology. In his discussion of the southern community in *William Faulkner: The Yoknapatawpha Country* (1963), Cleanth Brooks himself does much the same thing superbly well.

---

10. W. K. Wimsatt and Cleanth Brooks, *Literary Criticism: A Short History,* 713. Although no official distinction is made concerning the authorship of various parts of this book, we know that Brooks wrote the section on modern criticism. Faulting Fiedler for very different reasons, Charles R. Larson writes, "Ultimately—and I feel that this is the crux of the problem with Fiedler— . . . everything becomes a myth, and what started as a serious attempt to define *mythos* and its relationship to poetry has grown into a gigantic tumor which Fiedler has used not as an appendage of literature but as literature itself." See Larson's "Leslie Fiedler: The Critic and the Myth, the Critic as Myth," 141.

Although *Literary Criticism: A Short History* did not appear until five years after the publication of Fiedler's essay, Brooks's initial response to "Archetype and Signature" was almost immediate, coming in the winter 1953 issue of the *Sewanee Review.* Titled "A Note on the Limits of 'History' and the Limits of 'Criticism,'" this defense of New Criticism was actually the last installment in a running debate between Brooks and Douglas Bush over the meaning of Marvell's "Horatian Ode." While defending himself against the attacks of Bush's traditional historical scholarship, Brooks feels compelled to add a few words about Fiedler's more general assault on aesthetic formalism. In essence, he sees Fiedler's myth criticism and Bush's old historicism as opposite sides of the same coin.

Although he admits that Bush and Fiedler would find each other to be strange bedfellows, Brooks notes that both are attempting to restore biographical and historical considerations to the analysis of literature. Summarizing Fiedler's "neat, almost jaunty survey of recent literary history," Brooks writes, "If I may fill in some names, Mr. Fiedler might presumably see Mr. Bush as the thesis (the old-fashioned historical scholarship), me as the antithesis (the doctrinaire antibiographer), and himself as the triumphant synthesis."[11] There are, however, other ways of looking at the situation. Preferring dichotomy to dialectics, Brooks sees formalism as the only pure criticism and all other approaches as hybrids of nonliterary disciplines.

"In their concern for the break-up of the modern world," Brooks writes, "Mr. Bush, Mr. Fiedler, and a host of other scholars and critics are anxious to see literature put to work to save the situation." Although Brooks professes to share his adversaries' desire to redeem our disintegrating, deracinated culture, he thinks it dangerous to confuse religion and poetry. (He comes close here to branding Fiedler an Arnoldian moralist who wants to make a god of books.) Such confusion, he argues, serves neither God nor art: "[T]hough poetry has a very important role in any culture, to ask that poetry save us is to impose a burden on poetry that it cannot sustain. The danger is that we will end up with an ersatz religion and an ersatz poetry."

III

As impressive as Fiedler's theorizing about myth might be, the question remains: How useful is all of this in reading literary texts? The popularity and durability of New Criticism lies in its supreme utility. (There is more than a little truth to Christopher Clausen's contention that it enables a person with

---

11. Cleanth Brooks, "A Note on the Limits of 'History' and the Limits of 'Criticism,'" 357.

little imagination and learning to arrive at a plausible interpretation of a poem simply by mastering a few favored terms and techniques.) The test of a myth critic is whether his approach can help illuminate works of literature whose power is not fully explicable by other means or whether it finally degenerates into self-regarding schematics. Reading Sir James Frazer's *The Golden Bough* may tell us where T. S. Eliot got many of the symbols he uses in *The Waste Land;* it cannot tell us the literary value of those symbols. George Eliot realized one of the pitfalls of myth criticism when she created the character of Casaubon in *Middlemarch.* This dusty old pedant devoted his life to a futile search for the "key to all mythologies." In our own time, Joseph Campbell and Northrop Frye have claimed to have found such keys.[12]

Fiedler has wisely shied away from system building in an effort to read the particular patterns that give shape and coherence to our culture. At the same time, his observations are constantly rising to the level of generalization. In reading some myth critics (or critics of any persuasion, for that matter), one gets the sense that Procrustes is trying to fit the specific instance to the general paradigm. Fiedler at least gathers his evidence before presuming to tell us what it all means. As a consequence, his study of specific writers and specific books— e. g., "Come Back to the Raft Ag'in, Huck Honey!"—often tells us more about myth criticism than do his explicitly theoretical essays.

In his introduction to a new edition of *The Master of Ballantrae* (1954), Fiedler employs myth criticism to assess the literary worth of Robert Louis Stevenson. Can we find some way of redeeming Stevenson for high literature, or must we concede that a fondness for *Treasure Island* is "a minor subliterary vice, like reading detective stories" (*CE,* 1:297). (Although he would later renounce such elitist language, the very fact of his taking Stevenson seriously suggests how far removed Fiedler already was from the canons of high modernism and New Criticism.) To follow the lead of David Daiches and argue that, over the course of his career, Stevenson "progressed" from the romance to the novel really begs the question. We would have to concede, as Fiedler is unwilling to do, that the romance is an inferior genre. Also, we would still have no explanation for the power of those books of Stevenson's that are unquestionably romances.

To understand the appeal of a writer such as Stevenson, it is helpful to remember that Long John Silver appeared for years as a character in the "Katzenjammer Kids." One can hardly imagine Anna Karenina or Stephen Dedalus moonlighting in a comic strip. The reason that Long John Silver can get away with it is that "like other Stevensonian characters (Jekyll and Hyde,

---

12. See Joseph Campbell, *The Hero with a Thousand Faces,* and Northrop Frye, *Anatomy of Criticism.*

for instance), he exists, as it were, in the public domain—along with Thor and Loki, Hansel and Gretel." In other words, he has "an objective existence, a being prior to and independent of any particular formal realization." Thus, Fiedler concludes, "it is in the realm of myth, which sometimes overlaps but is not identical with literature, that we must look for clues to the meaning and unity of Stevenson's work" (298).

Unlike highbrow writers such as Joyce and Mann, Stevenson is not a sophisticated exploiter of mythic materials. Instead, he has more in common with popular entertainers such as Arthur Conan Doyle and Graham Greene. "Such naive exploiters of the mythic . . . preserve the 'story' and its appeal intact; in them the picturesque never yields completely to the metaphysical—and they can always be read on one level as boys' books or circulating-library thrillers" (298). The one myth that seems to run through Stevenson's work, giving it coherence and power in addition to mass appeal, is that of the Beloved Scoundrel. His books, from *Dr. Jekyll and Mr. Hyde* to *Treasure Island,* depict "the beauty of evil—and conversely the unloveliness of good." What makes this myth truly subversive is the fact that it is embodied, time and again, in books that are universally read and loved by children.

Even at this early point in his career, Fiedler was fascinated by writers who bridged the gap between elite and popular taste. In the late 1940s and early 1950s, the American novelist who seemed to epitomize such wide-ranging appeal was Robert Penn Warren. Unlike Faulkner, and to an extent Graham Greene, who wrote different kinds of stories for different kinds of audiences, Warren wrote books that were appreciated in both the academy and the marketplace. *All the King's Men,* a novel of undeniable artistic distinction, became a best-seller, won the Pulitzer Prize, and served as the basis for an Academy Award–winning movie. "For a work of real merit to win any of these doubtful distinctions is highly improbable," Fiedler notes; "and the compounded improbability of its winning all three is staggering" (*CE,* 1:339).

The mystery becomes even more impenetrable when one considers that Warren was by no means a literary populist. Along with Cleanth Brooks, he had rendered service to highbrow literature through his editorship of the *Southern Review,* which helped to establish the academic respectability of New Criticism during the late 1930s and early 1940s. Warren and Brooks had also elevated the tastes and exegetical skills of college sophomores with their New Critical textbooks, especially *Understanding Poetry.* The presence, at times the seeming ubiquity, of the metaphysical poets and T. S. Eliot in the college classroom was due in no small part to their efforts. And yet, here was Warren writing "serious fiction," which was devoured by readers of *The Robe* and *Dinner at Antoine's.*

What, then, accounts for Warren's improbable "crossover" appeal? Fiedler surmises that the mass audience will excuse a novelist for writing well, and even for taking an ironic and antisentimental view of life, if he is also totally committed to narrative. If the archetype and the story are one, any writer who can appropriate mythic material in a gripping narrative has a good chance of moving a popular audience. (In the *Poetics,* Aristotle himself stressed the importance of plot.) "To the naturalist, the pragmatist, the nominalist, plot can only be a 'machine' and must in honesty be abandoned; but to the believer in the reality of guilt and grace [an obsessive theme for Warren], the 'fable' with its immemorial reversals and recognitions is the formal vestige of a way of believing and a celebration of belief. The hunger for plot among the people is a hunger for ritual satisfaction, and the writer who can feed their hunger without condescension may satisfy them and his own alienated self at the same time" (344).

These early essays on Stevenson and Warren (along with "Come Back to the Raft Ag'in, Huck Honey!") suggest the extent to which Fiedler's view of myth criticism differs from that of more conventional figures such as Campbell and Frye. Although he pays occasional lip service to Jung, Fiedler is not particularly interested in finding a universal system of myth. The concept of archetype and signature allows him to identify characters and narratives that seem to belong to a particular culture or a particular age. Although a universal dream usually lurks behind the ritual story (the misogynistic appeal of male bonding in the Huck-Honey tradition, the seductiveness of evil in the world of Stevenson, the drama of guilt and redemption in the fiction of Warren), a particular type of signature is required to make this dream accessible in the form of literature. Fiedler is less interested in tracing the anthropological source of a given myth than in tracking the progress of that myth once it has become incarnate in song and story. He was finally driven to take popular culture seriously because he recognized that certain characters and situations pass so completely into our collective consciousness that they assume an existence independent of the formal works in which they originally appeared. It may well be a case of signature passing back into archetype again.

CHAPTER SEVEN

Discovering America

WHEN LESLIE arrived in Bloomington in the summer of 1952, he was coming west from Italy, not east from Missoula. Thanks to the Fulbright fellowship program, he had been appointed as a lecturer in medieval studies at the University of Rome. Although he had traveled to the South Pacific and to China during World War II, this was his first visit to the Europe he had dreamed of as a boy in Newark. He was accompanied by Margaret and his four children (a third son and a daughter had been born in Missoula), and he stayed long enough to produce a fifth. Although he had originally wanted to escape to a mythic Paris, he immediately fell in love with Italy and managed to extend his stay to a second year by teaching at universities in Bologna and Venice. It was in Italy that he almost died in his thirty-fifth year and that he first laid claim to the literature of his native land.

While overseas, Leslie formed a friendship with W. H. Auden, which would last for the rest of Auden's life. In the summers of 1952 and 1953, the Fiedler family vacationed on the island of Ischia, in the Bay of Naples. The island was beautiful and unspoiled, and in the summertime the local residents would move out into the countryside and rent their houses to tourists. Because no cars were allowed, one was forced to travel by horse and carriage. The expatriate community consisted mostly of refugee American artists and noblemen down on their luck—almost all of whom were gay. At the cafe where everyone gathered were two center tables. At one sat the Principe of Hesse, who would have been the next king of Italy, and at the other, W. H. Auden.

Although Leslie believed that intelligence was optional for poets, Auden was one poet who possessed this quality to an extraordinary degree. Leslie would try to tweak his Anglo-Catholic sensibility with anti-Christian remarks. For example, he would call Auden's attention to the fact that the man Jesus replaced on the cross was named Barabbas, which means "Son of the Father." Might the whole story simply be allegorical? When they tired of theological conversation, they would exchange fantasy books. Auden introduced Leslie

94

and his family to Tolkien's The Lord of the Rings, and Leslie gave the British poet Baum's *The Wonderful Wizard of Oz.*

There were many little towns on the island and a huge extinct volcano at its center. Mussolini used to spend his summers on Ischia, and his wife still lived there in 1952. The peasants would stop her in the marketplace and kiss her hand. The language spoken on the island was almost incomprehensible to Leslie; it sounded to him more like Chinese than Italian. Because there was not much else to do there, it was a good place to write. The Fiedlers lived in two houses, with a lemon tree right over the terrace of one of the houses. Leslie's daughter, Debbie, who was only two at the time, showed so much interest in what the neighbors were doing that, when she needed to pee, she would take her potty and set it outside the wall in front of the yard so she could sit and watch people moving up and down the road.

During part of the time that Leslie was in Bologna, Richard Blackmur was in town. A few years earlier, during one of his infrequent trips to New York, Leslie had run into Saul Bellow, who suggested that they go visit Mel Tumin at Princeton, and there Leslie met Blackmur. The visit turned into an orgy of eating, drinking, and talking. Thirteen years Leslie's senior, Blackmur was a good poet and an even better critic, who had made it in the academy without ever having attended college himself. Blackmur had attached himself to Princeton as a staff member of the Institute for Advanced Study and later as a lecturer in the creative arts program under Allen Tate. He became a resident fellow in the creative writing program and eventually a professor in the English department. He was much admired by the New York intellectuals for both his brilliant mind and his lack of formal schooling.

Leslie recalls that whenever Blackmur got drunk (which was a frequent occurrence) all his paranoia came out. He would begin by abusing blacks. After a few more drinks, he would start in on Jews. Then, when he was really deep in his cups, he would go after women. When he was completely gone, he attacked the entire human race. Blackmur was the sort of anti-Semite who always had to have a Jew in residence. Often it was Saul Bellow or Philip Roth or Leslie himself. With Blackmur in Bologna, Leslie was greatly tempted to stop by for a few drinks on the way to class. That regimen, along with the rich Italian food, plunged Leslie into an illness from which he nearly didn't recover.

When he contracted hepatitis at age thirty-five, Leslie assumed that his hard gemlike flame was simply destined to burn out early. He lay semiconscious for six weeks, almost wishing that someone would put him out of his misery. He was treated, though not cured, by a doctor who kept saying, "Now laugh at us Italians and our livers." After the disease ran its course, Leslie felt as if he had been reborn into a second life. But, when he walked down the street to get a newspaper at the corner kiosk, he nearly collapsed and had to crawl back home on his hands and knees. He remained very weak during a long convalescence. As he began to recover, he made up a song, which went: "You can easily tell he's not a lemon, cause the lemon never needs a shave."[1]

Early in his tenure at the University of Rome, Leslie discovered that the resident professor of English, Mario Praz, was reputed to be a *jettatore,* or caster of spells. "[A] postwar returnee to Rome after years of exile at the University of Manchester, [he] was referred to by all Italians who knew him not by his name, but as *l'Innominabile,* 'the Unnameable One,' because he was alleged to possess mysterious and even diabolical powers which, even when he did not wish it, interfered with the functioning of mechanical objects."[2] After his first face-to-face encounter with the unnameable one, Leslie found that his watch had stopped and could not be fixed.

Although Leslie assumed that he would be teaching medieval literature in Rome (his teaching at Missoula had never extended beyond the Renaissance), it was soon made clear to him that he was expected to teach American literature. At first, this expectation struck him as being arrogant and condescending. Did the Italians think that he was too provincial to teach anything other than his native writers? At NYU and Wisconsin, he had never even *taken* a course in American literature, preferring instead to concentrate in the more "scholarly" areas, which required at least the mastery of another language. Like the archetypal Americans who populate the international novels of James and others, Leslie Fiedler was now forced to confront his indigenous culture among the ruins of the Old World.

Of course, Leslie was not entirely unprepared for this experience. If he was not a professional Americanist, he was a passionate amateur. Given that he published in intellectual magazines and literary reviews rather than in strictly scholarly journals, he had inevitably written about American books past and present. If nothing else, "Come Back to the Raft Ag'in, Huck Honey!" established him as someone who had provocative things to say about the American literary tradition. The sense of pique that Leslie had initially felt about being asked to teach American books soon dissipated. As he recalls, "I became aware of the real desire in my students not merely to know but to identify with all that was unique in our books and the society which had produced them" ("Fulbright," 91).

Leslie discovered that the Italians were less structured than Americans in their approach to higher education. When he asked Carlo Itzo, his contact in Bologna, when his lectures were to begin, Carlo responded, "When would you like them to begin?" Leslie told him, and Carlo promised to post a note on the

---

1. Fiedler, interview with Jackson, June 10, 1989.
2. Leslie Fiedler, "Fulbright I: Italy 1952," 89. Subsequent references will be cited parenthetically in the text as "Fulbright."

bulletin board, so the students would know to be in the right room at the right time. When Leslie came on the appointed day, he found that Carlo had forgotten to make the arrangements. " 'Stab me. Kill me. Destroy me,' " he would say. 'Next week, I'll write it in a note and put it inside my watch.'" When the next week rolled around and he again saw Carlo, the Italian would sheepishly say, "Stab me. Kill me. Destroy me." On occasion, Leslie was tempted to do so.

In Italy an interest in American writers was at least in part a political gesture. For nationalist reasons, Mussolini had forbidden American literature. Consequently, being an Americanist was an act of anti-Fascist resistance. It was also an avant-garde assault upon academic elitism. American literature had been introduced to Italy by nonacademic creative writers such as Cesare Pavese and Elio Vittorini. Writing about American literature was a way of turning one's back on the insularity of old Roman culture and looking to the future. As Pavese put it, "America has no graveyards to defend." In a very real sense, Leslie, during his Fulbright fellowship year, introduced American literature to the academy in Italy. (More of his books have been translated into Italian than into any other language.) In 1952, there were no chairs of American literature in Italy. Forty years later, there were more than fifteen—several of them held by Leslie's former students.

Leslie arrived in Rome shortly after Cesare Pavese had committed suicide at the age of forty-two. Leslie knew Pavese only through his novels and his splendid translation of *Moby-Dick*. (Although inaccurate in literal terms, Pavese's translation maintains the spirit of the original, while managing to convey the cadences of Melville's English in a similarly poetic Italian.) One night in Torino, Leslie walked arm in arm with Gabrielle Baldini, both of them full of grappa, as Baldini pointed out where *Moby-Dick* had been translated and the balcony from which Pavese had thrown himself to his death. Like his American idol, F. O. Matthiessen, Pavese had left behind a note with a haunting line from *King Lear:* "Ripeness is all."[3]

Pavese's decision to take his own life seems to have been hastened by Matthiessen's suicide, "for in Matthiessen he thought he had discovered something of himself in pure American form, his own vision of the literature of the United States, his own desperate commitment to a politics of the masses, the terrible definition of maturity toward which he had been groping along his own lines" (*CE,* 1:363). Pavese was also shaken by his unrequited love for a Hollywood starlet, identified only as C (actually Constance Dowling), to whom he wrote some poems in the best American idiom he could muster. One, called "Last Blues," reads in part:

3. Leslie Fiedler, interview with Bruce Jackson, July 18, 1989.

> Twas only a flirt
> you sure did know—
> some one was hurt
> long time ago.
> Some one has died
> long time ago—
> some one who tried
> but didn't know.

Whatever the catalyst, Pavese was always fascinated by death. Fiedler tells us that "from the earliest pages, the diaries record his longing for suicide, the overture to the long flirtation, the approaches and withdrawals, the self-reproaches for cowardice and the desperate excuse that to kill oneself would be to lose the pleasure of looking forward to death" (*CE*, 1:362).

Pavese found in American literature, particularly in Melville, a special sort of symbolism, which was not at all like the aristocratic *symbolisme* of the French. Instead, Fiedler tells us, it was rooted in "a democratic faith that a 'colloquy with the masses' might be opened on the level of myth, whose unity underlies the diversity of our acquired cultures" (*CE*, 1:360). This engagement with myth in American literature made Pavese a kindred spirit for Leslie Fiedler, who was himself discovering his native writers largely through the prism of myth. Pavese's view of art, like Fiedler's, was fundamentally that of a myth critic. Thus, in describing Pavese's position, Fiedler reveals a good deal about his own evolving critical stance:

> Great literature, Pavese came to believe, moves us because what it reveals to us is felt as remembered as well as discovered, felt "for a second time"; yet the "first time" is known only by implication, in a sense never existed, except mythically, for it occurred before time began for us, in childhood when we do not know our experiences but are them. From this it follows that a work of literature, though it has to deal with parochial and local forms, things rendered as they are known "for the second time," does not finally depend for its force and conviction on "truth" of action, character or detail, but on how much of the daemonic energy of the myth survives its rationalization. (*CE*, 1:365)

The extent to which Leslie's own experience in Italy was bound up with American literature is suggested by his poem "The Whiteness of the Whale: Bologna, 1952." The poem begins in the parlors of the Bolognese (actually Blackmur's residence), as they rehearse the names of all who have "bled to dry the color of this colonnade"—not out of reverence, but simply "to allay / A lust for conversation." In the middle of the fifth line, the speaker (obviously Leslie himself) enters the colloquy:

> . . . . Yet here I fed
> As if to break the fast of ghosts, feasted
> Till my eyeballs bugged and frozen sweat
> Stood on the hot bulge of my brows, then drank
> Till morning in a garden where the dead
> Snails shrivelled in their pails of salt. "God bless Begonias!" sang my host.
>   "God bless," I said,
> "My bile."

As he describes his battle with hepatitis, Leslie contemplates the meaning of blood and his own lack of ancestral connection with the bloody history of Rome:

> Six weeks I lay in bed
> At odds with life in love with death.
> Red Cities turn us tallow-yellow, mallow soft.
> The knowledge of blood's color is forbid
> To us whose fathers fled from blood, left
> Colonnades like clots of serum for the shade
> Of sheds, of lofts, of sidings white as scars.

As an expatriated American, Leslie is an outsider, who plays the assigned role by eating and drinking too much—in the process turning himself from blood-red to jaundice-yellow. As a Jew, he is even more alienated from the Christian blood of Rome. The image of the Wandering Jew is somehow too tame. What he depicts is the Jew in flight. But now, as American and Jew, the speaker of the poem has come to Italy to teach a different history, bathed in a different color. As Melville tells us, white is a more universal and more ambivalent color than red. In a sense, it becomes the very image of our inmost self. The poem concludes with the recovered speaker returning to his vocation: "Risen at last, I took my notes by rail / Back to Bologna, back to my liver's hell, / And lectured on the Whiteness of the Whale" (*NFR,* 470).

I

When Leslie boarded the ship for Italy in 1951, he had in hand Hawthorne's *The Marble Faun.* He tells us it was a choice between that and Mark Twain's *Innocents Abroad,* between melodrama and comedy. Recalling his voyage, he writes:

> At first glance, shipboard life had seemed to promise pure comic Twain, and things threatened to reach a hilarious climax when we disembarked

briefly at Barcelona to make our first penetration of Europe. We had only a few hours ashore and everyone piled into the sightseeing buses at the dock. I found myself just behind a large, enthusiastic lady, almost purple with the strain of being an American. She had thrust eagerly down the gangplank but, getting her first whiff of the Old World, had begun holding her nose in ostentatious and growing disgust, until finally, in the shadow of her first cathedral, she had turned to all of us, imploring us to join in "God Bless America!" It was impossible to laugh; she was so obviously afraid. (*CE,* 1:92)

From the very start, it seemed that Leslie Fiedler's journey to Italy was destined to be a literary pilgrimage. The artifacts of American culture had given the Italians an image of our society that inevitably colored the way they viewed visitors from the United States. Those who were familiar with our high literature were introduced to an adversary culture that criticized the banality and philistinism of American life. Unfortunately, Italian intellectuals took the books of Theodore Dreiser, Sherwood Anderson, and William Faulkner far too literally. Rather than seeing them as evidence of the American tradition of dissent (and, thus, of the health of our society), Europeans had "an odd habit of reading our most poetic books as anthropological documents" (110).

The American intellectual abroad became a figure of exaggerated reverence and exaggerated pity. Any criticism of American culture he might make was taken as evidence of superhuman courage. To continue making such criticisms enabled the American intellectual to fulfill a stereotypical role for his European counterpart. It was only evidence of a truly independent mind that caused trouble. For an American to praise anything about his native land or cast doubt on the virtue of certain legendary American victims was to risk being taken for a propagandist. What was lacking in the view that European intellectuals took toward America was any sense of proportion. "Grant without qualification that American soldiers are ignorant, unacquainted with *The Scarlet Letter* and *Moby-Dick,* and your interlocutor will follow up by observing in a conspiratorial tone, 'It's easy for us [*us!*] to understand how such barbarians can be persuaded to use germ warfare against Korean peasants!' Or admit the abuses of Congressional investigating committees, and you will be expected to grant that the United States has resigned from Western Civilization" (112).

It was an article of faith among the European intellectuals Fiedler describes that the one true enemy of humanity was the bourgeoisie. Because American culture (both high and low) proclaimed the existence (perhaps even the dominance) of this beast, American intellectuals were viewed as traitors to their class in allowing the beast to live. What the cynical European could not abide was the suspicion that he would probably be no worse off in the land of Snopes and Babbitt than in the decadent Old World. Rather than admit this, it was far easier to make America into a mythicized image of everything he hated and to assume that the American who refused to join him in his orgy of abuse was acting in bad faith. In making such a refusal, Leslie declined to play the European version of the "Good American," or radical chic dissident.

At the level of popular culture, ordinary Italians embraced America, spawning homegrown imitations of *Life* and *Look* and American comic books (colored only on every fourth page because Italy was not as rich as America). Particular favorites of the Italians were Pecos Bill, "Jane Calamity," Donald Duck, and—preeminently—Mickey Mouse. Two-thirds of the films one saw advertised in Italy were of American origin, "despite the excellence of the Italian product and the substantial fine which an operator must pay if he does not show a certain proportion of Italian movies." "For most Italians," Fiedler notes, "the voyage to America is a cinematic one—a ritual more honored than the Mass" (96).

Italian writers who had been possessed imaginatively by America betrayed a strange ambivalence about the country. Emilio Cecchi, for example, read certain events in the daily newspapers as real-life analogues (or confirmations) of what he had encountered in Poe, Melville, and Faulkner. These writers "are welcomed by the Italian essayist as witnesses against their own civilization, whose barbarity he feels as a threat to his own." There was, however, a fascination and an attraction in American barbarity. The Italian writer's engagement with American literature might have begun with a search for depravity, but "it ends in [his] finding a utopia and a cue for emulation, . . . a secret hunger for the madness and primitive rage he chose to read into America" (100). In the late 1990s, an Italian student told Leslie that the two American writers to whom Italians feel closest are Jack Kerouac and Leslie Fiedler.[4]

For Italians, the first important critic of American literature was D. H. Lawrence. According to Fiedler, "Lawrence is for the Italians the Virgil of their infernal descent. It is impossible here in Italy to pick up a book or listen to a lecture on American literature that does not draw on *Studies in Classic American Literature.* . . . To an Italian, of course, the rhetoric of Lawrence's book (so committed and uncorseted and disturbing to the professor with a pipe) is an earnest that he is *simpatico,* on their side; and so their classic American literature, their Melville and Hawthorne and Cooper, are to this very day essentially Lawrence's" (102).

What makes American culture unique (and profoundly un-European) is the fact that our optimism is never merely official, but remains a deeply rooted condition of our national psyche. No matter how many falls we experience, we never quite lose the illusion of innocence, or at least the dream of perfectibility. This unrelenting Pelaginism will give us no rest.

4. Leslie Fiedler, interview with author, Feb. 27, 1999.

Among us, nothing is winked at or shrugged away; we are being eternally horrified at dope-addiction or bribery or war, at things accepted in other civilizations as the facts of life, scarcely worth a tired joke. . . . How absurd of our writers to have believed that only they were pained at the failure of love and justice in the United States! What did they think our pulp literature of violence and drunkenness and flight was trying symbolically to declare? Why did they suppose that the most widely read fiction in America asks endlessly, "Whodunit? Where is the guilt?" (126)

It is probably no accident that the first great practitioner of the "whodunit" in America also invented the image of the alienated artist for our popular imagination. Edgar Allan Poe helped to create the myth of the wounded Dionysian writer, which Hart Crane, F. Scott Fitzgerald, and others have been most willing to replicate. The pain of the scapegoat is real but also unavoidable. It is bred from the sort of naive idealism that continues to believe in the possibility of tragedy. For the most part, European intellectuals have moved beyond that point to a sort of fashionable despair. When they read American literature, it is often with a condescension that masks a secret yearning for the tragic vision they themselves can no longer articulate with a straight face. In American literature, the sophisticated European vicariously experiences "the encounter of the dream of innocence and the fact of guilt, in the only part of the world where the reality of that conflict can still be recognized" (128).

II

Shortly after his return to America, Leslie became a full professor at Montana State University. For several years, he had also been one of the most respected young critics in America. (In 1948, no less a figure than Lionel Trilling had confessed in his diary how desperately he wanted a talk of his to be praised by Fiedler.)[5] All that he seemed to lack was a book. Perhaps this was because Leslie insisted on seeing himself as primarily a poet and secondarily as a writer of fiction. With increasing frequency, however, he found that editors who would reject his creative work wanted him to review a book or write on some cultural topic. Eventually, he found that he had become a prolific and controversial critic almost in spite of himself.

With no publisher interested in the collection of poems he was circulating, Leslie finally agreed to offer a manuscript of critical prose to his friend Sol Stein. (The two had met through the American Committee for Cultural Freedom, of which Sol was executive director.) At the time, Stein was working

5. See Sanford Pinsker, "Leslie Fiedler, Freak," 184.

as an editor for Beacon Press, a largely secular publishing house owned by the largely secular Unitarian Church. In 1955, Beacon published its first three trade books—*Notes of a Native Son,* by Sol's high school classmate James Baldwin, the first American edition of George Orwell's *Homage to Catalonia,* and Leslie Fiedler's *An End to Innocence.* The theme announced by this title was one that had obsessed Leslie since his first published story on Al Eisner—the role of innocence in American life. The clear message running all the way through the book was that it was time for American culture to grow up and assume the maturity befitting a great nation.

In the same year that *An End to Innocence* appeared, R. W. B. Lewis published *The American Adam,* a book that explores the fascination of nineteenth-century American writers with the theme of innocence. Almost from the time Columbus made America accessible to the European imagination, many intellectuals and artists had come to view the New World as a second Garden of Eden and "the authentic American as a figure of heroic innocence and vast potentialities, poised at the start of a new history." In his epilogue, Lewis briefly discusses the persistence of the American Adam in twentieth-century American fiction. He even goes so far as to argue that "in most of what I take to be the truest and most fully engaged American fiction after the second [world] war, the newborn or self-breeding or orphaned hero is plunged again and again, for his own good and for ours, into the spurious, disruptive rituals of the actual world."[6]

Almost as old as the image of the American Adam have been the cautionary voices of those who believe that a return to innocence is neither possible nor desirable. When those voices came only from latter-day Calvinists preaching the doctrines of Original Sin and natural depravity, they could be dismissed as somehow un-American. (Emerson derided them as a "party of memory.") But it was not just Puritan theocrats who believed that life lived in the moral equivalent of a germ-free environment was less than fully human. Our most spiritually complex nineteenth-century novelists saw the fall into knowledge, with all its attendant dangers, as being necessary and potentially redemptive. If natural depravity is often accepted as a given in the Old World, the American is, almost by definition, destined to experience the *fall* from innocence. As Lewis has noted, the characteristic situation in Hawthorne's fiction "is that of the Emersonian figure, the man of hope, who by some frightful mischance has stumbled into the time-burdened world of Jonathan Edwards."[7] In *An End to Innocence,* Leslie Fiedler frankly aligns himself with this paradoxical and dialectical tradition in the American imagination.

6. R. W. B. Lewis, *The American Adam: Innocence, Tragedy, and Tradition in the Nineteenth Century,* 1, 197–98.
7. Ibid., 113.

An End to Innocence begins with Leslie's three controversial political essays from the early 1950s. These are followed by "Innocents Abroad," a section of four memoirs inspired by his Fulbright fellowship in Italy. The book then concludes with six discussions of American literary culture. Although only the first two of these, "Montana; or the End of Jean-Jacques Rousseau" and "Come Back to the Raft Ag'in, Huck Honey!" are widely remembered today, all six reflect the distinctive sensibility and voice that Fiedler had developed in a decade of publication since his return from the war. Like all critics worth reading, he identifies the essential qualities and limitations of the subject he is analyzing and places that subject in a broader cultural context. In the process, he tries to recover a usable literary past and to correct taste in our befuddled present.

"Images of Walt Whitman," which originally appeared in the January 1955 issue of *Encounter,* was published exactly one hundred years after the first edition of *Leaves of Grass.* When Ernest Hemingway declared that all American literature began with *Huckleberry Finn,* he was speaking primarily of modern fiction. The real beginning of the American poetic tradition came with *Leaves of Grass.* Whether modern American poets see themselves as descendants of Whitman or his mortal enemies is finally beside the point. He is the touchstone against which our poetry defines itself (a fact with which even so un-Whitmanesque a figure as Ezra Pound eventually had to come to terms). At the same time, the "Americanness" of Whitman is not itself entirely indigenous. Fiedler argues that "Walt Whitman's America was made in France, the Romantic notion out of Rousseau and Chateaubriand of an absolute anti-Europe, an utter anti-culture made flesh, the Noble Savage as a Continent" (*CE,* 1:164).

As Fiedler reminds us, to speak of Whitman is to speak of a many-faceted persona, a sort of cultural Rorschach test in which different interest groups see their own compulsions represented. At one level, Whitman depicted himself as the avatar of a new homegrown religion—a sort of "Mary Baker Eddy of American poetry" (154). (If America in the 1950s was a culture in need of maturity, the priestly Whitman was a figure to be shunned—either orthodoxy or unbelief was preferable to a kind of ersatz religiosity.) When he was not playing the role of shaman, Whitman was apt to be posing as the prophet of sexual emancipation or the quintessential democrat. Those who focus on the first of these roles are responding more to an image of swagger and braggadocio — e.g., his boast of having fathered a brood of illegitimate children—than to the tormented homosexual who never made it all the way out of the closet. Even more problematical is the appropriation of Whitman by political radicals. That a man who supported capitalism and despised trade unions should become a Marxist saint is surprising. That a poem by such a Yankee Doodle patriot as Whitman—"To a Foil'd European Revolutionaire"—should have been placed in the hands of Soviet troops fighting the American Expeditionary Forces in Siberia is nothing short of astounding.

At times, Whitman's image looms so much larger than life that one suspects it is larger than art as well. Whitman may share with Poe the dubious distinction of being his own most memorable creation. It is certainly a paradox that *Leaves of Grass* was originally conceived of as an anonymous poem. In many ways, Whitman would seem to be our least anonymous poet. And yet, to separate the "real" Walt Whitman from the self-created persona of the poetry is no easy task. Perhaps it is necessary only to acknowledge rather than explicate the disparity between man and myth. If Milton could nearly lose himself in the conventions of the pastoral elegy, Whitman may have achieved a similar self-effacement in the mask of the bard.

III

The closer we come to the present, the more difficult it is to make a proper assessment of any writer's worth. In a sense, the literary ancestors we choose to revere tell us more about the needs of our own time than about the achievement of a past era. In reflecting on the renewed interest in F. Scott Fitzgerald in the spring of 1951, Fiedler speculates that the postwar generation might well be atoning for the literary errors of the 1930s, when socially engaged writers, such as Steinbeck and Dos Passos, were seen as more serious than a Jazz Age playboy. With Hemingway knocked off the throne and none of the younger writers clearly his heir apparent, we were left only with the eccentric Faulkner (whose own best work was behind him) to play the role of great novelist. It therefore seemed necessary to reach back and rescue Fitzgerald for "our depopulated pantheon."

In American literature, nothing succeeds quite like failure. "We are," Fiedler notes, "behind a show of the grossest success-worship, a nation that dreams of failure as a fulfillment. The Christian paradox of the defeated as victor haunts our post-Christian world. None of us seems *really* to believe in the succeeding of success, though we do not know how to escape from its trap; and it has become one of the functions of our writers to supply us with vicarious failures for our second-hand redemption" (176). Although Fiedler does not say so explicitly, it is precisely our belief in innocence that makes a virtue of failure. Had Fitzgerald been successful in prostituting his talent in Hollywood, he would not have seemed the half-tragic, half-pathetic figure he has become in our popular mythology. (The year before Fiedler published his essay, Budd Schulberg had created a popular fictional version of Fitzgerald in Hollywood in his novel *The Disenchanted*.) Had he sobered up long enough to live into respectable old age, he would not have been the John Keats of our literature.

Facing the absence of a native aristocracy in America, Fitzgerald simply created the myth of the very rich as people different from you and me. Unlike Benjamin Franklin or Horatio Alger, Fitzgerald was more interested in the self-made man once made than in the process of the making. (We know very little about how Jimmy Gatz became Jay Gatsby.) "It is not money getters, but spenders, to whom Fitzgerald turned in his search for allies, out of a sense that the squandering of unearned money was an art, like writing, that squandering of an unearned talent; and that among the very rich there might be a perpetual area of freedom, like that in which the artist momentarily feels himself in the instant of creative outpouring." The truth that Fitzgerald realized is that in the life of the rich, as in the life of the artist, "there is a doom as absolute as its splendor." "To those who plead that Fitzgerald could not face up to life and success," Fiedler concludes, "it can be said that at least he kept faith with death and defeat" (182).

In contrast to Fitzgerald's idealization of the rich is the opposite tendency of some writers to make a hero of the bum. Fiedler sees Goethe's *The Sorrows of Young Werther*—"the first anti-bourgeois bourgeois novel"—as the archetypal book for such writers. It makes little difference whether or not those following in Goethe's tradition are even aware of his novel. Sensitive young writers everywhere are far too apt to see themselves as Werthers and to write about such characters in various disguises. Fiedler's "Dead-End Werther: The Bum as American Culture Hero" examines James Jones's *From Here to Eternity* as a prime example of this phenomenon.

Fiedler attacks the vulgar populism of Jones's novel in both moral and stylistic terms. In fact, for him, style and morality are closely related. *From Here to Eternity* has generally been called a naturalistic novel, which Fiedler takes to mean "nothing more spectacular than that it is badly written in a special and quite deliberate way" (184). Theodore Dreiser's work is the supreme example of such an approach to literature, while Henry James's embodies its antithesis. At the time that Fiedler wrote his critique of Jones's novel in 1951, and later when he included it in *An End to Innocence,* he clearly sided with the Jameseans. He believed it disingenuous to make an inept prose style into a mark of primitive authenticity. "One does not write in a state of nature merely for having disavowed the high traditions of his culture; he becomes rather the victim of the lower ones" (185).

Fiedler is no more taken with the substance of *From Here to Eternity.* Jones's compulsive celebration of the inarticulate rebel and his categorical distrust of civilization spring from the same sentimental view of the world that one finds in certain classic films of the 1930s, the blues, hillbilly songs, jazz, and Jack London's incarnation of the bum as artist. It is here that Jones "hopes to find that 'basic artless simplicity' which will be able to crash through the lies of bourgeois art, reach everyone at that core of loneliness which is our only real togetherness" (190). Although apolitical in any obvious partisan sense, Jones seems to be striving for a popular, accessible form of the proletarian novel. What he achieves is a middlebrow potboiler, which actually works better on the movie screen than on the printed page. The fact that Leslie Fiedler could find no redeeming virtue in such an approach to art (or acknowledge even a grudging appreciation for the popular media that inform Jones's vision) suggests what an uncompromising elitist he still was at this point in his career.

Fiedler concludes *An End to Innocence* with an essay titled "Adolescence and Maturity in the American Novel." Anyone who had been reading the book straight through would have had little trouble guessing where the author was likely to come down on the issue posed here. As we were moving into the second half of the twentieth century, it seemed that American fiction had come to the end of an era and was facing an uncertain future. Formerly revered writers, such as Sinclair Lewis, James T. Farrell, and John Dos Passos, seemed passe, and such writers as Sherwood Anderson and John Steinbeck appeared less formidable than they had just a few decades earlier. Even Hemingway and Faulkner were past their prime. Proletarian realism (if it had ever existed) was dead by the end of the 1930s, and its major practitioners—when visible at all—were seen "in a list of witnesses before a Congressional investigating committee, or on the masthead of a Luce publication" (198). The figures most likely to shape postwar American fiction were atavistic postnaturalists such as James Jones and Norman Mailer or sentimental liberals such as John Hersey and Irwin Shaw. The situation seemed far from encouraging.

At the highbrow level, the two dominant schools of contemporary fiction were associated with *Harper's Bazaar* (here understood as a synecdoche for slick fashion magazines) and *Partisan Review*. To Fiedler's mind, the most important writer of the former group was Carson McCullers, the most typical, Truman Capote. Fiedler regards the gothic homosexual sensibility of such writers as somehow descended from Faulkner's neurotic antifeminism. When this sensibility is most camp, it "appeals profoundly to certain rich American women with cultural aspirations, and is therefore sponsored in their salons and published decoratively in magazines that cater to their tastes" (201–2).

In contrast, *Partisan Review,* for all its lip service to high modernism, seemed less interested in style than in moral earnestness. While paying a kind of ritualistic homage to James and Faulkner, the magazine was more deeply influenced by Kafka. As long as it maintained its Eurocentric outlook, *PR* occupied a singular position in American culture without really being in the central tradition of that culture. Nevertheless, Fiedler discerned the beginnings of a new American tradition in the example of such *PR* writers as Lionel Trilling, Mary McCarthy, Delmore Schwartz, and above all others, Saul Bellow: "It is because the fictionists of this group are capable of seeing themselves with a characteristic irony, sad or brittle, because their world is complex and troubled enough to protect them from nostalgia and self-pity, that I see in them evidence of a movement toward a literature of maturity" (206–7).

As we look back on American fiction since the 1950s, we can see more clearly where Fiedler's predictions were on the money and where he missed the mark. Although Truman Capote continued to exercise considerable influence on the literary scene, he became less identifiably southern and more a naturalized citizen of Manhattan. At the same time, other writers from his native South—Flannery O'Connor and William Styron to name only two—became major American fictionists. Bellow would continue to produce brilliant novels and to verify Fiedler's ranking of him as the most talented of the *Partisan Review* writers. At the same time, the emergence of other American Jewish novelists—principally Bernard Malamud and Philip Roth—would cause critics, Fiedler among them, to speak of a Jewish Renaissance in American letters. What Fiedler failed to predict in 1951 was the influence the *New Yorker* would have on American fiction. In its pages, John Cheever and John Updike would redeem the suburban WASP as a proper subject for serious fiction, while the enigmatic J. D. Salinger would become the dominant literary voice of his generation for an entire decade.

Leslie Fiedler's reputation as the enfant terrible of American criticism is certainly not justified by the essays in *An End to Innocence*. Only "Come Back to the Raft Ag'in, Huck Honey!" could be regarded as an offense against orthodox literary taste. I suspect that that essay seems so important today less for what it said—or was misread as saying—at the time than for its seminal influence on Fiedler's criticism from the 1960s on. The voice that speaks to us throughout most of *An End to Innocence* is obsessed with achieving maturity and responsibility. To the extent that Fiedler confesses this to be a personal struggle, as he does in the political essays, he speaks with authority. (After all, from the time of Augustine on, the confession has been a venerable literary genre.) When he fails to admit the personal seductiveness of some of the literary and cultural forces he condemns, his pronouncements can sound fussy and doctrinaire, even—perhaps especially—when they seem correct. One is not entirely surprised that the book's dedication reads: FOR MY FATHER. *An End to Innocence* is the sort of book Jack Fiedler might have appreciated had he not died of cancer before having a chance to read it.

Leslie's maternal grandmother,
Perl Rosenstrauch

Leslie's parents, Jack and Lillian Fiedler

Leib Rosenstrauch with grandson Leslie

Jack Fiedler with sons Leslie and Harold around 1927

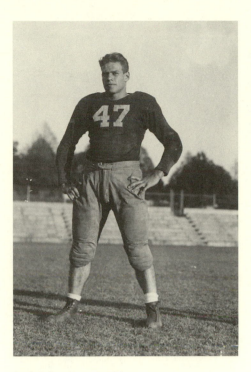

Leslie's brother, Harold

Leslie and his mother with Kurt, Madison, Wisconsin, 1941

Leslie with Rufus Coleman, the oldest member
of the Montana State English department,
Missoula, 1941

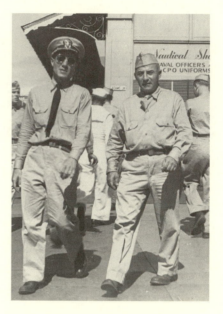

A very skinny Leslie on the left,
Honolulu, 1944

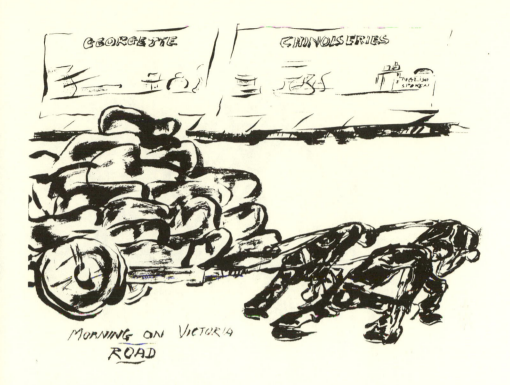

Original drawing by Leslie Fiedler, 1945

Original drawing by Leslie Fiedler, 1945

Leslie, Kurt, and Margaret at a
writer's conference, Salt Lake City,
1951

Leslie with Debbie, Kurt, Eric, and Michael, Rome, 1953

Leslie (center) and Kurt (left) in rehearsal for
Ali Baba, Missoula, 1955

PART TWO

CELEBRITY NUT
(1955–1971)

CHAPTER EIGHT

Eliezar Ben Leah

ALTHOUGH THERE were only about 30,000 Jews in Italy in the early 1950s, a disproportionate number were in positions of power and influence—from the leaders of the Communist Party to high-ranking businessmen and government officials. During his Fulbright tenure, Leslie discovered that he could usually recognize fellow Jews by their names. Anyone who was called after the name of a city or a town (e.g., "Milano") was likely to be Jewish. Although anti-Semitism seemed absent from Italy at this time, the culture remained overwhelmingly Christian. When his daughter Jenny was born, the maid who worked for the family sneaked her out of the house and had her baptized. When Leslie said, "But we are Jews," the maid replied, "Yes, but what is your religion?"[1]

In his essay "Roman Holiday," Leslie tells of the extraordinary efforts he made to find a Passover Seder while living in Rome. Like his grandfather Rosenstrauch, he wanted his offspring (particularly his two oldest sons, Kurt and Eric) to know of their heritage. ("Not that I believe, but so that you should remember!") His efforts were complicated by the fact that Passover coincided with Holy Week, Leslie recalls. "It was no use to remind my boys that, after all, the Last Supper was a Seder, too; nothing could redeem the sense of moving in loneliness against the current that flowed toward the great basilicas, the celebration of the Tenebrae, the washing of the feet, and the final orgy of Easter Sunday when half a million foreigners and Romans would stand flank against flank, the visible body of Christendom awaiting the papal benediction" (*CE,* 1:115).

As they searched for a Passover celebration, Leslie remembered some gossip he had heard about the chief rabbi of the modern Roman synagogue (built in the imitation Assyro-Babylonian style). He was of East European origin and

1. Fiedler, interview with Jackson, July 18, 1989.

119

therefore despised by the "old Roman" members of his congregation. When the Nazis came, he had to raise the ransom they demanded. Because all the rich Jews were in hiding, it was left to the pope to put up the money. Then, when the war was over, the aristocrats returned and began to conspire against their shabby leader. He later became a Catholic and lectured at the university.

When Leslie and his sons finally located a Seder, the experience seemed almost farcical. Old ladies were driven to the door in expensive cars and helped "trembling up the steps by their chauffeurs" (120). Three American boys (of the kind to refuse dinner invitations because they have promised their mothers to keep kosher) informed Leslie of the appalling heterodoxies of the Roman synagogue, about which he "can remember only the fact that it celebrates Bat Mitzvah, the equivalent of Bar Mitzvah but for girls" (121). Later, "three buxom waitresses in pink uniforms trimmed with the shield of David dashed frantically about with bowls of water for washing, herbs for dipping, etc., but they never managed to get anything to us on time, chiefly because the old ladies took so long waving them away; and we were often passed by completely, to the distress of my boys" (121).

On the way home, Leslie and the boys ran into an Italian Jewish couple, who were excited not by Passover, but by the success of a current transit strike. "This should be a lesson for De Gasperi and the Vatican, too," the husband said. When Leslie mentioned that he was returning from a Seder, the husband assumed that he was joking. Upon discovering that he was not, the wife gasped: " 'How can you do it? . . . Do you mean to say that in this day and age you tell your children—' she could hardly manage to say it—'you teach them that we're the *Chosen People?*' " (123).

I

If many of the New York intellectuals who came to prominence in the 1930s were Jews, most of them considered that fact to be irrelevant. Their ideal political and literary culture was both cosmopolitan and secular. Second- and third-generation American Jews were particularly eager to shed the stigma of their immigrant origins. This meant assimilation into some other ethos, be it the bourgeois environment of the American Babbitt or some bohemian ideal cobbled together from a reading of Marx and Kafka. By the end of World War II, however, this passion for voiding one's patrimony was no longer accepted without question. The experience of the Holocaust had taught Jews that they could not abandon their historical identity simply through an exercise of will. Even if they were eager to forget who they were, their persecutors were there to remind them. As a consequence, Jews of the postwar era began to reexamine the meaning of their heritage. The creation of the state of Israel may have been the most dramatic manifestation of this impulse, but one could also see the phenomenon at work in smaller ways in the lives of individual Jewish intellectuals.[2] After its founding by the American Jewish Committee in 1945, *Commentary* magazine became the major forum in which many of these Jewish intellectuals sought to relate their ethnic heritage to the larger culture of which they were a part.

It would hardly be an exaggeration to say that, in terms of reaching an audience of intelligent general readers (Jewish and Gentile alike), *Commentary* was Leslie's most important and reliable forum throughout the 1950s. Although many of his contributions were thoroughly secular in nature, several of his most important articles dealt with specifically Jewish topics. With the exception of his essay on Hiss and Chambers, probably nothing he wrote for *Commentary* created as much of a stir as a long essay he published in January 1951 on the Jewish-born French mystic Simone Weil.

By helping to introduce Weil's work to the American public, Leslie won prominent mention in *Time* and his first taste of national notoriety. He tells us that he received favorable responses from Herbert Read and Upton Sinclair and "even offers of audiences with the Pope and Sholem Asch, both of which temptations I managed finally to resist; in short, distinguished recognition and some comic relief." Moreover, Leslie has been told that "at the same moment that a doctor in the Celebes was sitting down to write me a note of appreciation, a professor in the Hebrew University . . . was hurling the *Commentary* containing my article through a window" (*CE*, 2:32).

Because we tend to associate modern Jews more with their secular achievements than with their religious piety, it seems hardly remarkable that Simone Weil was born into a family of prominent agnostic Jews. Nor is it surprising that during her early years she became committed to a rather conventional variety of Marxist socialism. (That is a familiar and comfortable pattern of experience.) What makes her into a memorable, even a scandalous, figure is her transformation into a Christian ascetic, who became a cult figure for Catholic existentialists.

The experience of Jewish people in a Christian society has usually ranged from peaceful coexistence to anti-Semitic persecution. On occasion, however, individual Jews have adopted the Christian faith. More often than not, this phenomenon has proved an uncomfortable experience. Even though Christianity derives from Judaism, it has been seen as primarily a Gentile religion ever since Saint Paul (who started out as a Jewish persecutor of Christians) sought to evangelize the Roman Empire. If anti-Semitism has been a frequent attribute of Christianity, the one common denominator that seems to unite secular and religious Jews is the fact that they are not Christian. Consequently,

2. For an extended discussion of this phenomenon, see Bloom, *Prodigal Sons,* 158–74.

any Jew who becomes a devout and articulate Christian is likely to be a figure of great curiosity in our society. Such was the fate of Simone Weil.

The reaction against Weil came from several sources. To begin with, her flirtation with the Roman Church has made her anathema to knee-jerk anti-Catholics of whatever background. Second, those who shared her earlier commitment to radical politics tended to regard any kind of religious conversion as a failure of political nerve, if not an example of dangerous neurosis. Finally, many Jews chose to view her religious odyssey as just another example of Jewish self-hatred. (There was enough evidence of latent anti-Semitism in her writing to lend credence to this notion.) In pondering the Weil legacy, Fiedler writes: "There has been going on, since the publishing of Simone Weil's work began, a struggle between her Jewish family and her Catholic literary executors, in which each would like by selection and emphasis to make it clear that at the end of her life she was clearly moving away from or toward the Roman Church." Fiedler managed to infuriate all sides in this controversy by writing sympathetically about Weil's religious views, while arguing "that she would never have become a Catholic because she found too great a 'Jewish' element in that church" (34).

Although Weil died in 1943 at the age of thirty-four, the extremity of her life and thought managed to generate passionate feelings a decade after her death. When she was five, at the height of World War I, she refused to eat sugar as long as it remained unavailable to the soldiers at the front. Later on, she went without socks because the children of workers could not afford them. As a young adult she worked as a teacher, "joining the workers in their sports, marching with them in their picket lines, taking part with the unemployed in their pick and shovel work, and refusing to eat more than the rations of those on relief, distributing her surplus food to the needy" (CE, 2:15–16).

When these gestures failed to get her teaching license revoked, Weil simply quit her post and joined the class struggle full time by taking a job at the local Renault auto plant. This lasted until her health gave out. What followed was a short period of rest, after which she set off for Spain to support the Loyalists, vowing never to use the gun that she was issued. In a ridiculously anticlimactic accident, she was injured by boiling oil and taken by her parents to recuperate in Portugal. It was here that she had the epiphany crucial to her conversion. When listening to a Gregorian chant at a time when her migraine was at its worst, she experienced a sense of Christ's passion. Shortly thereafter, she met a young English Catholic, who introduced her to the work of the British metaphysical poets. In particular, George Herbert's poem "Love Bade Me Welcome" took on for her the significance of a prayer.

Although her movement toward Christianity was sufficient to evoke hysteria among those who were bereft of any faith other than a liberal hostility toward faith itself, Simone Weil died before deciding to be baptized or making any gesture toward formal affiliation with a church. She saw herself as the ultimate outsider, whose particular martyrdom lay in remaining forever "at the intersection of Christianity and everything that is not Christianity" (9). Her Catholic friends, and many readers who never knew her, are convinced that, had she lived, Weil would have entered the Church and perhaps even have been canonized. As it is, she remains an unofficial saint for our time, speaking "of the problems of belief in the vocabulary of the unbeliever" (5). Because she wrote as well as lived her faith, she continues to witness for it from beyond the grave. The nature of her legacy is best summed up by Fiedler when he writes:

> As the life of Simone Weil reflects a desire to insist on the absolute even at the risk of being absurd, so her writing tends always toward the extreme statement, the formulation that shocks by its willingness to push to its ultimate conclusion the kind of statement we ordinarily accept with the tacit understanding that no one will take it *too* seriously. The outrageous (from the natural point of view) ethics of Christianity, the paradoxes on which it is based, are a scandal to common sense; but we have protected ourselves against them by turning them imperceptibly into platitudes. It is Simone Weil's method to revivify them, by re-creating them in all their pristine offensiveness. (23–24).

II

As a persecuted people, Jews have historically felt affinity with other victims of discrimination. In America, this has meant that the fates of blacks and Jews have often been linked because of their joint exclusion from "polite" WASP society. (As late as the 1950s, one could see signs along Miami Beach prohibiting "Negroes, Jews, and dogs.") It was probably not until the social upheavals of the 1960s that much attention was focused on possible disharmonies between America's two most excluded races. Nevertheless, prescient observers had detected warning signals much earlier. One of the most articulate voices on the subject belonged to James Baldwin. In "Negro and Jew: Encounter in America" (originally a review of Baldwin's *Notes of a Native Son*), Fiedler offers his own thoughts on the matter.

One of the major differences between American blacks and Jews concerns the way that they entered this country. According to Fiedler: "America is for the Negro a way into the West, a gateway to Europe. . . . The Jew, conversely, is the gateway into Europe for America" (*CE,* 1:454). An intellectual Negro such as Baldwin can admire Dante, Shakespeare, and Michelangelo, while realizing that even the most ignorant European is connected to Western culture in a way that he and his people will never be. Because their ancestors were kidnapped from Africa, they do not even belong to that continent, as the failed experiment in Liberia demonstrates. (It is not clear to what extent this situation has been altered by the cultural nationalism some black Americans have embraced in the years since Baldwin and Fiedler first wrote on this subject.) In contrast, the Jew seems to be the very embodiment of European culture. As Fiedler notes, "It is not merely that people of our blood, whether converts to Christianity or skeptics or orthodox believers, have been inextricably involved in the making of the European mind: Leone Ebreo, Maimonides, Montaigne and Spinoza and Marx—perhaps even St. John of the Cross and Christopher Columbus; but that we have haunted the mind of Europe for two thousand years as the black man has haunted that of America for two hundred" (455).

It is easy for WASP Americans to associate the primitive and "natural" black man with the satanic. (After all, "Black Man" was another name for the Devil in Puritan Massachusetts.) The Jew, even in his archetypal role as Christ killer, cannot be as readily viewed as diabolical. To do so would be to call Jehovah the Devil, which is something that no good Protestant American can do. Only romantic anti-Puritans, such as D. H. Lawrence and Sherwood Anderson, can successfully combine anti-Semitism with a sentimental glorification of dark-skinned people.

What came as something of a shock to many Jews in the 1950s was the extent of anti-Semitism among blacks themselves. Without much reflection, Jews had assumed that blacks were not capable of making subtle distinctions among different varieties of white people. Moreover, they had come to expect anti-Semitism only from groups more socially secure than they were. Finally, the Jews were probably the only category of white people who had done more good than harm to blacks. And yet, Baldwin writes with characteristic frankness: "[J]ust as society must have a scapegoat, so hatred must have a symbol. Georgia has the Negro. Harlem has the Jew."

If Baldwin was exposing a dirty little secret in 1955, the conflict between blacks and Jews had become an open and obvious issue by the mid-1960s. When Fiedler next visited this topic in print, it was in an essay published in the December 1966 issue of *Midstream* magazine. Here, he identified a variety of sources for black anti-Semitism. Among lower-class blacks, it tended to be a variation of that strain of white populism that sees the Jew as the prototypical capitalist exploiter. The most visible embodiment of this image for most poor blacks was the Jewish shopkeeper, who is physically located in the ghetto (a term borrowed from the experience of European Jewry) but who exists sociologically in a no-man's-land between WASP and black. Insofar as he is religious, or is imagined to be such, the Jew is an affront to both the black Christian and the black Muslim. The former perceives Jews as having both crucified Christ and heckled Simon of Cyrene when he helped carry the cross. The latter are "obsessed by the legendary notion of the 'Evil Jacob,' Israel the

Usurper—as well as the myth of Isaac before him doing poor Ishmael out of his heritage" (*CE,* 2:167).

At a deep mythological level, the Jew is neither white nor black but a third race. He is Shem, the son of Noah, trying at various times to pass as his black brother Ham or his white brother Japheth. To the extent that he is discriminated against by Japheth, Shem is allied with Ham; however, when he seeks to assimilate himself into Japheth's culture, it is frequently by baiting Ham. As Fiedler was prophetic enough to note, even the liberal Jew would eventually see his faith in human equality challenged by the intractable reality of black failure. Before "affirmative action" had become a national policy, Fiedler could see that blacks would ultimately need to demand "*special privilege* rather than equality if they were to make it at all in the very world in which the Jews have so preeminently flourished" (171).

If it had seemed possible in the mid-1950s to believe that racial tensions could be healed by "equal opportunity" and that black anti-Semitism was less powerful than the ties that bound oppressed blacks and liberal Jews, those convictions were far more problematical a decade later. Looking at the same situation, largely in response to conversations with James Baldwin, Norman Podhoretz had concluded that integration could succeed in America only if it led to such widespread miscegenation that consciousness of color would effectively disappear.[3] Without mentioning Podhoretz's controversial essay, "My Negro Problem—and Ours," Fiedler comes to much the same conclusion. His imagination is so moved by the number of Jewish girls giving birth to half-black babies, both in and out of wedlock, that he writes, "So naturally a new mythology is being invented, appropriate to that new solution; though like all new myths this one, too, contains within it the very old, indeed, the myth of the Jewish Daughter, Hadassah (renamed Esther, which is to say, Ashtoreth) dancing naked for salvation before the Gentile King" (173–74).

III

One of Fiedler's most comprehensive Jewish essays, "The Jew in the American Novel," was actually published as a monograph by Herzl Press in 1959. Although this was meant to be more of a survey than a theoretical discussion, its author's own tastes help to establish a canon of Jewish-American literature somewhat different from the consensus that existed at the time. In particular, Fiedler attempts to rescue such neglected novelists as Abraham Cahan,

---

3. This essay is included in Podhoretz's book *Doings and Undoings: The Fifties and after in American Writing.*

Daniel Fuchs, and Henry Roth and to challenge the esteem accorded to such popular but overrated figures as Ludwig Lewisohn and Ben Hecht.

Although the Jew has appeared as a figure in American fiction from the very beginning (since Charles Brockden Brown published *Arthur Mervyn* in 1799–1800), he was originally the creation of Gentile writers trying to come to terms with the stranger in their midst. (Even as late as the 1920s, Hemingway's Robert Cohn was a more compelling character and a more convincing Jew than any of the creations of Ludwig Lewisohn.) Appropriately enough, the first "Jewish-American" novelist was a Gentile named Henry Harland, who wrote under the pen name Sidney Luska. Along with such later authentic Jews as Cahan, Lewisohn, and Hecht, Luska wrote a kind of erotic fiction in which the problems of Jewish assimilation to American culture were posed in terms of sexual symbols. This theme, which Fiedler calls "Zion as Eros," would dominate the Jewish novel until it was replaced by the proletarian consciousness of the 1930s.

It seemed that the American novelists most celebrated in the 1930s were responding to the social crisis posed by the Great Depression. Because of the infatuation of many Jewish intellectuals with Communism, it is not surprising that Jews were among the major contributors to the proletarian and Popular Front literature of the period. Moreover, with the urbanization of the American novel begun by the Gentile Theodore Dreiser, the time was right for predominantly city-dwelling Jews to make their mark in American fiction. When we look back at the 1930s, however, Jews such as Edward Dahlberg, Leonard Ehrlich, Daniel Fuchs, Meyer Levin, and Mike Gold (the last of whom was called, with some justification, the "Al Jolson of the Communist movement") still seem less prepossessing than the Gentiles John Steinbeck, John Dos Passos, and James T. Farrell. In Fiedler's opinion, the two most important Jewish novelists of the decade were actually apolitical men who were largely ignored in their own time—Nathanael West and Henry Roth.

Jewish assimilation into the mainstream of American society took a quantum leap forward in the period following World War II. With the end of mass immigration, the Jewish population consisted increasingly of second- and third-generation Americans. At the same time, Hitler had decimated the Jewish population of Europe. Thus, Jews were becoming fully integrated Americans as never before. "No longer is our story that of the rise of an occasional David Levinsky," Fiedler writes, "but that of almost the whole Jewish people on the march toward the suburbs; of the transformation of essential Jewish life into bourgeois life" (*CE,* 2:98).

One of the consequences of this process was the emergence of Jewish literature at all levels of the cultural spectrum. At the lowest level, where overt anti-Semitism still had its strongest hold, the essentially invisible Jerome Siegal and Joe Shuster invented the first great comic book hero, Superman. Also science fiction, the first lower-middlebrow genre to challenge the hegemony of the Western and the detective story, was dominated by Jews. ("The notion of the Jewish cowboy is utterly ridiculous, of a Jewish detective, Scotland Yard variety or private eye, nearly as anomalous; but to think of the scientist as a Jew is almost tautological" [102].) It was at the middle and upper reaches of middlebrow culture, however, that Jewish writers gained greatest respectability.

Novelists such as Irwin Shaw, Herman Wouk, and Budd Schulberg lacked the philosophical depth, moral subtlety, and technical virtuosity that we associate with the highest art; however, they were literate enough and right-minded enough to be fashionable among upwardly mobile suburbanites. During the late 1940s and early 1950s, the anti–anti-Semitic novel (by both Jew and Gentile) was a particular rage, consisting of such pious liberal tracts as Arthur Miller's *Focus,* Laura Z. Hobson's *Gentleman's Agreement,* Mary Jane Ward's *The Professor's Umbrella,* and John Hersey's *The Wall.* Even the post–World War II antiwar novel (e.g., Irwin Shaw's *The Young Lions*) contributed to this trend by introducing the figure of the Jewish Sad Sack, who at the crucial moment proves just as macho as his WASP tormentors.

Finally, during the 1950s, two middlebrow Jewish writers created representative American prototypes of the period. In Marjorie Morningstar, Herman Wouk made a suburban Jewish housewife into a symbol of bourgeois respectability and interfaith tolerance, while J. D. Salinger gave us the ultimate sensitive and misunderstood adolescent in Holden Caulfield. In later years, Wouk (like Irwin Shaw before him) graduated to mastering the television miniseries, while Salinger disappeared into the mountain fastness of New Hampshire, where he could do his Zen meditations protected by barbed wire and guard dogs.

IV

Fortunately, the Jewish presence in American literature has not been confined to the ghetto of ethnic experience or even to the lowbrow and middlebrow levels of popular culture. During the 1950s and '60s, an increasing number of Jewish-American writers could be found at the very pinnacle of "serious" literature in this country. Like the so-called Southern Renaissance of a generation earlier, this phenomenon has been attributed to the social tension caused by the assimilation of an insular and traditional subculture into the mainstream of American life. Such upheaval creates the sort of introspection that produces a wide variety of literary effects—from broad comedy to high tragedy. As a critic, Leslie Fiedler has witnessed the rise and eventual demise of this Jewish Renaissance. As a Jew who remains proud of his cultural heritage, he has been a participant as well as an observer. Perhaps for this reason, the otherwise acerbic Grant Webster concedes that "in his more sober and scholarly moments Fiedler has traced and documented the entry of the Jew into our national literary culture better than anyone else. . . . Almost despite himself he is kind of an American Moses leading the Jewish intellectual community—his people—to the promised land of the republic of letters."[4]

Of all the major Jewish novelists to appear on the American scene after World War II, Norman Mailer was the least obviously Jewish. Mailer created an Irish American alter-ego named Sergius O'Shaughnessy in his novel *The Deer Park* (1955) and intended him to be the protagonist of a massive new novel he would never finish. (In the unfinished work in progress, Sergius is actually a character in the dream of an ineffectual Jew named Sam Slovoda, who is apparently another alter ego for Mailer.) But Mailer's most ambitious aspiration was to become as hip as the hippest Negro. In fact, in his controversial essay "The White Negro" (1958) he tried to construct an elaborate metaphysic around the white boy's desire to seem black. Although, in the late 1950s one could find instances of this desire everywhere—in Beats such as Jack Kerouac and Neal Cassady and rockers such as Elvis Presley and Jerry Lee Lewis—it took someone as manic as Mailer to make it the basis of a literary movement committed to marijuana, jazz, and the orgasm.

"The White Negro" was preserved for posterity in *Advertisements for Myself* (1959), a potpourri of Mailer's shorter writings in various genres—short stories, newspaper columns, editorials, pseudopoems, and fragments of drama. All of this adds up to Mailer's obsessive meditation on his own career. In his review of the book, Fiedler compares it to such other accounts of the defeat of a writer as Griswold's *Life of Poe* and Edmund Wilson's "recension" of Fitzgerald's *The Crackup.* "Mailer, however, is his own Griswold and Wilson, denigrating critic and adulatory surviving friend all in one" (*CE,* 2:124). In *Advertisements for Myself,* Mailer seemed to have found his ideal form and subject matter.

While Mailer was the least Jewish of the new Jewish novelists, Bernard Malamud was most closely linked in sensibility to the older tradition. This became apparent with his second novel, *The Assistant* (1957). (His marvelous but uncharacteristic first novel, *The Natural* [1952], featured a blending of baseball with the Grail Legend, reaching out—as Fiedler puts it—"with one hand to Ring Lardner and with the other to Jessie Weston" [*CE,* 1:325].) Fiedler believes that, in *The Assistant,* Malamud took up "the frustrated experiments of writers like [Daniel] Fuchs and Nathanael West." "In a strange way," he writes, "Malamud's novel *is* a belated novel of the thirties." It is only in the context of the depression that certain situations Malamud imagines make sense. "But how different *The Assistant* is from any novel *written* in the thirties!" (327).

---

4. Grant Webster, "Leslie Fiedler: Adolescent and Jew as Critic," 53.

Lacking the political agenda of the proletarian novel, Malamud's book also lacks its "note of hysteria" and "apocalyptic shrillness." Foregoing any obvious striving for humor, *The Assistant* seems deliberately underwritten. Nevertheless, it is a novel that can make the surreal (or at least the absurd) appear commonplace. While not a doctrinally religious writer, Malamud possessed a nonsecularist temperament along with the courage of his impulses.

Although a generation younger than Leslie, Philip Roth became something of a soul mate to his fellow Newark Jew. For years, the genuine literary excitement shared by Leslie and his high school classmates could not obscure the fact that the Newark they knew had produced no writer, "and hence no myth to outlive its unambitious public buildings, its mean frame houses" (*CE*, 2:119). To be sure, Stephen Crane technically hailed from Newark; however, his fictional cosmos consisted of "a smalltown Gentile world called Whilomville, not his native Newark at all" (119).

By the 1950s, it seemed already too late for a writer to immortalize the Newark that had existed twenty years earlier. That city had disappeared, never to be part of the mythic experience of a young writer, especially one whose own childhood and youth had been spent in the suburbs. Nevertheless, when Leslie opened Philip Roth's *Goodbye Columbus* in 1959, he found that a twenty-six-year-old fictionist had somehow re-created "my own remembered and archaic city." For Leslie, the shock and ecstasy of recognition almost obscured the other virtues and defects of Roth's novella.

> Maybe he has only dreamed that world, reconstructed it on the basis of scraps of information recollected from conversations with cousins or older brothers or uncles; or maybe a real city only becomes a mythic one when it is already dead. No matter—he has dreamed truly. In his nightmare vision, that is, a Newark very like the one from which I still occasionally wake sweating has been rescued from history, oddly preserved. At the Little Theatre across the Park from the Museum, Hedy Lamarr is still playing in *Ecstasy,* as she played for 39 weeks (or was it 79?) when I was sixteen. . . . [I]t is summer, of course, Newark's infernal season, in Mr. Roth's fictional city—and somebody's aunt and uncle are "sharing a Mounds bar in the cindery darkness of their alley, on beach chairs." It is possible to persuade oneself (though Roth does not say so) that with the proper coupon clipped from the Newark Evening News one could still get *three* transparent White Castle hamburgers for a nickel. (120–21)

The novelist whom Leslie had known longest was also the most important figure in the postwar Jewish Renaissance. By the time he published *Seize the Day* in 1957, Saul Bellow had become one of the few contemporary American novelists with whom it was "*necessary* to come to terms" (*CE*, 2:56). Not only was his actual achievement more formidable than that of any previous Jewish-

American novelist, he also came along at a time when Jews had so successfully broken out of the ghetto of ethnic literature that they were finally writing for a broad multicultural American audience. As we have seen, postwar Jewish writers such as Salinger, Wouk, Shaw, and the creators of Superman had accomplished a degree of assimilation that would have been incomprehensible to their predecessors. If others could take their Americanness more or less for granted, Jews were still striving to achieve that sense of entitlement. We find this tension at the heart of Bellow's work, particularly in his third novel, *The Adventures of Augie March* (1953).

Although Fiedler does not find *Augie March* to be as successful technically as the books that preceded and followed it (*The Victim* and *Seize the Day*), it poses the issue of Jewish-American identity with such boldness that it risks "the final absurdity: the footloose Jewish boy, harried by urban Machiavellians, the picaresque *schlimazl* out of Fuchs or Nathanael West, becomes Huck Finn; or, if you will, Huck is transformed into the foot-loose Jewish boy" (59). The milieu of *Augie March* "is Jewish-American, its speech patterns somehow molded by Yiddish, but its theme is the native theme of *Huckleberry Finn:* The rejection of power and commitment and success, the pursuit of a primal innocence" (61). Even if he does not know quite how to bring this story to closure, Bellow has ventured into territory uncharted by any previous Jewish novelist.

When Bellow is dealing with themes that are more familiar to Jewish writers, he manages to redeem them from cliché through his artistry and his vision. The reader of *Seize the Day* can't help being reminded of Miller's *Death of a Salesman*. "But how," Fiedler asks, "has Bellow made tragedy of a theme that remains in the hands of Arthur Miller sentimentality and 'good theater'?" Much of the transformation, Fiedler believes, is a function of style. Although Bellow is hardly an experimental writer, "there is always the sense of a living voice in his prose, for his books are all dramatic. . . . Muted or released, his language is never dull or merely expedient, but always moves under tension, toward or away from a kind of rich, crazy poetry, a juxtaposition of high and low style, elegance and slang, unlike anything in English except *Moby-Dick,* though at the same time not unrelated in range and variety to spoken Yiddish" (63).

In addition, Bellow possesses "a constitutional inability to dissolve his characters into their representative types, to compromise their individuality for the sake of a point" (63). As a consequence, his characters tend to be introspective, consciously struggling to assert their individuality in a society seemingly bent on denying it. "Their invariable loneliness is felt by them and by us not only as a function of urban life and the atomization of culture, but as something *willed:* the condition and result of their search to know what they are" (63–64). Not just Augie March but to a less obvious degree the protagonist of each of Bellow's fictions "is at once the Jew in perpetual exile and Huck Finn[,] in whom are blended with perfect irony the twin American beliefs that the answer to all questions is always over the next horizon and that there is no answer now or ever" (64).

Given their early ties with each other and Leslie's enthusiasm for Bellow's first four novels, one would like to think that their friendship deepened over the years as each man gained greater prominence in the literary world. If anything, the praise enjoyed by Bellow's subsequent work and his winning of the Nobel Prize for Literature in 1976 seemed to confirm Leslie's opinion that he was the most important American writer of his generation. Unfortunately, the two men drifted apart as the difference in their ideas about life and literature became increasingly apparent. On June 24, 1960, just after Leslie had published a review in *Poetry* magazine, in which he referred to the "marketable Jewishness" in Karl Shapiro's verse and the work of other unnamed American writers, Saul sent him an angry letter, which begins, "I really think you're *way* out. How you got there I don't know, but it's time to come back." To emphasize his point, Saul closes the letter with this admonition: "You had better think matters over again, Leslie. I'm dead serious."[5]

Reflecting on his former friend in 1989, Leslie remarked:

> Saul resented everything that happened to the world from the moment that modernism had been invented. He was against "angst"; he was against "alienation." He wanted to believe that the old bourgeois humanist values were still alive and well. That was bad, but even worse was the fact that, although I was one of the first people who ever wrote reviews of his books, which assessed him for what he was worth—at his true worth— after a while I stopped reviewing him. He's a very paranoid fellow, and he sat there saying, "Leslie isn't reviewing my books. Why does the bastard hate me?"

Some years after they stopped communicating with each other, a mutual friend named Seymour Betsky ran into Saul at the Reichs Museum in Amsterdam. "Leslie's in town," he said. "Would you like to see him?" Saul simply shook his head and replied, "Leslie Fiedler is the worst fucking thing that ever happened to American literature."[6]

---

5. See James Atlas, *Bellow: A Biography,* 291.
6. Leslie Fiedler, interview with Bruce Jackson, Apr. 22, 1989.

CHAPTER NINE

Heavy Runner

IF LESLIE'S IDENTITY as a New York Jewish intellectual made him an anomaly among Montanans, his residence in Montana made him something of a misfit among New York Jewish intellectuals. Had he conformed to the paradigm, he would have lived in "the City" or at least within commuting distance, and he would have spent most of his waking hours talking about an approved set of books and ideas with like-minded individuals. Their opinions might have differed, but their tastes would have been virtually identical. (In other words, his experience in Chicago during the early 1940s would have become a permanent way of life.) Despite his geographical distance from this insular environment, people persisted in stereotyping Leslie as part of the New York literary scene. As his sensibility increasingly chafed at such intellectual provincialism, he concluded that he had to make a personal declaration of independence.

In "*Partisan Review:* Phoenix or Dodo," which originally appeared in the spring 1956 issue of *Perspectives USA,* Leslie tried to give a fair and balanced assessment of the magazine with which he had been most frequently identified since his first appearance in its pages nine years earlier. The title of the article was apparently suggested in a letter Saul Bellow wrote to him on June 14, 1955. Expressing appreciation for the "kind mention" Leslie had given him in "Adolescence and Maturity in the American Novel" (just published in the May 2, 1955, issue of the *New Republic*), Saul goes on to say, "I don't consider myself part of the Partisan group. Not those dying beasts. They posed as Phoenixes but were always dodos."[1] Although the published essay mentions this exchange, it coyly identifies Bellow only as "the best of the younger American novelists," while admitting that "it was *Partisan* which almost alone

---

1. See Atlas, *Bellow,* 233; and Fiedler, *CE,* 2:43. This and other letters cited in this chapter are contained in Leslie Fiedler's private papers.

published him in the days when he was fighting to establish his reputation" (*CE*, 2:42).

Throughout what was then its twenty-year history, *PR* had sought to do what Leslie and others of his generation had aspired to do in their own careers—reconcile twin commitments to high modernist literature and revolutionary politics, as though they were simply different sides of the same coin. This impulse allowed *PR* to publish some of the most important and eclectic criticism to appear between the covers of any intellectual magazine in the 1930s and '40s. By the mid-1950s, however, the attempt to maintain an essentially schizophrenic identity had made the magazine seem dated and culturally irrelevant.

Although *PR* prided itself in being bohemian, its allegiance was to a bohemia that had long since been canonized by the academic establishment. More recent experiments in literary form were either ignored or dismissed out of hand. Even the embattled antiacademic stance of the magazine seemed willed and meretricious. More often than not, its editors and contributors were accepting teaching appointments at universities in the Northeast and elsewhere, while publishing some of their own best work in such unabashedly academic journals as the *Kenyon Review*. (Even in its earliest phase, *PR* drew much of its intellectual energy from Columbia University.) With the anti-Stalinist Left now virtually indistinguishable from the "vital liberal center," revolutionary politics itself had become ever more problematic for *Partisan Review*. Other than serving as a bastion of Eurocentric taste, *PR* appeared to have outlived its usefulness.

Not quite wanting to commit himself to the harsh conclusion that his argument seemed to demand, Leslie ends his essay on a conciliatory note: "It is a strange enough bird, the *Partisan Review*, a scraggier, shabbier, more raucous phoenix than we might have hoped for, and not one above crying out its own name at the top of its voice; but it is our only real contender for the title. Blasted into ashes by its enemies, mourned prematurely by its friends, despaired of by its own editors—it yet somehow survives; and that is, after all, the point" (55).

These temporizing words were not enough to allay the wrath of *PR*'s principal editors, William Phillips and Philip Rahv. On August 22, 1956, Phillips and Rahv sent Leslie an angry letter, which begins, "We want you to know that we think your piece on PR in the current PERSPECTIVES is malicious and in poor taste—all the more so because you yourself have benefited from the editorial policy you set out to malign." The letter continues in this vein for three paragraphs, accusing Leslie of disloyalty, disingenuousness, and a transparent desire to "play up to the genteel and now dominant factions on the literary scene."

Leslie must have responded almost immediately to this cry of grievance, because an even longer letter from Rahv, dated September 7, refers to such a response. Rahv begins by dismissing the notion that he and Phillips simply suffer from "a degree of paranoia" (apparently a quote from Leslie's letter), because everyone they have talked to saw the offending essay as an attack on *PR* rather than as a fair and disinterested appraisal of the magazine. One gathers that Rahv would probably have ignored a similar discussion of *Partisan Review* had it come from outside what he considered to be the *PR* family. ("To tell you the truth," he writes, "I reacted much less vehemently to the Hudson Review's open attack on us of some years back.") No doubt, Rahv's anger was also fueled by the realization that *PR* was no longer the dominant intellectual magazine it had been even half a dozen years earlier. As ungracious as it might have been for Leslie to say the things that he said, he was more often than not on target.

By the time he wrote his analysis of *Partisan Review,* Leslie's understanding of his own role as critic had begun to change. The subtitle of *An End to Innocence,* "Essays on Culture and Politics," was perfectly in keeping with the New York intellectual's view of the critic's vocation. By 1960, however, Leslie's second collection of magazine articles, *No! In Thunder,* was declaring itself to be "Essays on Myth and Literature." (The shift away from politics was telling.) Commenting on the direction his career had taken from 1955 on, Fiedler writes:

> Unlike my first collection, this one consists chiefly of literary theory, comments on literary works and reflections on the role of myth in art and society. I am glad this time to have moved politics to the periphery, not from mere snobbishness (though I do feel something hopelessly trivial in hunting one's subject in yesterday's headlines), but chiefly because I am by temperament and training committed to the world of the imagination rather than that of mere fact. I pledged myself in my first book to give to certain political documents "the same careful scrutiny we have learned to practice on the shorter poems of John Donne"; I pledge myself this time to approach the shorter poems of Donne (or Dante or Shakespeare or Whitman) with the sense that they matter quite as much to the self and the world as the execution of Caryl Chessman or even the suspension of atomic testing. (*CE,* 1:219–20)

At the beginning of the title essay of *No! In Thunder,* the author confesses a guilty secret: that he has always believed the creation and criticism of literature to be moral acts. Because an overtly moralistic approach to literature has long been considered reactionary (the sort of thing reserved for high church defenders of culture such as T. S. Eliot or Legion of Decency types), the disinterested critic is expected to refrain from homilies, "to speak of novels and poems *purely* . . . in terms of diction, structure, and point of view, remaining safely inside the realm of the formal" (*CE,* 1:221). And yet, as Fiedler rightly points out, an author's choices regarding the formal elements of his work imply a judgment about the experience he is rendering. Because such judgments have moral ramifications, an amoral criticism is *aesthetically* impossible.

Here, as in the essay "Dead-End Werther," Fiedler argues that morality and aesthetics are fundamentally related. "In the realm of fiction," he writes, "to be inept, whether unwittingly or on purpose, is the single unforgivable sin. To be inept is to lie; and for this, time and the critics grant no pardon" (222). His principal targets are middlebrow authors such as Leon Uris and Allen Drury and conscious antistylists such as James Jones and Jack Kerouac. Because such writers pander to the smug mediocrity of their audience, they win the sort of popularity and esteem that is denied to more serious and subversive writers. These latter artists usually experience one of two fates: they are either condemned as "dirty writers" or are misread and thus made classics for the wrong reasons. (If this analysis seems to minimize mythopoeic power and to denigrate popular taste, it should be noted that Fiedler would later consider "No! In Thunder" to be "an insufferably arrogant essay" [*WWL?*, 37].)

The refusal of the public to accept serious fiction is not an expression of prudery (American best-sellers have traditionally exploited sex) or even ignorance (the misreading of writers such as Faulkner and Pasternak is largely a willful act). It is rather a reaction against the perceived morbidity of our best writers. To Fiedler's mind, the morally committed writer is not only a superior craftsman but also an inveterate nay-sayer and iconoclast. "Insofar as a work of art is, as art, successful, it performs a negative critical function; for the irony of art in the human situation lies in this: that man—or better, some men—are capable of achieving in works of art a coherence, a unity, a balance, a satisfaction of conflicting impulses which they cannot (but which they desperately long to) achieve in love, family relations, politics." The irony is enhanced by the fact that perfectly realized works of art inevitably represent imperfectly realized aspects of life (love, family, politics, etc.). "The image of man in art, however magnificently portrayed—indeed, precisely when it is most magnificently portrayed—is the image of a failure. There is no way out" (225).

Fiedler is most emphatically not referring to what is commonly known as protest literature. Even when such literature is politically courageous, it tends to be a partisan indictment of specific social ills or suspect ideologies. "Even the attack on slavery in Twain's post–Civil War *Huckleberry Finn*—or, for that matter, in Mrs. Stowe's pre–Civil War *Uncle Tom's Cabin*—like an anti-McCarthyite fiction in the recent past or an excoriation of segregation right now, carry with them a certain air of presumptive self-satisfaction, an assurance of being justified by the future" (227). Fiedler sees these works, to the extent that they are regarded simply as protest literature, as easy or pseudo-nos, really disguised yeses. In contrast, the real nay-sayer is never partisan. On principle, he is willing to infuriate his friends as well as his enemies. As Melville observed of Hawthorne, "He says NO! in thunder; but the Devil himself cannot make him say *yes*" (*CE,* 1:226).

More than anything else, it is this spirit of ironic self-judgment that connects *An End to Innocence* with *No! In Thunder.* Although his approach to the issue is quite different, Fiedler's conclusion is remarkably similar to the one that Cleanth Brooks takes when he praises Dante for portraying more than one pope in Hell in *The Divine Comedy.* "Surely," Brooks writes, "there is more than mere propagandizing for a dogma and an institution in a view that can envisage Christ's vicar among the damned."[2] Dante's willingness to subject his most deeply held beliefs to the test of "ironical contemplation" is an essential part of what makes him a great poet. To use Fiedler's (and Melville's) terminology, he is willing to say "No!" in thunder.

In our own time, what differentiates a truly serious novel such as Saul Bellow's *The Victim* from such "earnest and humane tracts on anti-Semitism" as *Focus, Gentleman's Agreement,* and *The Professor's Umbrella* is its superior universality. Bellow believes "both Jew and gentile are simultaneously Victim and Victimizer. . . . Our Jewishness or gentileness, Bellow leaves us feeling, is *given;* our humanity is what we must achieve" (235). It is this striving for the complex and profoundly disturbing truth that constitutes the integrity of the serious novelist. "In the end," Fiedler tells us, "the negativist is no nihilist, for he affirms the void. Having endured a vision of the meaninglessness of existence, he retreats neither into self-pity and aggrieved silence nor into a realm of beautiful lies. He chooses, rather, to render the absurdity which he perceives, to know it and make it known. To know and to render, however, mean to give form; and to give form is to provide the possibility of delight—a delight which does not deny horror but lives at its intolerable heart" (238).

I

As we get further into *No! In Thunder,* we see that Fiedler's notion of myth is broad enough to include just about anything that interests him. Along with the title essay and the explicitly theoretical credos "In the Beginning Was the Word" and "Archetype and Signature," the most impressive selection is his discussion of the image of the child in literature. Called "The Eye of Innocence," it is a brilliant example of applied myth criticism. If childhood qualifies as a universal human experience, the ways in which it has been socially defined vary greatly from culture to culture and from age to age. In the image of the child, we see an interplay of archetype and signature as various cultures try to define what it means to be young and "innocent."

---

2. Brooks, *Well Wrought Urn,* 204.

The cult of the child, Fiedler tells us, was not possible as long as Western Christianity held to an absolute interpretation of Original Sin. "If one began by believing that an originally corrupted nature must be trained (cajoled and beaten) into the semblance of orderly virtue, he ended by being convinced that an adult had some chance of attaining goodness, the child little or none" (473). Romanticism not only rejected this traditional doctrine, but stood it on its head. Original Innocence now replaced Original Sin, and the process of maturation was regarded not as a climb toward Heaven, but as a fall from primordial goodness. In an age when the greatest compliment one could pay to an author was to say that he was secretly of the Devil's party, the child became not a candidate for damnation, but—as Wordsworth would have it—"father of the Man." Moreover, the child was the "one safely genteel symbol of protest" against bourgeois culture. For the romantic to glorify "the peasant . . . over the city dweller; the idiot or the buffoon over the philosopher; woman over man—and within the female sex, the whore over the bourgeoisie" (476), was to threaten middle-class values in a disturbingly obvious way. To love children, no matter how subversive the motivation, was simply to join ranks with decent people everywhere.

To the Anglo-Saxon mind, the supreme embodiment of childhood innocence is "the Good Good Girl, the blonde asexual goddess of nursery or orphanage, reincarnated from Little Nell to Mary Pickford" (477). In this figure, the worship of the female is combined with an idealization of virginity. Thus, the Divine Boy of orthodox Christianity has been replaced by a female counterpart "imagined not at the moment of birth but at that of death." What Fiedler is referring to here is the Protestant Pieta: "the white-clad daughter, dying or dead, in the arms of the Old Man, tearful papa or grandfather or wooly-haired slave" (478). In this shamelessly sentimental scene, we can indulge our prurient desire to violate, indeed destroy, an unbearable symbol of innocence. Also, in a culture where the Good Good Girl is deprived the refuge of the nunnery, it is only through death that her purity (and her maidenhead) can remain intact.

Although the Good Good Girl is a staple of both the British and the American imagination, the Good Good Boy remains an essentially Old World figure, "the juvenile reminder of a tradition of aristocratic culture," which Americans have left behind (481). Consequently American literature offers us no counterpart to Tiny Tim, Paul Dombey, or Oliver Twist. (The fact that Little Lord Fauntleroy was created by an American writer does not make him seem any less foreign.) Even as a pauper, the Good Good Boy strikes Americans as effete and priggish. When such a figure does appear in our culture, it is as an object of derision, a comic foil to the true American hero—the Good Bad Boy—Sid Sawyer in contrast to his brother Tom (or, one suspects, Ken Starr in pursuit of Bill Clinton).

The Good Bad Boy is the mischievous scamp who violates adult notions of propriety without ever doing anything seriously wrong. (One thinks of Dennis the Menace sitting in the corner with his teddy bear at his side.) Although the sissy is often called a "mama's boy," Fiedler argues that all American boys really belong to mother. The difference between him and the scamp is that "the Good Good Boy does what his mother must pretend to the rest of the world (even to herself) that she wants him to do, obey, conform; the Good Bad Boy does what she *really* wants him to do: deceive, break her heart a little, so that she can forgive him, smother him in the embrace that seals him back into her world forever" (481). Had the parable of the prodigal son been set in America, the forgiving parent undoubtedly would have been female.

According to the sentimental view of childhood, the one characteristic shared by the Good Good Girl and the Good Bad Boy is lack of sexual imagination. If evil is to be equated with the id and the child to remain a symbol of purity, then even the most innocent forms of genital curiosity have to be denied to those prepubescent icons. Other representations of the primitive or instinctual life could be divided into divine or demonic opposites: "Woman becomes the Fair Virgin and the Dark Lady, the Indian becomes Mingo and Mohawk, Pawnee and Sioux—Good Indian and Bad Indian!" (486). But the child, whose imaginative reality is explicitly defined by his—and particularly her—innocence, resists such bifurcation. Thus, childhood sexuality is dealt with obliquely or, more often, ignored altogether.

By the time we reach the mid-twentieth century, things have changed considerably. Whereas Twain was "squeamish about sex [but] utterly frank about violence," today's sentimentalists have reversed the equation (489). The sexual revolution has liberated the id from the superego, and material affluence has created a postpubescent extension of childhood known as adolescence: "The Good Bad Boy can get himself laid these days even in the fiction of Anglo-Saxondom, but he is no longer permitted to glory in beating up on the Jewish kid next door, or the minister's son or the overdressed stranger from the big city" (491). It is not surprising that, at the time Fiedler was writing, many of our more popular novelists were themselves overgrown adolescents—Good Bad Boys such as J. D. Salinger, laureate of prep-school angst, and Jack Kerouac, bohemian Huck Finn (or perhaps only Tom Sawyer) dreaming that he was Nigger Jim.

If the adolescent has replaced the child as moral exemplar in much contemporary literature, our vision has not necessarily become more sophisticated. (Huck Finn and numerous other nineteenth-century "children" were chronologically adolescents, but—because the category had not yet been invented—were never regarded as such.) We may simply have created another noble savage to serve as an indictment of civilization (here identified with the maturity of adult life). The James Dean prototype is a rebel without a cause not because his rebellion is gratuitous, but because it is too obvious to require a name. It is no longer the Good Good Girl who redeems us for bourgeois respectability, but the Good Bad Boy who leads us to existential authenticity.

As an outcast from society, the Good Bad Boy forms alliances with adults who are also outcasts. He might even learn the sacramental forms of rebellion (drink, indolence, and the like) from his adult mentors. The bonding of the child and the bum (as in William Faulkner's "Uncle Willy" and *The Reivers*) has become a commonplace in our national literature and our national life. As Fiedler suggests, the figure of Rip Van Winkle may well be "the Good Bad Boy grown old without growing up" (497). Unlike Peter Pan, who managed to remain a child in Never-Never-Land, Rip negotiates a passage from first to second childhood by sleeping through his prime adult years. Such a passage is even easier for the Negro or the Indian, because the Dame Van Winkles (and Miss Watsons) of this world have never considered the savage as more than a child—and sometimes as a good deal less.

For purposes of dramaturgy, the innocence of the child must be portrayed against a background of adult corruption. This results in a curious variation on the age-old theme of initiation. Traditionally, the rite of passage leads the child into adulthood and, thus, involves a loss of innocence. To an orthodox Christian or classical sensibility, such a process, though often painful, is both necessary and desirable. Theologically, this is the notion of the fortunate fall, the psychological equivalent of which is the basis for much of the tragic irony at the heart of canonical American literature. For the sentimentalist, however, innocence remains the supreme value. What is needed, then, is a form of initiation that introduces the child to the evil of the adult world without making him part of it. Here, the child "is not a participant in the fall, but a *witness,* only vicariously inducted into the knowledge of sin" (500).

The Child as Peeping Tom has become a familiar presence in modern literature. In works as diverse as Henry James's *What Maisie Knew,* Sherwood Anderson's "I Want to Know Why," Thomas Berger's *Little Big Man,* and even James Joyce's "Araby," children lose some of their illusions as a result of chance encounters with adult sexuality. The child thus acquires a knowledge of "evil," while maintaining his own innocence. Even when sexual contact does occur (as it increasingly has in recent literature), it is less a passage to maturity than an acted-out masturbation fantasy.

Until recently, real initiation in the American novel has been the result of violence, not of sex. In an almost exclusively masculine rite of passage, which takes place in the men's club environment of the wilderness under the tutelage of an old Negro or Indian, the boy kills "some woodland totem" by which "he enters into a communion of guilt with the natural world in which hitherto he has led the privileged existence of an outsider." Although this theme has been most frequently identified with Hemingway and Faulkner (who, in

"The Bear," made his backwoods mentor *both* an Indian and a Negro), it has also become a stock theme in popular outdoor fiction. "The boy with 'buck fever,' the kid trembling over the broken body of his first rabbit or the first bird brought down with a sling, is the equivalent in the world of violence to the queasy stripling over the whore's bed in the world of passion" (501).

Lately, sentimentality has had to make room for—if not entirely give way to—less genteel forms of romanticism. Thus, more insidious images of the child have begun to challenge the maudlin stereotypes of earlier times. The two principal characters in Henry James's *The Turn of the Screw* are children "through whom the satanic attempts to enter the adult world" (506). (This same notion would later be vulgarized in William Peter Blatty's *The Exorcist*.) In Vladimir Nabokov's *Lolita,* we have not a redemptive Good Good Girl, but a twelve-year-old nymphet, who seduces a middle-aged man. (This motif has long been a staple in the underground cult of child pornography.) Finally, in William Golding's *Lord of the Flies,* the parable of man's fall from Eden is reenacted by an all-child society stranded on a desert island. If the child represents the instinctive self, the id, then it must possess diabolic as well as angelic possibilities. The writers who have realized this "have come to believe that the self can be betrayed to impulse as well as to rigor; that an Age of Innocence can be a tyranny no less terrible than an Age of Reason; and that the Gods of such an age if not yet dead must be killed, however snub-nosed, freckle-faced or golden-haired they may be" (511).

More than anything else he had written up to this point, "The Eye of Innocence" indicates the general direction and specific qualities of Leslie Fiedler's critical muse. His command of intellectual history enabled him to show how something as common to humanity as the experience of childhood could take on radically different meanings as sensibility itself was altered. If the generalizations he makes strike some as too sweeping, the examples he cites are time and again both familiar and apt. One is reminded of the encyclopedic knowledge Randall Jarrell witnessed and the mesmerizing presence Jim Cox experienced at Bloomington in the summer of 1952. Fiedler's passionate involvement with ideas was becoming more evident in everything he wrote. By virtue of its length, "The Eye of Innocence" gave promise of what the Good Bad Boy of American literature might accomplish if he ever decided to compose a book of criticism rather than merely compile a collection of essays.

II

Although he prized his isolation from the literary culture of the East, Leslie did whatever he could to bring the best of that culture to Montanans. Initially, this involved addressing book clubs and women's groups. Then, when he took a turn as chairman of the English department in 1954, he made a determined effort to bring prominent writers to Missoula to read and speak. Although literary superstars were not able to command the sort of fees that are now routinely paid to the third-rate, Leslie still had a difficult time scraping up the sums required to bring visiting writers to Missoula. Fortunately, his personal contacts helped him lure celebrities who might not otherwise have considered venturing so far into the American frontier. For their part, Montanans knew how to respond to celebrity if not to art. Hundreds of people from around the state converged on Missoula and even pitched tents in the fields around campus just so they could say they were present when someone famous came to town.

The first writer to arrive was Leslie's friend from Ischia, Wystan Auden (by now, they had long been on a first-name basis). Although most of the audience found his poetry incomprehensible, the visit passed without peril until Auden was taken to a local steak house for dinner. When a bevy of college girls in formal gowns entered the restaurant, Auden "cried aloud among real estate agents and lawyers . . . : 'My dears, I know *exactly* how they feel. I used to be a *mad* queen myself' " (*BB,* 59). Fortunately, this comment passed without notice, and the local newspapers, impressed by the size of the audience at Auden's reading, gave the visit good press.

The next big-name author to hit town was William Faulkner. Although Leslie did not know Faulkner as well as he did Auden, he had met the Nobel laureate a few years earlier in the New York offices of Random House. Despite being a tiny man, Faulkner dominated any room he was in with the magnetism of his presence. When Leslie left Random House, he walked for several blocks in freezing temperatures before realizing he had left his overcoat behind. Leslie understood that, despite his deserved reputation as a difficult modernist writer, Faulkner had managed to appeal to a broad popular audience. Twenty of his short stories, some of them among his best work, had appeared in the *Saturday Evening Post,* which Leslie supposed was "the magazine most likely to be picked up by the common man when he has seen all the movies in town" (*CE,* 1:332). The breadth of Faulkner's appeal could not be explained as mere whoring for lucre. He was one of the few writers since the advent of modernism to have repeatedly bridged the gap between low and high art. In many ways, Leslie found him to be less an heir to James and Flaubert than a throwback to Dickens. He thought it would be interesting to see how the good people of Montana would react.

Following explicit instructions from Random House, Leslie rationed Faulkner's whiskey intake so that he would be able to fulfill his contract. Unfortunately, very few in the audience could hear a word he said. After the microphone level was adjusted to suit his small stature, Faulkner simply stepped so far back from the lectern that his address was inaudible to all but the first few rows of listeners. At a reception later that night, a young lady from Missoula asked Faulkner if A. B. Guthrie might one day write the Great Montana Novel, since "he loved the state so much!" To this the visitor from Mississippi replied: " 'To write about a place well, you must *hate* it!' And after a pause, he added, 'The way a man hates his wife' " (*CE,* 2:333). When Faulkner stumbled his way to the plane the next day, Leslie's two youngest daughters, confusing this big-name visitor with their friend from Ischia, waved their hankies at him and yelled, "Goodbye, Wystan."

Nearly a decade later, Leslie was confronted by a stranger to Missoula whose presence he had not brokered. One night in the early 1960s, he got an unexpected call at home. A voice said, "This is Willmoore Kendall. Do you remember me? I've been invited here to speak to the Young Americans for Freedom, and I've had just about as much as I can take from these pustular kids. I need to talk to somebody intelligent. Come to my hotel, but don't let anyone see you or know what you are doing." When Leslie got to the room, he found that twenty years had not changed his old acquaintance. The first thing Kendall said was "What ever happened to all those bright young men and their dull, dull wives?"[3]

If Willmoore Kendall might have been wary of any of his right-wing hosts seeing him consort with Leslie Fiedler, much of the left-wing intelligentsia had still not forgiven Leslie for his political essays in *An End to Innocence*. (Seen as a Commie at home, he was regarded as a Red-baiter abroad.) William Empson, whose literary disputes with Leslie were never as bitter as their political quarrels, wrote to him on January 4, 1956, with a comment that had been edited out of a letter he had sent to *Encounter*. (The digression about Leslie was simply not germane to the general topic of the letter.) "I see that dear Mr. Fiedler is still carrying on in your magazine," Empson writes. "Since it began, he has been positively praising whatever the reader is likely to think most disgusting in America at the moment. . . . Everybody likes a man to be gallant, but I don't think you are on to a really good line there. People might begin to think you were taking advantage of the young man's innocence." In his direct comments to Leslie, Empson accuses *Encounter* of being a magazine subsidized by foreign gold for the purpose of affecting opinion in England.

Responding to "my dear Empson" on January 18, Leslie writes, "We can afford to be frank with each other. There is, at least, no point in your posing as an objective, fair-minded, somewhat patriotic English citizen appalled at American propaganda. From my memories of your extraordinary speech at Bloomington, I am convinced that your arguments must be understood as

3. Fiedler, interview with Jackson, Apr. 22, 1989.

those of an apologist for a particular point of view. This does not, of course, prejudge them, but it puts them in a somewhat suspicious light. A man who believes the cooked-up reports about germ warfare in Korea would be willing to believe anything."

After three more paragraphs in which he tries to set Empson straight about what he had actually written concerning the Rosenbergs and other matters, Leslie assures his antagonist that he would never want to have to say in public some of the things he was being forced to say in this letter. He then concludes with a mild note of collegiality: "I remember with some pleasure as well as exasperation our discussions at Bloomington when you too were being subsidized by 'foreign gold,' and I hope that it will always be possible for us to keep open channels of communication." Leslie sent a copy of this letter to Stephen Spender at *Encounter,* along with his own observations. "I hope you have not been too troubled by this interchange," he writes. "The poor bastard, I am convinced, is more than half mad at the present point and certainly his reactions are, I am sure, not reasonable ones."

On February 10, Empson came roaring back with a rebuttal to Leslie's letter. He confesses to having been "playing by ear" (i.e., relying on faulty recollection) in what he said about Leslie's contributions to *Encounter* but thinks it "too much" to go back and look up the articles in question. In a long concluding paragraph, which appears to have been his last word on the subject, Empson tries to clarify the position he had taken the previous summer:

> Going back to my "extraordinary" speech in Bloomington, you must remember that Churchill had just flown over to Washington to try to prevent the Americans from causing a world war over Indo-China; at least the English thought he did, and succeeded in it. . . . The point about my wearing my Communist uniform, as I hope I made clear, was not that I had one (a matter of no interest) but that Churchill had paid me to have one, all through the Korean War. . . . Hence it seemed to me perfectly consistent to hurry back and do the Masque for the visit of the Queen to Sheffield, an extravagant bit of flattery which she thought pleasantly funny. I hope this makes my position more intelligible.

The doubleness of Leslie's life in Missoula was reflected in ways other than his ambivalent political identity. He was, among other things, "an Easterner in the West; a Jew in a Gentile world; an ex-Communist among those to whom the very word with or without an ex- was a curse; a liberal, which is to say an exponent of the third way, in a time of right-wing repression and left-wing lies; a lover of courage in a time of no heroes at all" (*BB,* 50). More than anything else, he thought of himself as an American. His experience in Italy had given him a new sense of national identity by forcing him to come to terms with

American literature and culture. Back among the original inhabitants of his own continent, however, Leslie realized that his Americanness must be won rather than merely assumed.

During Leslie's years in Missoula, the Indians were very much a persecuted minority. Montana's antimiscegenation laws were aimed at them rather than at the state's negligible black population. In many towns, Indians couldn't purchase a drink at a saloon. Ethnic stereotypes branded them as dirty, deceitful, and even subhuman. As the civil rights movement began to heat up in the rest of the country, Montana liberals had only the Indian to defend. Even if Leslie had not been moved politically by the plight of these victims, he almost certainly would have identified with the ancient sense of tradition and ritual— the presence of myth—in their culture. After all, both popular legend and the Book of Mormon have long held that the Indians are the lost tribes of Israel.

In 1956, his work on behalf of the civil rights of Indians led to Leslie's being adopted by the Blackfoot tribe. When he was given a traditional Indian bonnet during the induction ceremony, he thought that he would take it home with him as a souvenir. He then discovered that he had only temporary use of it. "They put it on my head," he recalls, "faced me into the sunset, said a formula, pushed me and told me to stumble, and I stumbled into Indianhood." Thereafter, when he participated in Indian meetings, Leslie would improvise a summary of what had been said. He remembers that "instead of saying what people had actually said, I would say what they had hoped to say or what they might have said, and they loved that."

The Blackfeet gave Leslie the name Heavy Runner, after a famous chief of the tribe for whom a mountain is named in Glacier National Park. (When his family later went to an Indian dance in Missoula, which featured a girl named Eleanor Heavy Runner, his kids kept screaming, "That's our cousin, that's our cousin!") "They told me in the ceremony," Leslie recalls, "that Heavy Runner had gone East and come back with the 'weapons of his enemies.' "[4] This was considered a better prize than killing a man or even taking his scalp. Leslie was struck by the fact that he was then preparing to leave Montana for a year's appointment at Princeton. The new Heavy Runner was to fill in for Richard Blackmur and to give the prestigious Christian Gauss lectures. Already he was challenging the received critical orthodoxy by asserting the primacy of myth in literature. What weapons he might bring back were anyone's guess.

4. Patricia Ward Biederman, "Leslie Fiedler: The Critic as Outlaw," 9.

CHAPTER TEN

From Princeton to Athens

THE ESSAY IN that rich and varied collection *No! In Thunder* that may shed most light on Leslie's own psyche is "Walt Whitman: Portrait of the Artist as a Middle-Aged Hero." Originally published as the introduction to the edition of Whitman's verse he edited for the Laurel Poetry Series, this essay was written at a time when Leslie himself was unheroically facing the crisis of being a middle-aged artist. Without knowing this, one might find the essay's emphasis merely puzzling and idiosyncratic. After all, so much of Whitman's bombastic optimism seems to inform *Leaves of Grass* that it might at first seem odd to focus on the poet's mid-life crisis. Nevertheless, Leslie argues that "the key poems of Whitman's book were written from sometime just before 1855 to 1860; that is, from the moment the poet approached his thirty-fifth year to the moment he left behind his fortieth." (*CE,* 1:288).

Leslie goes on to argue that Whitman's mid-life crisis remained more real for him "*as a poet* than the great national crises of secession and war, and [that] at the center of that personal crisis is a crushing sense of loneliness, of being unloved" (289). If the "I" who serves as protagonist for "Song of Myself" is a thinly disguised projection of Whitman himself, the ideal audience he creates—"The Beatrice he could never leave off wooing, the Penelope to whom he could never return"—is a considerably more ephemeral presence. "As the hero of [Whitman's] poem is called 'I,'" Leslie writes, "so the loved one is called 'you'; and their vague pronominal romance is the thematic center of 'Song of Myself.' It is an odd subject for the Great American Poem: the celebration (half-heroic, half-ironic) of the mating between an 'I' whose reality is constantly questioned and an even more elusive 'you.' The latter pronoun in Whitman's verse almost always is followed by the phrase 'whoever you are'" (290).

Since 1941, the man who wrote this essay had continually left and returned to Missoula, Montana, never feeling quite at home anywhere. He celebrated his fortieth birthday at Princeton, which was geographically less than fifty miles from the Newark of his youth but culturally a world removed. As March 8, 1957, approached, he was experiencing radical mood swings. During the preceding year, he had successfully grown a beard for the first time and begun regularly smoking cigars. He and Margaret were going through a rough spell in their marriage, even as Leslie kept falling in and out of love with various women (the "you" of his middle age?). His bar bill had never been higher.

Even worse, his son Kurt was experiencing a difficult adolescent rebellion. At the same time that he was receiving a first-class education at the Bronx School of Science, he was also being introduced to illicit drugs. And he would habitually run away. Fortunately, he would never go very far, usually calling Leslie from Mel Tumin's house and explaining where he was in whispered tones. Because he and Kurt had always been very close, Leslie was not prepared emotionally for what he knew intellectually was a common rite of passage for young males. Convinced that he was a failure as both husband and father, he threw himself even more energetically into his work. In the Christian Gauss lectures, he expounded on ideas about American literature that had begun to germinate in "Come Back to the Raft Ag'in, Huck Honey!" and had flowered during his two years in Italy. The end result would be a bounteous garden called *Love and Death in the American Novel*.

The students during his year at Princeton represented a marked contrast to those at Missoula. Whereas Montanans had names such as "Boone Sparrow," an aristocrat at Princeton might well be "Eberhart Faber IV." If the kids in Montana called Leslie "doc," those at Princeton would never have thought of calling him anything but "sir." (When he was first addressed in this manner, he looked around to see if there was an admiral in the room.) He remembers one young innocent telling him that a derelict had accosted his mother between the New York Public Library and her Park Avenue apartment and said: "Shit on you, you rich bitch." "Now why did he call her that, sir?" the student asked. It was all that Leslie could do to keep the old Newark radical in him from replying, "Perhaps because she was."

Its geographical proximity notwithstanding, the Newark of Bergen Street seemed as far removed as Montana itself from the "fake colonial austerity" of Princeton. Leslie's writing students, "well-tended, well-heeled Preppies all of them, understood that cultural distance and were given to handing in stories about how, feeling desperate, they had gone off to *Newark* to get laid—but encountering some sodden old Princeton alumnus at a bar, had been persuaded while there was yet time to return intact to their artificial paradise" (*BB,* 53).

John W. Aldridge, who had taught with Richard Blackmur in the Christian Gauss seminars at Princeton, wrote a fictionalized account of the place in his novel *The Party at Cranton*. In a book where most of the characters seem to be based on someone real, Leslie appears as the Dionysian Lester Fleischmann, who is engaged in an intellectual rivalry and sexual liaison with Miriam Hornblower, who is herself based on Mary McCarthy. Aldridge writes of Fleis-chmann and Hornblower:

> They were, in fact, so very much alike—even to the extent of knowing all the same people and sharing the same opinions about them—that it was almost impossible to tell their books apart, and reviewers were al-ways infuriating them by solemnly comparing a new work of one with a previous achievement of the other. Together they constituted—albeit with ferocious unwillingness—a sort of bicephalous Louella Parsons of the in-tellectual life, but exactly which was Louella and which Parsons was a question to which, considering the close similarity of their thoughts and works, no one took much time or trouble seeking an answer.[1]

On the night of the party that gives the novel its name, a carful of peo-ple accompany a drunken Lester as he drives Miriam to the train station. Af-ter Miriam is safely aboard the train for New York, Lester is discovered go-ing berserk in the deserted waiting room. First, he empties and demolishes a wastebasket and then throws it on the train tracks. Next, he rips the bars off the closed ticket window and proceeds to throw them like spears through the windows facing the street. "Then he caught sight of the illuminated cigarette machine standing in one corner, lurched over to it, raised his foot, and kicked the front of it, sending a spray of cigarette packages and glass fragments flying all over the floor." After a high-speed ride back into town, Lester proposes that everyone stop by his place for a nightcap. When his passengers decline and insist on being let out at the next street corner, "Lester at once obliged by violently wrenching the wheel, driving up onto the sidewalk, and coming to an instantaneous, bouncy stop not three feet in front of a large tree." After the passengers disembark, "Lester backed with a great scraping and roaring into the street, gave them one of his clean-cut Ivy League smiles and a cheerful wave, and went racing off into the darkness."[2]

On the fateful night of his fortieth birthday, Leslie found himself morose at a party in Princeton. No amount of food, drink, or literary gossip could bring him out of his doldrums. It was then that he had the sort of epiphany one usually only reads about. (One thinks of James's Lambert Strether telling a total stranger that he must live his life to the fullest before it is too late.) A woman, obviously in her late fifties, looked up from the piano she was playing to ask Leslie why he was so melancholy. When he explained, she gave him a knowing smile and said, "Don't worry, baby, fucking begins at forty."[3]

---

1. John W. Aldridge, *The Party at Cranton,* 148.
2. Ibid., 155, 156–57.
3. Fiedler, interview with author, Nov. 7, 1998.

I

It was during his year in Princeton that Leslie finally discovered New York. He traversed the forty miles between Princeton and Manhattan so frequently that he does not know to this day in which city he spent the most time. Not since the years in which he was hitchhiking between Madison and Chicago had he had the experience of living in two cities at virtually the same time. The New York Leslie inhabited in the mid-1950s was not that of *Partisan Review.* (His apostasy and excommunication had already taken place by then.) Instead, he was beginning to form friendships with a circle of editors associated with *Esquire* magazine. From this time until well into the 1970s, *Esquire* was trying to regain the literary prominence it had enjoyed when regularly publishing Ernest Hemingway and F. Scott Fitzgerald a generation earlier. Leslie was starting to move out of the closed sectarian world of the Jewish intellectual to find a broader market for his work. It was through such editors as Clay Felker, Rust Hills, Gordon Lish, and Alice McIntyre that he made this transition and also met other writers he admired—the last survivors of an older generation as well as some of the new kids on the block. He particularly remembers meeting an aging Dorothy Parker at an *Esquire* symposium. Just before they went on stage, she grabbed him and said, "Be nice to mother."[4]

Leslie's most notorious publication in *Esquire* was the story "Nude Croquet," which appeared in the September 1957 issue of the magazine. Although this tale was frank enough to get the issue in which it was published yanked from the newsstands in Knoxville, Tennessee, and to prompt the Dupont Company into withdrawing a dozen or more pages of advertising from the following issue, "Nude Croquet" hardly qualifies as erotic literature. If we define pornography as that which excites lust, Leslie's story is decidedly antipornographic in its almost clinical obsession with the sexual indignities of middle age.

"Nude Croquet" tells of a crazy, sad party attended by five couples, most of whom have known each other since their impoverished and idealistic youth. The host, Bill Ward, is a playwright whose comedy *All Buttoned Up* has been enough of a hit on Broadway to leave him financially independent and the owner of a gaudy mansion. (His young second wife, Molly-o, instigates the game that gives the story its title.) The other "creative writer" in the group is a poet named Leonard, who spends much of the party necking with his young trophy wife, Eva (pronounced Ay-vah). Although Marvin and Ascha Aaron are both original spouses, their relationship has developed into one of mutual recrimination. Marvin has gone from being a promising young critic to a disappointing middle-aged one. (It is by now apparent to everyone that neither

4. Letter from Leslie Fiedler to Mark Royden Winchell, Jan. 8, 1999.

his epic poem on the Wobblies nor his history of American culture will ever be completed.) The central character of the story is Howard Place (a successful painter based on Harold Rosenberg), whose longtime marriage to wife Jessie has survived his frequent infidelities. The one nonbohemian character is an underwear salesman named Bernie Levine. His plainspoken vulgarity makes him seem the most well adjusted guest at the party, until his wife, Beatie, reveals that Bernie, too, is deeply troubled, even as he seems bent on eating himself into an early grave.

Although it is a bit difficult at first to keep all ten characters straight in one's mind, the concentration achieved by unity of place and time and the richness of Leslie's controlling metaphor make "Nude Croquet" his most moving and coherent work of fiction. As its title suggests, the climax of the story occurs when the party-goers, far gone in alcohol and verbal abuse, decide to top off the evening with a game of nude croquet. When nubile, young Molly-o proposes the game, she sees it as nothing more than an act of zany abandon, à la Scott and Zelda Fitzgerald. (She has heard that such a game was once played at the Yaddo Writer's Colony.) For the older guests, however, the stripping of clothes both consummates and exacerbates the stripping of emotions that has gone on all night. As Ronald Bryden observes, "For them it is the necessary continuation of their truthfulness: they will show each other the veined flesh, the sagging bellies and shrunken arms of their dying bodies. Stumbling about by candlelight, in a half-darkness smelling of sweat and age, they perform a ritual reforging of intimacy into melancholy companionship in the face of death."[5]

The game ends when Marvin, who is the bitterest of the men and something of a klutz at croquet, falls flat on his face with an apparent heart attack. The lights are switched on, and Molly-o begins to scream. "One arm concealing her breasts, the other thrust downward so that her hand hid the meeting of her thighs, Molly-o confronted them in the classic pose of nakedness surprised, as if she knew for the first time what it meant to be really nude" (*NC,* 53). Left to ponder this radical transition in attitude, readers must decide for themselves what it means "to be really nude."

Obviously, the mildly decadent frolic that the young woman had in mind has turned into something that she had not bargained for. The simulated return to Eden is invariably a mistake for postlapsarian adults. Molly-o is naive enough to think that such a game can be restricted to fun. What she cannot deal with is the savage honesty that results. Also, as the woman with the most physical attributes and the fewest psychic scars to exhibit, she is flustered when the focus of attention shifts from the physical to the emotional. What she instinctively recoils from displaying is the nakedness of her own innocence. In

5. Bryden, *The Unfinished Hero,* 242.

becoming aware of that innocence, however, she may have taken the first necessary step toward losing it.

This story created an unprecedented stir in a place where people rarely, if ever, read anything Leslie wrote—Missoula, Montana. One anonymous pamphleteer took a rather prurient delight in quoting selected phrases from the story: "Pale flagrant breasts . . . rested one hand gently on her ass . . . she wore nothing underneath, no girdle, no pants . . . a little tuft of hair where the buttocks . . . nipples, not brownish or purple but really pink . . ." (*BB*, 74). The hackles of all decent Montanans (who had not yet forgiven Leslie for "Montana; or the End of Jean-Jacques Rousseau") were further raised when it was discovered that the author of "Nude Croquet" had published an equally explicit poem called "Dumb Dick" in *Partisan Review*. (This became, by all odds, Leslie's most widely circulated poem when it was quoted in full by his anonymous Torquemada.) It is difficult to imagine, however, that an intelligent reader could be stirred to anything but melancholy by such lines as the following:

> Love seethes to suds, seed runs
> Like whey in the raveled vein;
> Dumb Dick stands alone, or shrunken
> Sleeps. No matter. More than the stunned
> Wonder matters, more counts than who comes. . . .   (*NFR*, 467)

Unfortunately, when Leslie tried to defend the products of his muse he overestimated the degree to which his attackers might appreciate self-deprecatory irony. (His calling his apologia "On Becoming a Dirty Writer" was regarded as a confession of guilt.) In fact, the pamphlet attacking him triumphantly and uncomprehendingly reprinted the last paragraph of his essay. Leslie had written, "The authorities in Knoxville are apparently afraid that the game I describe might become a fad. . . . But they have clearly not read beyond my title, since my point is precisely how hard it is to strip naked—and how terrible! I had written a story, I thought, about youth and age, husbands and wives, success and failure, accommodation and revolt—and especially about the indignity of the failing flesh—all of which is, it seems to me, a dirty enough story, the dirty story we all live" (*BB*, 75).

II

From a creative standpoint, the most important product of Leslie's stay in Princeton was his first novel, *The Second Stone*, which appeared in 1963. Reviewing the book for *Critique*, Samuel Irving Bellman aptly describes the situation of some critics confronting a literary phenomenon such as *The Second Stone.* "Good, bad, or indifferent," he writes, "the novel cannot fairly be judged on its own merits, but must be read in the light of the massive body of socio-literary criticism Fiedler has produced in the past fifteen years."[6] A sufficiently resourceful critic would have an absolute field day finding many of Fiedler's favorite themes and images embodied in this novel. Whether the thematic material is adequately assimilated into a story, which compellingly depicts the experience of believable human beings is, of course, another question.

The essential situation depicted in Fiedler's novel is that of a love triangle involving the ultraliberal celebrity rabbi Mark Stone (a Jewish counterpart of Billy Graham and Fulton Sheen), his boyhood friend Clem Stone (no relation, but more about that later), and Mark's wife, Hilda. To heighten the symbolic resonance, the conflict is played out in Rome during the First International Conference on Love (organized by Mark and financed by a wealthy manufacturer of vaginal jelly with covert aid from the U.S. State Department) on April 30 through May 2, 1953—a timespan that coincides with the Communist celebration of May Day.

By setting *The Second Stone* in Rome (Hawthorne's Rome, as he readily confesses), Fiedler calls to mind the long tradition of international or expatriate novels in American literature. What is unclear is whether he is playing the international theme straight or whether he is writing a parody of the sometimes pretentious saga of the American abroad. Certainly Rome means different things to different characters. For Clem Stone, expatriation was originally a fashionable gesture against the bourgeois vulgarity of American life. But now, after six years of failing to write his war novel, he is no longer an angry young bohemian but a middle-aged poseur at the end of his tether. Mark, on the other hand, is a successful American "intellectual," who comes to Europe as a consumer of culture (his aging mother and her dentist-fiancé are more conventional tourists seeing the sights). Along with these American characters appears a smattering of anti-American Europeans, who make topical references to Eisenhower, Dulles, and lynchings in the South. And, of course, we have the picturesque ruins of Christian civilization ironically reminding us that we—or at least Fiedler's characters—live in a post-Christian culture. Presumably, it is a world so permeated by evil that no one is qualified to cast a first stone.

Fiedler's primary narrative task is to bring Clem and Hilda together as often and as passionately as possible yet still send Clem back to America without her at the end of their brief interlude. According to the conventions of American

---

6. Samuel Irving Bellman, "The American Artist as European Frontiersman: Leslie Fiedler's *Second Stone,*" 131.

popular culture (e.g., the film *Roman Holiday*, which is also the title of one of Leslie's essays on Rome), the American's romantic experiences in Europe are, almost by definition, temporary flings. Even in high literature, the American abroad usually finds him- or herself no more than a temporary resident. Individuals such as Hawthorne's Hilda and Kenyon or James's Strether may be sadder and wiser; others, such as Daisy Miller, are merely dead. Few live in Europe after its magic has disappeared.

At one level, Hilda's attraction for Clem seems to be based on nothing more complex than lust. With his own wife, Selma, back in America, he is a horny guy looking after his best friend's wife, while that friend is busy playing the role of international celebrity. (Hilda, for her own part, feels neglected by Rabbi Mark.) Apparently, there is nothing quite like the sight of monks' skeletons in an underground cemetery or the clammy floor of a ruined church to turn these two on, although they do delay their actual coupling until they reach Clem's filthy apartment.

With Fiedler, however, we expect more than mere soft-core pornography. What does Hilda, who shares the name of the snowmaiden in *The Marble Faun*, symbolically represent for her lover and her creator? Warming up to that topic, Clem tells her: "You deceived me. . . . I thought you were a *femme fatale* disguised as a snowmaiden. You're only a snowmaiden disguised as a *femme fatale* disguised as a snowmaiden." Then, a bit later: "You're not Lady Brett Ashley. You're Daisy Miller, Elsie Dinsmore, Marilyn Monroe."[7] Whatever else she may be, Hilda is the wife of Clem's oldest friend. The prospect of cuckolding Mark appears to represent no moral dilemma for Clem. Nor is it clear that he is seeking revenge for some offense Mark might have committed.

If anything, there seems to be a longstanding Huck-Honey relationship between Mark and Clem. (Although neither is exactly a man of color, Mark is a Jew and Clem a WASP.) It is interesting to note that, when Clem's ravishment of Hilda is at its height, "he could think only of Mark, of Mark and himself at sixteen" (120). Is Clem somehow possessing his boyhood friend by possessing that friend's wife? Six years prior to the publication of *The Second Stone,* Maggie tells Brick in Tennessee Williams's *Cat on a Hot Tin Roof* that she and Brick's friend Skipper "made love to each other to dream it was you."[8]

One cannot completely rule out the possibility that Clem and Mark are closer than lovers or brothers and more like doppelgangers. Originally Clem was named Marcus Stone, but to avoid confusion he changed his name to Clem, which is short for Clemens, Mark Twain's real name. Thus, Clem is

7. Leslie Fiedler, *The Second Stone: A Love Story,* 57. Subsequent references will be cited parenthetically in the text.

8. Tennessee Williams, *Cat on a Hot Tin Roof,* 57.

"the other [or second] Mark Stone." Except that Mark's family changed its name from Stein to Stone. So, Clem is actually the *real* Mark (or Marcus) Stone pretending to be Sam Clemens or Mark Twain, suffering from a writer's block. At the same time, the real Mark Stein is pretending to be Mark Stone or Dr. Kinsey, unwittingly funded by the State Department. (In the midst of this confusion, we have Nigger Jim, a black writer named Andrew Littlepage, defecting to the Commies on May Day.) The possibilities for literary exegesis are nearly endless.

If Mark and Clem are two badly divided halves of a single personality (Dionysus and Apollo or Chang and Eng), a figure who stands behind both of them is the author himself. When Clem contemplates writing about his affair with Hilda (under the Shakespearean title *My Second Best Bed*), the first sentence of his account is the same as the first sentence of *The Second Stone*. ("At first, Hilda, one hand pressed against the wall, had only retched.") Then, there is the debate over who actually wrote the avant-garde poem "In Vain from Love's Preakness, I Fly." The choices are (1) Mark (under whose name it was published); (2) Clem (who now claims credit); or (3) a collaboration of the two, which is Mark's present contention. As the cognoscenti know, the answer is (4) none of the above. "In Vain from Love's Preakness, I Fly" was published in the July-August 1951 issue of *Partisan Review* under the name Leslie A. Fiedler. It was this poem that caused Hilda to fall in love with Mark, and doubts about its authorship now prompt her to give herself to Clem.

Should we conclude that Clem can achieve the integrated personality necessary for his return to America only by destroying his Apollonian doppelganger (he has earlier thrown a "second stone" at him during a May Day riot) or at least by reducing him to a babbling idiot? In the concluding scene of the novel, Mark can be seen beating on Hilda's head and shoulders with a rolled up copy of *Thou* magazine, "unable to stop stuttering, 'I—I—I—I—'; though now it would have been hard to say whether he tried to begin a sentence, or merely, like his ancestors, wailed, '*Ai! Ai! Ai! Ai!*' " (302). In the midst of all this, everyone else in the room is frozen, except for Clem, who is crowing like a rooster. "Mark's hand rose and fell as if forever; Hilda bowed her head beneath the blows; and Clem cried cock-a-doodle to the room, the world. In a minute, he told himself, he would bark like a fox" (303).

Whether two such buffoons could ever be merged into the single author of "In Vain from Love's Preakness, I Fly" seems doubtful. But even if neither nor both equal Leslie Fiedler, nothing Leslie has written is more deeply personal than *The Second Stone*. He might owe the setting of the novel to his Fulbright year in Rome, but the character of Hilda is based on a woman with whom he began a twenty-five-year love affair while teaching at Princeton. Because she preferred to remain anonymous, *The Second Stone* is the only one of Leslie's books to appear without a dedication.

III

When Leslie left Missoula for Princeton in the fall of 1956, he gave up the last year of his term as chairman of the English department. During his two years in that position, he hired talented misfits who had gotten into trouble at their previous schools. (Even in a buyer's market, that was the only way to lure truly gifted people to an outpost as remote and provincial as Missoula.) As long as these individuals kept a low profile, their personal eccentricities were ignored. The only truly unforgivable sin in Montana was to be *locally* controversial. One could write countless articles on the Rosenbergs or the Hiss Case or homoerotic passion in *Huckleberry Finn* without attracting notice at home for the simple reason that few Montanans read the magazines in which those articles were published. It was only when one seemed to attack the state itself (as in "Montana; or the End of Jean-Jacques Rousseau") or publish a "dirty story" in a mass-circulation magazine that sparks would begin to fly. Even at that, Leslie probably could have regained his anonymity had he not decided to pick a fight with Carl McFarland, the president of the university, when he got back from Princeton.

Of the bold moves he tried to make as chairman, only one was actually blocked: his effort to hire a Negro professor. After the appointment had been cleared by vote of the department and all the appropriate university committees, Leslie wrote the applicant, Charles Nilon, a letter of appointment. Shortly thereafter, an ad hoc committee that was assembled to reconsider the job offer instructed Leslie to write a second letter nullifying the original one. Sensing that McFarland was behind this bit of treachery, Leslie threw down the gauntlet and assured the president that their fight had just begun.

The battle was delayed, however, by Leslie's year at Princeton. His physical removal from the situation and the change of life he was experiencing on the East Coast might have caused the controversy to blow over had Leslie not been appalled by the conditions he witnessed on his return to campus. Despite an overwhelming vote of confidence by the department, he had been replaced as chairman by Nan Carpenter, a southern lady who had strenuously opposed his policies, particularly his attempt to integrate the English faculty. (A bundle of contradictions, Nan was a Christian Scientist, who always said, "I'm holding a good thought for you, Leslie," and lent him money once when he was hard up.)[9] Too dispirited and timid to attack the administration, the faculty proceeded to take their frustrations out on one another. Rather than joining one of the impotent warring factions, Leslie decided to train his sights on the man responsible for the malaise. In the spring of 1958, Leslie got up before

9. Leslie Fiedler, interview with author, Feb. 26, 1999.

an audience of faculty and students and urged a vote of no confidence in the president of the university.

The odds against Leslie were long and the risks steep. It soon became apparent that the only possible outcome of this battle would be the president's departure or his own. Although the faculty groused endlessly in private about all the issues that typically stir academics ("such classically unresolvable questions as 'standards,' distinctions between in-state and out-of-state students, pay raises for present staff versus expansion"), no one but Leslie was foolhardy enough to attempt regicide (*BB*, 57). Indeed, while Leslie was at Princeton, 70 percent of the faculty had voted to support the administration he was now trying to topple.

The revolutionary zeal that Leslie had nurtured as a youth on Bergen Street had never before found a proper outlet. Having given up on the notion of reshaping society, he could now assume the role of hero or martyr in that unrepresentative microcosm of society that constitutes the university. As in his boy's fantasy, the battle lines were soon drawn. All the "progressive" forces (including a few hard-bitten Stalinists, who never thought that they would live long enough to support a contributor to *Partisan Review*) lined up behind Leslie, while all the reactionaries and know-nothings supported McFarland.

But the situation kept refusing to stay so neatly divided. Anti-Semites were in a particular quandary. Leslie was a Jew, but so too was McFarland, albeit a secret self-hating one who was trying to pass. And what was the Far Right to do? Leslie was a man of the Left, but McFarland had departed Montana as a young man to follow the New Deal to Washington, where he had served as special assistant to Attorney General Homer Cummings. Occasionally Leslie would get unwelcome fan mail from individuals who experienced obvious difficulty in sorting all the issues out. " 'I am glad someone is moving in on the president,' one such nut wrote, 'whose bosom friend is Bayard Rustin, the nigger jailbird . . . It makes you weep we have sunk so low.' " Another anonymously confided of Leslie's opponent: "he is a man who has a big head so bad . . . that you can't reach him with a ten-foot Pole. . . . He was Roosevelt's lawyer—that is enough said" (*BB*, 65). Even the expected Red-baiting was tinged with ambiguity. The Anaconda Copper Mining Company had such a good contract with the Stalinist-controlled Mine, Mill, and Smelters Worker's Union that it made sure no money was ever appropriated to enforce the anti-Communist legislation passed in the state during the McCarthy era. One could never be sure how a political controversy would be resolved in this state without a middle.

The issue came to a head when McFarland offered his resignation to the state board of education, thereby taking his fate away from the university itself and placing it in the hands of the Montana's top political and civic leaders. A controversy that Leslie had hoped would be resolved according to principle and reasoned debate was soon reduced to an exercise in political horse trading. As most of the state chose sides in the fight, Leslie was ostracized by former friends, hounded mercilessly by the press, and turned into a reluctant celebrity. When time came for the board to take its final vote, rumor had it that that body was split right down the middle. Consequently, the "Fiedler Faction" dispatched one of its most articulate supporters to make the case for McFarland's ouster. As the dissident spokesman was waxing eloquent about such high-minded ideals as the good of the university, one of the board members cut him short. " 'Fuck the Good of the University,' it is claimed he said, 'that's like Home and Mother. Who's on your side?" (*BB*, 69). When he was informed that the secretary of the Mine, Mill, and Smelters Worker's Union was supporting the anti-McFarland faction, the board member said, "You've got my vote," and the issue was settled. Leslie's cause had been saved by Montana's version of the Hitler-Stalin Pact.

Having stepped into the local spotlight, Leslie could no longer return to obscurity. Any time the forces of reaction needed a scapegoat for whatever was going wrong, the perfidious Fiedler was there to blame. Fortunately, his services were in sufficient demand elsewhere that he could usually get away for a year or more whenever he wanted to. One such opportunity seemed to present itself in the late summer and early fall of 1959. Throughout the mid-1950s, Elliot Cohen, the founding editor of *Commentary,* had suffered from bouts of depression. Then, in 1959, he took his own life. In addition to being a personal loss for Cohen's friends and associates, his death created an immediate crisis for *Commentary*. In an undated letter that was probably written some time in the summer of 1959, Albert L. Furth contacted Leslie on behalf of the publication committee for *Commentary*.[10] Subsequent correspondence indicates that the American Jewish Committee was seriously considering Leslie as a possible replacement for Cohen and that Leslie himself was at least initially interested in such an appointment.

Rather than give up tenure and permanently uproot his life for a position that might not work out, Leslie proposed taking a one-year leave from the university to come to *Commentary* as "Visiting Editor-in-Chief," with the prospect of taking on the job permanently if that seemed mutually agreeable. Although such an arrangement was acceptable in principle to the publication committee, Leslie was not the only candidate being considered. Irving Kristol, Daniel Bell, and Alfred Kazin had already refused the job, while Martin Greenberg and Norman Podhoretz were still in the running. Greenberg and Podhoretz had both worked on the magazine under Cohen and had developed rancorous feelings for each other. Greenberg was serving as acting editor until a final decision

10. The letters from Albert L. Furth to Leslie Fiedler are contained in Fiedler's private files.

could be made. Although he had left *Commentary* for a job with Looking Glass Books, Podhoretz was still in New York and still very much in the picture, even though he had convinced himself that he did not want the job.

In a letter to Leslie dated October 13, 1959, Furth confesses that the publication committee "remains on dead center" and apologizes for the exasperating delay in making a final decision. By this time, Leslie's initial enthusiasm had cooled to the point that he soon withdrew his candidacy and urged the committee to appoint Podhoretz as editor of *Commentary*. Although he appeared to remain uninterested in the appointment, Podhoretz met several times with the publication committee to discuss the future of the magazine and finally accepted the editorship in late 1959. Leslie knew Podhoretz to be an intelligent literary critic, who had studied under Lionel Trilling at Columbia and F. R. Leavis at Cambridge. He was also a skilled editor and a man of the Left in the tradition of *Partisan Review*. At the same time, he was sympathetic to the cultural radicalism of such iconoclastic figures as Norman Mailer, Paul Goodman, and Norman O. Brown. If Leslie himself could not be editor, he thought *Commentary* was in reliable hands with Norman Podhoretz at the helm.

The disappointment of not getting the editorship of *Commentary* was inconsequential compared to the trauma Leslie had experienced earlier that year when he learned of Walter Stone's completely unexpected suicide. (Walter's death and those of Al Eisner and Isaac Rosenfeld were the three losses that most affected Leslie's early life.) On the evening of March 11, Walter had been found hanged in a house where he was staying in suburban Hampstead, England. He was forty-two years old and an associate professor of creative writing at Vassar. The previous fall, he had received a faculty fellowship to do research at the British Museum and at Oxford and Cambridge. He left no note indicating the reasons for his desperate act. Leslie could only surmise that, having gotten everything that life could offer, Walter had discovered it was not enough. Leslie and Margaret had been so close to Walter and Ruth that the Fiedler children referred to the Stones as "foster father" and "foster mother."

Ruth later wrote a moving poem, called "Turn Your Eyes Away," about this wrenching experience. The first few lines read as follows:

> The gendarme came
> to tell me you had hung yourself
> on the door of a rented room
> like an overcoat
> like a bathrobe
> hung from a hook;
> when they forced the door open
> your feet pushed against the floor.
> Inside your skull

there was no room for us,
your circuits forgot me. . . . [11]

In addition to his wife, Walter Stone was survived by three daughters.

After Princeton, Leslie's next sojourn away from Montana consisted of a Fulbright Fellowship at the University of Athens during the 1960–1961 academic year. He remembers his time in Greece as an almost mythic experience. Early in his stay there, he discovered the name "Byron" carved on the pillar of an ancient temple. Although he suspected that this was a ploy by the local chamber of commerce, the romantic in Leslie wanted to believe that the great British poet had left his mark on this ancient ruin. Whether or not this was true, it seemed as if the skies were brighter and the seas bluer in Greece than anywhere else on earth. One day when Leslie was swimming in the Mediterranean, he suddenly saw a ship that looked as if it had just sailed out of the *Odyssey.* He swam out and climbed aboard, convinced that he had entered a land of enchantment.

The only thing about his time in Athens that Leslie found disconcerting was his experience at the university. The cultural literacy of his students was so low that he had to give them remedial instruction in Greek mythology before they could read Ezra Pound. Many of the students took pride in the clever ways they had found to cheat, and several of the women brazenly offered sexual favors in exchange for grades. But no amount of academic tawdriness could fatally detract from the allure of this magical place. A week or so before Leslie arrived, the local newspaper had run a story about the "foreign Dionysus" who was on his way. (He didn't have the heart to tell them that Dionysus is always, by definition, a foreigner.) At one point during his stay, he even dressed as Dionysus for a carnival and, with vine leaves in his hair, literally lost consciousness of his whereabouts and actions for more than a day.[12]

Leslie thought that one of the advantages of living in Athens was that he could be reunited with his brother, Harold, who was American consul in Istanbul. During their childhood, Leslie and Harold had been virtually inseparable. They had slept in the same bed and fought and loved each other as brothers do. But as adults, they had gone their separate ways. After being drafted in World War II, Harold had become completely committed to the military life. He had quickly moved into army intelligence and eventually joined the CIA after the war. A dead ringer for Charlton Heston, he had cut a dashing figure during the war as the commander of a tank company. He was known for jumping on to German tanks and prying the top open. Immediately after the war he was put in charge of maximum security prisoners at army prison camps. He

---

11. Ruth Stone, "Turn Your Eyes Away," 378.
12. Fiedler, interview with author, Nov. 7, 1998.

had an arsonist fire his furnace and was so tough that no one dared step out of line on his watch. A superpatriot who converted to Lutheranism, Harold had turned himself into a WASP. Still, Leslie had no idea how profoundly his brother had turned his back on his past. So, Leslie wrote him to propose that they get together at Christmastime. "Do you want to come here or shall I go there?" he asked. In reply, Harold sent him a letter saying, "This may come as a rude shock to you, but I never want to see you again in my life."[13]

By now, Leslie's own family was complete. After Kurt and Eric, his third son, Michael, had been born in Missoula in 1947. Then came the three girls: Debbie in Missoula in 1949, Jennie in Rome in 1952, and Miriam in Missoula in 1955. These six children grew up in Montana, far from Bergen Street and the experiences that had shaped their father as a youth. But unlike Harold, Leslie had wanted them always to know who they were as a people as well as who they might become as individuals. When his grandmother was dying, he took the infant Debbie to see her. They looked at each other and saw that their eyes were exactly the same—a pale blue like washed-out jeans. If there was a sense in which the Fiedlers would always be outsiders in Missoula, Leslie sensed that that would be true anywhere they lived. And after twenty years, Montana seemed as good a place as any to come home to.

13. Fiedler, interview with Jackson, June 29, 1989.

CHAPTER ELEVEN

American Gothic

IN 1984, LESLIE Fiedler told David Gates of *Newsweek:* "The typical pattern with one of my books . . . is that when it comes out everybody abuses it. Ten years later they're still abusing it but they've begun to steal ideas from it. Twenty years go by and they decide it's a classic, although nobody's ever said anything good about it."[1] This has clearly been the fate of Leslie's best known and most distinguished book, *Love and Death in the American Novel.* Having gone through its obligatory period of abuse decades ago, the book has long since taken its place as one of a handful of indispensable texts in the study of American culture. To appreciate its peculiar strengths, however, we need to understand why it was so widely vilified at the time that it was published.

As we have already seen, the serious study of American literature really didn't begin until the 1920s. Even then, the favored approach tended to be heavily social and political. When critics were not using our literature as a means of denouncing American life (a favored practice of bohemians and leftists alike), they were apt to be preaching an equally simplistic form of cultural nativism. Although it seems difficult to believe today, the first giant of modern American literary studies was the crudely populist Vernon Louis Parrington.

Perhaps reacting against the effete aestheticism he encountered at Harvard (where he graduated with Oswald Garrison Villiard and William Vaughan Moody in the class of 1893), Parrington was all too eager to evaluate literary works as cultural documents, which advanced ideas that he could either endorse or attack. Those writers who seemed largely indifferent to the great issues of the day (e. g., Henry James) were dismissed as "narrowly belletristic." Although Parrington died in 1930, the democratic nativism he represented struck many as particularly appealing in the days leading up to World War II. Throughout the war and its immediate aftermath, cultural jingoists followed

---

1. See David Gates, "Fiedler's Utopian Vision."

Parrington's lead in trashing insufficiently red-blooded literature, a category that included modernism in its "decadent" entirety. This point of view was expounded by such notables as Archibald MacLeish and Howard Mumford Jones, with the *Saturday Review of Literature* serving as their chief house organ.

Although more urbane and restrained than the *Saturday Review* patriots, New York Jewish intellectuals such as Alfred Kazin also joined in the celebration of American culture. In discussing Kazin's monumental study *On Native Grounds* (1942), Alexander Bloom writes, "[E]ven the political literature of the 1930s appeared much more *American* for Kazin than for the cosmopolitan, universalist intellectuals he followed. . . . Whereas the older [Jewish] critics began to accept gradually the role of American culture, Kazin took it as his main focus." While it was perfectly acceptable to denigrate particular writers and even entire periods or regions of American literature (Kazin was himself dismissive of the southern Agrarians and New Critics), there was a widespread belief from the 1940s on that ours was a fundamentally healthy and affirmative literary tradition.[2]

Appearing at the end of the 1950s, when national self-confidence was still high, *Love and Death in the American Novel* predictably offended many readers with what they took to be its brash irreverence toward our sacred literary culture. Although few went so far as a British reviewer who accused Fiedler of "fouling his own nest," both the academic and literary establishment took him to task for what they regarded as an overly pathological view of classic American literature. Malcolm Cowley, who had rediscovered the virtues of American life after his romance with Stalinism soured, went on the attack on the front page of the *New York Times Book Review* on March 27, 1960. At one point, he writes:

> I have thought at times of compiling a dictionary of synonyms for the use of college freshmen. Here are a few of the phrases guaranteed to impress young instructors: Never say friendship; say "innocent homosexuality." Never say curiosity; say "voyeurism," or refer to the curious man as a "castrated peeper." Instead of mourning for the dead, refer to "necrophilia." Instead of self awareness, speak of "narcissism." Remember that fun and games do not exist in the Freudian world except as "the symbolic enactment of sado-masochistic desires." Remember that family affection is merely a "repressed incestuous longing" and that chastity is "the morbid fear of full genital development."[3]

2. Bloom, *Prodigal Sons,* 136. By the time Fiedler wrote, a few prescient observers were already sensing serious strains in the pro-American optimism that had been fueled by the war against Hitler. Although his personal demons alone would have been enough to drive him to suicide, F. O. Matthiessen was also profoundly disillusioned by the extent to which the Cold War was dividing American society.

3. Malcolm Cowley, "Exploring a World of Nightmares," 40.

The attacks on Fiedler and his book were so persistent that, by the time Irving Kristol reviewed *Love and Death* favorably in the summer 1960 issue of the *Kenyon Review,* he felt compelled to devote the first half of his discussion to answering the charges made by other critics. Kristol suspected that Fiedler's Freudian vocabulary was merely the target rather than the true cause of the animus he had inspired. How else explain the fact that several of Fiedler's denigrators had lavished extravagant praise on Norman O. Brown's more radically Freudian book *Love against Death?* "My own inference," Kristol writes, "is that what these men object to in Fiedler is, above all, his manners. He is a writer who likes to strike bold postures, to splatter his pages with exclamation marks, to play the *enfant terrible* and *poete maudit,* to exaggerate for effect, to provoke without cause, to exhibit himself and to impose himself on the reader along with his ideas."[4] Kristol assured us that all of this would have gone over quite well in France, where there is a thriving tradition of amateur criticism among men of letters and literary journalists. Because Fiedler refused to conduct himself with the appropriate American solemnity, his attackers accused him of being inherently unserious.

Love and Death in the American Novel was such an obviously major work that those who had little good to say about it were often forced to articulate their objections at great length. It is ironic that even negative reviewers tended to hedge their criticism with enough grudging praise to provide ample blurb material. A perfect example is Richard Chase's long essay in the *Chicago Review,* "Leslie Fiedler and American Culture." Readers of the 1975 paperback edition of *Love and Death* were told (on the back cover) that Chase called the book "genuinely original . . . a work of lasting importance . . . a powerful indictment of our culture and modern culture in general." Turning to the full text of Chase's essay, however, we are not sure whether his comments, quoted out of context, were really meant as compliments. The author of *The American Novel and Its Tradition* (1957), Chase assures us that American fiction "is not merely a chronicle of nihilistic despair titillated up with a misplaced eroticism."[5]

Chase excoriates Fiedler for bombast, sensationalism, factual inaccuracy, and a failure to acknowledge his indebtedness to other scholars. According to Chase, Fiedler is "a run-of-the-mill Ph.D. candidate, a kind of archetype of the thousands who grimly and with what Fiedler calls a 'total moral commitment' nowadays study American literature and who submit articles to university quarterlies like *Modern Fiction Studies* entitled 'Theme and Structure in *Absalom, Absalom!*' or 'The Concept of Time in Sarah Orne Jewett.'" Even

---

4. Irving Kristol, "A Traitor to His Class," 506.
5. Richard Chase, "Leslie Fiedler and American Culture."

worse, Fiedler is absolutely profligate in his use of the exclamation mark: "He is the kind of author who can write: Herman Melville was born in New York in 1819!"[6]

There is a sense in which Fiedler not only anticipated but courted the controversy engendered by *Love and Death in the American Novel*. In reflecting on his book in 1967, he confesses to having gone deliberately beyond "the most ambitious and sensitive of our critics." Even if Parrington, Matthiessen, and Kazin "tried to buck the genteel tradition which insists that, after all, Poe was not *really* a drunkard or Hawthorne a melancholiac or Whitman a homosexual," they have nevertheless insisted "that our classic books are respectable politically, imbued with o. k. liberal sentiments." Fiedler, of course, will have none of that: "All these kindly and comforting lies *Love and Death* has eschewed—rejecting the conventional reasonable voice of our typical criticism along with its cliches of politics and good taste, and trying to become itself as wildly Gothic, as full of grotesque jokes . . . as, say, *Moby-Dick* or *Huckleberry Finn*. This is why the very form of *Love and Death* is novelistic. . . . My long, darkly comic study is a Gothic novel or it is nothing. Indeed, all criticism when really valid is literature, not amateur philosophy or inflated journalism."[7]

It is easy to see why Fiedler's book has most often been compared to D. H. Lawrence's *Studies in Classic American Literature*. As an instinctive, neo-romantic novelist, Lawrence was not expected to abide by the protocols of scholarship. Readers of his inspired and idiosyncratic book are not interested in footnotes and bibliography but in intuitions and judgments. Perhaps if Leslie Fiedler had been recognized in 1960 as primarily a creative writer rather than a critic and scholar, the literary establishment would have been less outraged by what he produced. But the irony of the situation is that only a scholar of immense learning and a critic of great perception could have written a book as inclusive and coherent as *Love and Death in the American Novel*. As suggestive as D. H. Lawrence's many insights may be, he could not have written the book that Fiedler wrought. In comparing Fiedler and Lawrence, Irving Kristol is certainly on the money when he says that Fiedler's "mind is more supple, more inquisitive, more far-ranging, more at home in the world of ideas." Kristol concludes that *Love and Death* "perhaps could not have been written, and certainly would not be as good as it is, if Lawrence had not previously produced his book; but it represents an improvement on the original."[8]

6. Ibid., 10.
7. Leslie Fiedler, "Second Thoughts on *Love and Death in the American Novel:* My First Gothic Novel," 10.
8. Kristol, "Traitor," 507.

I

"Between the novel and America there are peculiar and intimate connections." It is a memorable first sentence, to be sure. Not only does it announce the subject of the book, but it does so with the voice of authority. The paragraph continues in the same vein: "A new literary form and a new society, their beginnings coincide with the beginnings of the modern era and, indeed, help to define it. We are living not only in the Age of America but also in the Age of the Novel, at a moment when the literature of a country without a first-rate verse epic or a memorable verse tragedy has become the model of half the world" (23).

The concept of the "great American novel" is itself an implicit confession that prose fiction is the literary form best suited to the American experience. In large part, this is a function of history. For economic and social reasons well documented by Ian Watt and others, the modern novel came into being with the rise of capitalism and the middle class in eighteenth-century England.[9] Because this was precisely the time when America was developing a national identity, it was not surprising that the new genre was readily adopted by the New World.

In the first half of *Love and Death,* Fiedler concentrates on the way in which European prototypes were altered in the evolution of a distinctively American novel. (It is in the very act of relating our fiction to the larger context of European literature that Fiedler's book differs from all previous studies of the American canon.) According to Fiedler, the three basic paradigms available to eighteenth-century American novelists were the Richardsonian tale of seduction, the pseudo-Shakespearean epic of Fielding, and the Gothic romance of Monk Lewis. The first of these became the province of female sentimentalists, whose popular success has always exceeded their critical acclaim. The second "with its broad canvas, its emphasis upon reversals and recognitions, and its robust masculine sentimentality, turned out, oddly enough, to have no relevance to the American scene" (28). What has come to be regarded as "classic" American literature, therefore, is a variation on the Gothic. "Our fiction," Fiedler writes, "is essentially and at its best nonrealistic, even anti-realistic; long before *symbolisme* had been invented in France and exported to America, there was a full-fledged native tradition of symbolism" (28–29). It is this tradition that is the focus of *Love and Death in the American Novel.*

Before discussing the Gothic canon of American fiction, Fiedler traces the history of the novel's emergence in England and its transplantation to America. The point that he stresses throughout is the popular, bourgeois, individual-

9. See Ian Watt, *The Rise of the Novel.*

istic nature of the novel. The genre arose as a reaction to the class-conscious lit-erature of court and salon, was dependent upon mass production and a middle-class audience for its very existence, and was not even considered high art until the age of Flaubert and Henry James. Moreover, Fiedler reminds us, "the mo-ment at which the novel took hold coincides with the moment of the sexual division of labor which left business to the male, the arts to the female—thus laying up for the future the perils of Bovaryism, on the one hand, and on the other, the dictatorship of 'what the young girl wants' or, perhaps better, what her father thinks she *should* want" (42).

According to Fiedler, there were three levels of duplicity involved in the rise of the bourgeois novel: it represented the marvelous as ordinary, passion as piety, and entertainment as moral instruction. These evasions can be explained sociologically by the Puritan aversion to art and fancy. While literature was not totally outlawed, it had to be smuggled into the parlor in the guise of a sermon. The faith it served, however, was not that of Milton's stern Puritan despot, but rather "that secret religion of the bourgeoisie in which tears are considered a truer service of God than prayers, the Pure Young Girl replaces Christ as the savior, marriage becomes the equivalent of bliss eternal, and the Seducer is the only Devil" (45). In Fiedler's opinion, the religion of sentimental love is simply the Protestant manifestation of a process that had been developing in the Western psyche since at least the late Middle Ages.

Like the emergence of courtly love (and the more extreme forms of Mari-olatry) in eleventh-century Europe, the evolution of the bourgeois novel rep-resented "the inruption of the female principle into a patriarchal world, a revenge of the (officially rejected) Great Mother" (47). In the Catholic Mediter-ranean countries, the orthodox trinity of Father, Son, and Holy Ghost was enshrined in dogma, while the baroque trinity of cuckold, mother, and son was worshipped in art. By the same token, "it was on the religious marches of Europe, where mother-directed Catholicism and father-centered Protes-tantism met, in France, Germany, and England, that the novel especially flour-ished. . . . Committed to the Northern rejection of the Virgin, such men [as Richardson and Goethe] sought with special urgency to smuggle the mother principle back into their cultures. They were thus specially qualified to satisfy the secret hunger of the puritanical bourgeoisie, which demanded bootleg madonnas; it was the function of the early novel to supply them" (56).

Given the proper social conditions and a receptive mind-set, it required only a model narrative for the sentimental love religion to become myth for the Protestant middle class. Samuel Richardson (who is generally credited with having invented the English novel) actually provided complementary narratives—one comic and one tragic—in *Pamela* and *Clarissa*. Both involve a confrontation between an unprincipled seducer and a virginal young girl. In *Pamela* the heroine maintains her purity and is rewarded with marriage to the morally chastened aristocrat who had sought her favors illicitly. As Fiedler emphasizes, virginity is not itself a thing of value in the bourgeois worldview but rather a quality that makes the young woman worthy of the ultimate social good—marriage to someone of a higher station. And, if anyone should miss the underlying commercial ethic (which, in Fiedler's apt phrase, makes Pamela a "female Ben Franklin"), Richardson has subtitled his novel "Virtue Rewarded."

Although it is not as widely read as *Pamela, Clarissa* is perhaps even more potent as a mythic paradigm. Here, the Don Juan figure is not a roguish hero, nor is he finally made to capitulate to the bourgeois respectability of marriage. In the conflict of the chaste Clarissa and the rapacious Lovelace, we have a meeting of the immovable object with the irresistible force. After refusing Lovelace's overtures, Clarissa is drugged and violated. She nevertheless maintains the purity of her soul and dies a long, agonizing death. The blackguard Lovelace subsequently expires in a duel, but not before having a vision of Clarissa in Heaven and himself in Hell. This final vision blatantly exposes the Manichaeanism of the sentimental love religion. Although His name is often invoked, there is no supreme being here: "there are only man and woman in eternal conflict; for the divine principle has been subsumed in the female even as the diabolic has been in the male" (67).

The Richardsonian prototypes survived in American literature, appearing throughout the nineteenth century. The narrative in which they were originally embodied, however, lacked mythic power when it was transformed to an American setting. As Fiedler notes, "It is impossible to contrast domestic virtues with courtly ones in a country where there has never been a court, so that the essential Richardsonian conflict, which is also the dialectic of the form, is inevitably lost" (76). What has not been lost is the notion of female chastity as the apotheosis of virtue and the image of the suffering female herself as vicarious Christ—redeeming the penitent sinner (as in *Pamela*) or damning the impenitent one (as in *Clarissa*) by the purity of her example. These attitudes were consistent with the Puritan repudiation of overt sexual desire; however, they would not have achieved their specific form if the secularized sentimentality that was fast replacing Puritan theology had not also supplanted the patriarchal God of the old religion with a new female anima.

Although one can find numerous variations of Clarissa in the high canon of American literature, her most obvious presence is in the popular novel. The sad fate of the wronged maiden was a stock theme in pulp tearjerkers well into the twentieth century (until the sexual revolution made that theme passé). Viewing sexual violation from the other side of the bed were pornographers who pruriently depicted the act of seduction itself (pornography simply being the dark side of sentimentality). Because women in American fiction generally lacked the moral and physical stamina of Clarissa, those who maintained their virtue were either saved melodramatically from the buzz saw by dashing young heroes or—like the Good Good Girl—dispatched from this vale of tears before the onset of puberty.

Turning his attention from the Richardsonian novel of seduction to the Gothic romance, which is at the heart of his study, Fiedler shows terror replacing love as the essential theme of fiction. There were clear problems, however, in transferring the Gothic romance from Europe to America. Although the image of the maiden in flight and the ambiguous hero-villain presented no difficulties, there were no haunted castles in the New World nor any established class system to provide the historical and social background on which European Gothicism thrived. What was needed was a set of indigenous symbols that would evoke a distinctively American sense of Gothic terror. The man who would discover (or invent) this set of symbols was the first important American novelist, Charles Brockden Brown. Whether or not his own work is finally judged a success, Brown created the romantic image of the American writer and, through his influence on Poe and Hawthorne, helped to shape the course of American fiction.

Just as Brown adapted the Gothic novel to the American scene, James Fenimore Cooper remade a later prototype, the historical romance, in the image of the New World. Although it is sometimes regarded as a subgenre of the Gothic (both are concerned with the past and with making the marvelous credible), the historical romance represents a crucial difference in outlook. For those writing in the tradition of Cooper and Sir Walter Scott, the savage and primitive are largely purged of their demonic associations and sometimes even established as moral norms. Like the Gothicist, the "white romantic" is fascinated by the quaint and picturesque, but his attitude is more likely to be one of nostalgia than of horror. In the historical novel, "hero and heroine flee not projections of their feared inner selves but real enemies, genuine conspiracies, external dangers. . . . The historical Romance (and its companion form, the Romantic narrative poem as practiced by Byron) represents the sight-seeing of the middle classes before cheap and speedy transportation had made it possible for them to do it in the flesh" (163).

By appropriating the landscape of the Gothic novel, the plot and theme of the historical romance, and some of the character types of the Richardsonian tale of seduction, Cooper proved himself a great synthesizer of adult literary traditions. As Fiedler notes, however, those works of his that continue to live tend to be regarded as children's—or more specifically—boys' books. That is a fate that Cooper's Leatherstocking Tales share with the first two parts of *Gulliver's Travels, Robinson Crusoe,* some of Scott (e.g., *Ivanhoe*) and Dickens (e.g., *Oliver Twist*), and much of Robert Louis Stevenson (e.g., *Treasure Island* and *David Balfour*).These books have certain characteristics in common: "all of them have male protagonists, adult or juvenile; all involve adventure and isolation plus an escape at one point or another, or a flight from society to an island, a woods, the underworld, a mountain fastness—some place at least where mothers do not come; most of them involve, too, a male companion, who is the spirit of the alien place, and who is presented with varying degrees of ambiguity as helpmate and threat" (181). That such a pattern would be repeated again and again in classic American novels is, of course, a point that Fiedler had been making ever since he first published "Come Back to the Raft Ag'in, Huck Honey!" in *Partisan Review* a dozen years earlier.

The archetype of interethnic male bonding first made its appearance in American literature in the figures of Cooper's Natty Bumppo and Chingachgook. From the time of Cooper on, the prototypical American hero (particularly in the pulp Western) has shunned both women *and* civilization as a single threat to his freedom. In *The Last of the Mohicans,* Natty—who is here known as Hawkeye—suggests rather unconvincingly that his lack of desire for the opposite sex is due to his unfamiliarity with society and its conventions of courtship. Later on, he asserts that the bond that joins him to Chingachgook's son Uncas is stronger than that which unites man and wife. Then, after the death of Uncas, he renews his vow of fealty to Chingachgook. As Fiedler notes, the culturally plausible expedient of mating Natty with an Indian squaw is prevented by Cooper's implacable fear of miscegenation.

If Cooper represents the chaste male couple of the wilderness novel in the characters of Natty and Chingachgook, he uses the main action of *The Last of the Mohicans* to depict the darker and more pervasive fear of interethnic rape. Although Cooper skirts the issue, it is clear that Magua—the bad Indian—is intent on violating Colonel Munro's daughter Cora. It is just as clear that Cora and the good Indian Uncas are attracted to each other. Rather than transgress the sacred color line, Cooper has both Indians die without possessing their beloved. (Hawkeye will not even allow the Indian mourners the consolation of imagining Cora and Uncas joined in the hereafter.) The crowning irony is that Cora also must be killed off to prevent her from mating with a white man (which is no immediate threat, because the matinee idol Duncan Heyward prefers her blonde sister, Alice). This is not because Cora is a Good Good Girl whose maidenhead must be preserved at all costs, but because she is the product of her father's liaison with a light-skinned Negress. Insofar as she is white, she cannot have an Indian lover; insofar as she is black, she cannot have a white husband. Thus, in what is ostensibly an historical romance, or only a boy's adventure book, Cooper gives narrative embodiment to what would become our culture's subconscious preoccupation with race and sex.

II

Having established some of the ways in which Brown and Cooper adapted European literary models to American circumstances, Fiedler devotes the second half of *Love and Death in the American Novel* to the later adaptations that have given our classic literature a tradition of its own, different from but continuous with that of our mother country. One such adaptation was Nathaniel Hawthorne's transformation of the Richardsonian tale of seduction into a series of Gothic romances, which depict adult heterosexual passion more forthrightly than any other American fictions prior to Henry James.

In Richardson's fable, chastity and suffering were united in the single figure of Clarissa. (It was the very preservation of her chastity that caused Clarissa's righteous suffering.) In Hawthorne's *The Blithedale Romance* and *The Marble Faun*—and numerous other American narratives—the Clarissa prototype has been divided. The virgin is represented as an ethereal blonde-haired snowmaiden—Priscilla in *The Blithedale Romance* and Hilda in *The Marble Faun*—while the suffering female—Zenobia in *The Blithedale Romance* and Miriam in *The Marble Faun*—is a dark-haired lady of passion and sensuality. (Hardly original with Hawthorne, this polarity appears in Cooper's *The Last of the Mohicans* in the characters of Alice and Cora Munro.)[10] Although he is too much a child of the Puritans ever to show the dark lady triumphant, Hawthorne generally made her a more interesting figure than her pale opposite. Like Milton, he was secretly of the Devil's party.

The one Hawthorne novel from which the snowmaiden is completely absent is *The Scarlet Letter*. Here, the sensuous and suffering dark lady exists without a virgin foil. However, Hawthorne stops short of suggesting that feeling is itself redemptive. (Dimmesdale is saved by the confession that brings his death, and Hester is consigned to the role of Protestant nun.) The novel seems to be less concerned with passion as such than with its moral ramifications. The fall of Hawthorne's characters is postulated rather than enacted. Fiedler notes that "Hawthorne is the only American novelist of classic stature who deals centrally in his most important works with the seduction theme; yet there is no seduction scene . . . in any of his works!" (224–25).

After Hawthorne the seduction tale was relegated to popular literature for several decades, only to be revived for "serious" fiction by Stephen Crane and Theodore Dreiser in the guise of naturalism. In his discussion of *Sister Carrie*, Fiedler demonstrates that Dreiser was more a sentimentalist than the libertine he was accused of being. Although he does not kill Carrie off (as Crane had done with Maggie), he shows her come to an ambiguous end and Hurstwood fatally punished for his transgressions. Dreiser shared the bourgeois notion that the loss of virginity was the worst fate that could befall a girl; however, the censors were more concerned with the fact that Dreiser dealt with illicit sex

---

10. This dichotomy has almost become a cliché in popular culture. Consider, for example, the characters played by Grace Kelly and Katy Jurado in the film *High Noon*.

than with the attitude he took toward it. In reality, Dreiser's gingerly treatment of passion is considerably less subversive than his indictment of American society: "What makes *An American Tragedy* particularly American is the fact that Clarissa falls prey not to Lovelace but to Horatio Alger!" (254).

After a discussion of the Good Good Girl and the Good Bad Boy (which is largely, though not exclusively, a recycling of "The Eye of Innocence"), Fiedler devotes a chapter to the treatment of women in American fiction. Perhaps because the books he considers were all written by men, this chapter is titled "The Revenge on Women: From Lucy to Lolita." The point he makes here is that one of the corollaries of the innocent homoeroticism of the American novel is a seeming inability to deal with women as fully developed, three-dimensional characters. (The polarization of women into snowmaidens and dark ladies is one symptom of this problem.) Although Henry James is frequently cited as a notable exception to this misogynist tradition, his novels are also filled with sexual stereotypes.

Fiedler argues that the conventional dichotomy between virginal and worldly women—complete with appropriate color scheme—is a staple of James's best novels. What James adds is the international slant, which identifies the snowmaiden as an innocent American and the dark lady as a worldly European (of course, Hawthorne had originated this distinction in *The Marble Faun*), "or more precisely, the American girl who has remained true to her essential Niceness and the American lady who has fallen to the level of European cynicism and moral improvisation" (305). The Jamesean nice girl seeks a European husband, not because she wants to escape the moral constraints of her homeland, but because she is eager to share them: "to naturalize her bridegroom to the American ethos, as Clarissa or Pamela had sought once to naturalize their lovers to the world of bourgeois values." Conversely, the "not-quite-nice American girl . . . seeks to yield herself up to Europe and its ways, as do Kate Croy or Charlotte [Temple] or Madame Merle. To Henry James the Fair Maiden, the Good Good Girl[,] is quite simply America itself—her whiteness the outward manifestation of our mysterious national immunity to guilt, which he feels as at once lovely, comic, and quite terrible" (305–6).

In the high literature of our own age, the pale virgin has all but disappeared, only to be replaced by her wicked alter ego—not the dark lady, but the coquette. The bitch goddess of the twentieth century masquerades as an innocent fair-haired child, but she is not above using her teasing sensuality for personal gain. Unlike the dark lady, she is motivated less by passion than by cold calculation. If James's fair maiden represented one image of America, the bitch goddess of F. Scott Fitzgerald symbolized a quite different one. Sharing the first name of James's Daisy Miller, Fitzgerald's Daisy Buchanan is actually "an odd inversion of Clarissa-Charlotte Temple-Maggie Verver; no longer the abused woman, who only by her suffering and death castrates her betrayer, but the abusing woman, symbol of an imperialist rather than a colonial America" (312–13).

In Fitzgerald's fictional world we have a mythically realized image of the female, but "little consummated genital love." ("In his insufferable early books," Fiedler writes, "the American institution of *coitus interruptus,* from bundling to necking a favorite national pastime, finds at last a laureate; and even in his more mature works, his women move from the kiss to the kill with only the barest suggestion of copulation between" [316].) With Hemingway, we have the opposite situation: he is very fond of depicting the sex act but has a difficult time conjuring up believable women as partners. Consequently, his sex scenes range from the brutal to the ludicrous. Although he is most at home in the wilderness men's club, Hemingway's particular version of machismo involves frequent sexual conquests. He simply cannot think of anything to do with the women once they have satisfied the male libido.

Like so many of his American predecessors, Hemingway employs the cliché of the dark lady and the fair; however, in his mythology, neither is a virgin. The dark lady, who is usually Indian or Latin, is a kind of mindless, subservient geisha girl descended from Melville's Fayaway (the exotic Polynesian playmate of Tommo, the author's alter ego in *Typee.*) These women are essentially "painless devices for extracting seed without human engagement." Conversely, the Anglo-Saxon woman (whether she is literally blonde or not) is invariably the bitch goddess, who uses her allure to assert power over, and thus symbolically castrate, the men in her life. Neither female prototype is much more than a projection of the masculine subconscious. The Anglo-Saxon coquette represents the fear of (or masculine desire for) emasculation; while "through the Dark anti-virgin . . . a new lover enters into a blameless communion with the other uncommitted males who have possessed her and departed, as well as with those yet to come. It is a kind of homosexuality once removed, the appeal of the whorehouse (Eden of the world of men without women) embodied in a single figure" (318).

We find a more limited variation on American misogyny in the writings of William Faulkner. With seemingly nothing good to say about white women of childbearing age, Faulkner mythologizes (some would say sentimentalizes) maternal black women, such as Dilsey in *The Sound and the Fury* and Aunt Mollie in *Go Down, Moses*—a book dedicated to his own family servant Mammy Caroline Barr. These women, even more than Faulkner's flawed males, represent a moral norm in his fictional universe. In Yoknapatawpha County, the dark lady is not an exotic seed extractor but a surrogate mother.

Elsewhere in American literature, not even motherhood is sacrosanct. (In a literary tradition where the bitch goddess can impersonate the Good Good Girl, it is perhaps best to regard *all* women as suspect.) From Mary Glendinning in Melville's *Pierre* to Mrs. Ellis Burden in Warren's *All the King's Men* (and one might as well add Sophie Portnoy in Roth's *Portnoy's Complaint*), certain mothers have, through their excessive solicitude, assumed the role of castrating bitch. Literary matricide makes the revenge on women complete.

With women—or more specifically, matriarchy—identified as the enemy, the only satisfactory human relationship left is between males. Fiedler begins his support for this thesis with a discussion of Rip Van Winkle's flight from petticoat government and then moves through a whole pantheon of latter-day Rips—from Hemingway and Faulkner to Dagwood and Jiggs. It is within this context that Fiedler expands on the more limited theme of interracial homoeroticism. Although *Huckleberry Finn* had supplied the title for his earlier essay on this topic, Fiedler finds male bonding to be a much more explicit theme in *Moby-Dick*. According to this reading, the love story of Ishmael and Queequeg serves as a foil to the Faustian tragedy of Captain Ahab. Only Melville's great mythopoeic powers redeem the former story from sentimentality and the latter one from melodrama.

Having expatiated on eros, Fiedler returns his attention to thanatos in a chapter that begins with a discussion of Poe's contributions to American Gothicism. (Actually, as the poet laureate of necrophilia, Poe manages to unite eros and thanatos into a single myth.) Fiedler concludes that Poe's Gothicism is limited by his failure to deal with the ultimate source of blackness in American literature—the Negro. As more successful counterexamples, he cites the Melville of *Benito Cereno* and the Twain of *Pudd'nhead Wilson*. (Although *Huck Finn* is interracial, Nigger Jim is closer to being an Indian in blackface than a southern Negro.) To Fiedler's mind, Poe's greatest accomplishment in the realm of myth was to create the image of the *poete maudit* in his own likeness.

One of the more fascinating and controversial arguments that Fiedler makes in *Love and Death* is that the Faust figure has maintained a continuing presence in the American novel. Certainly, Melville's Captain Ahab and Faulkner's Thomas Sutpen—with Flem Snopes as his farcical counterpart—would seem to fit this prototype; however, others whom Fiedler cites are more problematical candidates. Only if we expand our notion of the Faust myth to include everyone who is of the Devil's party (or, in purely secular terms, everyone who has flouted society's concept of right and wrong) can we fit Hester Prynne and Huck Finn onto this Procrustean bed.

Of the major characters in *The Scarlet Letter*, Chillingworth most resembles the mad scientist who sells his soul to the Devil. Yet, in terms of his role in Hawthorne's novel, he is *already* damned, perhaps even the Devil himself. Dimmesdale does experience a fall, though it occurred before the novel begins. Like Faustus, Dimmesdale is plagued by excessive pride; but, unlike the diabolic doctor, he repents and chooses salvation in the end. Although Hester remains unrepentant, and even tells Pearl that the scarlet letter is the Devil's mark on her, she—like Dimmesdale—has fallen for passion rather than for knowledge. Hester may believe herself damned for her sin, but Hawthorne does everything he can to convince the reader otherwise. The true guilt of Hester and Dimmesdale lies not in their fornication (Chillingworth's obvious impotence renders them technically innocent of the more serious charge of adultery), but in their prolonged separation from each other. (This, if anything, is what constitutes their mutual violation of "the sanctity of a human heart.") By the end of the novel both characters have repented of this transgression, and both are "saved." At worst, Hester is a Faust *manqué*.

The same is even more true of Huck Finn. He may be deadly earnest in his resolve to "go to Hell," but his Mephistopheles is nothing more sinister than his memory of Jim's loyalty and kindness. Also, like Hester and Dimmesdale, Huck "falls" for passion—or compassion—rather than knowledge. Finally, if Hawthorne was Puritan enough to think fornication a sin, Twain was not Confederate enough to think the same of freeing a slave. Unlike Hester and Dimmesdale, Huck has never done violence to the sanctity of a human heart. In order for the Faust myth to work, one must believe—or at least suspend disbelief—in both the reality and justice of the protagonist's damnation. The audience of *The Scarlet Letter* and *Huckleberry Finn* can believe in neither.

III

Because the first edition of *Love and Death in the American Novel* and *No! In Thunder* appeared in the same year, many readers were discovering Fiedler as both a myth critic and a scholar of American literature at about the same time. One thing that was immediately apparent was that his concept of myth did not aspire to the level of universality claimed by Joseph Campbell and Northrop Frye. Fiedler is quite content to talk about myths that exist in only one culture or perhaps only in one regional subculture. The concepts of archetype and signature suggest that when a universal pattern of experience becomes song or story, its individuating characteristics may differ radically from nation to nation and from era to era. Male bonding, for example, is an experience that has existed in many different places and at many different times; however, it has assumed a particular form and meaning in American life. This realization has led some purists to argue that Fiedler uses the terms *myth* and *archetype* too broadly when he is actually talking about communal dreams and fantasies. For a literary critic, however, it is perhaps best to err on the side of specificity. The more generic the myth one envisions, the less connection it has even to the imaginative life of a real people. Critics such as Campbell and Frye are really not dealing with myth at all, but with what W. K. Wimsatt has called "the myth of myth."[11]

At the opposite extreme from those detractors who find him insufficiently orthodox (which is to say universal) in his approach to myth are those who fault Fiedler for generalizing at all. It is far too easy to find important American novels and distinguished writers who do not conform to Fiedler's schematics.[12] But to renounce generalization is really to give up on the possibility of criticism. We would be left with a series of discrete reading experiences lacking any connection with each other. (I believe that it was this fatal flaw that kept the neo-Aristotelian approach to criticism from catching on outside of the University of Chicago.) No account of something as pluralistic as the American literary tradition can hope to be all-inclusive. Perhaps Fiedler's major strategic error is his tendency to sound too often as if he has found the key to all American mythologies. But that very brashness is part of his appeal. Whatever he may be, he is no mealymouthed temporizing scholar who cannot make an observation or render a judgment without hedging it in with a thousand qualifications.

There are several reasons why *Love and Death in the American Novel* has become a classic despite the bad press it has suffered. For one thing, Fiedler is that rare critic who combines a discerning literary intelligence with a broad knowledge of other fields. Psychological and sociological criticism of literature are often so deadly because the practitioner is writing primarily as a psychologist or sociologist (or, worse yet, an ideologue), who is simply *using* literature to support some extraliterary argument. Because Fiedler loves and understands literature, he can use these other fields without being dominated by them. It is one thing to be able to say that certain kinds of books have been produced and revered in America. It is far more difficult to say why. Fiedler gives us the model of someone who has asked that question and has come up with some plausible answers. By opening up American literary criticism to questions of race, gender, and sexuality, he has become a kind of sorcerer's apprentice— giving rise to much that is good and a lot that is bad in cultural criticism. Leslie Fiedler is one of the few critics of our time who has made a difference.

11. In "Northrop Frye," Wimsatt writes, "The Ur-Myth, the Quest Myth, with all its complications, its cycles, acts, scenes, characters, and special symbols, is not a historical fact. . . . [S]uch a monomyth cannot be shown ever to have evolved actually, either from or with ritual, anywhere in the world, or ever anywhere to have been entertained in whole or even in any considerable part. We are talking about the myth of myth" (97).

12. For example, Malcolm Cowley writes that these theories don't "work at all with a whole galaxy of novelists whom Fiedler dismisses as 'middlebrow': William Dean Howells, Edith Wharton, Willa Cather, Sinclair Lewis, James Gould Cozzens, or anyone else who tries to present normal Americans." See Cowley's "Exploring a World of Nightmares," 1.

CHAPTER TWELVE

East Toward Home

ON THE DAY THAT *Love and Death in the American Novel* was supposed to appear in 1960, its publisher (Criterion Books) went bankrupt. Although the book was in print, all the copies were locked in a warehouse. Fortunately, Criterion was bought out by Dell, and the book was belatedly distributed. At well over six hundred pages, the sheer bulk of the volume was intimidating. Over the next few years, that fact (not the outraged reviews) convinced Leslie that a revised edition was needed. He had seemingly thrown everything he knew about the American novel and its European antecedents between the covers of this book. A deeply personal volume (its use of first person scandalized many righteous scholars), it grew out of Leslie's years in Rome and Princeton, when his engagement with American literature seemed inseparably bound up with the crises of his personal life. Looking back on *Love and Death* with a measure of detachment, he admits that "I am sometimes annoyed at how hard it presses or how pleased it seems with its own insights" (*LD*, 7).

Although he resisted the temptation to change the language and tone of the book, Leslie began to prune, sacrificing digressive allusions for a more direct line of argument. By removing one or two sentences from paragraph after paragraph, he managed to slim the tome down by well over a hundred pages. In this effort, he was continuing the surgery performed on the first edition by his friend and editor Catherine Carver. (Without the revisions she suggested, the first edition probably would have been eight to nine hundred pages long.) Leslie had first met Katy Carver when she held an editorial position at *Partisan Review*. She had begun her career thinking herself a writer, only to discover that her greatest talent lay in sharpening and clarifying the prose of others. Throughout her career with various publishers, she continued to do freelance work for Leslie, Saul Bellow, and a few others in the circle of friends she called her "boys."[1]

---

1. Fiedler, interview with author, Nov. 5, 1998.

Beyond trimming the book, Leslie rearranged some of its contents. In the original edition, for example, a third section had consisted of extended discussions of *The Scarlet Letter, Moby-Dick,* and *Huckleberry Finn.* In the second edition (published in 1966), these discussions were worked back into the main body of the text. As Leslie explains in the preface to the second edition, "I have done this first of all because I believe that is where they best fit, but also because I have a hunch that some readers of the earlier edition never reached them at all—and they are of critical importance to the total meaning of my book" (7).

In revising *Love and Death in the American Novel,* Leslie implicitly conceded that it was not necessary for him to say everything he had to say in that one volume. Because American novels continued to be produced, *Love and Death* was, by definition, only part of an ongoing project. That project had begun with "Come Back to the Raft Ag'in, Huck Honey!" and had continued with every review or essay Leslie published about an American writer. By 1964, he found that he had enough to say about contemporary American literature to warrant a book that would extend (and to some extent modify) the arguments made in *Love and Death.* Suggesting an imminent apocalypse—or perhaps just a sea change in literary fashion—he called the book *Waiting for the End.*

Appropriately, the point of departure for this new book was the passing of the two most formidable American novelists of the twentieth century. To be sure, by the time Ernest Hemingway and William Faulkner died within a year of each other in the early 1960s, their best work was long behind them. (Fiedler writes, "In a sense, each received the Nobel Prize posthumously, though both lived long enough to accept it with thanks."[2]) Each man had dissipated his talent to the point that physical death was somehow anticlimactic. Nevertheless, the final reality of that physical death forced us to ponder all that the "old men" had meant to us. In approaching this topic, Fiedler suggests that the badness of the later Hemingway and Faulkner is ironically a key to what was always most essential about these writers.

If they ended their careers by parodying themselves, it was because their styles were never far from something like parody. At their best, both men were capable of savage irony—Faulkner in his depiction of the Snopes family, Hemingway in his Sherwood Anderson travesty *The Torrents of Spring* (a novel that most critics do not esteem as highly as Fiedler does). "We should not, then, be surprised that, having exhausted the worlds they began by caricaturing (and having succeeded in those very worlds at the same time), the two comic geniuses of our century ended by caricaturing themselves" (10).

---

2. Leslie Fiedler, *Waiting for the End,* 9. Subsequent references will be cited parenthetically in the text as *WE.*

Fiedler finds it more than a little ironic that Faulkner should have died just before the region that he immortalized in fiction became the center of national controversy. The reference here is not just to the general struggle for civil rights in the South but to the specific confrontation in Faulkner's hometown of Oxford, Mississippi, "where, just after his death, Federal troops were deployed to insure the registration of a single, indifferent Negro student in a less-than-mediocre university. It is as if history itself were subscribing to Faulkner's view of the South—his notion of a baffled aspiration to the tragic, nurtured by dreams and memories, falling away always, in fact, into melodrama or farce" (11). The town that considered Faulkner something of a civic embarrassment during most of his life has not hesitated to capitalize on his memory in the years since his death. For many Americans, the South that Faulkner hated passionately enough to understand, and hence redeem in the alchemy of his art, belongs forever to the town drunk of Oxford, Mississippi.

If Faulkner is an example of the success of failure (he was not widely known at the time he was doing his best writing, and all of his books were out of print by the end of World War II), then Hemingway is more nearly a case of the failure of success. He was, in Fiedler's opinion, both liked and disliked for the wrong reasons: "[H]is truest strengths presented themselves all along in the guise of weaknesses, his most disabling weaknesses in the guise of strengths" (12). Fiedler regards Hemingway's macho posturing as meretricious and diversionary because his real value was as a poet of terror. (In an earlier essay, Fiedler had expressed his impatience with "those young writers from Rome or Palermo or Milan who write in translated Hemingwayese about hunting and *grappa* and getting laid—but who have no sense of the nighttime religious anguish which makes Hemingway a more Catholic writer than most modern Italians" [*CE,* 2:345].) The true Hemingway is not so much a bull as a steer, and so it is only fitting that the protagonist of his greatest novel, *The Sun Also Rises,* be impotent.

Hemingway's downfall began when the swagger and bravado that had originally been his defense against the abyss became the standard by which he measured his life and art. By abandoning "the role of the anti-hero, the despised Steer, in whose weakness lay his true strength, Hemingway became first a fiction of his own contriving, then the creature of articles in newspapers and magazines, as unreal as a movie star or a fashion model. And it was the unreal Hemingway who wrote the later books, creating a series of heroes no more real than himself: men who sought rather than fled unreal wars, and who, in the arms of unreal women, achieved unreal delights" (*WE,* 15). Fiedler suspects that Hemingway's defense became his reality, simply because it is too difficult to sustain the mood of Ecclesiastes, the experience of the void. If a dark night of the soul follows the saint's vision of God, how much darker must the night be "when the initial vision is itself of nothingness" (15). When the pose could no longer be sustained—Hemingway's mind and body were both deteriorating at the end—his only alternative was to leave off vicarious dying for the real thing.

Although talented writers continued to publish traditional novels in the 1950s and '60s, they repeatedly disappointed our expectations. There was no breakthrough work to take the form in a new direction, as we had seen at the beginning of the modernist era. In various ways, our most experimental writers appeared to be declaring the death of the novel. As Fiedler notes, there are various ways to do that: "to mock it while seeming to emulate it, like Nabokov, or John Barth; to reify it into a collection of objects like Robbe-Grillet; or to *explode* it, like William Burroughs, to leave only twisted fragments of experience and the miasma of death" (170). Like Marshall McLuhan, Fiedler was convinced that the death of the novel was implicit in its birth. As a machine-made, mass-produced, mass-distributed commodity, it was the beginning of popular art. Thus, it was only a matter of time before technology would develop storytelling media that did not require print. When we speak of the death of the novel, we are talking about the end of the Gutenberg era, because the novel was "the last narrative art-form invented, or capable of being invented, for *literates*" (172).

I

At the same time he was singing a requiem for the novel, Fiedler was finding surprising vitality in what until recently had seemed the moribund genre of American poetry. Consequently, *Waiting for the End* concludes with some enthusiastic comments about those whom Fiedler considered to be the most promising American poets of the late 1950s and early '60s, along with appropriate homage to their most influential predecessors. At the time, two towering figures appeared to exemplify the divided state of American poetry: Ezra Pound and Robert Frost.

Long before he made his infamous radio broadcasts for Mussolini, Pound had committed a more fundamental treason against American culture. Although Americans have often looked favorably upon the enemies of democracy, Negroes, and Jews, they have been less tolerant of those who violate middle-class notions of artistic decorum. The fact that most Americans who knew Pound to be a traitor and a madman had never read *The Pisan Cantos* or any of the other flagrantly modernist poems written under Pound's influence (e.g., Eliot's *The Waste Land,* Crane's *The Bridge,* and Williams's *Paterson*) is quite irrelevant. Because we know in a very general way that modern poetry has come to consist of "fragmented, allusion-laden, imagistic portraits of an

atomized world" we implicitly judge Pound when we censure this development (185).

The poet whom twentieth-century America embraced just as passionately
as it repudiated Pound was Robert Frost. Despite his early expatriation in England and his contempt for bourgeois life, Frost was shrewd enough to write in
conventional verse forms about subjects that had been regarded as properly
poetic since the time of the romantics. Frost was loved by those "who hated
all other living poets . . . [precisely] because he seemed to them a reproach to
those others who made them feel inferior with their allusions to Provencal and
Chinese poetry, their subverted syntax and fractured logic, their unreasonable
war against the iambic, their preference for strange, Mediterranean lands and
big cities" (188).

Although Fiedler's growing sense of literary populism would seem to put
him more in Frost's camp than in Pound's, he praises both men for having
written "certain lines which no literate American, perhaps no educated man
anywhere, will willingly forget" (190). At the same time, he criticizes both
for having pursued their own legends so assiduously that they have alienated
themselves from certain people who will not read them and have just as egre-
giously endeared themselves to those who will read—or misread—them for
the wrong reasons.

To my mind, Fiedler's most valuable comments on American poetry come
in a chapter called "The Unbroken Tradition." Perhaps this discussion would
be more appropriately called "The Unbroken Traditions," because Fiedler
identifies four ongoing lines of development in American verse, beginning
in the nineteenth century. These four schools of poetry have followed the
respective examples of Longfellow, Poe, Whitman, and Emerson and can be
associated in a very general way with the four mythic regions of our country.

At first glance, the influence of the most popular American poet of the nineteenth century—Henry Wadsworth Longfellow—would seem to be limited
to his own era. At the time Fiedler was writing, no American poet of any
stature saw himself as an heir to the Longfellow tradition. (With the subsequent rise of neoformalism in American verse, such a generalization no longer
holds true.[3]) Nevertheless, that tradition has blended itself with a whole body
of popular poetry and song, which is "the nearest thing to a common culture we
possess" (197). Such Longfellow chestnuts as "The Children's Hour" and "The
Village Blacksmith" are as well known as "The Night before Christmas" and
the songs of Stephen Collins Foster. If highbrow modernists shunned the di-
dactic content and conventional prosody of Longfellow, it was with an awareness that they were defining themselves *against* the model that he provided.

3. See Dana Gioia, "Longfellow in the Aftermath of Modernism."

For the mass audience of his own day, however, Longfellow represented a genteel version of eastern "culture." He had studied at the best universities in Europe and was professionally engaged in elevating the tastes of the sons of America's ruling class as the first professor of modern literature at Harvard. Because his most popular poetry was so accessible, ordinary men and women could get in on the act. That the populace took to him more readily than they did to the histrionically egalitarian Whitman suggests that Americans are motivated less by class solidarity than by a desire for upward mobility. Along with the transparency of his verse, Longfellow's elitism assured his popularity. As the purveyor of what was taken to be a European standard of culture, he was our quintessential eastern poet.

Because he was both a Gothicist and a dandy, Edgar Allan Poe can be seen as the father of a significant tradition in southern culture (so much so that Allen Tate wrote an admiring essay called "Our Cousin, Mr. Poe"). Although his influence on highbrow American literature is considerably more extensive than that of Longfellow, Poe made it into the canon in a roundabout way. He has always been a favorite poet of children and young adolescents, but adult Americans have found him "at once too banal and too unique, too decadent and too revolutionary, too vulgar and too subtle, all of which is to say, too American, for us to bear except as reflected in the observing eye of Europe" (199). And it is through that eye that he has come back to us. Sophisticated modern poets such as Pound and Eliot, who would regard Poe as a crude versifier—the "jingle man," as Emerson called him—freely acknowledge the influence of Poe's French admirers Baudelaire and Mallarmé. What all of these poets share is an antirationalist symbolic imagination, which sometimes verges on surrealism. "It is not entirely fortuitous," Fiedler notes, " . . . that the only poet writing in English who succeeded in imitating Poe's rhythm and diction with real faithfulness is that composer of nonsense verse for children, Edward Lear" (193).

Our most self-consciously *American* poet was, of course, Walt Whitman. For Whitman, being an American meant severing one's cultural ties with Europe and finding poetic inspiration in the indigenous materials of our own country. (He considered the United States themselves to be the greatest poem.) Although he lived his entire life in the East, Whitman was mythologically a poet of the American West. Because the West is always coextensive with whatever might be the current frontier, it maintains a fixed archetypal significance even as its physical boundaries change. As a poetic personality, Whitman projected himself forward in both time and space. It was only through conquering time and space that one could achieve cosmic unity at a higher level of being. To find the passage not only to India, but to more than India, was ultimately the manifest destiny of the spirit. Whitman's truest descendants were not only those who emulated his style in life and art, but those who shared his passion for exploration—actual Westerners such as Carl Sandburg and Vachel Lindsay and spiritual pioneers such as Allen Ginsberg and his fellow Beats.

The final line of American verse that Fiedler identifies is the least obvious but most enduring and continuous of the four. Although it actually begins with Edward Taylor in the seventeenth century, Fiedler names it for Ralph Waldo Emerson, because "it is Emerson who brought it to full consciousness, at the very moment when the schools of Longfellow and Poe and Whitman were defining themselves for the first time" (210–11). This line runs from Emerson through Emily Dickinson to Edwin Arlington Robinson, Robert Frost, and the early Robert Lowell. (Because Taylor's verse was not discovered until the 1930s, it apparently represents a confluence rather than an influence.) Although Longfellow and Emerson were both New England Brahmins, Longfellow was identified more with cosmopolitan Boston and Emerson with provincial Concord. In other words, Emerson and company are not eastern but *northern* poets. Robert Frost implicitly acknowledged as much when he published a volume called *North of Boston.*

"For Emerson," Fiedler writes, "the poet is neither dandy nor domesticated paraclete; he is, rather, a lonely philosopher or magician; a rebel, perhaps, as much as Whitman's mythical poet, but one, in Frost's phrase, 'too lofty and original to rage'" (212). This line of poetry, particularly in the hands of Robinson and Frost, always scanned and frequently told a story. Moreover, it is about the only body of American verse that deals with nature as observed reality rather than as symbolic construct. (To some extent, this can be said of the poetry of the Agrarian South as well.) If the poetry of Whitman is based on a European myth of America and that of Longfellow and Poe on American myths of Europe, the Emersonian line is more authentically homegrown. Because it lacks the flamboyance of Whitman, the elegance of Poe, and the rhythmic didacticism of Longfellow, it is a tradition that critics have found difficult to pigeonhole. Although it could be argued that Fiedler himself pigeonholes with too much ease, making generalizations that are at once too broad and insufficiently inclusive, he does what all good critics do for the familiar—he reads it new.

II

In a favorable and discerning review of *Love and Death in the American Novel,* Benjamin DeMott noted that Leslie Fiedler, "though not yet called to any of the genuinely voluptuous chairs of American literature, has consolidated his position as the most controversial professor of literature in America since Irving Babbitt."[4] This description was fraught with irony. A scholar with Leslie's distinguished record of publication should have been in great demand in academia; however, the very qualities that made him a well-known critic caused timid English departments to shy away from him. Typically, if there was one person in a department enthusiastic about pursuing Leslie, there would be someone else just as adamantly against him. If only he had been "controversial" in a safely conventional way, all could have been forgiven. Instead, he made the mistake of ruffling feathers in too many opposing camps. The only university administrator who repeatedly tried to persuade him to leave Missoula was Tom Adamnowsky, who ran a program in American literature at the University of Toronto. But, Leslie declined to abandon Montana only to become a "landed immigrant" in Canada.

For all its provincialism, the Mountain West had come to be a familiar setting for Leslie and his family. The pay was lousy, but he could get academic leave any time he wanted to teach in Rome or Athens or Princeton. Also, there were a few authentic westerners who seemed intent on proving their independence and sophistication by supporting him. For example, in the midst of his battle with President McFarland, Leslie had received an invitation to visit the White family (owners of one of the largest ranches in the state) in Two Dot, Montana.

The owner of the ranch was a tough guy with a lot of money; he branded and castrated his own cattle and drove around his spread in a Cadillac because he said it was higher off the ground than most other cars and would miss the bumps in the field. (Although the younger generation of Whites were all Goldwater Republicans, the grandmother kept a picture of FDR on her bedroom wall.) The family, which sent its son to Princeton and its daughter to Wellesley, seemed for all the world to have stepped out of Fitzgerald's "A Diamond as Big as the Ritz." When Leslie spent the night at the ranch, he awoke in the morning to find a pile of *Partisan Review*s next to his bed.[5]

For the most part, however, Leslie's life in Missoula was becoming numbingly predictable. After the publicity surrounding his victory over McFarland, he was permanently cast in the role of a gadfly in Montana education. At the very time that Benjamin DeMott characterized his tone as "more appropriate to a half-starved young writer on 4th Street than a man making good money in Missoula," the state board was chopping two hundred dollars off his proposed seven hundred dollar pay raise. Leslie observed ruefully "how ignorant the big outside world was of our little inside one, and how abjectly I had allowed myself to be lost in its parochial concerns." He "had become, in fact the Montanans' Leslie Fiedler rather than my own, thus turning what had been at the

4. Benjamin DeMott, "The Negative American," 193.
5. Fiedler, interview with Jackson, Aug. 9, 1989.

start an escape from the prison of my old self into just another cell, though this time a mountain madhouse rather than an urban jail" (*BB,* 85). Then, in 1964, Albert Spaulding Cook, new chairman of the English department at the State University of New York at Buffalo, gave him a call.

Prior to the 1960s, public higher education in New York had scarcely seemed to exist. Certainly, the Empire State had nothing to compare to California's university system. When Nelson Rockefeller was elected governor, that situation began to change. Convinced that ordinary citizens, not just persons of wealth such as himself, deserved a first-rate university education, Rockefeller began establishing public campuses across the state. In several instances, this involved the state takeover of an existing college. What had been known for years as the University of Buffalo (or just UB) became the State University of New York at Buffalo. A private school of no distinction was being transformed with millions of tax dollars into a cosmopolitan university, unrecognizable to most of the local citizenry.

There was no conscious decision to make the English department the crown jewel of the new state university. That situation developed because Al Cook had not only a blank check but a vision of what an English department ought to be. When he was told that he could hire seven full professors, he knew exactly the sort of people he wanted. Whether they had Ph.D.s or other traditional scholarly credentials meant little to Cook. He believed that an English department should be staffed by writers. His definition was broad enough to include critics and literary intellectuals, as well as poets and novelists. These people were not just adornments who were called writers-in-residence and assigned courses in creative writing. They were the faculty. In Cook's judgment, anyone who could write a book could teach a book. Although he was himself a churchgoing Episcopalian of stern morality and conventional lifestyle, he tolerated the personal eccentricities often exhibited by productive writers. Tell Cook that a man was a drunkard, an atheist, and a sexual libertine, he would simply ask, "But what has he written?" The first of the seven full professors Cook hired was the Black Mountain poet Charles Olson. The second was Leslie Fiedler.

The big names Al Cook brought to campus helped him attract outstanding junior faculty during one of those rare periods in the profession when good entry-level jobs were plentiful. Bruce Jackson remembers meeting Al at a party during his own next-to-last year in graduate school at Harvard. "You're going to be looking for a job next year," Al said. "Call me and maybe we can work out something for you at Buffalo." When Jackson appeared skeptical about coming to a school that had not yet earned a first-class reputation, Al said, "We've hired Charles Olson, Leslie Fiedler, and John Logan. . . . Buffalo is more interesting than you think." After he finished his degree, Bruce received offers from Penn, UCLA, and MIT; then he got a call from Al Cook. "Have you taken a job yet?" he asked. When Bruce indicated he had not, Al said, "Since I talked to you we hired C. L. Barber, Lionel Abel, John Barth, and Robert Creeley."[6] At that point, Bruce knew that Buffalo was the most exciting place in the country for a young English professor to begin his career.

Leslie had been more difficult to convince that Buffalo was the place to be. For all its deficiencies, Montana had been a sort of home for over two decades. In particular, the Fiedler kids had established ties they were reluctant to break. Nevertheless, Al persuaded Leslie to come to Buffalo to teach summer school in 1964. Like most of his ventures away from Missoula, Leslie found this an intellectually stimulating experience. Bright students were the rule rather than the exception, and all sorts of interesting people seemed to pass through town. For example, Leroi Jones was there that summer. (Leslie could never bring himself to call his fellow Newark native Amiri Baraka.) In one conversation about *Moby-Dick,* Jones said, "Don't talk to me about that fuckin' whale. It was white!"

Admittedly, few such conversations could be had in Missoula. Nevertheless, at the end of the summer, Leslie was ready to head back west. "Give us more of a chance," Al Cook pleaded. "Teach here for a year. If you don't like it, then you can go back to Montana." When the year was up, Leslie knew that he had found a new home. Even though Montana State made a halfhearted effort to keep him, the true Montana opinion of his departure was probably "good riddance." Hearing the news of Leslie's move east, an old Indian fighter observed: "That goddam Fielder [*sic*]. I always knew he would run out on us some day" (*BB,* 88).

III

Although he had amassed a distinguished record of publication by the time he left for Buffalo, Leslie still considered himself a teacher who wrote rather than a writer who taught. (Over thirty-six years after his departure from Missoula, Leslie was one of sixteen professors featured in an article titled "Teachers Who Change Lives" on the university's official website.)[7] From the time he first stepped in front of a college classroom at the University of Wisconsin in 1939, he had tried to enlighten and entertain his students—or at least to allay their boredom. As a writer and public lecturer, he simply addressed an expanded audience of students—the reading and listening public. In *What Was Literature?* he says, "[T]he teacher, that professional amateur, teaches not

6. Bruce Jackson, "Buffalo English: Literary Glory Days at UB," 9.

7. The testimonial to Leslie was written by Ruth Carrington (B.A. '51, M.A. '67). "Teachers Who Change Lives," *Montanan* 18, 2 (winter 2001) <www.umt.edu/comm/wol>.

so much his subject as himself. If he is a teacher of literature, he provides for those less experienced in song and story, including the reluctant, the skeptical, the uncooperative, the incompetent, a model of one in whom what seemed dead, mere print on the page, becomes living, a way of life—palpable fulfillment, a transport into the world of wonder" (114).

During his final years in Montana, Leslie began celebrating what he provocatively calls "academic irresponsibility." His point was to question the limited defense of academic freedom that is implied by the notion of a counterbalancing sense of responsibility. In practical terms, this meant that only certain kinds of speech and thought would be tolerated. Even during the McCarthy era, very few tenured professors were persecuted for strictly political views; however, unconventional personal behavior almost always got academics into trouble.

Leslie dissents from this tepid compromise, with its ever-shifting standards of permissibility, by arguing that freedom of thought and expression, if it is to have any meaning, must be absolute. The only "responsibility" that such freedom entails is the willingness to defend the intellectual cogency of one's position and to remain open to new evidence and differing points of view. This is far from a libertine position because it imposes on the professor the full burden of his freedom. "Above all," Leslie writes, "when his ideas are proved wrong, to his own satisfaction, in the debate with those who challenge him, he must feel free to confess his error without in any way diminishing his right to have held those ideas; for he has never had any real freedom at all unless he has been free from the start to be wrong and unless he remains free to the end to change his mind" (*CE*, 2:378).

Defenders of the counterculture and partisans of the political Left had little trouble endorsing Leslie's position when the enemies of freedom came from the conservative tradition they instinctively distrusted. (To protest Harvard's firing of Timothy Leary from its psychology department for his championing of LSD and marijuana was an exercise of righteous liberal indignation.) But they often failed to show equal vigor in defending victims on the other end of the political spectrum. To Leslie's mind the most conspicuous failure of liberal professors "has been their refusal to protect the dissident right-wingers among them from antilibertarians on our side." Without naming names, he cites the difficulties his old acquaintance Willmoore Kendall experienced at Yale. "Surely one of the most scandalous events of recent academic history," he writes, "has been the quiet dismissal of a distinguished rightist teacher of political science from an equally distinguished Ivy League college, whose own silence was bought by buying up his contract and whose colleagues' silence apparently did not have to be bought at all" (372).

The man who had once advocated a "liberalism of responsibility" and had decried the pervasive adolescence and immaturity in American literature was now taking a cautious second look at the counterculture. If his disdain for the writings of Jack Kerouac did not blind him to genuine literary talent among the alienated young, his perception of that talent was sometimes largely intuitive. Back when he was still living in Missoula, Leslie had served on the committee that dispensed Woodrow Wilson fellowships to students in the Northwest. Typically, if the committee had twenty scholarships to give, eighteen went to students from fashionable Reed College, who had shaved their beards, cut their hair, and put on coats and ties for the occasion. One year, Leslie was impressed by a rough-hewn young applicant who looked like a wrestler and who struck him as more genuine than the young con artists he was accustomed to. It took all Leslie's powers of argumentation to persuade his colleagues to award a fellowship to this young man. Because he was successful, Ken Kesey entered the graduate program at Stanford University and wrote *One Flew over the Cuckoo's Nest*.

In the late 1960s, Leslie's role as an educational reformer took him to Paris, where he and the French critic Hélène Cixous helped to plan an experimental branch of the University of Paris. (Leslie stayed at her apartment, and when her maid saw him—in his robe, with his beard and flowing white hair—get up to go to the bathroom in the middle of the night, she swore that she had seen either Saint Joseph or God himself.)[8] This new school was designed to open up the canon by teaching American literature of both the elite and popular variety, while deliberately courting the sort of difficult students who were not being well served by the more traditional academy. Unfortunately, the time for this revolution had come and gone. The program never got off the ground. Even the plumbing in the new buildings did not work properly, and poststructuralist criticism had replaced American studies as the new rage in France.

The critical theorists who now dominated the French academy actually made the old establishment in America look good to Leslie. This newer crowd seemed more interested in their own jargon and attenuated arguments than they did in the joys of song and story. Fractious faculty meetings would end with each side screaming "Ideologue!" at the other. (As far as Leslie could see, the accusation did indeed fit both sides.) They joined ranks only when some outsider questioned their control of literary study. Not long after Leslie had made some disparaging comments about the theorists, he got a call at his residence. The anonymous caller said, "We know you have been late for class twice this week." Perhaps out of embarrassment, one old-line French scholar took Leslie aside and told him that there were no real Frenchmen in this new wave of critics—"only Jews or faggots or both."

8. Fiedler, interview with author, Feb. 25, 1999. Except where otherwise indicated, the information in this section of the chapter comes from this interview.

Of this crew, the "faggot" for whom Leslie felt the most admiration was Michel Foucault. He spoke in a genuine language, not some arcane code, and he seemed to be a real human being—a *mensch* in Yiddish terminology. When Foucault gave his inaugural lecture in Paris, the auditorium was filled with several hundred people come to witness an historic occasion. What seemed new to the French, however, had already been exported to some of the more adventurous universities in America. Leslie sat in the third row that night, listening to ideas he had heard Foucault advance the previous year in Buffalo.

IV

Over three decades later, survivors of the late 1960s and early '70s remember the Buffalo English department as a magical place, where nearly anything could happen. When Bruce Jackson arrived in September 1967, he recalls seeing a thin man sitting "quite still at a grey metal desk, staring down at a lined yellow pad." When Bruce asked him where the main office was, the man exploded. " 'I'm not here to answer questions!' he screamed. 'Why do all you people ask me questions? Why don't you all just leave me alone?' He slammed the door shut with his foot." When Bruce found someone who was willing to give him directions, he learned that the thin screaming man was John Wieners, a poet who was not even an official member of the department. "What's he doing here? In a faculty office," Bruce asked. "Writing poems, I guess," his guide replied.[9]

In those days, the Buffalo English faculty was housed in two long sheds (known, for no apparent reason, as Annex A and Annex B) on a campus just off Main Street. (With the exception of the medical school, the university has since moved to a more remote location in suburban Amherst.) These were spartan, crowded accommodations (little better than quonset huts). But it was also a place where highly creative people were constantly arriving on the scene. Some would remain to become fixtures in the department, while others were only passing through.

One of the early casualties was the first full professor Al Cook hired. At six feet, six inches, Charles Olson was an imposing physical specimen (Leslie would get a crick in his neck just looking at him); however, by the mid-1960s, this literary pioneer had become little more than a name whose best work was behind him. Although he abhorred regular hours and the other demands of a steady job, the salary Cook was offering him ($15,000 a year) was too good for a financially impaired poet to turn down. Also, Olson was given the sort

9. Jackson, "Buffalo English," 10.

of flexibility and indulgence he would have found in no other department. In deference to his sleeping habits, Cook allowed Olson to convene his two classes once a week in the late afternoon.

If some of Olson's students became ardent disciples, others were treated in a manner that would prompt lawsuits today. One revealing class session is described by his biographer, Tom Clark:

> In the notorious first meeting of his fall 1963 Modern Poetry seminar, Olson started class by having students identify themselves. When it came the turn of one rather small and delicate-seeming young woman, the new distinguished professor interrupted, "I once knew a woman who looked like you: one brown eye, one blue." He then casually added, as an aside to the men in the class, "The only thing you can do with a woman like that is fuck her." The young woman rose to her feet, replied flatly, "You couldn't," and stalked out.[10]

Olson deteriorated quickly after his wife died in a car crash in March of 1964. He began living in the University Manor Motel, just across the street from the campus, where he would hold office hours in various states of undress. By the winter of 1965, he was such a physical and mental wreck that a colleague, Jack Clarke, had to take over his classes in midsemester. Although Al Cook left the door open by emphasizing that Olson was on sick leave, he never returned to Buffalo and died in 1970.

Other appointments proved equally problematic. John Logan was an accomplished poet, author of such highly respected books as *Cycle for Mother Cabrini* and *Ghosts of the Heart*. Unfortunately, he was also a hard-core alcoholic whose sexual misbehavior created frequent scandals on the streets of Buffalo. (Leslie remembers the department getting calls from the police concerning Logan's sordid entanglements with local newsboys.) He would amaze his colleagues by showing up drunk at readings, only to deliver a flawless performance once he mounted the platform. Logan retired early and died relatively young.

Dorothy Van Ghent enjoyed an even briefer stay at Buffalo. A Communist poet from the 1930s and an expert on the nineteenth-century novel, she found it difficult to keep a job. She was on the verge of being fired from an assistant professorship at the City University of New York when Al Cook offered her a position as tenured full professor at Buffalo. Because she was rarely sober after noon, she was given morning classes. For one phenomenal year, Dorothy turned out to be a brilliant teacher, although she irritated Leslie by calling him at three in the morning when she couldn't sleep and by making passes

10. Tom Clark, *Charles Olson: The Allegory of a Poet's Life,* 306.

at all three of his sons. (She was in her fifties at the time and strongly attracted to adolescents of both genders.) In what would have been her second year at Buffalo, Dorothy Van Ghent took leave and traveled to Rome. She died there and, like Keats, was buried in the Protestant cemetery.

For all his flamboyance and iconoclasm, Leslie Fiedler was a force for stability in this volatile environment. He was able to compartmentalize his life to the point that play never seriously interfered with work. Also, over time, his colleagues began seeking his advice on academic matters, large and small. It was on Leslie's recommendation that the department gave Dwight Macdonald a visiting appointment. This proved a popular move at several different levels. Older faculty remembered Macdonald as one of the most important independent radicals of the 1930s and '40s. Students were more likely to be familiar with him for his leadership in the movement against the Vietnam War or his movie reviews in *Esquire*. (Leslie had used his influence with Alice McIntyre to get him that position.) The fact that Macdonald was never a proper academic scarcely seemed to matter in the bohemian atmosphere of the Buffalo English department. The only thing that disconcerted Leslie was Dwight's genteel anti-Semitism, which became most apparent when he was drinking—as he was most of the time.[11]

Three other acquaintances of Leslie's who ended up on the Buffalo faculty were Lionel Abel, Robert Creeley, and John Barth. Although Lionel had moved, with so many Jewish intellectuals, to the neoconservative Right, his basic personality was little changed from what it had been when he was a Trotskyite in Chicago back in the early 1940s. Bruce Jackson remembers him always chewing on thick red toothpicks called Stim-u-dents. As Bruce recalls, "A regular feature of nearly every [departmental] meeting was Leslie Fiedler waiting until the end of an argument by everyone else to say something eminently sensible, whereupon Lionel would say, his New York accent coming from way back in his palate and halfway up his nasal passage, 'Lessslee, that's the STOOPesdest thing I've ever hearrrrd.' His Stim-u-dent would wiggle up and down."[12] If nothing else, his salary at Buffalo enabled Lionel to buy a proper set of false teeth.

If Lionel Abel had been a friend of Leslie's youth, Bob Creeley had scarcely been an acquaintance when he and Leslie were both at Harvard. (Only years later did Leslie realize that one of the most highly respected poets of the 1960s had been the quiet undergraduate who sat in the back of F. O. Matthiessen's poetry class.) While the change in literary fashion from high modernism to more open verse had served Creeley well, later developments—such as the

11. Fiedler, interview with author, Feb. 26, 1999.
12. Jackson, "Buffalo English," 11.

rise of language poetry—would make his work seem less revolutionary with each passing year. Nevertheless, Creeley was always more interested in his art than in literary politics. (As Leslie has observed, he is one poet who doesn't wish every other poet dead.) One nostalgic evening, when Leslie, Creeley, and Allen Ginsberg were feeling the weight of their advancing years, all three men spontaneously remembered the opening line of Wyatt's famous lyric: "They flee from me, that sometime did me seek."

Leslie had met John Barth back in the 1950s when he was teaching at Princeton and Barth was on the faculty at Penn State. By the 1960s, Barth had become one of the most exciting experimental novelists in America. Although Al Cook was undoubtedly skeptical about postmodernist fiction, Barth fit the profile of people he recruited. Lacking a Ph.D., he had spent twelve years at Penn State without rising above the rank of associate professor. At Leslie's urging, Cook gave Barth a tenured full professorship and began using his name to recruit top-flight younger faculty and graduate students. As Barth noted years later, "more than any other single factor, it was Leslie's presence there that tipped my scales Buffaloward."[13]

Despite his fame, Jack Barth was a genial individual, who soon became one of Leslie's near neighbors and closest friends. Also, Leslie had done much over the years to promote an appreciation of Barth's work. In his review of Barth's first novel, *The Floating Opera* (1956), Leslie had accurately characterized it as an example of "provincial American existentialism," at a time when Barth himself was not certain what those terms meant. Sixteen years later, when Barth's novel *Chimera* (1972) was nominated for the National Book Award, Leslie was one of the five jurors making the selection. But he soon realized that the rest of the panel did not seem favorable to Barth. (Leslie even phoned him ahead of time to inform him that he didn't have a prayer.) Jack was therefore surprised when a divided jury decided to give him half the prize. When pressed for an explanation, Leslie cheerfully confided to his friend: "You had two for you and two against you, . . . and I drank the swing-vote under the table."[14]

Although Leslie and Creeley have remained at Buffalo, most of the other stars of the late 1960s and early '70s are now gone. Dwight Macdonald and Lionel Abel retired, and both have since died. Al Cook left for a position in comparative literature at Brown, while the distinguished Shakespearean C. L. Barber departed for the University of California, Santa Cruz. Both are now dead. Jack Barth returned to his native Maryland, where he now teaches writing seminars at Johns Hopkins. Other notable figures came and went— including a future poet laureate of the United States, Robert Haas, and South

13. John Barth, "The Accidental Mentor," 139.
14. Ibid., 141.

Africa's most impressive living novelist, J. M. Coetzee. Others simply seem to have disappeared. The last time Leslie saw John Wieners, he was standing in rags on a street corner in Manhattan, watching five hundred of the world's most famous people enter the Plaza Hotel to attend Truman Capote's masked ball.[15]

15. Fiedler, interview with author, Feb. 27, 1999.

CHAPTER THIRTEEN

True West

WHEN LESLIE visited Montana in 1969, he felt less a tourist from the East than a native returning home. Ironically, he had never known that feeling of belonging when he lived in Missoula. He was struck first by the surface familiarity. Little had changed in either the natural or man-made landscape. His observations in "Montana; or the End of Jean-Jacques Rousseau" seemed as disconcertingly true as they had when he made them twenty years earlier: "There were the same wooden faces under the broad-brimmed Stetsons and the bright colored headscarves bulging over half-concealed curlers" (*CE,* 2:338). The only innovation seemed to be the newly acquired fad among teenage boys to run coyotes down with their motorcycles.

A few of the old structures were gone: "a new bridge replacing an old one from which a friend once nearly jumped to her death; a new highway scarring the side of a hill where my two oldest boys at five or six or seven used to play among poisonous ticks for which we would search the hairline at the back of their necks just before bedtime" (338). What Leslie would have liked best "would have been a trip to the Buffalo Preserve at Moiese and a last encounter with the old albino bull, into whose unreadable blear eyes I used to look through the wire fence, feeling myself each time I returned a little more like that totem beast—a little shaggier, a little heavier, a little whiter" (339). But in the critic's absence, the beast had died.

The school hadn't changed much, although it was now called the University of Montana. Leslie found himself "looking up at the 'M' made of whitewashed stones on the side of Mount Sentinel, and wondering who had won the five dollar prize this year for suggesting 'the best new tradition'" (339). The house where he used to live was still owned by the Unitarian Fellowship. He was pleased to discover that they had faithfully retained the four-toed foot that he and his boys had painted on the fence as their family emblem. Whether it continued to bug the neighbors as it had in his own time would have to be a question for another day. Intent on finding the Missoula he most fondly remembered, he went around to the bars where he used to drink, only to discover two of them completely gone and a third transformed into a bohemian coffeehouse.

Although Leslie avoids the explicit cliché, the lesson underlying his experience is that you can't go home again. The scenarios played out in one's imagination never seem to conform to script in real life. He had seen himself entering the Maverick and finding Spider still behind the bar—"his flattened pug's face turning slowly from side to side as he kept an eye out for trouble; and his back to the pasted-up clipping on the mirror behind him, the article in which I had mentioned his saloon" (341). But Spider was not there to say "Hey, Professor" and buy him a bourbon and ditch. The Maverick was dark and empty, and one "could see nothing between the boards nailed over its broken front window" (341).

All that is left are memories: of Dorazi's, "where the Indians had felt free to come even when they were still being hassled in other bars"; of the Sunshine, "where—with a couple of electrified guitars and a mike—one indistinguishable cowboy group or other had so filled the place with sound that walking in cold sober felt like walking into a well" (340). With fondness, Leslie remembers staggering out of the doors of the Sunshine "one night, as blind drunk and happy as I have ever been in my life, my wife sagging on my arm, equally happy I hope (it was, I recall, a wedding anniversary); and there were a pair of cops waiting to greet us—and, in that lovely time before the fall of us all—to drive us home in jovial solicitude. 'Now take it easy Doc, you're gonna be all right in the morning'" (340–41).

I

Not long after this trip back to Missoula, Leslie observed, "[I]t is a Montana landscape I see when I close my eyes, its people I imagine understanding, or more often misunderstanding me. And in this sense, I have to think of myself as a Western writer."[1] It was in his second novel, *Back to China* (1965), that Leslie had first used the Montana setting in his fiction. Here, the contemporary Mountain West serves as time present, against which the memory of China immediately after World War II is juxtaposed. The novel's protagonist, a philosophy professor named Baro Finkelstone, has had himself sterilized in atonement for the bombing of Hiroshima and spends the next twenty years seeking to maintain his youth by doing dope with his male students and sleeping with his female ones.

1. See John Wakeman, ed. *World Authors 1950–1970* (New York: H. H. Wilson, 1975), 469.

Baro (perhaps a pun on "barren") is another one of those rootless Jews who have become fixtures in the contemporary American novel. Fiedler adds an exotic twist, however, by removing this character from a conventional urban environment. The only reminder Baro has of that environment is his left-wing Jewish colleague Hilbert Shapiro. Although the locals have these two confused to the point that they sometimes receive each other's hate mail, Shapiro is a priggish and self-righteous political activist, whereas Finkelstone is a hedonistic free spirit. In addition to being alienated from Jewish stereotypes, Baro doesn't seem to belong to any alternative culture. When he attends a worship service of the Native American Church, he finds not the ten lost tribes of Israel, but a peyote cult with overtones of fundamentalist Christianity.[2]

In one sense, Baro is an all-too-familiar figure in American life (and particularly American college life)—the postmenopausal hippie. The only difference is that his vasectomy has brought about an early change of life. Unable to procreate, he becomes a surrogate father to young bohemians whose ways he apes. Moreover, he is able to copulate at will without fear of the responsibilities of paternity. Before his operation, he had refrained from interracial sex, even to the point of fleeing an orgy between fifty soldiers and fifty geisha girls, but afterward he pulled a fat Oriental nurse into bed with him. It comes as little surprise that his main playmate in Montana is the Japanese widow of an Indian beatnik he had befriended. (The lad dies in a motorcycle wreck before the novel begins.) As a kind of pleasure and penance, Baro pumps his sterile seed into this girl while looking at two movie stills from *Hiroshima, Mon Amour* tacked to her bedroom door.

If Baro finds sexual ecstasy with a Japanese dark lady, it only stands to reason that he has known frustration with a WASP snowmaiden. In this case, it is his wife, Susanna, an upper-class Episcopalian, whom he has neglected to inform of his operation. Feeling guilty and unfulfilled because of her inability to conceive (there are references to an abortion she had years earlier), Susanna turns frigid and starts popping tranquilizers and guzzling half gallon bottles of sherry. One night, in a drunken stupor, she either seduces or is seduced by one of Baro's students. (Presumably, her husband was out either dropping acid or getting it on with some Oriental lovely.) Later that night, she and Baro have one of their infrequent comminglings of the flesh, and when she discovers she is pregnant, she thinks the child is his.

If there is something a bit naive about the effort of Faulkner's Ike McCaslin to achieve racial atonement through celibacy, Baro Finkelstone's halfway gesture is downright sophomoric. It is only fitting that this postmenopausal hippie

---

2. An earlier version of this episode was published in *Esquire* under the title "Bad Scene at Buffalo Jump." See *Nude Croquet,* 251–65.

should finally become a "father" through the action of one of his surrogate children. In a thematically apt, if somewhat contrived, ending, husband and wife become reconciled through this act of infidelity. Baro "remembered his grandfather having told him once that in Jewish law a child begotten by a rapist was considered the child of his mother's husband: a legitimate heir, a true son of Israel, a partaker in the covenant. And he thought, no longer troubled but amused, how among the orthodox, the impotent and sterile must have prayed for a *pogrom,* an assault on their women that would leave them fathers but not cuckolds."[3]

In many respects, *Back to China* is a moving and engrossing novel. Fiedler has drawn abundantly on his own experience in both China and Montana. (Even the book's typography suggests the difference between East and West: the Montana scenes are rendered in narrow blocks of print with wide right margins; the memories of China are set in more conventional format.) The physician who performs Finkelstone's vasectomy, Dr. Hiroshige, is a composite of the man who had been framed as a war criminal in Tientsin and the professor who had organized a party for Leslie and "fifty of his closest friends." No doubt, the students, colleagues, and Indians with whom Baro associates in later life are based on either real people or character types Leslie encountered in Missoula. It would be wrong, however, to see Baro as his creator's alter ego. Whatever Leslie may have thought about Hiroshima, he always took seriously the biblical injunction to be fruitful and multiply. Also, accusations to the contrary notwithstanding, he was never the drug-taking, student-screwing professor that Baro becomes. Even if Baro is meant to be a somewhat sympathetic protagonist, he is also a deeply flawed individual.

The problem with Baro as a fictional character is that the motivation for his two most important acts in the novel—his sterilization and his later acceptance of Susanna's pregnancy—seem ambiguous and arbitrary. His most emotionally wrenching experience in China was the arrest of Dr. Hiroshige, but it came *after* his surgery. The effect of Hiroshima on his conscience and consciousness is postulated but never convincingly rendered. One who has witnessed the gruesome scenes depicted in John Hersey's *Hiroshima* might want to do penance; however, Fiedler spares us an up close glimpse of the horror. Unlike Ike McCaslin, Baro just doesn't seem the type to make great symbolic sacrifices. One could imagine him going under the knife for the satyric purposes the operation eventually serves but not for the misguided idealism that the novel seems to insist upon.

Baro's newfound affection for his wife is also hard to fathom. Her almost accidental tryst with one of his more obnoxious students can hardly make her

3. Leslie Fiedler, *Back to China,* 247.

more lovable, even if her conviction that the child is Baro's seems moderately endearing. We cannot even be certain that Baro as surrogate father will settle down and be faithful to her. If his seemingly gallant acceptance of her and her child effects no change in his behavior, then that action becomes as pointless as his original sterilization. The only plausible explanation of Baro's character is to see him, even in his compulsive pursuit of pleasure, as essentially masochistic. "[H]e has a total of one clear goal in life," Guy Daniels writes, "to hate his cake and eat it."[4]

II

The central virtue of *Back to China,* which is its author's genuine feeling for the experience of deracination in the contemporary Mountain West, is also evident in his next major work of fiction—three novellas published in 1966 under the title *The Last Jew in America.* In this sequence of interrelated narratives—"The Last Jew in America," "The Last WASP in the World," and "The First Spade in the West"—Fiedler creates the mythical Lewis and Clark City, located somewhere between Montana and Idaho. The title narrative concerns itself with the abrasive friendship that unites three old men who were the first twentieth-century Jewish immigrants to settle in the town. Because Louie is dying in a Catholic hospital, Jacob attempts to persuade Max to help him organize a bedside Yom Kippur service, which will include the largely secularized Jewish males of the community.

His refusal to be assimilated into the prevailing WASP culture causes Jacob Moskowitz to think of himself as the last Jew in America. He still speaks with an accent and moves his hands when he talks, but his ethnicity is really a matter of degree. He had lost his religious faith many years before as a boy in Russia. (His most vivid childhood memory is of his mother's anguished reaction when she catches him deliberately breaking the Yom Kippur fast.) For many years, Jacob devoted himself to the terrestrial faith of Communism, but that too proved to be a g-d that failed. Now seventy, he maintains the cultural trappings of Judaism with the same defiance that had prompted him to repudiate its spiritual substance so many years before. The bedside ritual that he orchestrates turns into something of a farce when Louie becomes positively apoplectic upon realizing that there is a crucifix on the wall of his room. (He insists that his fellow worshippers wrap it in a towel from the bathroom.) And yet, the service is well attended, which suggests something about the residual solidarity of persons who have nothing in common other than their Jewishness, even if they are not quite sure what Jewishness is or means.

4. Guy Daniels, "The Sorrows of Baro Finkelstone," 27.

On the way out of the hospital, Jacob and Max—a successful businessman and a former Stalinist—debate the prospects of an afterlife. To show his disdain for such superstitions, Max sells his share of the hereafter to Jacob for a nickel. Realizing that Max's Catholic wife will insist that he repurchase his share of eternity, Jacob sits by the phone awaiting Max's call as the story closes. Although Jacob professes to know what Max will want and how he will respond to the request, the actual conversation is left for us to imagine. As we do so, the biblical analogue that springs to mind is that of Esau selling his birthright to his brother Jacob for a mess of pottage. Like the biblical Esau, Max is a practical man who undervalues spiritual things. It is significant that Jacob Moskowitz was himself referred to as "Esau" when his enraged mother caught him breaking the Yom Kippur fast. Perhaps Fiedler sees almost all contemporary Jewish Americans—even those named Jacob—as Esau figures, bereft of their birthright and condemned to a nomadic existence.

Like "Nude Croquet," "The Last Jew in America" suggests that the novella is the form in which Fiedler works best. (The two companion pieces in the same volume tend to support that notion as well.) His imagination is so rich that, in the novel proper, he is tempted to go off in too many different directions. At the other extreme, his conventional short stories are often underdeveloped. In "The Last Jew in America," he is dealing with characters he knows well. (Jacob is quite obviously based on Joe Kramer, to whom the entire book is dedicated.) Fortunately, this includes a knowledge of their inner motivations, as well as their external mannerisms. The narrative also dramatizes some of the themes that have engaged Fiedler in his nonfiction writing.

In particular, Jacob's resistance to assimilation (what Fiedler has elsewhere referred to as the second Holocaust) seems a heroic but doomed struggle. The bedside service he organizes for Louie is only his most recent attempt to remind the aging Jews in Lewis and Clark City of the heritage they have abandoned. "But behind every Jewish male whom Jacob trapped, lurked the unseen presence, the threat of that man's wife, usually a gentile, so that their encounters smacked inevitably of a tryst, an indiscretion, an extra-marital affair without status or future; and each ended, therefore, in mutual recriminations and anger."[5] In contrast, members of the younger generation have not had a chance to forget their heritage—because they never knew it in the first place. One of the most poignant moments in the story occurs when Jacob discovers his young daughter coming down the street and prepares to embrace her. Upon seeing him, she abruptly leads her companions down a different path to avoid him. Contemplating this snub, Jacob tells himself:

5. Leslie Fiedler, *The Last Jew in America,* 15. Subsequent references will be cited parenthetically in the text.

He had only demanded of her: *Love me! Love me!,* as if he were a father like the fathers in her schoolbooks, like the father of Dick and Jane, who plays baseball with his kids, who owns a dog and drives a car. He had never thrown a baseball, he hated and feared dogs, and had never learned to drive, relying on [his wife] Leah. So what had he expected? What had he deserved? Yet when Catherine had failed to love him enough and had run around a corner to hide, he had only sulked, reproaching her with silence—he who found words for whatever he needed except in his own house. (31)

Thematically, "The Last WASP in the World" is in many respects the obverse of "The Last Jew in America." Whereas Jacob Moskowitz is an eastern Jew adrift in a WASP West, Vincent Hazelbaker is a western WASP immersed in a Jewish East. A native of Lewis and Clark City, Vin has become a celebrated New York poet, whose wife, two main mistresses, and assorted groupies are all Jewish. The action of the story takes place on the day and night of the wedding of his goddaughter (who, according to her mother's insinuations, is his real daughter as well). The wedding reception is itself such a comedic tour de force that it almost makes the rest of the story—strong as it is—seem anticlimactic. As the rabbi who performed the ceremony asks to be excused, Vin can see him "struggling to bring his wristwatch up into view out of the surrounding tangle of elbows and arms and fists full of whisky glasses that had already begun to slop over onto the purple and gold and green of his prayer shawl. 'In just fifty-five minutes I must be on the plane for Alabama. Selma, you know.' At this evocation of the spirit of Civil Rights, his face lit up with a glow as it had not at the earlier mention of God" (56).

At the reception, Vin more than lives up to his reputation as a lush and a womanizer and ends the evening trying to persuade his three-woman harem to service him simultaneously. Maintaining a kind of self-protective female camaraderie, they decline and leave him to fantasize about golden Western shikses. In particular, Vin Hazelbaker remembers a recent poetry reading in Lewis and Clark City. After the literary festivities, he had been taken by a young professor to a beatnik coffeehouse on the site of the old Western bar where he had had his first sexual experience many years before. (The girl was a young Indian whore named the Princess, a kind of demythologized Sacajawea whom he remembers having done for him "what no one afterward would ever do for him worse."[6]) There, he is picked up by a female Jewish graduate student, who walks him back to his motel and stays for a quick tumble in bed. The girl

6. This is, of course, an ironic allusion to Hemingway's story "Fathers and Sons," in which the protagonist remembers his initiation into sex with an Indian girl ("she did first what no one has ever done better").

he really remembers from that evening, however, was a pale WASP student who praised his rather pedestrian poetry reading and who reminded him of the girl he sought everywhere—"a friend, a compatriot, a relative, among the alien heads of the darker, more vivid types who clustered to hear him. . . . He would never sleep with such girls, feeling himself in relation to them a father, a priest, a ministering angel in a dream" (107).

We have here again the dichotomy of snowmaiden and dark lady. The latter exists for sex, the former for worship. Having become satiated with sex, the romantic Vin still dreams of the pure, ethereal, unattainable western girl. For him this figure is epitomized by Ardith Eugenia Sparrow, the pale and fawning coed he had met in Lewis and Clark City. Early in the story we learn that Vin is distressed by a letter he has received from Miss Sparrow; however, Fiedler withholds the contents of that letter from us until the very end. It is then that we discover that the chaste WASP goddess has written, *"I want you to fuck me. I want to be screwed by you"* (118). Disillusioned and drunk, Vincent Hazelbaker lies in bed, a phone in his hand but no number to dial and a cry for help on his lips.

Although the West may simply be an alien environment in "The Last Jew in America" and an elusive dream in "The Last WASP in the World," it is the essential thematic landscape of "The First Spade in the West." If Fiedler is trying to say that the utopian West is quite literally nowhere, then it is appropriate that this most western of his fictions focus on that ultimately displaced person the American Negro. Fiedler's Ned York, who is descended from the black guide who accompanied Lewis and Clark, owns his own cocktail lounge in Lewis and Clark City and hopes to impress his children by being named Kiwanis Man of the Year. When he occasionally entertains his customers with a rendition of "When I Was a Cowboy," they think that it is a novelty; however, Ned realizes that the song belongs to no white artist but to the legendary black folksinger Leadbelly.

In terms of our basic racial stereotypes, any successful black businessman is a source of irony. (This was the premise behind the long-running television sitcom *The Jeffersons*.) In the course of Fiedler's narrative, we see Ned arguing politics with a liberal beatnik who is the leader of his house band, currying favor with the richest white woman in town, and ejecting a disreputable Indian slut from his bar. The latter character is what Vincent Hazelbaker's first love, the Princess, has become—what Fiedler has called elsewhere a sort of "anti-Pocahontas."[7]

After a night of hard drinking, which ends at Ned's bar, the aging matriarch of the town and her gigolo boyfriend—secretly her new husband—are

---

7. See Leslie Fiedler, *The Return of the Vanishing American,* 150–58. Subsequent references will be cited parenthetically in the text as *RVA*.

too drunk to drive back to their home in the mountains. Ned chauffeurs them home and is drafted into hauling the old crone's ashes, while her husband is passed out on the living room floor. The experience proves too much for the bride, who dies of a heart attack. Fortunately, the cuckold's homosexual paramour—Ned's bandleader—shows up and helps Ned dump the husband's nearly comatose body in the nuptial bed. The novella closes with the gaudy public funeral of Mrs. Elmira Gallagher, complete with "traditional" western honor guard. "There they were," Fiedler writes, "in full cowboy outfits, all four of them, because that was the way Elmira had wanted it: chaps and bandannas, high-heel boots and spurs, and a ten gallon hat on the chair right behind each of them, the works. . . . Standing there dressed like cowpokes [were] a beatnik from the East, a little sheeny with a shoe clerk's moustache, a big fat queer who'd struck it rich, and a spade" (190–91).

Lewis and Clark City exists on what Fiedler has called the "third frontier," where pop images of the West are not only exploited for profit but have become a kind of ersatz reality. Because the pop West is a product of invention, there is theoretically no reason why the four improbable members of Mrs. Gallagher's honor guard should not pose as cowboys. This closing scene is simply the most obvious and most elaborate of the many parodies to be found in "The First Spade in the West." In the bedroom tryst of Ned and Mrs. Gallagher, we have an hilarious inversion of *southern* obsessions. Instead of the black man raping the white woman, we have the white woman seducing the black man. There is even an echo of Thomas Dixon, Jr., in Elmira's telling Ned that, when she was a child, "they taught us girls to be scairt of negras like they was some kind of wild animal like a gorilla or something" (160). Then, we have the obvious reversal of gender roles when the old woman dies from a too strenuous sexual encounter with a younger man.

Curiously, the central western myth of interethnic male bonding is absent from this story. Mrs. Gallagher's widower and his boyfriend manage to escape from petticoat government along with the old woman's money; however, these two are of the same ethnic extraction, live in civilization, and serve as comic figures, not as moral norms. Moreover, Ned York is no Nigger Jim or Chingachgook, but an honorary white man who has sold out to the dream of bourgeois success. From a mythic standpoint, then, "The First Spade in the West" is most significant for what it fails to depict. It is not even a straightforwardly antimythic tale. Fiedler seems to be saying that the old myths are now so dead that even in satire they can be evoked only obliquely.

III

Toward the end of the 1960s, Fiedler noticed that the Indian, who was a more truly invisible part of our national life than Ralph Ellison's Negro, was beginning to appear with astonishing frequency in mainstream American literature. Among the writers he mentions are John Barth, Thomas Berger, Ken Kesey, David Markson, Peter Matthiessen, James Leo Herlihy, Leonard Cohen, and "the inspired script writers of *Cat Ballou*." These artists (and Fiedler himself in *The Last Jew in America*) have "been involved in a common venture: the creation of the New Western, a form which not so much redeems the Pop Western as exploits it with irreverence and pleasure, in contempt of the 'serious reader' and his expectations" (*Return,* 14). Fiedler explores this phenomenon in his third venture into literary anthropology, *The Return of the Vanishing American* (1968).

Early in this book, Fiedler asserts that "geography in the United States is mythological." Hence, much of our literature has "tended to define itself—topologically, as it were, in terms of the four cardinal directions: a mythicized North, South, East, and West" (16). This tendency toward literary regionalism was no doubt a function of the immensity of the North American continent. Unlike Europe, America is a big land with a short history. Consequently, it is possible to think of our fiction, like our poetry, as being northerns, southerns, easterns, and westerns.

The northern is exemplified by the novels of William Dean Howells (one thinks particularly of *The Landlord at Lion's Head*) as well as a little of Henry James—for example, *The Bostonians*—and, "supereminently, Edith Wharton's *Ethan Frome*" (17). This type of story "tends to be tight, gray, low-keyed, underplayed, avoiding melodrama where possible—sometimes, it would seem, at all costs. Typically, its scene is domestic, an isolated household set in a hostile environment. The landscape is mythicized New England, 'stern and rock-bound,' the weather deep winter: a milieu appropriate to the austerities and deprivations of Puritanism" (16). Such a world seems to come off less well in prose fiction than in the narrative poetry of Robert Frost, Edwin Arlington Robinson, and (more recently) Robert Lowell. (Fiedler might also have added John Greenleaf Whittier to the list.) Perhaps its supreme embodiment, however, is in Henry David Thoreau's extended prose poem *Walden*.

In contrast to the icy reserve of the northern, the southern is a blood-hot genre, which actively seeks melodrama. To Fiedler's mind, the southern is an indigenously American form of Gothic. The ruined mansions of Europe have simply been replaced by decaying plantation houses. (Because he wrote before the Civil War had laid waste to the plantations, Poe had to set his horrors in a "mythicized Europe.") Fiedler goes on to argue that "what the Church and feudal aristocracy were for European Gothic, the Negro became for the American variety" (18).[8]

---

8. One assumes that by this he means that the Negro is a source of evil in the southern mind. But surely that is true only of some Negroes in some southern novels. The good darky is, of course,

What makes the southern perhaps the most successful of our topological fictions is its ability to function equally well as highbrow literature (Edgar Allan Poe through William Faulkner to Truman Capote and Flannery O'Connor) and as mass entertainment (beginning again with Poe and running through those narratives that Fiedler would later dub specimens of the "inadvertent epic": Thomas Dixon Jr.'s *The Clansman,* re-created as D. W. Griffith's *The Birth of a Nation,* and Margaret Mitchell's *Gone with the Wind,* as both novel and movie). "The Southern has always challenged the distinction between High and Pop Art, since not merely Poe, its founder, but such latter-day successors of his as Faulkner and Capote [and, one might add, Tennessee Williams] have thrived in the two presumably sundered worlds of critical esteem and mass approval" (18).

Far from trying to bridge the gap between canonical and popular literature, the typical eastern tends to be self-consciously elitist. "Basic to [its] worship of High art," Fiedler writes, "was the dogma that there are some books, in fiction chiefly those of James, . . . an appreciation of which distinguishes the elect from the vulgar, the sensitive from the gross, and that those books can be known immediately because a) they are set in Europe, b) they mention other works of art, often so casually that only the cognoscenti know them without the aid of footnotes, and c) they are written by expatriates" (20–21). What is at work here is a reversal of the American Adam's movement west. By returning to the sophisticated, decadent, Old World environment of Europe, the American is able to appear more "innocent" than in his native habitat. It is thus as a tourist that the American is most identifiably American. In these days of cut-rate airfares, Daisy Miller has been replaced by the gawking suburbanite with loud shirt, louder children, and ubiquitous camera.

The regional subgenre that has held the greatest fascination for Fiedler (and probably for Americans in general) is the western. It embodies what is at once the most familiar and most elusive of the topological myths. To Europeans, the West was originally coextensive with the entire New World. (By discovering America, Columbus replaced their nightmare images of dragons and sea monsters lurking at the boundaries of a flat earth with the concept of the West.) With the settling of the New World, however, each region that had once been considered west in turn became east. Thus, the West that Columbus discovered finally becomes a mirage, one that ultimately leads us back to Asia. It is, in the words of Walt Whitman, a "passage to India." Both the oldest and newest of our mythic regions, the West is simultaneously everywhere and nowhere.

---

a staple of the plantation novel from Thomas Nelson Page to Margaret Mitchell. Also, as Fiedler himself would demonstrate in the second section of *What Was Literature?,* the bad nigger represented the threat of "rape from below," whereas the aristocrat in the traditional Gothic novel posed the spectre of "rape from above."

When Fiedler speaks of the American West, he is thinking of the region between the Mississippi River and the Rocky Mountains. "The heart of the Western is not the confrontation with the alien landscape (by itself this produces
only the Northern), but the encounter with the Indian, that utter stranger for
whom our New World is an Old Home" (21). Because of the radically strange
and alien nature of the Indian, he is the one element of the American experience that white Europeans have never been able to assimilate. Whether he is a
survivor of the Lost Continent of Atlantis, a remnant of the wandering tribes
of Israel, or some extraterrestrial being, he is the ultimate other. He may have
a soul, but—as D. H. Lawrence concluded—"*not* one precisely like our own,
except as our own have the potentiality of becoming like his" (22).

According to Fiedler's definition, the western refers neither to a region nor
a direction, but to our encounter with the savage other. "So long as a single
untamed Indian inhabits it," Fiedler writes, "any piece of American space can
become to the poet's imagination an authentic West" (26). Of course, the corol-
lary of this notion is that, once the Indian has disappeared as a mythic presence
in the American imagination, the Western will become a defunct genre (a fate
that already seems to have befallen the Northern and the Eastern).[9] And yet,
the western is so deeply embedded in our national subconscious that it refuses
to go gentle into that good night. It is constantly being resurrected from two directions: from the past in the form of historical fiction—even of the debunking
variety, such as Thomas Berger's *Little Big Man*—and from the future in the
form of science fiction tales, which are really cryptowesterns, "space operas"
instead of "horse operas."

IV

After America began to be settled, Fiedler argues, four myths arose that
collectively created our image of the Far West. These are "The Myth of Love in
the Woods," or the story of Pocahontas and Captain John Smith; "The Myth
of the White Woman with the Tomahawk," which is based on the experience of Hannah Duston, a New England woman who was captured by Indians and fought her way to freedom; "The Myth of the Good Companions in
the Woods," the Paleface/Redskin version of the Huck-Honey motif, derived
from the youthful friendship of fur trader Alexander Henry and the Indian

9. In the 1950s and 1960s, James Baldwin wrote fiction of expatriation; however, the racial emphasis of his narratives makes them less easterns than cosmopolitan southerns. Even more recently,
we see a pattern of European/American connections in the work of John Irving. The tradition of
the northern seems to have been domesticated out of existence, leaving us with only the commuter
fiction of Cheever and Updike.

Wawatam; and "The Myth of the Runaway Male," first imagined by Washington Irving in "Rip Van Winkle."

Beginning with the last of these myths, Fiedler duly acknowledges that the Rip Van Winkle prototype goes back many centuries in German legend but argues that a distinctively American element was added to the story in Irving's retelling. This is the battle of the sexes, a conflict that Fiedler contends is the American equivalent of the class struggle in European culture. Although Irving's story is set in New York, it is mythologically less a northern than a western. Rip's antagonist is not the climate or the land, but petticoat government. (It was Irving who invented that marvelously evocative term.) By fleeing from the hearth into the wilderness, Rip becomes the comic version of the womanless American hero. In effect, Irving has taken the Teutonic legend of the enchanted sleeper and, by adding a shrewish wife, turned it into "a comic inversion of the legend of the Persecuted Maiden—a corresponding male fantasy of persecution, appropriate to a country that likes to think of itself, or endures being thought of, as the first matriarchy of the modern world" (56).

But neither the escape from petticoat government nor the flight into the wilderness are themselves sufficient to make what Fiedler would consider a complete western. "What makes the Rip myth finally eccentric—and just a little irrelevant—is Irving's failure to dream for Rip appropriate good companions to whom he can flee" (59). It remains for Cooper to complete the western myth by providing Natty Bumppo such a companion in the form of Chingachgook. If one suspects that Fiedler is engaging in special pleading on behalf of the Huck-Honey motif, it is only necessary to consider the fate of the Rip story when it was transferred to the stage by Joseph Jefferson. In the melodramatic version of the tale, Rip returns not to a dead but a chastened wife. Instead of a profound depiction of the misogynist myth, we simply have *Pamela* with the sex roles reversed—the shrew is not defeated, only converted.

If "Rip Van Winkle" belongs to the literature of masculine protest, then Pocahontas—as she is re-created by Captain John Smith—seems more at home as goddess of the sentimental love religion. However, her willingness to sacrifice herself redeems not the alien lover, but her own father.[10] This is because the white sensibility that has created the story begins by defining the Indian as a savage in need of salvation. Thus, Pocahontas betrays her own people out of love for the paleface. In another part of the legend, she even slips away from camp to warn the white community of impending attack. (Although Fiedler does not make this point, it seems that the Pocahontas myth is roughly equivalent to one half the Romeo and Juliet story.) In our own time,

---

10. In the politically correct Disney version, Pocahontas converts a WASP John Smith to multiculturalism and ecological awareness.

the sentimental nature of her legend has become so distorted that Pocahontas herself has been transformed into a high camp icon of the mod Western.

Hannah Duston is an icon very different from Pocahontas. (With his flair for schematics, Fiedler sees her as a version of the anti-Pocahontas.) According to the story, she was captured by the Indians when her wimpish husband absconded with seven of their eight children, leaving her and an infant to fend for themselves. (The Indians, of course, bashed the infant's brains out against a tree, as Cooper would have his bad savages do in *The Last of the Mohicans.*) Not only did this intrepid lady eventually escape from her captors, but she took a bounty of scalps with her as well. If Pocahontas represents the possibility of interracial love, Hannah Duston embodies the reality of interracial strife.

In the American version of the Rip Van Winkle myth, we have seen a dominant wife and a passive husband; however, in the Hannah Duston story, the wife becomes a heroine rather than a comic butt. Fiedler describes the statue of Hannah Duston in Haverhill, Massachusetts, as "the stone figure of a longskirted, sunbonneted woman with a tomahawk raised aloft in her delicate hand—so like the standard Freudian dream of the castrating mother that it is hard to believe it has not been torn down long since by some maimed New England male just out of analysis" (91).

As we have noted, "The Myth of the Good Companions in the Woods" is a variation on the central thesis of "Come Back to the Raft Ag'in, Huck Honey!"; however, it acquires additional resonance by being juxtaposed to the other western myths. The friendship of paleface Alexander Henry and redskin Wawatam, originally chronicled in Henry's *Adventures* and preserved for high literature in Thoreau's *A Week on the Concord and Merrimack Rivers,* is obviously antithetical to the "Woman with the Tomahawk." Not only does Henry's experience give us an image of interracial love, but it is one that is achieved in the wilderness in flight from petticoat government. (In contrast, Mrs. Duston brings petticoat government *into* the wilderness.) Wawatam also differs from Pocahontas, in that his gender removes the threat of miscegenation and domesticity. His relationship with Henry makes the European into a quasi-Indian, whereas that of Pocahontas with John Smith makes the Indian into a quasi-European.

Although the bonding of Alexander Henry and Wawatam is the real-life paradigm for an enduring motif in American fiction, few writers since Cooper have actually made the colored antiwife an Indian. (Fiedler suspects that Cooper may have doomed the genre he helped create by portraying his Indians elegiacally, as the last of a dying breed.) What we have instead are crypto-Indians disguised as members of other races—Melville's Queequeg as a South Sea Islander, Twain's Jim as a runaway slave. (Twain's practice is explained by his hatred of real Indians.) Consequently, attempts to redeem the western for high literature have tended to be problematic. Fiedler demonstrates that

Poe's one venture in this genre—*The Journal of Julius Rodman*—is "a hopeless jumbling together of the Southern and the Western, to the detriment of both" (129), and that Walter Van Tilburg Clark's moving novel *The Oxbow Incident*—whose chief villain is an ex-Confederate general and most important colored man a Negro—is finally not a western "but an anti-Southern in a Western landscape, . . . an illustrated sermon *against* lynching" (142).

When the western once again became an acceptable genre in high literature, the tone had become irreverent and debunking. Fiedler sees the roots of the "New Western" in Hemingway's first published novel. A farce about Indian life masquerading as a parody of Sherwood Anderson, *The Torrents of Spring* exploits "the clichés and stereotypes of all the popular books which precede it, . . . bringing the full weight of their accumulated absurdities to bear in every casual quip" (147). The next notable attempt to make the western into self-conscious camp can be found in Nathanael West's satirical description of a drugstore cowboy and a Yiddish Indian in *The Day of the Locust*. For reasons that seem to baffle Fiedler, this inchoate genre did not reach fruition until 1960 when John Barth's *The Sot-Weed Factor*—a burlesque of the Pocahontas myth—gave rise to a whole spate of New Westerns, which produced neither a new myth nor an antimyth, but rather an antistereotype.

If there is an obvious weakness in *The Return of the Vanishing American,* it is in the brevity of Fiedler's discussion of specific New Western texts. His delineation of the various western myths is so fascinating and suggestive that one expects a full-scale application of those myths to the relevant literature (maybe not on the order of *Love and Death in the American Novel,* but certainly more than he gives us).[11] Also, there are Wests other than the one dreamed of by those in flight from the East. The place must also have a meaning for those families who have lived there for generations, for whom it is neither a failed paradise nor an alien landscape but, quite literally, home. (Joan Didion's first novel, *Run River* [1963], and much of her nonfiction writing about the Sacramento of her childhood reads more like southern literature—though not exactly the Fiedlerian "Southern"—than anything produced by the four western myths.) There is a considerable tradition of agrarian writing set in the American West—from Willa Cather to Edward Abbey and beyond—for which Fiedler's four myths are largely irrelevant.

Even if we take it on its own terms, the New Western that Fiedler writes and extols is not so much mythic as mythological—more signature than archetype.

---

11. Thomas Berger's *Little Big Man* is itself a treasure trove, which would reward detailed analysis. (The hint of fabulation in Jack Crabb's point of view—combining the ambiguity of Young Goodman Brown with the wish-fulfillment of Walter Mitty—along with the novel's pseudoscholarly narrative frame turns *Little Big Man* into a metahistorical tale.) Also, since Fiedler wrote *The Return of the Vanishing American,* such Native American writers as N. Scott Momaday, James Welch, and Louise Erdrich have come into their own.

Like Robert Penn Warren and Graham Greene, the writers of the New Western have responded to the loss of original archetypes by exploiting the formulas of popular culture for "serious" purposes. But the seriousness of their purpose is itself undercut by a kind of self-referentiality that makes the New Western actually postwestern, as well as postmodern. The stuff its dreams are made on consists not so much of nineteenth-century myths as twentieth-century images, manufactured for movies and television.[12] When the vanishing American returns, it is not as Chingachgook or even as Tonto, but as Chief Bromden, tossing a control panel through the asylum window in *One Flew over the Cuckoo's Nest* before returning to the privileged insanity of his tribe.

12. In reviewing *The Return of the Vanishing American,* Kenneth Rexroth writes, "Speculation based on the analysis of myth and symbolism can make anything out of anything. . . . I've camped with hundreds of Indians and slept peacefully in canyons swarming with wildcats. I am just a Westerner, and I can't recognize the Dark Savage Forces that haunt Leslie Fiedler." See Rexroth, "Ids and Animuses," 4, 47.

CHAPTER FOURTEEN

Innocence Reclaimed

WHEN LESLIE moved to Buffalo, he soon realized that he had made, at best, a partial return to the East. Buffalo was a former frontier town, still a couple hundred miles west of the Atlantic Ocean. But, like Newark, it was also an industrial, working-class city. His grandfather Rosenstrauch had lived there in 1904 (sixty years before Leslie's own arrival), and his mother had briefly attended the public schools, where German was taught as a second language. (At home, she had given names to the rats who shared their flat in one of the poorer sections of town.) Leslie also discovered that his father's brother lived in Buffalo and ran a cigar stand in the Erie Bank. (This branch of the family had become so completely assimilated that they did not even know they were Jews.) Leslie even had a cousin who was named Leslie Fiedler.

The WASP aristocracy, which had run Buffalo in the nineteenth century, had gradually lost numbers and power. By the time Leslie arrived, many of them had moved out to the suburbs, leaving control of the city to the Italians and the Poles and ownership of Buffalo's elegant old houses to new arrivals— managers of electric power plants, cancer researchers at Roswell Clinic, and— occasionally—college professors. Needing to shelter a family of six children, Leslie bought a large three-story house at 154 Morris Avenue, in a pleasant residential neighborhood just off Main Street. It had been built in 1904, the year Leon Rosenstrauch lived in Buffalo.

If Newark could boast of Stephen Crane and Philip Roth, Buffalo seemed devoid of a literary tradition. Scott Fitzgerald had lived there briefly as an infant when his father worked for Proctor and Gamble, but the city has no presence in his work. (At the end of *Tender Is the Night,* Dick Diver retreats to a series of ever smaller towns in upstate New York.) Of slightly greater significance is the fact that, in 1870, Sam Clemens spent the first year of his married life in Buffalo, where he owned part of the *Buffalo Express.* When he and his new wife, Olivia Langdon, arrived in Buffalo for their honeymoon,

Clemens was distressed by the opulence of the "boardinghouse" where they were to spend their wedding night. As he was trying to figure out how he would pay the rent, his wife informed him that the "boardinghouse" was actually their new home—a gift from her father, a wealthy coal merchant from Elmira, New York.

Despite this auspicious beginning, the Clemenses left Buffalo a year after their arrival. Sam did not like being a newspaperman and eventually sold his share of the *Express* at a $10,000 loss. (In his *Diaries of Adam and Eve,* he envisions Niagara Falls as paradise and one of the seediest suburbs of Buffalo as the region of exile.) More than a decade later, an official of the Erie County Public Library wrote the city's former resident to ask if he had a manuscript he would be willing to donate to their collection. He replied that he did, if the library would pay the postage. Upon opening the package from Clemens, the librarian was disappointed to find that the manuscript was not the best-selling *Innocents Abroad* but a newly completed book called *Adventures of Huckleberry Finn.*

The wealthy WASP residents of Erie County, who could afford Ivy League tuition, had never sent their children to the old University of Buffalo. Catholics of sufficient means and grades were more likely to attend a nearby church school, such as Niagara or Canisius. Thus, the student population of UB had been drawn largely from working-class Protestant and Jewish families. (The school was derisively referred to as Jew-B.) These kids were generally headed for careers as dentists, pharmacists, accountants, public school teachers, technicians, insurance agents, and real estate lawyers. Not only were they sober and career-oriented, they were also mostly drawn from the surrounding community. The comfortable mediocrity of the school made it a familiar and unthreatening part of local life. Its faculty had few intellectual pretensions, only a desire to join the country club and be invited to the cocktail parties of Buffalo's most prominent families.

The coming of the new university system drastically changed town/gown relations in Buffalo. More professors than ever could now afford to live in the fashionable neighborhoods of the city. Many of these professors were from elsewhere, and their unconventional habits did not always sit well with longtime residents of the old neighborhoods. (For example, it was something of a culture shock to see various Fiedler children meditating naked in their backyard.) But suburban life also had a way of domesticating the new arrivals. Leslie had made the transition from political activist and street corner speaker to highly paid professional. With a huge mortgage, a swimming pool, and the prospect of an endowed chair in the near future, he seemed to have made it. Then, one spring night in 1967, his new middle-class respectability came crashing down around him.

I

On May 19, 1967, *Time* magazine ran a story about the use of illegal drugs on the nation's campuses. Called "Potted Ivy," the story reads, in part: "At State University of New York at Buffalo, Critic-Novelist Leslie Fiedler, 50, was arrested in his home during a pot-and-hashish party, together with his wife, his 26-year-old son, the son's wife and two 17-year-old boys. Fiedler, who will be tried on drug charges next month declared that 'What's really involved is not a criminal proceeding but an attempt to limit my freedom of speech.'" As Norman Mailer would say, let us leave *Time* to find out what really happened.[1]

In 1967, Leslie and Margaret Fiedler had six children, ranging in age from twelve to twenty-six. Given the reality of American culture at that time, it was inevitable that these offspring would come in contact with marijuana, either as users or friends of users, or—more likely—as both. Like millions of other parents, the Fiedlers had to decide how to confront this situation. Leslie's own experience growing up made it highly unlikely that he would emulate his father's stance toward the longhaired men and—occasionally—shorthaired women who were testing the boundaries between liberty and license. (If he had rebuked his father by writing a defense of the flapper when he was age ten, Leslie was not about to attack the bohemian life now, just because he appeared to be a bourgeois homeowner.) Leslie recalled that Jack Fiedler had been particularly adamant about the issue of narcotics. As a pharmacist, he claimed that he could walk into any room and identify the hopheads by looking into their eyes. His son simply preferred to look the other way.

Even if he had had no children, Leslie would have opposed the prohibition of marijuana on the merits of the issue. The scientific evidence convinced him that pot was no more dangerous than the bourbon and cigars he preferred. Historical experience suggested that any attempt to outlaw a substance desired by a sizable percentage of the population would make criminals of otherwise law-abiding citizens, while creating profits for more hardened, better connected criminals. In the case of marijuana, it was not even necessary to rely on a professional class of bootleggers. Pot could be grown practically anywhere by practically anybody without the health hazards associated with bathtub gin. The greatest threat associated with marijuana was to the freedom of those hapless individuals apprehended smoking it. Consequently, when a student organization called LEMAR was formed to work for the legalization of marijuana, Leslie volunteered to be its faculty advisor. At the time, he did not think that

---

1. "Potted Ivy." Norman Mailer writes, "Now we may leave *Time* to find out what happened," after beginning *The Armies of the Night* with a distorted account of his behavior which was printed in *Time*.

he was courting anything more than a measure of unpopularity for asserting his First Amendment rights on behalf of a controversial cause.

Michael Amico, assistant chief of detectives and a night school graduate of the old University of Buffalo Law School, was the representative voice of older Buffalo. "I want the world to know," he announced, "that in Buffalo you can't violate the narcotic laws and get away with it."[2] What particularly bothered Amico was the fact that, if Leslie and LEMAR had their way, there would be no more narcotic laws to violate. In a public debate with advocates of legalization, Amico had said, "Don't worry kid—when we get you LEMAR guys, it's going to be on something bigger than a little pot-possession." "Yeah," he continued, "—there are some of those professors out at U. B.—bearded beatnik Communists. I wouldn't want any of my kids to go out there, but that's all right—they'll be gotten rid of" (*BB,* 135).

In April of 1967, Leslie began to notice that his phone was fading in and out. Some cars kept turning around in nearby driveways; others, belonging to no one in the neighborhood, seemed to be parked for long periods of time near the Fiedler house. One particular bread van began to haunt the neighborhood. What Leslie did not know was that, in February, the Buffalo Narcotics Squad had decided to launch an investigation against him and his family. To facilitate the investigation, narcotics officers had gone to the mental ward of a Buffalo hospital and recruited a sixteen-year-old homeless girl, Marsha Van der Voort, who had gone to school with Leslie's daughter Jenny. (Marsha bragged that she had been in the Fiedler house many times and that she could drop in any time she wished.) Beginning in March, Marsha began appearing, disappearing, and reappearing at the Fiedler house "with a set of unconvincing and contradictory stories about what exactly had happened to her (she had been in the hospital for a V. D. cure; she had been in jail; she had been confined to an insane asylum; she had been beaten up by incensed old associates)" (*BB,* 136–37). All the while, she was wired with a two-way radio, about the size of a package of cigarettes, with a concealed antenna. Any conversation within earshot of this device was monitored by cops in the mysterious bread truck, now parked across the street.

What was probably the ultimate indignity occurred when Marsha—armed with her listening device—shared wine and unleavened bread at the Fiedlers' Passover Seder. Remembering that evening, Leslie writes:

> The ironies are archetypal to the point of obviousness (one of my sons claims we were thirteen at table, but this I refuse to admit to myself), embarrassingly so. I prefer to reflect on the cops in their listening post (in the bread van?) hearing the ancient prayers: "Not in one generation alone have they risen against us, but in every generation. . . . This year we are

2. "Potted Ivy."

slaves, next year we shall be free!" I cannot resist reporting, however, that at the end of the evening, the electronically equipped "friend" said to me breathlessly, "Oh, Professor, thank you. This is only the second religious ceremony I ever attended in my life." (My wife has told me since that the first was the lighting of Channukah candles at our house.) (137)

After six weeks of surveillance, the narcotics squad obtained a search warrant from a judge of the Erie County Court. This warrant was issued on the strength of an affidavit maintaining "that there was probable cause for believing that certain property was being used or possessed at the Fiedler residence as a means for committing certain narcotic crimes." With only one day left in the ten-day life of the warrant, six police officers burst into 154 Morris Avenue at 10 P.M.. on the evening of April 28. Leslie remembers that he and Margaret were downstairs, getting ready to accompany Kurt and his wife, Emily, to a movie. (Eric was taking a bath.) After discovering small quantities of marijuana and hashish, the police placed six people in the house under arrest. Leslie and Margaret were charged with violating an old and obscure ordinance against maintaining a premise, "knowing that it is intended to be used for committing . . . a public nuisance."[3]

II

The nature of the charge against Leslie refuted the notion that he was himself a user of marijuana. During their six weeks of electronic surveillance, the police had gathered no information suggesting that he smoked pot. Although they strongly suspected that marijuana could be found on the premises, they waited until the search warrant was about to expire before making their move. Rather than running the risk of coming up empty-handed, they sent Marsha Van der Voort into the house to plant the illegal weed just prior to making their entrance. The fact that the police knew just where to look for their evidence and managed to find it without tearing up the house seemed more than mere coincidence. While the police were conducting their "search," Leslie was detained in his study on the first floor of the house and interrogated without having been read his Miranda rights. In the course of the interrogation, he denied ever having smoked marijuana himself but admitted to having been in the presence of those who did. According to one of the arresting officers, "his response was this is my house and my children. They can do what they want."[4] On the basis of that admission, Leslie was charged with breaking a law that was designed primarily to prohibit opium dens.

3. Herald Price Fahringer, *Appellants' Brief,* v.
4. Ibid., 6.

Leslie, Margaret, Kurt, Emily, and two friends of the Fiedler children were taken down to the Erie County jail to be fingerprinted and booked. While he was being incarcerated, Leslie realized that, seventy-three years earlier, Jack London had been in this same jail on a charge of vagrancy. As Kurt played his guitar and sang protest songs behind bars, Leslie called Richard Lipsitz, husband of the English department secretary and one of the most prominent attorneys in Buffalo. After Lipsitz dispatched his partner Herald Price Fahringer to the lockup, Leslie made bail and returned home to find Jack Barth straightening up his kitchen and stocking his refrigerator with beer.

The presumption of innocence is a venerable American principle, which applies only to criminal punishment. Anyone even suspected of certain kinds of misbehavior is likely to find himself subject to all sorts of noncriminal sanctions. Not long after Leslie's arrest, there was talk of suspending him from teaching, pending an investigation. This was nipped in the bud when the members of his department announced that they would not meet their classes if he could not meet his, and both the student senate and the graduate student association threatened to strike in sympathy if the need arose. Leslie himself made a personal appeal to President Meyerson—going over to his house, hugging his wife, patting his kids on the head, putting his arm around Meyerson, and saying, "Remember Martin, a man is innocent until proven guilty." Unfortunately, the community off campus was not as easily wooed.[5]

Shortly after his arrest, Leslie was informed by the Traveler's Indemnity Company that his homeowner's insurance was being canceled. No explanation was given other than the bald statement that his account was not wanted. Without insurance, he would not be able to maintain his mortgage and would probably lose his home. He then secured insurance from Manufacturers and Traders Trust, which also canceled without explanation in a few weeks. With their backs against the wall, the Fiedlers went to an independent agent, asking him to find some company that would insure their house. Although the agent was encouraging, he never called back and managed to be out of the office whenever the Fiedlers tried to get in touch with him. On the ninth day of a ten-day grace period, Margaret phoned the mortgage department at their bank to learn that the day before the insurance agent had told the bank he had been unable to insure their house. The next day, with the bank breathing down their necks, the Fiedlers secured a policy from Allstate Insurance. Two weeks later, that policy, too, was abruptly canceled. Meanwhile, the legal maneuvering continued in the criminal case, with Leslie scheduled to leave in August to teach at the University of Amsterdam in the fall and the University of Sussex in the spring.

5. Fiedler, interview with author, Feb. 26, 1999.

In an effort to alert the wider intellectual community to his plight, Leslie published a long essay called "Exhibit A: On Being Busted at Fifty" in the July 1967 issue of the *New York Review of Books*. Although this would be Leslie's only publication in the *New York Review,* it provided precisely the sort of forum he needed. To make his case in *Playboy* or *Ramparts* would have been to preach to the converted.[6] What remained of the New York intellectual community— and those who liked to think of themselves as part of that community—read the *New York Review of Books* as religiously as they had read *Partisan Review* twenty years earlier. Before long, moral and financial support began to come in from all over—from unexpected sources as well as from the usual suspects. In addition to left-wing academics, members of the Road Vultures Motorcycle Club, an assistant to Barry Goldwater, and the conservative columnist William F. Buckley, Jr., all contributed to the Fiedler Defense Fund.

While Allstate finally relented and reinstated Leslie's homeowner's insurance, New York Life canceled a life insurance policy one of its slick-talking salesmen had cajoled Leslie into buying.[7] Even more amazing, his application for a Diner's Club card was rejected. No automobile company would let him purchase a car on credit, nor would any bank approve a loan for that purpose. In a society predicated on debt, being required to pay cash for all purchases reduces one to second-class citizenship. And Leslie had still not been convicted of the single misdemeanor violation with which he had been charged.

If local persecution were not bad enough, Leslie learned through the rumor mill that the rector of the University of Amsterdam had become so alarmed by media coverage of the drug bust that he had decided to revoke Leslie's appointment as a Fulbright lecturer for the fall of 1967. (This was later confirmed by an evasive and legalistic communication from the rector himself.) With the schedule of the Buffalo English department rearranged to accommodate his absence, Leslie was preparing to depart for Europe in precarious legal and financial straits and without a promised job for the fall.

III

For Leslie, getting out of the United States at this point in his ordeal was like fleeing the belly of the beast. The American Council of Learned Societies

---

6. A laissez-faire attitude toward recreational drug use was part of the hedonistic "Playboy Philosophy." The left-wing readers of *Ramparts* would have opposed the drug laws because they represented an infringement on civil liberties. By this time, Leslie was publishing in both these mass-circulation magazines.

7. Bruce Jackson persuaded Larry Pierce, who was in charge of drug education for the state of New York, to intervene with Allstate to get Leslie's house insurance restored. I gleaned this information from my interview with Bruce Jackson and Diane Christian on July 10, 1999.

had agreed to pay the airfare to Europe that his Fulbright grant would have covered had he not been stiffed by the rector of Amsterdam. However, when he arrived at Heathrow Airport in London without a work permit in hand, customs officials almost sent him back to Buffalo. In the end, they gave him permission for a twenty-four-hour stay in England. This proved long enough for him to board a flight for the south of France, where one of his future colleagues at Sussex had offered him refuge at a vacation home where he was spending the summer.

After ten days of seclusion—only Herald Fahringer had his address—and much-needed rest, Leslie returned to England physically relaxed and mentally alert. Although he still could not produce a work permit, he was able to talk the immigration officer on duty into granting him a thirty-day grace period. Because the University of Sussex had found some classes for him to teach in the fall, Leslie was neither a vagrant nor an undesirable alien. When he arrived in Brighton, where the university is located, he discovered that his work permit had arrived in Buffalo the day after his departure. It had since been returned to the University of Sussex and was awaiting him on his arrival. He was now a "properly registered resident alien, complete with a year's visa and a National Health Certificate" (*BB,* 188). Not only were there classes for him to teach at Sussex, but a lecture series at University College in London assured him further employment and intellectual stimulation during his exile.

Back at home, the drug case was taking some interesting new twists. On August 25, Marsha Van der Voort called Herald Fahringer's office, saying that she had heard he wanted to talk to her. Arrangements were immediately made for a supreme court stenographer to record her statement. In a characteristically rambling and incoherent manner, Marsha admitted under oath to having planted the marijuana that the police had seized at the Fiedler home the preceding April. This admission should have been sufficient to get the case dismissed without trial. But, at that point, the cops began leaning on Marsha. By the time of the hearing to suppress evidence, on January 28, 1968, she was recanting the admissions she had made to Fahringer and lying in open court. No doubt, the police had warned her that her statements to the defense counsel opened her to charges of perjury for her original testimony. Given her fragile psyche, they were able to convince her that it was the defense, not the prosecution, that had been harassing her. Also, as payment for her cooperation, they had offered to send her to beautician's school.[8]

Leslie's response to his time in England was typically ambivalent. He lived in an elegant old house on Montpelier Road. It was filled with rickety and raffish furniture, faded prints of mysterious ancestors who had once lived there,

---

8. Fiedler, interview with author, Feb. 26, 1999. Except where otherwise indicated, the remaining information in this chapter comes from that interview.

and many old books—including a Fourth Folio of Shakespeare. Brighton itself seemed like a cross between Princeton and Coney Island. Describing life there, Leslie writes, "Walking through the tangle of decayed streets quite near our own, I would remember Pinky's obscene record in Graham Greene's *Brighton Rock;* strolling past the Metropole Hotel, I would think of Mr. Eugenides' invitation for a weekend in Eliot's *The Waste Land* . . . ; and returning home, I would pass a buttoned-up neighbor walking his dog and dreaming of the next book about Brighton, full of old ladies and middle-aged queers and muscular young men with short tempers" (187).

Although Leslie had hoped that Sussex would be like the redbrick universities that had produced the new wave of British writers (Kingsley Amis et al.), he soon discovered that it aspired to be another Oxford or Cambridge. The students came primarily from the upper classes with the centuries of prejudice that that entailed. When teaching a class in the American Jewish novel, he asked his students why they thought there was no similar tradition of Anglo-Jewish fiction. "Because," one young lady replied, "our Jews have so much money they don't need to write books."

One day, when he was in his colleague Marcus Cunliffe's office, Leslie was introduced to a vaguely familiar man in his sixties. It was Alger Hiss. Although Leslie was certain that Hiss knew what he had written about him, no mention was made of that long-ago essay or the even more remote case that had occasioned it. The two men confined themselves to small talk and academic gossip. The whole time, Leslie was struck by an expression on Hiss's face that he had seen only rarely in his life. It was the guilty man's facade of innocence. The Buffalo teenager who stole the collection of silver dollars Leslie had brought with him from Montana had worn such an expression. "Not only am I innocent," it said, "but innocent in a way that you could never begin to understand."

Because of a relatively light and flexible schedule at Sussex, Leslie was able to travel around Europe and speak before various audiences in 1968. He spent part of the spring in Paris. (Although the French had generally ignored his work, *Le Monde* featured a prominent and favorable review of *The Return of the Vanishing American* while he was there.) Leslie gave the last lecture—on Thoreau—at the Sorbonne before all the universities were shut down by a general student strike. He was also in Czechoslovakia long enough to celebrate that country's brief independence from Soviet rule and meet the young playwright Vaclav Havel.

The 1960s proved to be a turning point for many American intellectuals. Those who had been devoted to Trotskyism in the late 1930s, who had written for *Partisan Review* and the *New Leader* in the late 1940s, and had graduated to *Commentary* and *Encounter* in the late '50s more often than not found themselves drifting to the political Right by the late '60s. To the extent that the New

Left had a political ideology, it seemed like nothing so much as neo-Stalinism. One could not be an anti-Communist—even a liberal anti-Communist—and sing the praises of Castro and Ho Chi Minh. Although it would take another decade for Irving Kristol, Norman Podhoretz, and company to accept the label "neoconservative" and to embrace the Reagan wing of the Republican Party, the cultural battles of the sixties pushed them inexorably in that direction. One might wonder why Leslie Fiedler, having shared so much of the neoconservatives' intellectual history, chose to follow such a different path.

A clue to the differences between Leslie and those old friends is suggested by the fact that Norman Podhoretz's memoir, published in 1967, was called *Making It,* whereas Leslie's account of his life, which appeared two years later, was titled *Being Busted.* While Leslie was playing the role of bohemian rebel in the provincial backwaters of Montana, the resident New York intellectuals were becoming respectable and, if not rich, at least comfortable in postwar America. The institutions of liberal democracy seemed to have worked for them. If they had once seen themselves as barbarians at the gates, they were now doing very well inside the gates.

In contrast, Leslie's respectability was far more tenuous. In some quarters, he was seen as a major critic, in others as a controversial enfant terrible. Perhaps for that reason, he could get temporary teaching positions at the great universities of the world without ever being called to a permanent appointment at any of them. Had the unconventional and visionary Al Cook not been at the helm in Buffalo, Leslie might have spent his entire career at Missoula. Any danger of his becoming a bourgeois suburbanite once he arrived in Buffalo was eliminated when the police invaded his home in April 1967.

Even as a pariah and outlaw, Leslie went only so far in embracing the youth culture. The political cant of the New Left held little appeal for him. Unlike such professors as H. Bruce Franklin and Noam Chomsky, he did not become infatuated with revolutionary Communism. (That enthusiasm was confined to his first adolescence.) If anything, he had come to believe that all politics was little more than the opium of the people. "[W]hen I am not, like my favorite models Rip Van Winkle and Huckleberry Finn, on the lam," he writes, "I am neither pledging allegiance to the red-white-and blue nor chanting, '*Ho—Chi-Min,*' only saying with Bartleby the Scrivener, 'I would prefer not to,' which is good unmelodramatic American for the satanic Latin of '*Non serviam*' " (*BB,* 234). Leslie may have grown a beard in the late 1950s and long hair in the late '60s, but both would be so common by the late '70s that one could no longer discern a man's politics from the amount of hair on his face or head. And whenever a member of the counterculture would start to think that Leslie was one of them, he would politely refuse a turn on the joint that was making its way around the room.

IV

Leslie's first extended critical analysis of the counterculture had come in June of 1965 at a "Conference on the Idea of the Future," held at Rutgers University.[9] The situation was fraught with irony. The anti-Stalinist Committee for Cultural Freedom, which sponsored the conference, seemed like a relic from another era. (*Ramparts* magazine, for which Leslie had just begun writing, would soon expose both the committee and Irving Kristol's old magazine *Encounter* as fronts for the CIA.) Not surprisingly, several of the veteran cold warriors who spoke at the conference spent most of the time looking for the future in the past, in "the defunct revolutions of the thirties and even 1848" (*BB,* 157).

Rather than be a redundant presence on the podium, Leslie decided to begin "not with long-rehearsed reflections on the literary generation of Eliot and Pound and Yeats and the tradition of the Marxian Left, but with my still raw reactions to the literary generation of Allen Ginsberg and Robert Creeley and Ken Kesey, and the not-yet-traditional modes of revolt foreshadowed in the Dionysiac explosion on the Berkeley campus of the University of California" (158). The characteristic ambivalence of his presentation pleased no one. The young felt that he "had come close enough to what they were up to to understand it, and had then finked out short of total commitment," while his older listeners believed that "having come close enough to understand meant that I had crossed the line, gone over to the generational enemy" (158). In perhaps the final, crowning irony, Leslie's talk was published that fall in *Partisan Review,* a magazine he had declared a dodo nearly a decade earlier.

This lecture, which Leslie called "The New Mutants," depicts the youth culture as proudly obscurantist and hedonistic. The young are not simply rejecting bourgeois values in favor of a more idealistic vision of the good. Rather, they are celebrating madness, polymorphous sexual perversity, and an apocalyptic sense of their own importance. What Leslie gives us is an almost clinically convincing portrait of the counterculture—one that might be recognized as valid by everyone from Timothy Leary to Norman Podhoretz. What is lacking is a clear sense of the speaker's own attitude toward what he is describing. It is easy to understand why partisans on both sides of the issue were uncertain of where he stood.

Eight years later, Leslie would revisit many of the issues first raised in "The New Mutants." By the time "The Rebirth of God and the Death of Man" appeared in the winter 1973 issue of *Salmagundi,* his own drug bust and the protracted legal ordeal that followed had brought him much closer to the culture

---

9. According to the *Oxford English Dictionary,* it was in this lecture that the term *postmodernism* was first applied to literature.

he was only observing in "The New Mutants." (Although a sense of engagement is conveyed in *Being Busted,* one comes away from that book with a much more equivocal view of the drug culture than of the arbitrary police power seeking to repress it.) In the later essay, the metaphysicians of the counterculture (as opposed to the lumpenheads, who were content to get stoned and laid without giving thought to the cosmic ramifications of their lifestyle) still come across as antinomians. Here, however, they are depicted less as human mutants than as religious reformers.

Although Fiedler does not use the term, what he describes is a contemporary form of gnosticism. Early in the essay, he notes that, after the revolutionary shift in values that occurred during the 1960s, he found it much easier to teach Dante. It was no longer necessary to explain to students what was meant by vision and why one might wish to pursue it at the expense of other more tangible values. He admits, however, that the adherents of the new religion were seeking their vision in the here and now, not in some eschatological future. They were involved in a kind of inverted mysticism, which celebrated rather than denied the flesh. Psychedelic drugs (peyote, in the case of certain American Indian cults) replaced the bread and wine of Holy Communion. Instead of the Christian Bible, Milton, and *Pilgrim's Progress,* the scriptures of the new ecclesia consisted of *The Tibetan Book of the Dead,* the *Whole Earth Catalog, The I Ching,* J. R. R. Tolkien's Ring trilogy, a macrobiotic cookbook, selected volumes by Kurt Vonnegut and Herman Hesse, Castenada's *Teachings of Don Juan, The Kama Sutra,* and selected comic books.

Toward the end of this long essay, it seems as if Fiedler is breaking out of his apparent detachment. In words that would bring joy to the heart of a neo-conservative, he writes,

> Yet how can we bring ourselves to applaud without reservation a group of believers who offer us a kind of salvation, to be sure, a way out of the secular trap in which we have been struggling, but who are themselves ridden by superstition, racked by diseases spread in the very act of love [and this was before AIDS], dedicated to subverting sweet reason through the use of psychedelic drugs and the worship of madness, committed to orgiastic sex and doctrinaire sterility, pursuing ecstasy even when it debauches in murder, denying finally the very ideal of the human in whose name we have dubbed our species *Homo sapiens*?[10]

But for Leslie to leave matters there, on such a note of stern rebuke, would have meant chastising too many young people for whom he felt genuine affection, including members of his own family. And so, he proves himself fi-

---

10. Leslie Fiedler, *Tyranny of the Normal: Essays on Bioethics, Theology and Myth,* 27. Subsequent references will be cited parenthetically in the text as *TON.*

nally more willing to trust experience and instinct than mere reason. When his first grandson, Seth Wystan (named for Adam and Eve's third son and W. H. Auden), was born in the late 1960s, Leslie decided that the infant should be circumcised "like all of his male ancestors for three thousand years" (28). Although a white-robed doctor from a nearby Protestant hospital was recruited to perform the surgical procedure, Leslie himself presided over the religious ritual at a local commune in the presence of a congregation of mostly hippie goyim, who were "bearded and sandaled and robed quite like my own ultimate forebears." At the point in the ceremony when Leslie said to the baby, who actually bled in full view of all, his pain dulled by his first sip of wine, "I say unto you, *'In your blood live!'/* Yes, I say unto you, *'In your blood live!'* " he recalls that the blond-haired, blue-eyed young man who stood behind him responded "Heavy trip, man!" and fainted. "It was a response written in no prayerbook, but it was the right response. Because for once, for the first time in my fifty years of life, a *Brith,* a commemoration of our ancient Covenant with the God we thought dead was really *happening!*" (29).

V

When *Being Busted* appeared in late 1969, it was dedicated to the infant Seth. Leslie was back in Buffalo, and the drug case had yet to be resolved. (By the time that he and Margaret were finally brought to trial—on April 1, 1970—the other persons arrested had all gotten off with suspended sentences or fines.) In a sense, the book was an inevitability. When a writer wishes to make sense of his experience, he writes about it. Also, any royalties from the book would help defray mounting legal expenses. Nevertheless, a criminal defendant takes a risk when he speaks about his case before it is adjudicated—especially if he does so in print. *Being Busted* is more a work of the poetic imagination than it is a legal brief; however, zealous prosecutors were quick to introduce passages taken out of context to demonstrate Leslie's criminal intent. Not only did the court allow the prosecution to do so, it prevented the defense from introducing potentially exculpatory passages.

In one passage the prosecution found particularly damning, Leslie seems to admit to the charge against him. He writes, "Once deciphered, 'maintaining a premise' turns out to mean creating a context, a milieu, an intellectual atmosphere in which the habits of the young are understood rather than condemned out of hand; their foibles responded to with sympathy and love rather than distrust and fear; the freedom necessary to their further growth sponsored and protected rather than restricted and crushed by an appeal to force and the intervention of the police" (159). Of course, his point is that he is being tried for a state of mind, which could not possibly be criminal in and of itself. Unfortunately, the jury that tried the case—including a juror who slept through the proceedings—was considerably less sophisticated than the audience for whom the book was intended.

As a meditation on the first fifty years of Leslie Fiedler's life, *Being Busted* is an engaging book, which inhabits some middle ground between the light of common day and a dream landscape. Although there is a strong sense of place, very few names other than Leslie's own are mentioned, and those only in passing. The critical reaction to the book has been mixed, depending to some extent on one's sympathy for the counterculture and the effort to legalize marijuana. The most perceptive critics, however, have realized that pot was simply the occasion, not the point, of the story.

Writing in the *New Republic,* Reed Whittemore makes a dubious comparison in expressing his admiration for the Fiedler persona: "What interested me in his book," Whittemore observes, "more than the details of his being busted, and the implications for all of us of the experience to which he has been subjected, was his massive cool. I don't know how cool he was *really* in the face of the recent indignities, but with pen in hand he displays enormous detachment from his own problems, a detachment rather modelled after Henry Adams. The book might better be called *The Education of Leslie Fiedler,* with the chief lesson being learned that the spoken word is dangerous after all."[11] Of course, this is the one lesson Henry Adams seems not to have learned in his interminable lament about the failure of his education. Adams undervalued the life of the mind in a way that Leslie Fiedler never has. If Adams was an eighteenth-century dinosaur trapped in an uncongenial age, Leslie is the Darwinian hero, struggling to adapt to changing circumstances so that he will not become extinct.

Writing twenty years after the publication of *Being Busted,* James Seaton compares Leslie Fiedler, not with Henry Adams, but with a previous version of Leslie's own self. The critic who had urged an "end to innocence" and argued for a "liberalism of responsibility" in 1955 now seemed to be arguing for the virtues of innocence and irresponsibility a decade and a half later. Near the end of *Being Busted,* Leslie writes, "That judgment was and remains 'innocent': collectively and individually innocent, not only of the absurd police charges (about which there was never any real doubt), but also of having in any essential way failed our own personal codes." "To make this clear to everyone," he continues, "my wife and I intend to keep insisting not just that we are 'not guilty,' which is a legal formula only, but that we are 'innocent,' in the full sense of the word" (249).

In response to this declaration, Seaton writes, "But such protestations of total innocence were exactly what troubled Fiedler about Hiss and the Rosen-

---

11. Reed Whittemore, "Tough Martyr," 27.

bergs. The issue is not whether anybody in Fiedler's house ever smoked grass. The issue is to what extent Fiedler regained the pose of innocence that in *An End to Innocence* he had ascribed to his own generation. In *Being Busted* and in later works Fiedler indeed assumes a pose of political innocence, of one unimplicated in the complexities of political life, the pose of a permanent outsider."[12]

This is a telling observation only if one disregards the specific circumstances of the situations involved. It is one thing for a Soviet spy to deny charges of espionage; it is quite another for an indulgent parent to deny that he is running the legal and moral equivalent of an opium den. To believe that Alger Hiss and the Rosenbergs were metaphysically "innocent" one must believe that spying for the Soviet Union should have been a legally permissible activity. To believe in Leslie Fiedler's "innocence," one need only hold that a parent ought not to be jailed for failing to inform on an offspring for using a substance that shouldn't have been banned in the first place.

Despite Leslie's and Margaret's claims of innocence, the jury returned a verdict of guilty on April 9, 1970. On April 30, Margaret was fined $500, while Leslie was ordered to serve six months in prison. (Leslie suspects that the judge who sentenced him might have been trying to send a message to his own daughter, who was herself a user of marijuana.) Over the next two years, Leslie's legal bills continued to mount. On May 25, 1971, his appeal to the Erie County Court was denied and his sentence affirmed. Although he tried to push the whole matter to the back of his mind, Leslie was convinced that he would eventually be spending time in the slammer.

In the spring and summer of 1972, five years after his arrest, Leslie's conviction was reviewed by the New York Court of Appeals. From a strictly procedural standpoint, the case against him appeared questionable. For one thing, the prosecution had introduced information gleaned from electronic surveillance of the Fiedler house without ever producing the undercover agent who obtained that information. Thus, the defense had had no opportunity to cross-examine Marsha Van der Voort or to introduce the admission she had made under oath to planting the marijuana that was seized during the arrest. There was even some doubt as to whether the cops could have heard anything through their eavesdropping that would have justified a search in the first place. An electronics expert hired by the defense sent someone into the Fiedler house with a listening device similar to the one Marsha had carried, stationing a listener outside the house at the same place where the police had been. Although the cops claimed to have heard incriminating conversations from the third floor of the house, the defense witness could hear nothing but the clicking of billiard balls. Moreover, the listening device employed by the

12. Seaton, *Cultural Conservatism*, 114.

defense used a nine-volt battery, whereas the police had used only a four-volt battery.

When the appeals court rendered its verdict in July of 1972, Leslie walked free for a reason more basic than any of the procedural issues raised. Speaking for a 5 to 2 majority of the court, Judge James Gibson declared that "no crime had been charged or proven." The law that Leslie was accused of violating applied only to a building that the owners specifically maintained for criminal purposes. "It was never contemplated," Judge Gibson wrote, "that the criminal taint would attach to a family home should members of the family on one occasion smoke marijuana or hashish there." Finally getting it right, *Time* titled its account of the decision "Being Unbusted."[13]

Although this whole dreary experience destroyed any lingering respect Leslie might have had for the judicial system, his arrest put him on much friendlier terms with the Buffalo police. Having undergone a rite of passage, he was now familiar to them in a way that more law-abiding members of the community were not. (A dozen years after his conviction was reversed, Leslie told David Gates of *Newsweek* that the police "know me. . . . They don't feel I'm a square anymore. There's a funny way in which cops distrust respectable citizens."[14]) When *Being Busted* appeared, one of the arresting officers came by the house to get "the professor" to autograph his copy of the book. Appreciating the absurdity of the situation, Leslie inscribed it, "To an old buddy."

13. See "Being Unbusted."
14. Gates, "Fiedler's Utopian Vision."

Leslie presiding over a Seder

(left to right) David Ben Gurion, Philip Roth, Margaret, and Leslie, Tel Aviv, 1962

Leslie meets Golda Meir, Tel Aviv, 1962. "She gave me orange juice when I said I needed a drink," he recalled.

Leslie and Margaret confer with their attorney, Herald Price Fahringer, on the night of the drug bust, 1967

Leslie finally gets his chair, 1974

Leslie at a literary conference in the late 1970s. Robert Bly is next to Leslie, and Joyce Carol Oates is third from Leslie's left.

Leslie and Sally in Dublin in the 1970s

Leslie in New Delhi in the 1970s

Leslie with Ishmael Reed

Leslie with Ray Federman in the SUNY–Buffalo English department in the 1970s

Leslie with Camille Paglia at Fiedlerfest, Buffalo, 1995. *Photo by Bruce Jackson.*

Leslie with Allen Ginsburg at Fiedlerfest. *Photo by Bruce Jackson.*

PART THREE

STARTING OVER
(1971–)

CHAPTER FIFTEEN

Sacred and Profane

IN THE MID-1960s, Leslie's old friend Sol Stein formed his own publishing company, Stein and Day (the "Day" being a pseudonym for Sol's wife); it would be Leslie's exclusive book publisher for more than a decade. *Back to China, The Last Jew in America,* the second edition of *Love and Death in the American Novel, The Return of the Vanishing American, Nude Croquet,* and *Being Busted* all appeared under the Stein and Day imprint. Then, in 1971, Sol Stein published *The Collected Essays of Leslie Fiedler.* At the very least, this title was misleading. Far from being a comprehensive edition of the several hundred essays Leslie had published up to that point, the two volumes represented only the criticism he wished to preserve. The first volume consisted simply of a reprinting of *An End to Innocence* and *No! In Thunder.* The second required Leslie to go back and rescue old magazine pieces from dusty periodical rooms and to decide what order, if any, was formed by these fugitive writings.

As might be expected, one cluster of essays concerns "Jewish writers, chiefly but not exclusively Americans, as well as reflections on the plight of such writers when they abandon the traditional tongues of their people, holy or secular, to address the Gentile world in the language of the Gentiles" (*CE,* 2:xi). Appropriately, this section of the *Collected Essays* is called "To the Gentiles."[1] In what would prove to be a premature statement, Fiedler writes, "[T]his section must be understood as valedictory, my farewell to a subject which has concerned me for a long time, but which seems to me at the moment exhausted, both in terms of my own interests and that of the young audiences who no longer find in Jewish experience viable images of their own character and fate" (*CE,* 2:xi). Even had he stopped writing on Jewish topics at this point (which he did

---

1. The following year, Stein and Day published this and the other two sections of volume two as separate paperback books.

not), the very fact that Fiedler wanted to preserve this testimony to the Gentiles suggests that Leib Rosenstrauch's grandson could not easily forget from whence he came.

In introducing "To the Gentiles," Fiedler says of "Master of Dreams: The Jew in a Gentile World" that here "I have come as near as I suspect I ever shall to a final mythical definition of the situation which defines me as well as many of the writers whom I most love" (3). Beginning with the biblical story of Joseph, this essay argues, the primary archetypal role the Jew has imagined for himself in a predominantly non-Jewish culture has been that of the dream master. The point is made explicitly in the sixth satire of that goyish poet Juvenal, where in the midst of an inventory of all the tempting goods on sale in Rome, he tells us that "'for a few pennies' one can buy any dream his heart desires 'from the Jews'" (176). Because Joseph experienced both persecution and success as a result of his dreams (and his ability to interpret the dreams of others), his story is broad enough to explain the peculiar position that Jews have traditionally occupied in the Western, Gentile world.

Fiedler does make a strategic qualification when he admits that the image of dream master is more often a Jewish self-perception than a Gentile stereotype. "When the Gentile dreams the Jew in his midst, . . . he dreams him as the vengeful and villainous Father: Shylock or Fagin, the Bearded Terror threatening some poor full-grown *goy* with a knife, or inducting some guileless Gentile kid into a life of crime." This is because "Shylock and Fagin are shadows cast upon the Christian world by that First Jewish Father, Abraham, who is to them circumcizer and sacrificer rolled into one—castrator, in short" (177). The Jewish imagination, however, always sees Abraham releasing his son before the moment of intended sacrifice. In turn, that son, Isaac, becomes the father of Jacob, who is the father of Joseph. Although Joseph himself had offspring, he lives in the mythic memory not as another father, but as the favorite son who makes good and thus provides salvation for both the Gentiles and his own family. That this schematic description can also be applied to Jesus— who for Christians is the salvific favored son of God—suggests why the biblical Joseph is so important to the Jewish imagination and why he is a luxury that the Gentile mind—insofar as it is shaped by Christian myth—cannot afford.

Although Fiedler claims that this archetypal formulation holds up for the entire history of Jewish/Gentile relations, he is chiefly concerned with the literary Jew in the modern world. For our time, the role of Joseph the dreamer has been divided into the two figures of physician and artist—i.e., Sigmund Freud and Franz Kafka—"which is to say, the Healer and the Patient he could not have healed, since he is another, an alternative version of himself" (178). As doctor and scientist, Freud represents the rational mind wrestling with the forces of the unconscious, which are largely produced by our conflicts with our parents. In his masterwork *The Interpretation of Dreams,* "obsession is turned into vision, guilt into knowledge, *trauma* into *logos*." As victim and seer, Kafka represents the power of the imagination to apprehend that which cannot be understood, to confront that which cannot be overcome. "Between them, Kafka and Freud, the crippled poet and the triumphant savant . . . have helped to determine the shape of Jewish-American writing in the first half of the twentieth century" (182).

Although Fiedler's ensuing discussion mentions the work of Delmore Schwartz, Allen Ginsberg, and Henry Roth, his primary focus is on Nathanael West's *The Dream Life of Balso Snell* and Norman Mailer's *An American Dream*. West's novel is a highly surrealistic account of a tour through Western civilization as it is preserved inside the Trojan horse. It is significant that the vehicle of culture is Greek and that the Jewish protagonist can enter it only through the anus. "Not for him, the High Road to Culture *via* the 'horse's mouth,' nor the mystical way of 'contemplating the navel'; only the 'Acherontic' Freudian back entrance: the anal-sexual approach. 'Tradesmen enter by the rear' " (183). For all its sophomoric obscurity and vulgarity, *Balso Snell* is significant for being an apprentice work that introduces themes West would develop more skillfully in his remaining fiction.

The narrative line of Mailer's novel is considerably easier to follow; however, it too deviates from realism. If West's Balso Snell is an American Kafka, Mailer's Stephen Rojack more nearly resembles a hip Freud. Rojack is a former Congressman, a television personality, and a professor of "existential psychology." Not only has he won public respect and adulation, but he also fulfills his private fantasies. This involves doing battle with three shikses, who represent various aspects of Potiphar's wife. His own wife is an arrogant upper-class bitch, whom he murders in a fit of rage. Before disposing of the body, he finds time for a quick tryst with the German maid, whom he enters from the same orifice that took Balso Snell inside the Trojan horse. His last conquest is of a blonde girl with the suggestive name of Cherry. Before he can totally possess her, however, he must fight off a black man who threatens him with a knife. The macho Jew defeats the spade but finds his victory to be Pyrrhic when the enraged friends of his assailant murder the golden girl in revenge. The novel closes with Rojack making a phone call to Cherry in Heaven. At this point, she evokes the image of the ultimate dream shikse and cinematic sex goddess by telling him that "Marilyn says to say hello."

I

In calling the next section of his *Collected Essays* "Unfinished Business," Fiedler confesses that there are topics he has not yet fully explored; some he never will. Among other things, we find in this grab bag of essays fragments of books Fiedler thought he might one day write. One of these would have dealt with the literature of the 1930s. This was, of course, the period of his adolescence, when his literary sensibility was being shaped. The affinity he feels for that decade gives his writing about it an affecting personal quality; however, it might also account for what he regards as a fatal lack of detachment. "I cannot write a full scale work on the thirties," he confesses, " . . . not now anyhow, because I am still too deeply involved with memories and feelings still out of my control" (195). In lieu of the full-scale work he could not write, Fiedler gives us some fascinating notes toward a revisionist history of the 1930s seen from the perspective of the late 1960s.

At one level, the notion of literary periods is as arbitrary as that of literary regions; however, it is possible (at least for Fiedler) to speak of the dominant myths of particular times, even if those myths do not change like clockwork with the passing of each decade. "The Radicalism of the sixties, like that of the thirties," Fiedler writes, "is influenced by the Bohemia which preceded it, and with which it remains uncomfortably entangled; and it differs from its earlier counterpart precisely as the one Bohemia differs from the other" (238–39). What makes the situation even more complex and paradoxical is that one of the principal legacies the bohemia of the 1950s bequeathed to the radicals of the following decade was the "memory" of an underground '30s fundamentally different from the overtly political era represented by the likes of Dos Passos and Steinbeck (both of whom had turned to the right by the 1960s).

Fiedler regards Nathanael West, who was virtually unknown during his lifetime, as one of the most important American writers of the 1930s. Although nominally a leftist, West was actually an absurdist and con man, whose bleak existentialist vision was at odds with the political millennialism fashionable among writers of his time. Not until the late 1950s were West's novels brought back into print, perhaps because it took the shadow of the bomb for his cynical foretaste of apocalypse to seem credible. His reputation was revived by the Beats of that era and enhanced by the literate radicals of the 1960s.

Although the radical and avant-garde literature of the 1930s constitutes the tradition with which Fiedler is most familiar, he recognizes—as many commentators do not—that there was a very different but equally powerful literary movement under way at approximately the same time in the American South. (That is why he calls one of his essays "The Two Memories: Reflections on Writers and Writing in the Thirties.") If contemporary Jewish novelists such as Saul Bellow were influenced by the literature of the radical 1930s, other contemporary writers (Fiedler mentions Truman Capote and Marshall McLuhan by name) were nurtured by the contemporaneous Agrarian tradition.[2]

---

2. Although many fine southern writers (Eudora Welty, Flannery O'Connor, Peter Taylor, and the charter Agrarians Donald Davidson, Andrew Lytle, and Robert Penn Warren—to name only

In addition to the most obvious regional and ethnic differences, the radical and Agrarian 1930s were separated by opposite myths. The radical vision existed in the tension between "the terrible fact of the present and the dream of a barely possible future" (258). In contrast, the Agrarians were caught between "an equally dismal actuality and the dream of a manifestly unreal pure past." "Nonetheless," Fiedler argues, "the manifestos of the Agrarians tell the kind of lie which illuminates the truth of the fiction of Faulkner and Warren and [John Peale] Bishop, even as the Marxist manifestos tell the kind of lie which illuminates the truth of the novels of Nathanael West and Henry Roth" (258–59).

Fiedler's last "unfinished business" pertaining to the 1930s is to praise the book he calls "Henry Roth's Neglected Masterpiece." Fiedler begins his essay, which originally appeared in *Commentary* in 1960, by confessing that Roth's novel *Call It Sleep* was not entirely unnoticed when it appeared in 1935. One reviewer, whom he does not identify, called the book "a great novel" and hoped that it would win the Pulitzer Prize, " 'which,' that reviewer added mournfully, 'it never will' " (see *CE,* 2:271). In fact, H. L. Davis's *Honey in the Horn* won the Pulitzer for 1935, while Clara Weatherwax's *Marching! Marching!* won the first, and only, award given by *New Masses* for the proletarian novel of the year. These two prizes help to substantiate Fiedler's contention that the literary turf in the 1930s was pretty much controlled by the leftists, on the one hand, and the southern Agrarians, on the other. Considered "too poetic" by the former camp, Roth's novel was ignored entirely by the latter.

In 1959, Fiedler had declared *Call It Sleep* to be "the best single book by a Jew about Jewishness written by an American, certainly through the thirties and perhaps ever" (*CE,* 2:96). Despite the plausibility of this assessment, even some critics who were hoping for a flowering of Jewish American literature were cool to Roth's novel. Apparently, he had made the mistake of depicting the vulgarity and poverty of New York ghetto life with an unseemly realism. Not only had he offended the sensibilities of ethnic boosters, Roth had compounded the grossness of what he portrayed by rendering it through the sensibility of a child. Making precisely this point in 1960, upon the belated republication of *Call It Sleep,* Fiedler writes, "Its vulgarity . . . is presented as *felt* vulgarity, grossness assailing a sensibility with no defenses against it" (275).

If grossness and vulgarity were all that Roth's novel had to recommend it, the obscurity it so long suffered would have been warranted. Fortunately, there is another quality in *Call It Sleep,* which is the opposite of vulgarity

---

a few) had been influenced by the Agrarian social vision, Truman Capote and Marshall McLuhan seem like strange choices. Despite his early southern gothic fiction, Capote was more at home in Manhattan than in Alabama by the 1960s. It is true that the Canadian McLuhan did revere the Agrarians early in his career; however, his real fame was as a prophet of the post-Gutenberg culture.

but which requires the existence of vulgarity to achieve its fullest resonance. Fiedler notes an observation of C. M. Doughty, which Nathanael West quotes in *The Dream Life of Balso Snell*: "The Semite stands in dung up to his eyes, but his brow touches the heavens." It is this paradox that helps us understand the quintessentially Jewish nature of Henry Roth's novel. "Indeed," Fiedler writes, "in Jewish American fiction from Abraham Cahan to Philip Roth, that polarity and tension are present everywhere, the Jew mediating between dung and God, as if his eternal function were to prove that man is most himself not when he turns first to one then to the other—but when he touches both at once" (276). *Call It Sleep* is finally a religious novel because it shows us something like the sacred amid the profane, without slighting the reality of either.

II

From the Rosenbergs to Montana, from science fiction to academic freedom, very little that has engaged Fiedler's imagination goes unrepresented in "Unfinished Business." It is not surprising that almost all the essays in this section deal in some way with American literature and American culture. (Even a discussion of Jaroslav Hašek's *The Good Soldier Schweik* is as much about the American literary response to war as it is about Hašek's novel.) One of the best of these essays deals with an American writer whose myth and influence remained strangely compelling, even as his physical reality was overtaken by literary paralysis and self-inflicted death.

In early November 1960, Leslie Fiedler and his Montana State colleague Seymour Betsky made a pilgrimage to Ketchum, Idaho, to see the dying Ernest Hemingway. Although the ostensible purpose of the trip was to persuade Hemingway to speak at their university, Leslie and Betsky were actually "seeking the shrine of a God in whom we were not quite sure we believed" (345). The occasion was particularly difficult for Leslie because, in his critical writing, he had balanced his praise of Hemingway with honest censure of the novelist's more glaring faults. (At a symposium in Naples ten years earlier, he had told an Italian admirer of Hemingway: "yes—sometimes he puts down the closest thing to silence attainable in words, but often what he considers reticence is only the garrulousness of the inarticulate" [345].) And Hemingway was notorious for reading the critics.

One affinity that Leslie felt with Hemingway was that both men were outsiders who had come to live in and identify themselves with the American West. (Montana State was the university from which Robert Jordan had departed for the Spanish Civil War in *For Whom the Bell Tolls*.) It was only fitting that Hemingway had now returned to Sun Valley to die, "and it was scarcely ironical that his funeral be held in a tourists' haven, a place where the West sells itself to all comers" (345).

Although Hemingway had never written a book set in the Mountain West, all his books were informed by the same values as the television Western: "The West he exploited is the West not of geography but of our dearest and most vulnerable dreams, not a locale but a fantasy, whose meanings do not change when it is called Spain or Africa or Cuba. As long as the hunting and fishing is good and the women can be left behind." This was the West of Gary Cooper, an actor with whom Hemingway was as closely identified as Tennessee Williams with Marlon Brando, and one whose face, "in its inarticulate blankness, [was] a living equivalent of Hemingway's prose style." Along with many others, Leslie "was moved by Hemingway's telegram offering Cooper odds of two to one that he would 'beat him to the barn' [i.e., die first]" (346).

What we get in Leslie's description of Hemingway ("An Almost Imaginary Interview: Hemingway in Ketchum") is the picture of a frail man who is old before his time. We find *TV Guide* and *Reader's Digest* on his coffee table; and when he tries to play the gracious host, offering his guests "Tavel—a fine little wine from the Pyrenees," he simply degenerates into self-parody. It soon becomes evident that, if Hemingway had ever been capable of speaking in public, those days are now gone. It is difficult enough for him even to write. At the end of that awkward encounter, the Hemingways drove their guests back to town to pick up Betsky's car. Among the chores that Hemingway had to do in town that morning was go to the bank. But because it was Saturday, the bank was closed, and Hemingway was reduced to rattling the closed glass doors. " 'Shit,' he said finally to the dark interior and the empty street," Leslie reports, "and we headed for our car fast, fast, hoping to close the scene on the first authentic Hemingway line of the morning. But we did not move quite fast enough, had to hear over the slamming of our car door the voice of Mrs. Hemingway calling to her husband (he had started off in one direction, she in another), 'Don't forget your vitamin tablets, Daddy' " (354).

In coming west to die, Hemingway reversed his earlier journey to Europe, a trip that had itself become almost obligatory for American artists long before his lost generation of expatriates appeared on the scene. A case in point is Mark Twain, whom Hemingway had praised for having begun American literature with *Huckleberry Finn*. As difficult as it may be to remember, our most American—and one of our most *western*—writers achieved his earliest fame with a travel book on Europe—*Innocents Abroad*. And, from that point on, the image of Europe would recur frequently in his work: from nonfiction books such as *A Tramp Abroad* and *Following the Equator* to such novels as *The Prince and the Pauper, A Connecticut Yankee in King Arthur's Court, Personal Recollections of Joan of Arc,* and *The Mysterious Stranger.* Even in *Huckleberry*

Finn, Huck and Jim encounter sham European nobility in the King and the Duke, who seem only slightly more ridiculous than the presumably genuine Italian counts in *Pudd'nhead Wilson.*

Innocents Abroad is primarily concerned not with Europe as such, but with the reaction of the American tourist to Europe. For this reason, Fiedler compares the persona "Mark Twain" with Christopher Newman, protagonist of Henry James's *The American,* which was published in 1877, only eight years after Twain's book. Like "Mark Twain," Newman was the sort of American who could suffer an "aesthetic headache" while lounging in the Louvre, "convinced from the start that the fresh copies of the Old Masters being made by various young ladies right before his eyes were superior to the dim and dusty originals" (308).

The one artifact of Old World culture that finally commands Twain's reverence is the Sphinx. While gazing upon it, he notices "a wart or an excrescence of some kind" and hears "the familiar clink of a hammer." It is a fellow tourist trying to take a souvenir home from "the most majestic creation the hand of man has wrought." "Confronted with this absolute sacrilege," Fiedler writes, " . . . all Twain can conceive of doing is call a cop." In the process, he merely proves "just how ineffectual such sanctions are against the American tourist's irrepressible need to chip away piece by piece the Old World he does not dare confess bores him; but what else was there for Twain to do in response— except, of course, to write a book" (311).

Because Mark Twain was neither the first nor the last of our writers to reveal his essential Americanness against the touchstone of Old World culture, Fiedler has tried repeatedly, since his Fulbright fellowship in Italy, to define what our encounter with Europe teaches us about the way we see ourselves. He again turns to that topic in one of his most provocative essays, "Caliban or Hamlet: A Study in Literary Anthropology." As his old *Partisan Review* editor Philip Rahv had done in his famous essay "Paleface and Redskin," Fiedler attempts to divide classic American writers into roughly Apollonian and Dionysian categories. He goes beyond Rahv, however, in relating this distinction to the images that Europeans harbor of Americans and that Americans harbor of themselves. Because these images are rooted in literature but have extraliterary ramifications, Fiedler draws upon what he calls literary anthropology to argue that Americans have been viewed alternately as either Caliban or Hamlet.

As Fiedler would remind us in *The Return of the Vanishing American* (which was published two years after the original appearance of this essay), "America" was a realm accessible to the European imagination for nearly three hundred years before the "United States" came into being. During this time, one of the most mythically potent attempts to visualize the "brave new world" across the sea was *The Tempest,* a play that Leo Marx has called "Shakespeare's American Fable."[3] Even today, many Europeans share Shakespeare's vision of the indigenous American as Caliban, *"l'homme sauvage* of an already existing mythology transplanted to the New World: part Indian, part Negro, all subhuman" (293). Thus, when Americans—particularly American writers—are most primitive, nativist, and provincial, they are closest to validating the European stereotype of them. (This may go a long way toward explaining European enthusiasm for such examples of American popular culture as country music, hard-boiled detective novels, and Jerry Lewis.) It is no accident that Swift's persona gives an American credit for his "modest proposal."

When John F. Kennedy was assassinated, Europeans—and many Americans—found it easier to attribute the act to a brutish Caliban than to "a lonely and isolated individual who is diseased or deranged in mind" (see *CE,* 2:286). And yet, in declaring Lee Harvey Oswald to have been the lone assassin, the Warren Commission opted for the latter paradigm—for Hamlet over Caliban. Paradoxically, Americans are most themselves not when they are attempting to verify an image that Europeans created for them even before they existed as a people, but rather when they "permit themselves . . . freely to ransack their whole cultural heritage (Hebraic-Hellenistic-Renaissance-Romantic, all that they share with Europe); and when they end choosing . . . at first hand whatever they will" (289). When this has happened, Fiedler maintains, the image of Hamlet has been most often chosen.

The Hamlet analogy, like that of Caliban, is influenced by our relationship to Europe. It enables us to play, however, not the rebellious slave, but the wronged son. I suspect that, insofar as we think of ourselves only in the context of America, the Adamic prototype is our most compelling self-image. But, when we feel the tug of the umbilical cord that ties us to our Old World mother, we become that second Adam, Christ, or even that second Christ, Hamlet: "For archetypally speaking, Hamlet is Christ after the death of God" (292). America's compulsion to save the rest of the world (particularly the Western or European world) from whatever particular monster happens to be at the gate is the impulse of a dutiful son.

At the time Fiedler was writing this essay (mid-1960s), the Dionysian-Redskin-Caliban image was in vogue. Whitman seemed a more vital model than Eliot; the Beats and their various spin-offs still represented an important cultural influence; and even such elegant stylists as Norman Mailer and James Baldwin were remaking themselves as holy barbarians. (Although Fiedler mentions only Karl Shapiro, the transformation was also taking place in

---

3. Leo Marx, *The Machine in the Garden,* 34–72.

American poetry, as early formalists such as Robert Lowell and Robert Penn Warren were experimenting with more open and confessional verse.) In the next three decades, the introspective, self-referential Hamlets of postmodernism came to dominate high, canonical literature, with popular culture increasingly becoming the domain of Caliban. Predictably, Fiedler chose to follow the living beast rather than the dying prince.

III

Superficial observation would suggest that Leslie Fiedler's career as a critic can be divided neatly into periods. From the late 1940s until the mid-1950s, he was a *Partisan Review* intellectual, making the obligatory transition from Trotskyism to liberal anti-Communism. Then he emerged as a leading myth critic. In the 1960s, he really hit his stride as a revolutionary interpreter of American literature, and finally, late in the decade, he discovered popular culture and began an assault on the literary canon, which has been going on ever since. As James Seaton put the matter: "It is a striking example of the— often unacknowledged—influence of Fiedler that he is both a shaper of one consensus and a source for its challenger."[4]

But closer scrutiny suggests how arbitrary those distinctions are. Leslie's interest in myth dates back to the poem he wrote about Mercury and the invention of the lyre when he was still a child. (For that matter, he wrote "Archetype and Signature" at the same time he was writing his political essays.) Also, his most famous single statement on American literature ("Come Back to the Raft Ag'in, Huck Honey!") comes at the very beginning of his career. Even his engagement with popular culture began early—when he scandalized the literary world by publishing an essay on comic books in the August 1955 issue of *Encounter.*

Had this essay ("The Middle against Both Ends") been nothing more than a discussion of comic books, it would have become dated as quickly as the genre itself, which Fiedler believes was "killed, perhaps, by the tit-magazines, *Playboy,* etc.—or by T.V., on which violence has retreated to the myth from which it began, the Western" (*CE,* 2:416). What survived the demise of comic books was the impulse to censorship, which had fueled the middlebrow assault on that medium in the first place. Although highbrow intellectuals would go to the barricades to defend *Ulysses* or *Lady Chatterley's Lover* from the philistine attacks of the Parent Teachers Association and the Legion of Decency, those same intellectuals would often join the attack on popular culture. The

---

4. Seaton, *Cultural Conservatism,* 105.

highbrows might have had First Amendment reservations about outright sup-pression, but their defense of standards just as effectively anathematized liter-ature that failed to make it into the canon. What the middlebrow rejects on ethical grounds, the highbrow repudiates for aesthetic reasons.

Fiedler included "The Middle against Both Ends" in the final section of the second volume of *Collected Essays*. Published under the title "Cross the Border—Close the Gap," the eight selections gathered here constitute a defin-itive—some would say anticlimactic—declaration of independence from the critical strictures associated with high modernism. Fiedler was not just pur-suing a newer approach to criticism (he had done that from the beginning of his career), he was also questioning the very concept of serious literature, as it had prevailed in England and America since the early years of the twenti-eth century. If modernism was dead, so too was an essential part of his own literary education. Rather than seeing this as merely an end, Fiedler tends to regard it as a new beginning. In the introduction to "Cross the Border—Close the Gap," he writes, "Like many in my generation, I have been *thrice* born—first into radical dissent, then into radical disillusion and the fear of innocence, finally into whatever it is that lies beyond both commitment and disaffection" (*CE,* 2:405).

The title essay of "Cross the Border—Close the Gap" begins with a sharp attack on the adequacy of the old New Criticism to deal with the sort of liter-ature that was becoming increasingly common in America during the 1960s. Specifically, Fiedler identifies "the unconfessed scandal of contemporary liter-ary criticism" as the vain attempt to "explain, defend, and evaluate one kind of book with standards invented for a different kind of book" (461). "The second or third generation of New Critics in America," he writes, " . . . end by prov-ing themselves imbeciles and naïfs when confronted by, say, a poem of Allen Ginsberg, a new novel by John Barth" (462).

What Fiedler is calling for here sounds very much like the amateur criticism he was extolling nearly two decades earlier. "[A] renewed criticism certainly will no longer be formalist or intrinsic," he writes; "it will be contextual rather than textual, not primarily concerned with structure or diction or syntax, all of which assume that the work of art 'really' exists on the page rather than in a reader's passionate apprehension and response" (463). Examples of this "newer" criticism can be found as far back as Longinus's *On the Sublime*. In more recent times, Nietzsche's *The Birth of Tragedy* demonstrates the critic's ability to use works of art as occasions for creating other works of art. Among his contemporaries, Fiedler is particularly impressed not so much by the ap-proaches as by the voices of such disparate figures as Marshall McLuhan, Nor-man O. Brown, and Charles Olson. The more comic, irreverent, and vulgar the criticism the better. As a prime example, he cites the opening line of a book review by Angus Wilson: "Everyone knows that John Rechy is a little shit."

If he had found amateur criticism appealing a generation earlier, Fiedler now found it essential for appreciating the literature of postmodernism (a term from the world of fine arts that he himself was the first to apply to song and story).[5] If one of the achievements of modernism was to create a high literature remote from popular taste, the decline of modernism has seen the genres of popular culture appropriated by serious writers. The "New Western" Fiedler discusses in *The Return of the Vanishing American* is a notable example of this phenomenon. So too are the genres of science fiction and pornography.

As early as "Archetype and Signature," Fiedler had suggested that for the modern writer, cut off from ancient systems of myth, one source of archetypal material lay in the formulaic genres of popular culture. Needless to say, this is not quite the same thing as endorsing pop culture in its undiluted, hardcore form. Although Fiedler would eventually do precisely that, he was not quite ready to do so in "Cross the Border—Close the Gap." Consequently, most of the writers he discusses here are highbrows who are parodying the pop material they use. Vladimir Nabokov's *Lolita,* Terry Southern's *Candy,* William S. Burroughs's *Naked Lunch* and such recently legalized older works as D. H. Lawrence's *Lady Chatterley's Lover* and Henry Miller's *Tropic of Cancer* might have been considered dirty books, but they probably would not have been carried in authentic porn shops. The sort of scandal created by Philip Roth's *Portnoy's Complaint* led to the best-sellers' list, not to social or legal ostracism. Ironically, it was only in popular entertainment itself that censorship was still practiced. As Fiedler had observed in an earlier essay, "if giving offense be the hallmark of the *avant-garde,* Lenny Bruce is the last *avant-garde* artist in America" (*CE,* 2:458).

While "literary" writers were mining the treasure troves of popular culture, several pop artists were trying to close the gap from the other direction. Rock singers such as Bob Dylan, John Lennon, and Frank Zappa insisted that they should be taken seriously as poets. The same was true of certain commercial musicians who billed themselves as "folk artists," including the early Dylan, Leonard Cohen, Richard Fariña, and scores of others whom Fiedler does not name. If modernism widened the breach between poetry meant to be read and songs meant to be sung, it seemed that postmodernism was attempting to repair our sundered culture. In his enthusiasm for this development, however, Fiedler seems not to have noticed how tentatively it had begun. When highbrow writers were not blatantly slumming in the world of pop, there was still an element of self-conscious "camp" in their productions. By the same token, one gets the impression that the hippie bards who wished to be regarded as seri-

5. *Oxford English Dictionary,* 12:201.

ous writers were just as self-consciously going uptown—sort of like the stand-up comedian who does a soliloquy from Shakespeare to prove that, down deep, he is really a dramatic actor.

Because America does not have an indigenous high culture in the same sense that even a second-rate European nation does, our literature has invariably seemed either derivative or childlike. Fiedler had made this point with a mixture of bemusement and alarm from "Come Back to the Raft Ag'in, Huck Honey!" to *Love and Death in the American Novel,* which is to say, from the late 1940s to the early 1960s. By the time we get to *Waiting for the End,* in the mid-1960s, he seems to have concluded that, in the aftermath of modernism, the very immaturity of American culture might no longer be a liability. He makes this point even more explicitly in "Cross the Border—Close the Gap." In noting, once again, that our classic books tend to be boys' books, he writes, "But suddenly this fact—once read as a 'flaw' or 'failure' or 'lack' (it implies, after all, the absence in our books of heterosexual love and of the elaborate analysis of social relations central to the Continental novel)—seems evidence of a real advantage, a clue to why the Gap we now want to close opened so late and so unconvincingly . . . in American letters" (472).

Popular culture has always been open to magic and fantasy. (One of its functions is to provide ordinary people with various avenues of escape from the tyranny of the quotidian.) Prior to the advent of realism, this was true of "serious" literature as well. Hawthorne and Poe could write convincingly about the supernatural. Even writers who did not flagrantly violate the laws of nature could bend them with impunity. Then came Mark Twain and his insistence on narrative probability. From the end of the Civil War up through the 1950s, overtly antirealistic writing was largely confined to the nursery, to the ghettos of "genre" literature (e.g., romances and science fiction), and to such non-Gutenberg modes as stage melodrama and action films. Any highbrow—or even middlebrow—writer seeking to transgress these boundaries would surely have been scared away by Twain's devastating lampoon of such heresy in "Fenimore Cooper's Literary Offenses."

One of the central achievements of postmodernism has been to make fantasy once again accessible to serious literature. Among other things, this has meant that the underground life of the imagination, which had been banished from high American writing for nearly a century, was now redeemed for respectability. But then, Fiedler suggests, this may well have been the authentic American tradition all along. "It has been so long since Europeans lived their deepest dreams," he writes, "—but only yesterday for us. . . . [T]o be an American (unlike being English or French or whatever) is precisely to *imagine* a destiny rather than to inherit one; since we have always been, insofar as we are Americans at all, inhabitants of myth rather than history" (472, 473).

IV

By the time he published *What Was Literature?* in 1982, Fiedler was claiming that his most ostensibly theoretical writings ("In the Beginning Was the Word" and "Archetype and Signature") were actually intended to be parodies of academic pretentiousness, while his more outrageous work (e.g., "Come Back to the Raft Ag'in, Huck Honey!") was his most truly serious. If this is so, one hardly knows what to do with such a challenging and eclectic essay as *"Chutzpah* and *Pudeur."* Originally written in 1969, this essay is the concluding selection in "Cross the Border—Close the Gap." When we consider that, in 1960, "Archetype and Signature" and "In the Beginning Was the Word" occupied a similarly climactic position in *No! In Thunder,* we might well regard *"Chutzpah* and *Pudeur"* as an index of how far Fiedler's theoretical sensibility had developed over the watershed decade of the 1960s.

Early in his essay, Fiedler acknowledges the tradition in which he is working. Viewing literature in terms of a neat dichotomy is a venerable critical practice, two of the more recent examples of which are Matthew Arnold's concept of Hebraic and Hellenic and Philip Rahv's more parochial denomination of Paleface and Redskin. Fiedler's effort is distinguished from those of Arnold and Rahv because he sees his polar terms as referring not to two discrete categories of literature (or writers), but to two complementary aspects of the creative process. His approach here tends to be more Freudian than Jungian; but, in its mixture of high and low rhetoric, scholarly erudition and vernacular crudity—indeed of *pudeur* and *chutzpah*—this essay is most unmistakably Fiedlerian.

Pudeur is a French term that refers to a sense of modesty and tact, particularly in sexual matters. Psychologically, *pudeur* seems most appropriately connected with anality. Early toilet training teaches one the propriety of excreting in private. By the same token, writing is for many artists much of the time —and probably for all some of the time—primarily an act of concealment. It may be an assertion of the ego, but it is one that is done in terms of conventions (some inherited, some improvised) that conceal the personality of the author. Because the mask of traditional literary forms is largely inaccessible to modern writers, we find such contrived versions as "the reticence of Emily Dickinson, the endless qualifications of Henry James, the playful assault on syntax and punctuation of e. e. cummings" (*CE,* 2:519).[6]

Against the decorous French term Fiedler opposes the vulgar Yiddish one. *Chutzpah* could well be defined as a brazen lack of modesty, an urge to exhibit

6. For a classic discussion of the masking function of the pastoral elegy, see John Crowe Ransom, "A Poem Nearly Anonymous," *The World's Body* (New York: Scribner's, 1938), 1–28.

rather than conceal the self. If literature arises generically from the interaction of archetype and signature, it emerges psychologically from the dialectical clash of *chutzpah* and *pudeur*. One suspects that Fiedler's more recent pair of terms is not wholly unrelated to his earlier one. To talk about archetypes as the stuff of our collective unconscious serves the *pudique* function of hiding the individuating aspects of the poet's personality. At the same time, the artist's signature can be seen as a product of his *chutzpah*. Although one characteristic might seem dominant in particular writers or even in particular ages, the tension between *chutzpah* and *pudeur* is always present and "plays a large part in determining our essential double view of what it is the artist says or does or makes" (517).

The two literary forms that best exemplify the dialectic between *chutzpah* and *pudeur* are the pornographic poem and that enigmatic figure that has been called everything from a riddle to a (metaphysical) conceit. On the one hand, we have the arrogant, *chutzpahdik* poet (Walt Whitman, Allen Ginsberg), who "must first be condemned as 'the dirtiest beast of the age,' then, not cleared of that charge but found through it, and loved for it." On the other hand, "the shamefast poet . . . must first be blamed for his *obscurity,* then without being absolved, found through it and loved for it, quite like Gerard Manley Hopkins." Fiedler further develops this unlikely pairing by reminding us of Hopkins's declaration of his spiritual affinity with Whitman: "It is as close to confessing the particular guilt that dogged him, the homosexuality he shared with Whitman, as Hopkins could come; but it is also a reminder of the sense in which *chutzpah* and *pudeur* are originally and finally one, two faces of a single ambivalence" (533).

How far such ventures in psychobiography actually take us in understanding the verse of poets as rich and complex as Whitman and Hopkins is, of course, an open question. If Hopkins is doing nothing more than alluding to that *pudique* term *affectional preference,* then the dialectic between *chutzpah* and *pudeur* is reduced to the contrasting personae of "flaming fag" and "closet queen." Fiedler is generally on more solid ground when dealing with cultural myth rather than with sexual pathology. And it is at the level of cultural myth that the concepts of *chutzpah* and *pudeur* prove most suggestive.

When building the Tower of Babel, Fiedler notes, men experienced a fall not "from grace into morality" but "from the Tongue into many tongues, from 'Revelation' to 'literature' " (521), perhaps even from archetype to signature. In a sense, *chutzpah* and *pudeur* are simply different responses to the fall at Babel. The swagger of the poet who dares to say "I" and to say it in the vernacular is a profane celebration of the fall to literature. In contrast to this act of celebration is a tradition of shame, which believes that, if only the vernacular can be suppressed, we can find our way back to unity. The ordaining of Latin as the holy tongue of the Catholic mass was an attempt to reverse Babel, an act of ecclesiastical *pudeur*. In the humanistic religion of high culture, the attempt to make a literary canon of books written in an elevated vernacular may be a similarly wishful act of historical regression.

Reflecting on the current situation, Fiedler writes, "Without an adequate faith to justify it, any venture at defining a canonical literature, like any attempt to separate a sacred language from a profane is revealed as one more spasm prompted by the castrating shame which has been haunting Western Art ever since the first Western artist set out to sing of sex and the 'I.' The chill that freezes the marrow of worshippers at the altars of High Art is not just the cold that possesses all empty churches, but the zero weather of the Eternal Winter, which sets a new generation of readers to shivering even in our superheated classrooms and libraries" (539). It would be nice to believe, with Levi-Straus, that one can reject the extremes of Eternal Summer and Eternal Winter (of *chutzpah* and *pudeur?*) for the balanced periodicity of the seasons. Fiedler argues, however, that we have lost the rhythm of the seasons "in a world of air-conditioning and travel so rapid that summer and winter are hours rather than months apart" (540). (For that matter, only in art, never in nature, are perfect harmony and equilibrium achieved.) Thus, if one must choose between extremes, Fiedler will opt for the summer of Dionysus over the winter of Apollo. Like the Bacchae themselves, he sees in the orgy a utopian image of community.

CHAPTER SIXTEEN

Till the Tree Die

EARLY IN THE third chapter of *The Great Gatsby,* Nick Carraway remarks:

> I believe that on the first night I went to Gatsby's house I was one of the
> few guests who had actually been invited. People were not invited—they
> went there. They got into automobiles which bore them out to Long Is-
> land and somehow they ended up at Gatsby's door. Once there they were
> introduced by somebody who knew Gatsby and after that they conducted
> themselves according to the rules of behavior associated with amusement
> parks. Sometimes they came and went without having met Gatsby at all,
> came for the party with a simplicity of heart that was its own ticket of
> admission.[1]

For nearly a decade, a 1960s' equivalent of Gatsby's parties took place at 154
Morris Avenue in Buffalo every Fourth of July. At first, the guests were invited
friends of Leslie and Margaret Fiedler and however many of their six children
happened to be living at home. But pretty soon the word got around that this
was the place to be. Carloads of people would arrive from Buffalo and the
surrounding area and, in some cases, from neighboring states. The festivities
would begin some time around noon and would continue until midnight or
later. The center of activity would periodically shift from the poolroom on
the third floor of the house to the swimming pool out back. As the revelers
got progressively intoxicated on their substance of choice, they would settle on
a victim to be thrown, fully clothed, into the pool. The celebration was not
considered complete without loud music and at least a couple of visits from
the local police. On one occasion, Michael Fiedler tossed a watermelon rind
through a neighbor's open window.

---

1. F. Scott Fitzgerald, *The Great Gatsby,* 45.

A frequent guest at these bashes was Allen Ginsberg, who always seemed to bring an entourage with him. Although Allen had been born in Newark, he was a decade younger than Leslie and had spent his boyhood in Paterson, New Jersey. Leslie had long known Louis Ginsberg, Allen's father, a high school teacher who ran a citywide poetry club in Newark, but Leslie and Allen did not meet until much later, when they were both well-established literary provocateurs. One day during Leslie's Fulbright year in Athens, Allen came knocking on his door. He was making a pilgrimage to India and thought it high time the two made each other's acquaintance. Whatever reservations he might have had about the Beat movement and the emerging counterculture, Leslie immediately responded to Allen's personal warmth and sincerity. Despite his status as a celebrity, there was nothing pretentious or condescending about his manner. (Gore Vidal, who had also visited in Athens, seemed both—lecturing Leslie about how Jews didn't understand homosexuals, until he disappeared into the night with a handsome young boy from Missoula, who was also passing through town.) More than anything else, Leslie's growing friendship with Allen introduced him to the youth revolution of the 1960s.

If Allen's presence always seemed to brighten the occasion, the people he brought with him were a mixed lot. His fellow Beat poet Gregory Corso, who was a frequent companion, seemed to think that iconoclasm consisted primarily of being rude and offensive. Timothy Leary, on the other hand, was usually good for a laugh—whether you were laughing with him or at him. There was a part of him that was a charming Irishman. However, by the time he had been fired by Harvard and had become a full-time guru and professional nut, Leary had degenerated into self-parody. As a matter of principle, Leslie was uncomfortable with any religion newer than the Old Testament, and he was never entirely certain whether Leary was a remarkably gifted con man or a victim of his own delusions. Seeing him perform in the flesh before a convention of the National Student Association failed to settle the matter. "After a false start or two intended to tease us to full attention," Leslie recalls, "he appeared draped in a white robe and accompanied by an utterly stoned Black acolyte, who sat cross-legged throughout, playing a Beatles record on a portable player between his knees" (*BB,* 156).

As much as he might enjoy the company of some of the wild men of the 1960s, Leslie realized that they lacked a belief in evil and a sense of tragedy. To appreciate his ambivalence about the decade one might well begin with "Song from Buffalo," a poem that he published in 1975. The detached but sympathetic speaker realizes that it is finally impossible for one who has seen the Holocaust, even at a distance, and walked on the sands of Iwo Jima to sing the Songs of Innocence with a straight face. The poem reads as follows:

In the evening they came to my cavern
Where I lay with the bones of the dead,
Saying: *Sing us a song of rejoicing*
Come out of the web of your head
But I listened to whispers from nowhere
And whispered my answer instead—

At nightfall they came to my cavern
Crying: *Sing us a song for the streets*
Sing a song without rhyming or heartbeat
Since only madness is sweet.

But I'd died on the ovens at Belsen
And killed where the black lava sand
Covered small yellow men I had murdered
And buried my own severed hand.

I cannot sing with my head in an oven
And my fingers awash in the sea
My head turned to ash in an oven
And the ghosts of old friends eating me.

Dear Allen, I remember your singing
By the edge of the algae-dark pool,
And Gregory casting the *I Ching*
And nodding out in his drool.
It was mud I toiled in he told me
And his mouth unwound like a spool . . .   (*NFR,* 472)

I

The one political cause to win Leslie's active support in the late 1960s was the struggle of the Ibo people to break away from Nigeria and establish an independent nation. He had long been interested in literature written in English by Africans and found that most of the best of it was produced by members of the Ibo tribe—foremost among them, of course, being Chinua Achebe, whom Leslie has repeatedly nominated for the Nobel Prize. (Although his masterpiece *Things Fall Apart* is regarded by critics as the best novel written in Anglophone African, Achebe has never gotten the call from Stockholm.) The fact that the Ibos were part of Nigeria, indeed the fact that there was such a "nation" as Nigeria, was largely an accident of British imperialism. As long as the Ibos remained in Nigeria, it seemed inevitable that they would continue to struggle with the northern tribes for control of the country. A military coup that had brought an Ibo faction to power in January 1966 was countered by a successful coup of northerners in July of that year. After repeated efforts at negotiation brought only further bloodshed, the eastern (Ibo) region of Nigeria announced its secession from the federal state on May 30, 1967. With that decree the Republic of Biafra was born.

The effort to get the United States government to take some notice of Biafra proved disheartening. Because Leslie had once taught in a summer program at Harvard organized by Henry Kissinger, he traveled to Washington to lobby Kissinger, who was now national security advisor to President Nixon. As he later indicated in an undated letter to Miriam Reik, president of the Committee for Biafran Artists and Writers, "the position of the State Department and especially of their African desk . . . is that there must be a single unified Nigeria, even if this means the death in war or by starvation of every single Biafran." Kissinger, who reminded Leslie of Dr. Strangelove, was interested only in discussing politics on the nation's campuses. Leslie recalls that "I had a hard time stopping his speeches about how participatory democracy leads to Caesarism long enough so that I could make mine about the plight of Biafra."

Leslie's old Montana friend Mike Mansfield, who was now majority leader of the Senate, was much friendlier and more attentive. "One of the things that made Mansfield favorably disposed," Leslie observes, "was a visit he'd had a few days before from a group of Holy Ghost Fathers—one of whom happened to be his cousin. We should have more Irishmen in the Senate!" Unfortunately, Mansfield believed that "as long as the pressure in Vietnam was on, it seemed hard to believe that much notice would be given to a little war in Africa in which we have few direct interests."[2]

Although the Biafrans were mostly Christian and their adversaries mostly Islamic, Leslie had come to regard the Ibos as the "Jews of Africa"; not only were they literate and well educated, but they also charged a thirty-five dollar landing fee of planes that brought their supporters in through enemy fire. After traveling to the area himself, he became hopeful that the tribal animosities that fueled the war could be resolved in a million years, although he feared it might take a million and a half. On January 12, 1970, the nation of Biafra was crushed, and Nigeria was once again under a unified bloody dictatorship.[3]

Leslie's relationship with Americans of African descent has been long and mostly friendly. His claim to have acquired his platform style from black street preachers was confirmed by Houston Baker and Henry Louis Gates, who jokingly accused him of being the academic equivalent of Elvis Presley—a

2. The Holy Ghost Fathers was a Catholic religious order with a mission in Biafra. This letter is contained in Leslie Fiedler's private papers.

3. Except where indicated, information in this section comes from the author's interviews with Leslie Fiedler on Feb. 26–27, 1999.

white man who stole the black man's act. During his long tenure at Buffalo, he formed particularly warm friendships with two gifted black writers— Samuel P. Delaney and Ishmael Reed. Although Delaney had gone to the Bronx High School of Science at the same time as Kurt Fiedler, neither Leslie nor Kurt knew him at the time. (While at Harvard, Kurt did become friends with the aspiring black novelist William Melvin Kelley, who told Leslie: "Kurt is good; for what, I don't know; but he's good."[4]) Delaney is one of a small number of experimental writers who have combined science fiction and postmodernism. Reed is a Buffalo native, whose work reflects the full range of black experience, not just racial protest. Drawing on folklore, fantasy, parody, myth, and popular culture as well as the conventions of serious literature, he is more often compared to avant-garde writers such as William Gass, Thomas Pynchon, and Donald Barthelme than to Richard Wright and James Baldwin. At various times, Leslie was instrumental in persuading both Delaney and Reed to take teaching positions at Buffalo.

Leslie has always believed that true racial equality cannot be defined in terms of political correctness. It requires, among other things, the ability to call a son of a bitch a "son of a bitch," even if he belongs to a minority race. On one particular occasion, he found an indirect way of doing just that to one of America's secular saints—Martin Luther King, Jr. While sharing a platform with King, a young representative of the militant organization SNCC (Student Non-Violent Coordinating Committee), and the truly saintly Dorothy Day, Leslie felt an immediate distrust of King. As he later recalled, King would "grab any female ass that came within reach of him, especially if it was white." Speaking on the same program with him, Leslie felt as if he were in a play with another actor who never misses a chance to upstage everybody else; and listening to his oratory, Leslie felt as if he were listening to platitudes he had heard a thousand times before. When it came Leslie's turn to speak, he did not confront King directly but managed to imply that he was a kind of Uncle Tom. Obviously impressed, one militant black in the audience stopped Leslie on his way out and paid him one of the highest compliments he has ever received: "Man, you're one mean motherfucker."[5]

Because of his association with the New York literary community, Leslie would periodically run into James Baldwin. One of the first times the two had contact was when Leslie was sailing to Rome for his first Fulbright fellowship in 1952. He noticed a familiar face among the people on the dock. It was Jimmy

---

4. Fiedler, interview with Jackson, May 7, 1989.

5. Leslie's sense of déjà vu may be attributable to King's lifelong practice of plagiarism. The most complete scholarly discussion of this phenomenon can be found in Theodore Pappas, *Plagiarism and the Culture War: The Writings of Martin Luther King and Other Prominent Americans* (Tampa: Hallberg, 1998).

Baldwin, putting his sister on the ship to Europe. Because she had grown up in an insular environment in Harlem, Baldwin was a bit apprehensive about her traveling alone. Leslie promised to take care of her and promptly delegated the task to his capable son Eric. Later, it seems that Leslie would find himself at parties where Baldwin and Norman Mailer were either falling out or making up with each other. Although interracial homosexuality was an essential part of Baldwin's lifestyle, he didn't think very highly of "Come Back to the Raft Ag'in, Huck Honey!" His criticisms, however, were made behind Leslie's back. In face-to-face encounters, he was invariably charming, even deferential. On one memorable night, Leslie caught an uncharacteristic glimpse of Baldwin's personality when he sang gospel songs in Alice McIntyre's apartment while Alice accompanied him on the banjo.

II

Had he not become an English professor and literary critic, Leslie almost certainly would have gone into the theater. During his adolescence in Newark, drama was inextricably intertwined with his political activity. The young Stalinists with whom he associated studied the Stanislavsky Method and produced plays that tended to be long on propaganda and short on art. As a street corner speaker, Leslie was a consummate performer, who needed the immediate response of an audience. As he observed six decades later, "the motion has to go back and forth from the stage to the audience, from the audience to the stage."[6]

Drama also served as Leslie's introduction to cultures very different from his own. Many of Leslie's high school classmates who were involved in theater were homosexuals. Through them, he glimpsed a world where fifteen-year-olds could mingle on an equal footing with well-established middle-aged professionals—often at parties attended by such closeted luminaries as Tallulah Bankhead and Johnny Weissmuller. Leslie would later discover that even straight entertainers often had something to hide. His friend Eddie Cohen, who changed his name to Eddie Jurist when he became an actor and writer during the golden age of television, became embroiled in the quiz show scandals of the 1950s. Once Leslie received a free set of the *Encyclopedia Britannica* for supposedly contributing a question to the show *Whiz Kids*. Apparently, Eddie had written the question himself and signed Leslie's name to it.

6. Leslie Fiedler, interview with Bruce Jackson, Apr. 8, 1989. Additional information in this section comes from the author's interview with Leslie Fiedler on July 9, 1999.

Leslie's passion for theater did not diminish during his years in Missoula. (He was particularly in demand for "ethnic" roles, such as that of the mad ballet master in Kaufman and Hart's *You Can't Take It with You.*) As a result, he formed friendships among theatrical people, including one with a young actor from Brooklyn named Carroll O'Connor. After failing to break into the Irish theater, O'Connor received a scholarship from Montana State in the early 1950s. While there, he acquired both a wife and a renewed sense of his vocation as an actor. One of the first productions in which he performed after his departure from Missoula was a stage version of James Joyce's *Ulysses,* directed by Burgess Meredith. O'Connor played Buck Mulligan to Zero Mostel's Leopold Bloom. Although his talent was not in question, Carroll O'Connor seemed doomed to play small character parts, always hoping for the big break that might never come.

After his arrival in Buffalo, much of Leslie's acting took place off-campus. In October 1966, for example, he narrated Stravinsky's *Oedipus Rex* for the Buffalo Philharmonic Orchestra. The following year, he appeared in Paul Valéry's *My Faust,* produced by an Off-Off-Broadway group called the Theatre for Ideas. This organization specialized in reading performances of intellectually challenging works by writers such as Brecht, Giraudoux, Bellow, and Lowell. Although Valéry died before finishing *My Faust,* the three long acts he did complete raise the paradoxical issue of Satan's loss of power in the modern world (not because the world has grown more holy but because it has lost its capacity to believe in myth). In what might have been regarded as typecasting by the director Maurice Edwards, Leslie played the title role, while John Simon portrayed Mephistopheles. Reviewing the play in the February 16, 1967, issue of the *Village Voice,* Joseph LeSueur writes, "Valery's conception of Faust as an inflated pedant was beautifully realized by Fiedler, while Simon's hissing, disdainful Mephistopheles was the devil incarnate."[7]

In addition to performing on the stage, Leslie had appeared on talk shows since early in the history of television. When he was living in Missoula, he was a frequent guest on a Canadian program called *Fighting Words,* hosted by the drama critic Nathan Cohen. The show usually featured intellectuals who would discuss an unattributed quotation. On one program, the subject for discussion was something that Leslie himself had written but failed to recognize. Another time, he was paired with two Canadian critics who were not yet widely known—Northrop Frye and Marshall McLuhan.

Because of his broad range of interests and his predominantly oral imagination Leslie proved to be as natural a performer on television as he was on

7. Joseph LeSueur, "Theatre: *My Faust.*"

the lecture circuit. "There was a moment during the '60s," he recalls, "when the format of the *Merv Griffin Show,* for instance, had come to include—along with an aging actress, a current pop music star, and a stand-up comedian—a visiting 'nut,' at that point usually Allen Ginsberg or Norman Mailer, or occasionally, as it turned out, me" (*WWL?* 19). After about his third appearance on the Griffin show, Leslie was informed that he would have to join AFTRA (the American Federation of Television and Radio Artists). He continued to enjoy courting a popular audience until one day he and Louis Untermeyer were bumped from the show because the other performers had gone on too long. Some young assistant producer came back to the green room to break the news to them. He walked up to Untermeyer, who was very old and very distinguished, slapped him on the back, and said, "Well, that's show biz." *If that's show biz,* Leslie thought, *I've had quite enough of it,* and he never appeared on the Griffin show again.

One of Leslie's most interesting and rewarding talk show experiences was on November 15, 1974, when he was the sole guest on William F. Buckley, Jr.'s, *Firing Line.* Although Leslie and Buckley were hardly ideological soul mates, they both took ideas seriously and neither adhered too rigidly to a single party line. (Buckley had, after all, contributed to Leslie's legal defense fund.) Besides, after a steady diet of the *Merv Griffin Show,* it was a luxury to engage in serious and uninterrupted discussion for an entire hour. When Buckley sent a car around to bring him to the studio, Leslie ended up having to pay the road toll because the driver had no money other than marked hundred dollar bills; he was an off-duty narc moonlighting as a chauffeur.[8]

Leslie's one big opportunity to appear on the silver screen came in the spring of 1978. When he was in Los Angeles pushing his most recent book on the Sandy Barron television show, he mentioned that he had always wanted to be an actor. Shortly thereafter, he got a call from the independent film producer Wanda Appleton, who was planning a fantasy film called *When I Am King.* Although this was a low-budget production, it did include a pair of well-known second-tier Hollywood actors—Aldo Ray and Stuart Whitman. The two young principal characters, Jack and Jorinda, share a fantasy about their exploits in a land that might have been imagined by the Brothers Grimm. In the role of Eyalo, Leslie got to wear pink tights and a smock, drive a circus wagon, and speak such deathless lines as: "Come, little one. . . . Look at the juggler. Leonardo is a wonder this day. Look!"[9] Leslie was paid $785 a week for two and a half weeks of filming and was put up at a hotel that could have come right out of Nathanael West's *The Day of the Locust.* Over twenty years later, *When I Am King* has yet to be released.

8. Fiedler, interview with author, Nov. 7, 1998.
9. Wanda H. Appleton, *When I Am King,* 25.

One advantage of Leslie's stint in Hollywood was the opportunity to renew contact with his old student Carroll O'Connor. By the early 1970s, Carroll had become perhaps the biggest star on network television for his role in the groundbreaking situation comedy *All in the Family*. Although a liberal himself, Carroll gave such an engaging and human portrayal of the bigoted Archie Bunker that he struck millions of viewers as a more sympathetic figure than his politically correct daughter and son-in-law, played by Sally Struthers and Rob Reiner. In 1972, one could see T-shirts and bumper stickers proclaiming support of Archie Bunker for president. Many signs were marking the end of the 1960s. The popularity of *All in the Family* was one of them.

Through Carroll, Leslie was invited to authentic Hollywood parties, where he met such celebrities as Burgess Meredith, Shirley MacLaine, and Larry Hagman (who was beginning what seemed an unpromising television series called *Dallas*). Leslie recalls Shirley MacLaine as being incredibly patronizing and self-important—always dropping names, saying things like, "When I saw Fidel last, he said to me. . . ." Hagman, on the other hand, he found an intriguing fellow, who somehow seemed younger than his actual years—perhaps because his mother, Mary Martin, had once played Peter Pan.

Despite his lone venture into the cinema, Leslie never broke entirely free of the role of college professor. (It is perhaps fitting that his most enduring presence on screen came not in an absurd low-budget fairy tale, but in the mainstream film *Exposed*—where Nastassja Kinski clutches a copy of *Love and Death in the American Novel* to her bosom, and a fictional teacher writes a sentence from that book on a fictional blackboard.) It was a role he redefined for an age in which the boundaries between education and entertainment were becoming blurred.

Born too late for the carnival sideshow or the Chautauqua circuit, Leslie would eventually bring his inspired barbarian routine to lecture halls across America. According to Benjamin DeMott, it went something like this:

> He rocks slightly as he speaks, his veins stand forth and his face sweats—
> a clever, bearded, tanned face. Mephistopheles one second, Santa Claus
> the next, the Saint Saens Samson after that. He seems almost to hum to
> himself, his rhythms and bits take on a Lenny Bruce beat, self-enjoyment
> sweeps up the room—good humor, vivacity. Even in his moments of
> scrinched-up, tortured, small-boy—cruelly-punished pain, the man's
> larger-than-life quality and relish of self are constant. Here before you,
> folks, here in this barrel torso sits the soul of the last appetitive, red-
> skinned, thoroughly nonacademic academic on earth.[10]

---

10. Benjamin DeMott, "A Talk with Leslie Fiedler," 9.

III

In the figure of William Shakespeare, Leslie's interests in both theater and literature were ideally joined. In the early 1980s, he even participated in a series on the BBC, in which actors in Elizabethan costume appeared before Elizabethan sites and recited Shakespeare's sonnets, accompanied by comments from scholars and critics. (Although the series was never finished, Leslie's segments with John Hurt and Ben Kingsley were among those aired on British television and remain available on tape.) By this time, his reputation as an iconoclastic reader of Shakespeare was well established.

Back in 1948, when he first delivered "Shakespeare and the Paradox of Illusion" as a lecture before the English Institute, Leslie had confidently predicted that he would someday expand upon its themes in much greater detail. By the time he published the lecture in *No! In Thunder* in 1960, however, he confessed in a footnote: "I no longer believe I shall really come to terms at great lengths with Shakespeare, but I leave the hope of 1948 in the text to remind myself of what seemed possible twelve years ago" (*CE,* 1:268). Another twelve years had to pass for that project to seem possible once again. In the introduction to "Unfinished Business," he writes, "Just six months or a year ago, I would have included among these scraps from unfinished books an essay or two on Shakespeare, but suddenly I am in the process of writing that presumably unfinishable book" (195). A year later, he published *The Stranger in Shakespeare*.

The stranger, according to Fiedler's definition, is one who resembles us closely enough to be recognizable as a member of the human family, while seeming alien in other important respects. For men, the original stranger is the woman. The attempt to come to terms with her presence in "a culture whose notion of the human is defined by males" takes many different forms, the simplest and most vulgar of which is female impersonation.[11] This phenomenon, which survives today principally in tawdry burlesque routines, is both an example of one of the central impulses behind all drama (the desire to express one's fascination with the stranger) and a remnant of one of the customs of Shakespeare's time (that of boys playing girls' parts). The various levels of sexual identity in Elizabethan comedy become even more confused when female characters assume the disguise of men. In *As You Like It,* for example, "the boy who has been playing Rosiland playing she is Ganymede playing Rosiland, steps out of his role and stage-sex to speak the Epilogue." (47).

Shakespeare was obsessed with the woman as alien long before he developed the sophisticated technique displayed in *As You Like It*. In his first play—

---

11. Leslie Fiedler, *The Stranger in Shakespeare,* 19. Subsequent references will be cited parenthetically in the text.

Henry VI, part one—he introduces three diabolic Frenchwomen (the Countess of Auvergne, Margaret of Anjou, and Joan of Arc), all of whom are "bent on betraying the male champion of the English" (47), and all of whom could have been portrayed by the same actor. Of these, the most significant mythically is Joan. Because she has been canonized by the Roman Church and can claim such distinguished literary admirers as Friedrich von Schiller, George Bernard Shaw, Jean Anouilh, Eugène Sue, and Mark Twain, it is something of a novelty to observe Shakespeare's depiction of her as a demonic transvestite, who was indeed guilty of witchcraft. At a time when renewed interest in the occult makes it again possible to believe in witchcraft, this neglected play of Shakespeare's apprenticeship is winning a new and appreciative audience.

In *The Merchant of Venice,* we also see women dressing as men, but without the homoerotic overtones of *As You Like It* or the demonic ones of *Henry VI.* The stranger in this dark comedy or problem play is not the woman but the Jew. In his discussion of *The Merchant of Venice,* Fiedler tries to rescue the mythic character of Shylock from those who would make him into nothing more than a victim of anti-Semitism or would condemn Shakespeare for not having done so. In the story of Shylock and his daughter Jessica, Fiedler argues, Shakespeare has grafted "onto a pre-Christian folk tale elements derived from the official mythology of the Christian church, though much altered in the course of popular transmission" (117).

Specifically, Shylock is a variation on Abraham, the Jewish father with a knife in his hand. (Because the Jews have been blamed for killing Christ, Abraham is more apt to be remembered by Christians at the point of sacrificing his son than at the moment of reprieve.) In contrast, Jessica is the Jewish maiden who is a good, even redemptive, person to the extent that she is a bad (i.e., treacherous) daughter to her Jewish father. In short, she is a prototype of the Virgin Mary, who by being immaculately conceived and remaining perpetually chaste, is free of any connection with Jewish patriarchy, and who, in her response to the Annunciation, became the first Christian.

Shylock, of course, is not really a merchant of Venice but a moneylender. The merchant who gives the play its title is the equivocal and frequently ignored Antonio. By reading *The Merchant of Venice* as Antonio's play, Fiedler gives us a character who bears an uncanny resemblance to the even more obscure Antonio of *Twelfth Night.* In the comic resolution of the play three young couples are rewarded with marriage, while three older men are frustrated in their deepest desires and excluded from the community of bliss. Shylock is defeated in court and condemned to become a Christian; Portia's father fails to preserve his daughter's virginity with the riddle of the casks he had conceived prior to his death; and Antonio, while gaining both his life and his fortune, is finally more an abandoned father or spurned lover than a successful merchant.

Finding *Othello* to be another of Shakespeare's more mythically resonant plays, Fiedler reminds us that the sources from which this story was drawn did not envision Othello as ethnically black. That innovation was Shakespeare's own unique contribution to the fable, and its significance is more symbolic than racial. Fiedler believes that Shakespeare was not trying to conjure up the largely American nightmare of miscegenation but rather to suggest that Othello is "at the furthest possible cultural remove from the girl he loves and who loves him. . . . It is no mere mistake, however, but the mythmaking instinct of the popular audience which demanded that the destroyer of the most elegant of Patient Griseldas appear in black-face (and she in white, her pallor as much a mask as his swarthiness) in order that they seem as unlike as possible" (173).

Fiedler suggests that structurally we should consider *Othello* two plays—a one-act comedy followed by a tragedy in four acts. The comedy ends in typical enough fashion with the young bride escaping her protective father in order to elope with her beloved. In this case, however, the beloved is not Prince Charming but the beast, and the marriage brings not comic resolution but a bridge to the ensuing tragedy. To complicate matters further, it is a tragedy that comes perilously close to being a bloody farce. Othello (who is mismatched with Desdemona in age as well as race) is busy playing the imagined role of cuckold, while Desdemona is dreaming herself Griselda.

The figure who orchestrates this tragifarce is Iago, who controls the action from the beginning of act two until the midpoint of act five. During this period of control, he plays something very like the Shakespearean fool, accusing Desdemona of faults that the behavior of the other women in the play would seem to suggest are common female weaknesses. As fool, he utters generally applicable platitudes, which in the particular case of Desdemona prove tragically untrue. Thus, he is less fool than devil, and consequently, morally blacker than Othello. For this reason, Fiedler thinks that Othello should be played by a white man in black face and Iago by a black man in white face. In a film production, the colors could progressively bleach and darken until the two characters have symbolically merged roles by act three and reversed them by act five.

Although there are no Africans, Jews, or demonic females in *The Tempest,* Shakespeare's final play exists against a mythic backdrop that makes it, among other things, his definitive statement on the role of the stranger. The magical island on which the action of the play transpires is located on an imaginative continuum that stretches east to Africa and west to America. The two characters who connect us with Africa never appear on stage. One is Claribel, daughter of the king of Naples, who has taken a Tunisian for a husband. (At one point, the king even sees his present misfortune as a judgment on him for having approved the match.) The other is Sycorax, a witch from Algiers who is Caliban's mother. America, on the other hand, is an unspoken presence, the archetypal brave new world being settled by Europeans at the time Shakespeare was writing *The Tempest.*

In Caliban, we see an imaginative linking of the Negro and the Indian. This mythic monster (whose name, of course, is an anagram for "cannibal") is the most alien of Shakespeare's strangers because he is a humanoid composite of so many feared outsiders. If Othello's marriage to Desdemona does not quite suggest the horror of miscegenational rape, then Caliban's attempted violation of Miranda clearly does. Should we accept Fiedler's notion that Europeans instinctively view America as a Caliban culture, then there may be a special ambiguity in Prospero's final reference to Caliban: "this thing of darkness I/Acknowledge mine." Because the phrase "This thing of darkness I" ends one line of verse, it seems "for a moment completely to identify the occultist Duke with the 'savage and deformed slave'; . . . as if, through Prospero, all Europe were accepting responsibility for what was to remain forever malign in the America just then being created by conquest and enslavement" (249).

IV

At the time he was writing *The Stranger in Shakespeare,* Leslie's thirty-two-year marriage to Margaret was finally falling apart. In many ways, things had been troubled from the very beginning. Their passionate relationship had been characterized by anger as well as love. Years later, Leslie wondered if their greatest intimacy had not been when they were fighting. At least at those moments there had been some degree of communication. The fact that Leslie volunteered to serve in World War II during a period when he and Margaret had not been talking for several days suggests that the fights were often more productive than the silences that followed them. Perhaps because their rejection of bourgeois values had been part of their initial attraction to each other, the couple tried to maintain an independence and autonomy that would have been difficult enough in a marriage of two highly compatible people. As it was, Leslie and Margaret seemed always to be operating with fundamentally different worldviews.

For all his flamboyance and seeming certitude, Leslie Fiedler is a profoundly ambivalent man. (At one time he joked that his epitaph should read, "He was nothing if not ambivalent.") Al Cook once summed up Leslie's character well when he said that he was always in the middle of the road, but more often than not, it was a road that hadn't been built yet. This quality of mind accounts for the lively dialectic in much of his writing, but it also makes him somewhat enigmatic. In contrast, Margaret desperately needed something to believe in. Having grown up with two inadequate fathers, she spent much of her adult life looking for a source of authority that could give coherence and order to her life. Leslie was no doubt correct in saying that he converted her not from Stalin to Trotsky but from Stalin to himself. Unfortunately, it is as difficult for a man to be a guru to his wife as it is for him to be a hero to his valet.

In addition to being insufficiently sympathetic to his wife's many intense but short-lived enthusiasms, Leslie spent much of his married life trying to experience the youth the depression had denied him. This inevitably meant falling in love with various women. Because he was an incurable romantic, these were infidelities of the heart as well as the flesh. He might have been totally sincere in vowing everlasting chastity in the letters he wrote Margaret from the South Pacific, but things have a way of looking different on dry land. While in China after the war, Leslie developed a crush on a popular singer who was known as the Japanese Dinah Shore. (Her signature song was "Those Beautiful Chinese Nights.") It was only after she told him that she had a son old enough to be in the Japanese army that his ardor cooled.

Leslie's desire to surround himself with beautiful women is not that hard to understand. In his case, however, normal fantasy was enhanced by a childhood in which even the closest members of his own family told him he was ugly. (It is no accident that, when he remembers his brother Harold, he sees a dead ringer for Charlton Heston.) What sweet revenge to walk down Fifth Avenue with a lovely woman—say, Margaret and Alice McIntyre—on each arm. The marriage suffered considerable stress during Leslie's midlife crisis from 1952 to '57. Between the ages of thirty-five and forty, he sought in the arms of other women the sort of comfort he wasn't getting at home. He remembers the summer he spent at Bloomington in 1952—while Margaret and the children were back in Rome—as more of an erotic than a literary experience. (One might guess as much from reading "Pull Down Vanity!") And the year at Princeton was a time when Leslie's personal life seemed to be coming apart, even as *Love and Death in the American Novel* was coming together.

Why did a marriage that had weathered so many crises collapse after three decades? If there was any catalyst, it was the drug bust and the radically different reactions of Leslie and Margaret to this experience. When Leslie first visited Herald Fahringer's office, he noticed a picture of Sacco and Vanzetti over the desk. "That is not the idea, at all," he said. "I want to win, not be a hero, much less a martyr." On the other hand, he believes that, given the chance, Margaret would have made the opposite choice. It was for this reason that he made certain she did not testify.

When Leslie learned that his kids were smoking dope, he took the news in stride without becoming a user himself. Typically, Margaret swung from one extreme to the other. At first, she was horrified to think that her children were violating the drug laws—under her own roof, no less. But her way of dealing with the situation was finally to embrace the counterculture as fervently as she had other causes. She eventually formed a sibling relationship with her offspring, smoking dope herself. Finally, she convinced her brother Paul, a respectable executive with an engineering firm, that the drug culture was superior to the conventional life he was leading and that he should switch from whatever he was then selling and concentrate on pot instead. When he was finally caught, Paul ended up serving a considerable term in the state penitentiary.[12]

Although Margaret had left Leslie many times (to seek shelter not with her mother but with her aunt), she had always come back. And Leslie had welcomed her, not wishing to admit failure in such a significant part of his life as his marriage. A steady stream of little disagreements could be borne, indeed had been borne. But what was finally unendurable was the knowledge that when a big challenge came along, he and Margaret were driven further apart rather than closer together. Having passed age fifty, Leslie felt that he had made it to the top of the hill and was on his way down. If he was to begin life over again, he would have to cut his losses soon. One final bit of philandering forced a crisis.

On his way back from Biafra in 1968, Leslie stopped in Dublin for a James Joyce conference. While there, he went for a drink in the Lincoln Tavern one evening, where the man on the next bar stool, Sean Mac Reamoinn, introduced him to a remarkable young woman named Nuala O'Faolain. Nuala had grown up as one of nine children in a dirt-poor North Dublin family. Nevertheless, she earned scholarships to University College, Dublin; the University of Hull; and finally Oxford. When she met Leslie, she was teaching in the English department at University College, Dublin, and was between men.

Nuala and Leslie struck up a friendship, which lasted for several years. In her memoir *Are You Somebody?* Nuala recalls, "Leslie came and rescued me once when all my money was stolen in Venice. I went and rescued him at a party in New York, when a beautiful girl who had been hitting Norman Mailer in the face was getting ready to hit him, too. He looked like Neptune, and he was a proper Jewish patriarch in his personal life." They saw the movie *Beyond the Valley of the Dolls* together and made a joint presentation at a Joyce seminar held in a palazzo in Trieste in 1970. "I remember standing on the podium," Nuala writes, "singing 'Put another nickel in, / See Our Lady in the skin, / All I want is loving you / and music, music, music.' The school playground ditty was central to some new reading in *Ulysses* we had thought up in a bar."[13] At one point during the conference, Nuala was so drunk that she set her hair on fire when she leaned back against Hugh Kenner and tried to light a cigarette.

---

12. Fiedler, interview with author, Feb. 26, 1999.
13. Nuala O'Faolain, *Are You Somebody: The Accidental Memoir of a Dublin Woman,* 105–6, 106.

Probably the most memorable excursion that Leslie and Nuala shared was a trip to see the legendary film director John Huston at his home in East Galway. Huston was a friend of Alice McIntyre's, and she had told Leslie to "look John up" if he ever got a chance. He had almost done so when he was living in Missoula and Huston was filming *The Misfits* with Clark Gable and Marilyn Monroe in Nevada. But, when he was on his way there, Leslie got a telegram saying, "Marilyn in hospital. Don't come." Now, in July 1969, he and Nuala arrived at Huston's Georgian manor, set in a landscape of big fields and stone walls, in time to watch the gray-and-white televised image of Neil Armstrong stepping onto the surface of the moon.

Much of the talk that weekend was about Marilyn. She had become addicted to sleeping pills in the belief that, if she got enough sleep, she would keep her looks. "[W]hile she was half sedated by them, Paula Strasberg would read her lines to her, over and over. The next day, Marilyn would take barbiturates to counteract the sleeping tablets and finally arrive on the set. And she would know her lines. She'd know the main words in them and how long they were. She would know the exact rhythm of each line. But she would get the tenses all wrong."[14] Huston was convinced that Marilyn would never have killed herself had she found something "socially useful" to do.

Although there was a wife or mistress and several silent children in residence, they all lived in another house, and Huston communicated with them by telephone. At first, Huston did not know what to make of Leslie, who was not seeking an interview or a job—only conversation. (He was even more baffled by Nuala, because she was Irish and female and carried her clothes in a paper sack.) In addition to being a director and actor, Huston was also an amateur artist, whose paintings of women all looked like his daughter Angelica. The one passion Huston and Leslie shared was for cigars, and before Leslie left, Huston drew a picture of him on the cedar lining of a cigar box. It resembled John Huston much more than it did Leslie Fiedler.

The fact that Leslie had an Irish girlfriend probably bothered Margaret less than the fact that he had taken that girlfriend to see John Huston. She believed that such a trip was the prerogative of the wife, not the mistress. This breach of etiquette, along with all the other differences that were surfacing, fatally disturbed the equilibrium of the marriage. The alternating rhythm of quarrel and reconciliation, which had lasted for more than thirty years, was replaced by an environment of sustained hostility. When he published *The Stranger in Shakespeare* in 1972, the deteriorating marriage was very much on Leslie's mind. In act five of *Cymbeline,* Imogen appears to her husband Posthumus in male disguise. Taking her for a presumptuous boy, he strikes her to the ground. "Why

14. Ibid., 107.

did you throw your wedded lady from you?" she asks. *"Hang there like fruit, my soul, / Till the tree die!"* is his reply. Leslie uses these words of Posthumus as the epigraph to his book, which he dedicates: "To Margaret: Act V." The previous fall, he had told Margaret to get out and stay out, before kicking her down the front steps of their home.

On her own, Margaret soon showed up at Attica to join protestors who were picketing that infamous prison. Later, she traveled to Cuernavaca, Mexico, to sit at the feet of the radical education reformer Ivan Ilyich. By the early 1980s, she was living at the Rajneeshpuram commune in rural Oregon. This religious community consisted of followers of Bhagwan Shree Rajneesh, an Indian guru in his early fifties, who claimed to have achieved spiritual enlightenment at the age of twenty-one. (Among other things, he believed that two-thirds of the human race would be dead from AIDS by the year 2000 and exhorted his followers to wear both condoms and rubber gloves while making love and to avoid kissing.) Over the next three decades, the Bhagwan spread his doctrines from India to the Western World—Germany, Japan, Australia, Holland, England, and finally, Canada. Then, in 1981, he purchased six million dollars' worth of land in a sparsely populated section of Oregon and moved in with several thousand devotees and a fleet of luxury automobiles. Along with other worshipers of the Enlightened One, Margaret would take her turn riding a helicopter into the clear Oregon sky, from which she scattered rose petals as the Bhagwan, in one of his twenty-seven Rolls Royces, passed on the road below.[15]

---

15. Fiedler, interview with author, Feb. 26, 1999.

CHAPTER SEVENTEEN

Eleanor Mooseheart

IN THE FALL of 1971, Sally Smith Andersen was a single mother of two young sons with an uncertain future. She had lost her initial bid for tenure in the English department at the University of Illinois and was apprehensive about the prospects of her second and final chance. Although she was a promising poet, it was unclear how much her publications in that genre would advance her academic career. Just to be safe, she resolved to go job hunting at the next meeting of the Modern Language Association, which was to be held in Chicago between Christmas and New Year's. In the meantime, Ruth Stone—who was a guest professor at Illinois that year—had invited Sally to spend Christmas with her in Brandon, Vermont.

As Sally became a more committed poet, she began to look upon Ruth as a mentor. During Ruth's time in Illinois, she and Sally gave readings together and struck up a warm friendship. The older woman was not only a more experienced and successful poet, she was also Sally's guide to a world that seemed more sophisticated than any she had previously known. Sally had had a conventional Middle American upbringing with periodic visits to family in southern Illinois and Mayfield, Kentucky. The only real celebrity in her family was her great aunt, Alice Hegen Rice, who wrote *Mrs. Wiggs of the Cabbage Patch*. Christmas in Vermont seemed just the sort of interlude to take Sally's mind off the precariousness of her personal and professional life.

Sally and Ruth set out from Champaign-Urbana, Illinois, in Sally's car, driving all day and well into the night; snow fell steadily and the roads grew increasingly hazardous. As was her habit when traveling back to Vermont, Ruth intended to spend the night at Leslie's house in Buffalo. Because Sally had never met Leslie, her impressions of him were based entirely on his work. Having recently read *Being Busted,* she asked Ruth, "Does Leslie Fiedler use drugs?" "Absolutely not," Ruth replied, "but he has one foot in the alcoholic grave." (Given the fact that both Sally's father and her ex-husband had been alcoholics, this was not an auspicious introduction.)

As it turned out, Leslie was not even at home but was off attending a bar mitzvah in Holland. Margaret was gone by now, and the house, which could only be described as a crash pad, was occupied by various Fiedler children and assorted friends. Because no one was in charge in Leslie's absence, Sally had to go from room to room, searching for a place to sleep. In each room a ritual kept repeating itself: two wild-haired hippie heads (one male and one female) would pop up from under the covers. She finally sacked out on the floor of a room on the third story. The next morning, practically starving, Sally looked for something to eat in the kitchen. All she found was a single piece of lasagna, which was being saved for Leslie upon his return from Amsterdam. One of the kids had painted on the kitchen wall: "You are always welcome in my home."

Before starting the final leg of the trip to Vermont, Sally purchased snow tires for her car. Unfortunately, the people who sold them to her didn't speak English. It was not until she got to Ruth's property in Vermont and one of the wheels fell off her car that she realized the snow tires were the wrong size. The first evening in Vermont, Sally and Ruth slept in the barn with another ad hoc commune of young people—including Michael Fiedler, who had recently been in jail in Israel and had brought back a very bad and very contagious case of head lice. The house in Brandon was scarcely an improvement over the barn. The pipes had frozen, so there was no running water, and Sally had to go to the local beauty parlor to get her hair washed. The carcass of the Thanksgiving turkey was rotting in the refrigerator, and Sally discovered, much to her chagrin, that the previous occupants of the bed in which she slept had had crab lice. But it was a lively household, filled with painting, poetry, and song. Several of the kids purchased arty Christmas presents for Sally at a combination thrift and antique shop.

Given the condition of her car, Sally flew to Chicago for the MLA convention. On the second day of the gathering, a graduate student from Illinois invited her along to Leslie Fiedler's talk on Shakespeare. After the talk, Sally introduced herself to Leslie and thanked him for letting her stay at his home. They retired to the hotel bar and agreed to meet later that night to attend the parties being thrown by their respective departments. Such parties are traditionally held during the "cocktail hour," before anyone has had a chance to eat supper. Starting at the Illinois party, Leslie and Sally began guzzling drinks on empty stomachs. Because Leslie had already had a good start and Sally was an inexperienced drinker, they were both soon in their cups. (Upon departing the jammed hotel suite, Leslie accidentally stepped in a wastebasket.) After more drinks at the Buffalo party, they both became a little disoriented. They finally got some supper somewhere, but Sally figures she probably didn't eat much of it because, when she woke up the next morning in Leslie's hotel room, she discovered a steak in her pocket along with some carrots and celery sticks from the Illinois party.

Sally and Leslie spent the final two days of the convention together. This forced Sally to miss a dinner engagement at the home of a dear friend, who has not spoken to her since, and Leslie to cancel a scheduled appearance on the Irv Kupcinet radio show. When Leslie flew back to Buffalo, Sally had to try to make sense out of what had just happened. She had fallen madly in love with a charismatic man old enough to be her father. (She was born the year that Leslie and Margaret got married.) Did he feel the same or was this just a convention dalliance? Her friend Yvonne Noble, who taught at Illinois and had seen Leslie operate at previous conferences, told Sally that she would have to act like an adult. Not only would Leslie not call her, he probably wouldn't even remember her name.

Three days later, Yvonne Noble was proved wrong. Leslie called and invited Sally to accompany him to a party in New York. The party turned out to be a reception for Yevgeny Yevtushenko at the New School for Social Research. She bought a beautiful new dress, held up by a snap that was always coming undone. Then, the day before the party, her face broke out in a rash. (She later concluded that this was an allergic reaction to tetracycline.) In a panic, she went to the cosmetics counter at a nearby department store and purchased a remedy called Charles of the Ritz Disaster Cream. Unfortunately, she did not realize that the cream was supposed to be applied the night before it was needed. Consequently, Sally found herself at an elegant reception with a dress that kept coming unsnapped and a face that appeared to be caked with greasepaint. In the center of the room, Leonard Bernstein was playing the piano, while Bob Dylan was off in a corner playing his guitar.

It was at this point, with Sally's confidence at low ebb, that Allen Ginsberg and Gregory Corso walked in. Upon seeing Sally, Gregory said, "One of Leslie's concubines, I presume." Enraged, she hit him with her rolled-up program and almost burst into tears. Seeing that she was distraught, Allen put his arm around her and kept telling her in comforting tones: "Remember, all is maia. All is illusion." Rather than meeting the other celebrities in attendance, Sally spent much of the rest of the evening fuming in the ladies' room, as Puerto Rican maids helped her scrape Disaster Cream off her face.

I

During the spring semester of 1972, Leslie spoke a total of three times at the University of Illinois. One of these occasions was a poetry reading, which almost didn't come off when the luggage with his poems wound up in Nome, Alaska. He and Sally got his published poems from the library, and he managed to talk a good bit between delivering each one. The romance blossomed, even as practical obstacles kept Leslie and Sally from making a permanent commitment to each other. For one thing, Leslie's children were still hopeful that their parents would reconcile. This created some awkward moments, especially after Debbie Fiedler decided that she wanted to resume her education by enrolling at Illinois. She also moved in with Sally so that she could observe the budding relationship. On one of Leslie's visits, she handed him a letter from Margaret suggesting that they get back together. All that Sally could do was sit there hoping she was not a home wrecker. Meanwhile, her own children (Soren, ten, and Eric, six) wanted their mother to themselves and resented this strange man in their lives. On one occasion, Eric placed himself on the couch between Leslie and Sally and pummeled Leslie with his little fists to get him to move as far away as possible.[1]

If Sally was by now the prime candidate to be the next Mrs. Leslie Fiedler, it was because she had jumped to the head of the queue. Although Leslie had been temporarily smitten with many women over the years, his most enduring relationship had been with Alice McIntyre. It was she who had first gotten him to write for *Esquire* and thus had introduced him to a popular audience. During his year in Princeton, their romance became so intense that it looked as if Leslie's marriage to Margaret might end at that point. Dealing with the situation in the only way she knew how, Margaret became close friends with Alice as a way of interposing herself between her husband and the other woman. *The Second Stone* is the only one of Leslie's books with no dedication, because the dedication would almost certainly have gone to Alice, who was the model for Hilda Stone. He thought of her as his muse, and she thought of him as her rabbi.

In a strange way, Leslie's relationship with Alice was inextricably bound up with his marriage to Margaret. Between them, these two women gave him what neither was capable of giving alone. (The situation of Vincent Hazelbaker and his longtime harem in "The Last WASP in the World" is imaginatively pretty close to Leslie's own experience.) With Margaret out of the picture, Leslie's relationship with Alice would inevitably change. It had gone on so long and so far that it would either have to progress to marriage or end entirely.

The more he thought about living permanently with Alice, the more Leslie realized how different they actually were. He liked his women to be beautiful and a little crazy, but somehow Alice was too much of both. Her clothes were always the most stylish and her hair always the right tint. Her physical perfection, which seemed alluring in a mistress, was a bit threatening in a potential wife. After she left *Esquire,* Alice moved back to her native California. Never one to tolerate a daily routine, she spent most of her time writing largely unpublished poetry. With Sally telling him to fish or cut bait, Leslie traveled to

1. Sally Fiedler, interview with author, Feb. 27, 1999.

California to find out if his twenty-five-year relationship with Alice was finally over. After his return, they never spoke to each other again, although a mutual friend will occasionally get drunk and call Leslie to tell him that he is still the love of Alice's life.[2]

In the summer of 1972, Sally and her two boys came to Buffalo to spend some time in Leslie's household. Although various Fiedler offspring were in and out of town, the only one who was living permanently at Morris Avenue was Leslie's youngest child, Miriam, who was always called Mimo after a character in Bernard Malamud's *The Natural*. (When Malamud was teaching at Oregon State and Leslie was still at Missoula, the two had been so close that Leslie's kids referred to Malamud as "Uncle Bernie.") Mimo, who was seventeen in the summer of 1972, married sixteen-year-old Bob Konrad at the Fiedlers' annual Fourth of July party. Shortly thereafter, while Soren and Eric Andersen were spending some time with their father, Sally and Leslie took a trip to Europe, where they saw Kappy and other expatriate friends. The sojourn concluded with a three-week stay in an old monastery on an island off the coast of Greece. Although the facilities were rustic (two cots, a jug of water, and no indoor plumbing), the setting was beautiful. With his drug conviction recently reversed and his divorce from Margaret imminent, Leslie appeared to be a free man. It was now up to Sally to determine whether she should make this radical change in her life. She decided to go back to Illinois to teach in the fall and contemplate her future.

Rather than irrevocably burn her bridges behind her, Sally sought a leave of absence for the spring of 1973. She moved back to Buffalo with Soren and Eric and, despite the opposition of her children and his, she and Leslie were married—by a justice of the peace at the same courthouse where his drug case had been initially tried six years earlier. (Leslie's mother observed that her son needed two young children like he needed a hole in the head.) They left the courthouse just as the police were changing shifts. "Congratulations Professor," several familiar cops shouted jocularly. "Just don't spend your honeymoon in Buffalo."

In addition to Leslie and Mimo, the only other member of the Fiedler household to bridge the departure of Margaret and the arrival of Sally was Leslie's dog. In his poem "To My Old Dog Chuki: A Love Story," Leslie recalls the time when

> My then beloved wife managed—
> "Accidentally," she explained at great length—
> To knock you into the half-frozen pool

---

2. Fiedler, interview with author, Feb. 26, 1999.

Backing up in her shiny new car
Really suspecting, I guess,
That we loved each other more
Than either of us did her.

Although she was already "half-blind, lame, and incontinent," Chuki managed to survive this disaster

Long enough to lie—
Twitching feebly and dreaming
No doubt of the old days
By the Blackfoot—
Safe in the lap of my brand-new beloved. . . . [3]

As Jack Fiedler could have told Sally were he still alive, life with Leslie would prove to be a series of shocks and surprises. For one thing, he never locked his door at night, thinking someone might need him. On several occasions, someone did. One night, about a month into the marriage, Leslie and Sally were awakened late at night by a pounding on their bedroom door. When Sally opened the door, she was confronted by a young black man, who appeared to be seven feet tall and to weigh three hundred pounds. Before she could gather her wits to ask him who he was, she heard Leslie say, "What do you need, Homer?" Homer had been a high school friend of Leslie's daughter Jenny. On this particular night, both he and his probation officer were too drunk to find their way home. Leslie, who slept in the nude, threw on a robe, walked Homer downstairs, pointed in the direction of his home, and said, "Drive that way."

One morning, some months later, Sally went to check on seven-year-old Eric. Curled up next to Eric in his single bed was a young writer whom Leslie had tried to encourage. The last anyone had heard of him, he had been confined to a mental hospital. Apparently, he had stolen an attendant's uniform and an ambulance and had broken out of the asylum. Having no place else to go, he drove the ambulance to Morris Avenue, parked it in the driveway, and crashed in a random bedroom. Although he was relatively harmless in the Fiedler house, the young writer did threaten some other people during this unauthorized furlough from bedlam.

A few weeks later, Sally came downstairs for breakfast and found a borderline psychotic fighting with her eleven-year-old son, Soren, over a glass of orange juice. Not knowing what to make of the situation, Soren kept saying (in his frightened little boy's voice), "But it's mine." Finally, in his own manic,

---

3. Typescript in the possession of the author.

high-pitched voice, the psychotic began mimicking Soren: "It's mine, mine, mine!" Sally did her best to interpose herself between her son and his tormentor, only to learn later that the young intruder's greatest hostility was toward women. (Once when Leslie was out of town, Sally had to talk him out of burning down their house.) From one of the most prominent families in Buffalo, this man had been writing a dissertation with Leslie for at least twenty years.

Sally was not the only one to experience culture shock. When it came time for Leslie to meet her family, he felt as if he were Woody Allen cast in a very bad movie about the Old South. Not long after their wedding, the couple visited Sally's step-grandmother, Betty, and her sister, Rubal, in Mayfield, Kentucky, at a house that looked as if it belonged in a Faulkner novel. (Although it had seemed like Tara when Sally was a child, it now more nearly resembled Thomas Sutpen's decaying mansion.) At the door, they were met by Parthenia, an old black maid who appeared to have come right out of central casting. Throwing her arms around the new Mrs. Fiedler, Parthenia gushed, "I'se so glad to see you Miz Sally."

Betty and Rubal—both in their mid-eighties—were dressed to the nines and sitting before a fire during a sweltering summer. As they sipped bourbon and ate English biscuit, they made a fuss over Leslie as the man who "saved our little girl." Later, over a dinner of fried chicken, lima beans in cream sauce, and strawberry shortcake, Betty casually observed, "You know Sally, they're letting Jews into the country club. I guess somebody's got to pay for the new eighteen-hole golf course." As Betty went on about this fat and vulgar Jew, Sally experienced a crisis of conscience. Was this the point at which a person of principle would say, "My husband is Jewish"? (Even Soren and Eric seemed to be uncomfortable.) But, when Sally looked over at Leslie and saw the merriment in his eyes, she relaxed—knowing how he must be enjoying the absurdity of the moment.

While Leslie could take high camp enjoyment in the Old South, he found the New South depressingly like the rest of the suburban Sunbelt. This was never more true than when he attended a conference on the American Future in West Palm Beach, Florida, November 15–16, 1974. The conference was organized by Mel Tumin and sponsored by IT&T, with the covert purpose of persuading influential politicians and industrialists to establish a state university in that part of Florida. The participants included three Nobel Prize winners, the civil rights leader and Washington insider Vernon Jordan, radical feminist Kate Millet, Sidney Hook, William F. Buckley, Jr., and Arthur M. Schlesinger, Jr. Leslie's panel, on popular and elite culture, consisted of himself, Truman Capote, Harold Rosenberg, and Lionel Trilling.

Although the conference did not succeed in getting a new university built, it did produce some memorable results. For one thing, Leslie came so far out of the pop culture closet that he ended up arguing with Lionel Trilling about the value of soap operas. In addition, he got to see his tall new wife dance with Truman Capote, who didn't seem to rise much above Sally's waist. Leslie also found himself functioning once again in the role of cultural interpreter. Although the pop culture superstars found it difficult to talk with the old-time Jewish intellectuals, Leslie could serve as a mediator between the camps. Finally, he saw a great blow for America's future struck that weekend when the resident middle-aged feminist introduced Mel Tumin's sixteen-year-old son to the mysteries of sex.[4]

II

For years now, Leslie has referred to his second marriage as the "Reign of Sally." It is perhaps ironic that a critic famous for celebrating the flight from petticoat government in American life and literature has submitted himself so readily to a conventional domestic regime. But, as we have seen, Leslie is a man of ambivalence and paradox—if not outright contradiction. And, as anyone who has spent time in her tactful and sweet-tempered presence can see, Sally is no Dame Van Winkle. If her family is correct in believing that Leslie saved Sally, there is a sense in which she saved him as well.

As troubled as his marriage to Margaret might have been, it is difficult to imagine Leslie accomplishing as much as he did as a single man. Even when he strayed from the bounds of monogamy, it was hard for him to remember a time when he was not a husband and father. These roles gave his life a stability it would otherwise have lacked. He conceived of "Come Back to the Raft Ag'in, Huck Honey!" while reading *Huckleberry Finn* to Kurt and Eric; however, he would have had an infinitely more difficult time writing this essay and his other criticism had he not had a wife to run the household and keep the kids at bay while he was working. If the breakup with Margaret freed him from the major source of conflict in his life, it also robbed him of a familiar part of his identity. Although the experience may not have been as traumatic as the midlife crisis he had suffered at Princeton twenty-five years earlier, neither did he find it altogether comfortable to be a bachelor for the first time in his adult years. The word soon spread among women he would kiss at parties to keep their teeth clenched if they did not wish for the intimacy to extend beyond a perfunctory gesture of greeting.

When Sally entered his life, the good bad boy, now in his mid-fifties, was finally ready to settle down. The house on Morris Avenue was soon restored

---

4. Fiedler, interview with author, Feb. 27, 1999; Sally Fiedler, interviews with author, Feb. 27, 1999, July 10, 1999.

to a degree of cleanliness and order. If Leslie's wild friends were still welcome there, even they sensed that the 1960s were over. The Fourth of July parties became less frenetic and eventually stopped. By the mid-1970s, Leslie was listing the date of his marriage as 1973 and identifying himself as the father of eight children! Sally made it clear, however, that she would not have another four so that he could be the patriarch of a Jewish tribe.[5]

As the only one of Leslie's biological offspring still at home, Mimo had witnessed the last agonizing months of her parents' marriage and was not ready for a stranger to take her mother's place. If the original family could not be salvaged, she at least wanted her father to herself. In a strange way, those early years of conflict ultimately brought Mimo and Sally closer together. When they didn't end up killing each other, they became instead the best of friends. Today they stay in touch with an ease and frequency that amuses the telephone-shy Leslie.

If marriage to Leslie represented a radical change in Sally's personal life, her career was altered in far more problematic ways. As an assistant professor at the University of Illinois, she was trying to climb the academic ladder. To give up both the hope of tenure and the ability to move to wherever a suitable job might materialize is tantamount to leaving the profession. She could always teach as an adjunct instructor at SUNY-Buffalo or one of the other local colleges, but that would mean low pay and even less prestige. She and Leslie team-taught one creative writing class, but she had mixed feelings about the experience. The pleasure of sharing a "fun" course with her husband was undercut by the realization that their students called him "Dr. Fiedler" and her "Sally."

Fortunately, Buffalo is the location of several elite preparatory schools for both boys and girls. In the late 1970s, Sally secured a position at the Nichols School, a formerly all-male institution, which had just gone coeducational. Although "nurturing" even bright adolescents is not quite the same as "mentoring" graduate students, it beats teaching freshman comp at night school. The job at Nichols seemed to give Sally a career and an identity of her own without having to sacrifice her roles as wife and mother. Besides, there were professional advantages to being Mrs. Leslie Fiedler. When it came time to schedule visiting speakers, it helped to have a husband who counted some of the most prominent writers in the profession among his personal friends. At least in theory, it seemed like a real coup when Leslie persuaded Allen Ginsberg to bring his act to Sally's school.

Had he chosen to do so, Allen probably could have given an unforgettable but inoffensive reading. (A sophisticated prep school, after all, is not the same

5. Jackson and Christian, interview with author, July 10, 1999.

as a fundamentalist religious academy.) But every radical worthy of the name finds it a special joy to gross out would-be liberals. (In his address to the Harvard Divinity School, Ralph Waldo Emerson managed the seemingly impossible task of getting himself branded a heretic by a bunch of "Unitarian theologians.") Surely, Sally should have sensed trouble when Allen mentioned that he would be sharing the bill with his longtime boyfriend, Peter Orlovsky. Although Ginsberg himself has written on a range of topics, Orlovsky seems fixated on the scatological and the homoerotic—including such evocative lyrics as "Jerking Off Allen Ginsberg in Tangiers." It promised to be a memorable occasion.

When Allen and Peter came to town, they stayed at Morris Avenue. Remembering their visit two decades later, Sally simply describes them as "wild and woolly." Peter, who was suffering from a cold, constantly chewed garlic, which made his presence in a closed car nearly unbearable. The two were scheduled to read twice at the Nichols School—once in the afternoon for the students and then again in the evening for the general public. As was his custom, Allen burned incense on the stage and punctuated his reading with instrumental music and Oriental chants. He read a tribute to his late father, which included frank descriptions of his own sexual practices. Peter went further over the line, with a long poem about "shit" and even more graphic sexual passages. When the roof didn't fall in and the students responded with polite applause, rather than a mass walkout, Sally thought she was home free. "Should we be careful this evening?" Allen asked. Not wanting to seem a prude or a censor, Sally told him to use his own best judgment.

Apparently, word had gotten around about the afternoon reading. Consequently, the headmaster and trustees of the school were in attendance, along with a sizable number of parents and seemingly half the city of Buffalo. The atmosphere was so tense that one could almost smell the wire burning in the walls. On this occasion, many people did get up and walk out—including the headmaster's wife. Leslie and Sally's next-door neighbor Larry Desaultels recalls overhearing two blue-haired ladies who did stay for the entire reading conversing on the way out. "I certainly hope there wasn't as much 'sucking' and 'fucking' when they read for the young people this afternoon," one said to the other. After an emergency meeting of the board of trustees, the headmaster was sacked and replaced with a bluenosed Puritan who insisted on prior approval of all visiting speakers.[6]

The common thread through the stages of Sally's professional life was her poetry. In her collection *Eleanor Mooseheart* (1992), she reflects humorously

---

6. Sally Fiedler, interview with author, July 10, 1999.

on the mundane challenges of domesticity and (in so doing) gives us a unique perspective on her marriage to Leslie. Most of the conflicts Eleanor encounters involve her husband, Horace. They argue over such things as whether the cat should be put out in the snow at night or whether the animals really mind if they eat meat. A sense of mortality pervades a few of the poems. In "Figuring It Out," Eleanor tries to imagine what life will be like without Horace, who is obviously older than she, while he claims that it means she secretly wants him dead. "A Time for Decisions" has Eleanor thinking about burial preparations for herself and Horace as she puts their dead cat to rest under the begonias and Horace growls about the bills for the cat's chemotherapy. In "An Old Story," Horace spends hours each day reading obituaries for such familiar names as Broderick Crawford, Bernie Malamud, and Otto Preminger. ("'They're dropping like flies,' he mutters.") Eleanor tries to take his mind off this fixation by preparing his favorite dishes, no longer flirting with the man across the street, and reminding Horace of his old girlfriends. But the best strategy is to call him by his favorite name. "'Hey there' —she says, / 'King of the Beasts!'"

One particularly memorable poem concerns the different ways in which men and women deal with the physical effects of aging and of the concessions women inevitably make in the process. Although a feminist sensibility is evident here, the light tone makes the message all the more compelling. "Cold Wave" reads as follows:

> Horace and Eleanor are fighting
> about the heat.
> He has been chilly of late,
> and Eleanor's life is just
> one long hot flash.
> He pushes the thermostat up,
> she sticks her head out
> the bathroom window.
> He piles on the covers,
> she strips off her nightgown
> and dangles her feet over
> the edge of the bed.
>
> We've got to compromise, Eleanor thinks.
> That is the way it is in a marriage.
> I give a little, he gives a little.
> She begins to wear lighter clothes.
> She ices her cranapple juice.
> She walks out in the snow without her galoshes.
> She floats her wrists under

the cold-water tap.
Horace is downstairs
building a fire.[7]

III

In addition to freeing him from a legal threat, the reversal of Leslie's drug conviction also removed a stigma that had kept him in a precarious position in the Buffalo English department. Although his colleagues supported him throughout his ordeal, the university regarded the entire case as a public relations problem. As much as the department might have wanted him as chairman, the university was not about to give serious administrative responsibilities to a convicted drug offender. Moreover, distinguished professorships that were endowed with private money usually required at least the tacit approval of the donor. As a practical matter, this meant being acceptable to well-heeled WASPs. As a controversial Jew, Leslie would have been a hard sell under the best of conditions. His drug sentence put him indefinitely beyond the pale.

When the drug case was finally resolved in Leslie's favor in July 1972, the university was prepared to give him the endowed chair he so richly deserved. Unfortunately, even a verdict of legal innocence was not sufficient to persuade any private donor to fork over the necessary money. So, the university created a special chair out of funds coming directly from the president's office and even offered to let Leslie name the position. Although the "Huckleberry Finn professorship" struck the authorities as being a bit too informal, they finally agreed to let Leslie call himself the "Samuel L. Clemens Professor." Unlike so many academic chairs, this was created especially for the person who holds it and will cease to exist when Leslie retires.

One of the benefits that went with the Clemens chair was a private secretary to assist Leslie with his various professional endeavors. (Given his hatred of the telephone, he was also delighted to have someone to field his calls.) In November 1972, Leslie hired Joyce Troy, who was looking for work after having spent her earlier adult life raising a family. Not only was she unfamiliar with academia and the literary profession, Joyce had not even completed her B.A. degree. Perhaps for that reason, Leslie proved to be an ideal employer and mentor. Years later, Joyce remembers his patience as she was feeling her way in this new world. (He did not even chastise her when she began a letter to the literary journal *Salmagundi* with the greeting: "Dear Mr. Magundi.") Over the next three decades, Joyce would become such a fixture in Leslie's office that

---

7. Sally A. Fiedler, *Eleanor Mooseheart,* 27, 33.

those who had business with him would come to rely upon her almost as much as he did. In addition to typing his manuscripts, securing permission to use a wide range of copyrighted material, arranging his travel, and making sure that he got paid for his many lectures, Joyce has kept track of Leslie's publications since 1970. Anyone ambitious enough to compile a Fiedler bibliography will have to begin by checking her voluminous files.

Not long after arriving in Buffalo, Leslie helped found the Empire State University, a program that enabled older adults to complete their education by giving them credit for "life experience" and assigning them to work with personal tutors. (One of Leslie's charges in this program confessed to him that she had done time for killing her mother, whom she had accidentally shot while aiming at her father.) After working under him for many years, Joyce finally completed her own degree in the Empire State program under Leslie's direction. It was something of a thrill, after having listened to him for so long, to have him listen to her.[8]

On September 1, 1974, Leslie finally began a three-year term as chairman of the Buffalo English department. Unlike his tenure at Missoula, he did nothing to rock the boat in his new position. The university was progressive, even by his own iconoclastic standards, and he got along well with the administration. After the heady days in which Al Cook had built the department, the mid-1970s proved to be a time of retrenchment. Although Leslie was more than a mere caretaker, he knew how to delegate responsibility and refused to take the job home with him. The administrative work was no great burden. What he found most unpleasant were the glimpses the job gave him into the difficult sides of people's personalities. It was like being a priest without the power of absolution or a psychiatrist without the ability to prescribe therapy.

It is not easy for an administrator to deal professionally with personal friends. Leslie discovered this when much of his time as chairman was taken up with complaints by or about Bruce Jackson. Bruce had come to the department shortly after Leslie's arrival and had proved a faithful friend during the drug case and many other personal crises. (He had even accompanied Leslie to California for his final confrontation with Alice McIntyre.) Bruce's first marriage began to fall apart about the same time as Leslie's final split with Margaret. Then, not too long before Leslie met Sally, Bruce became involved with Diane Christian, whom he would later marry. A former nun, Diane was beginning a new life as both a secular woman and an English professor. (When she and Bruce finally wed, Leslie pointed out that she had now been married to two Jews.) Like Leslie and Sally, she and Bruce were starting life over together in the early 1970s.

8. Joyce Troy, interview with author, July 9, 1999; Leslie Fiedler, interview with author, July 8, 1999.

Perhaps the acid test of Leslie's friendship with Bruce came in his three years as chairman. Twenty-five years later, neither man could recall the specific points of controversy. (It has been said many times that academic politics are so vicious because the stakes are so low.) Whatever strains may have existed at the time, the whole period seems rather farcical now. "I spent half my time dealing with everyone other than Bruce," Leslie recalls. Bruce himself simply says, "I can usually get my way because I have a forceful personality and I know how to argue. None of that worked with Leslie."[9]

If chairing the department was more a civic duty than a new career path, Leslie's interest in the direction of the profession had remained constant at least from the time that he had directed the humanities program at Missoula. As he once put it, "I spent the first half of my career trying to break down the barriers between academic disciplines and the second half trying to tear down the walls between elite and popular culture."[10] This latter effort was on display at a meeting of the English Institute in 1979. The program that Leslie and the African American critic Houston Baker had organized was ostensibly to deal with two topics—"English as a World Language for Literature" and "The Institution of Literature." The implicit common denominator of papers delivered under both of these headings was the effort to "open up the canon."

In his contribution to the program, Leslie discussed the institution of literature as it is found in the academy. Although the vestige of a literary culture exists outside the academy, increasingly, "literature is effectively what we teach in departments of English; or conversely, what we teach in departments of English is literature."[11] This is because writers and critics of "serious literature" have essentially been absorbed by the academy. Until early in the twentieth century, professors of literature were old-line philological scholars, who believed that only the classics were worthy of study (preferably in the original Greek and Latin). When they did express preferences for literature written in living languages, it was usually for the safely genteel and sentimental. The first great revolution in English studies came when this old guard was overthrown by defenders of modernism and scholarship was replaced by "criticism." Leslie sensed that that revolution had run its course and that another one, equally radical, was needed.

Even when they considered themselves political populists, the defenders of modernism—and its preferred exegetical method, New Criticism—were hardcore cultural elitists. *Partisan Review* might have seemed schizophrenic in its twin commitment to political revolution and literary hierarchy, but Marx himself was devoted to traditional high culture. Consequently, the defense

9. Jackson and Christian, interview with author, July 10, 1999.
10. Fiedler, interview with author, July 8, 1999.
11. Leslie Fiedler, "Literature as an Institution: The View from 1980," 73.

of cultural standards, as embodied in the modernist canon, became common ground for literary academics of various political persuasions. Whether their ideal society was the Agrarian South or a more perfect Soviet Union, they shared common citizenship in the Republic of Letters. This exclusive club effectively denied admittance to anyone who confessed a liking for most of the songs and stories that have moved the masses over the ages. Particularly taboo was any entertainment that had become accessible to a mass audience through media more recent than the Gutenberg press. In fact, the split between elite and popular culture had become so pronounced that the book no longer seemed to be the final form for any text. Mass literature became films or popular songs, while "serious" fiction and poetry were turned into classroom exhibits.

Leslie wished to reverse the modernist revolution by returning to a time when the most sophisticated members of society and the groundlings could both respond to the same songs and stories. Art has many functions in society, but marking differences in class should not be one of them. Of course, it is one thing to seek a literature that can bridge the gap between elite and popular culture; finding it is quite another matter. Leslie's earlier work (which he has not completely repudiated) suggests that the solution surely does not lie in finding some sort of happy medium in middlebrow culture. Neither does it lie in subjecting popular art to the same kind of deadly critical approaches that have threatened to make elite literature unreadable. (That is why Leslie eventually stopped attending the annual meetings of the Popular Culture Association.) What he eventually did was to return to an insight he had first ventured in his plea for amateur criticism in the *Kenyon Review,* which was to see if myth criticism could help to reunify our sundered culture. At the same time he was developing this position, he brought his own brand of amateur enthusiasm to the study of popular genres. On occasion, this involved venturing into those same genres himself.

CHAPTER EIGHTEEN

Mutants New and Old

THE SAME YEAR that he became chairman of the Buffalo English department, Leslie published his third novel, *The Messengers Will Come No More*. The book contains two dedications: "To Sally / who broke the block / with love"; and: "To Phil / who showed the way, / with thanks." If Leslie's many friends and colleagues knew who Sally was, probably few would have been able to identify Phil as Philip José Farmer, a writer who successfully combined the lowbrow genres of science fiction and pornography. (One of his books— a "feral-man anthology" called *Mother Was a Lovely Beast*—is dedicated to Leslie.) Although he had read science fiction for years, it was not until the mid-1960s that Leslie began discussing it in print. (A few comments in *Waiting for the End* constitute the first tentative breakthrough.) His son Eric had introduced him to the genre, and in turn, Leslie had tried to convince Eric that highbrow writers such as Kafka were actually writing science fiction before the term was invented. In fact, Leslie has argued that "the history of science fiction is essentially the history of a name."[1]

Although futurist fantasy had been written since ancient times (some literary historians cite Plato's work as a forerunner of sci-fi), science fiction as we know it was impossible before the revolutionary technological developments that took place late in the Victorian era. Jules Verne and H. G. Wells—both of whom began writing at the end of the nineteenth century—are regarded as the inventors of modern science fiction, although some devotees believe that the genre was anticipated in some of Poe's tales. The term *science fiction* itself was coined by Hugo Gernsback, editor of *Amazing Stories* magazine in 1929. What Gernsback had in mind was "a charming romance intermingled with scientific fact and prophetic vision" (*Dreams,* 11). This definition was consistent

---

1. Leslie Fiedler, *In Dreams Awake: A Historical-Critical Anthology of Science Fiction,* 11. Subsequent references will be cited parenthetically in the text as *Dreams*.

with the Victorian separation of fiction into novels and romances and seemed to be generally accepted until the 1930s, when most American writers who considered themselves hardcore science fictionists insisted that they were essentially realists and even progressive social satirists (an image fully endorsed by Gernsback's successor, John W. Campbell). It is probably no accident that the golden age of American science fiction coincided with the New Deal of Franklin Roosevelt.

If the pioneers of American science fiction found it comforting to think of themselves as writing in the tradition of liberal realism (as defined by, say, V. L. Parrington), it was in denial of the awkward fact that they were dealing in technological fantasies that appealed more to a right-wing Nietzschean imagination than to the pieties of social democracy. (Robert Heinlein is the second favorite novelist of American libertarians, ranking only behind Ayn Rand.) As Leslie himself put the matter in the introduction to his anthology of science fiction, *In Dreams Awake:*

> At first . . . , American s-f sought to deny the dangerous ambiguity of its deep fantasies by denying, in the name of "realism," all fantasy. Yet a basic appeal of the genre surely lies in its creation of technologically oriented mythologies to replace the older ones made obsolete by science. In order to survive, however, such mythologies had to be presented as if they were rooted not in "wonder" and dreams but in "extrapolation" from scientific "fact." Science fiction may be a literature of dreams, but its dreams are those of men dreaming they are awake. (15)

Although highbrow British writers such as H. G. Wells, Aldous Huxley, George Orwell, C. S. Lewis, William Golding, and Anthony Burgess have been able to do science fiction with no loss of cultural status, American practitioners of the form were originally considered vulgar hacks. When Leslie used to attend their conventions, he saw a small and incestuous group of people who swapped wives, mistresses, friends, and enemies, while upholding the image of the American writer as a world-class drunk. The first generation of American science fictionists (Robert Heinlein, A. E. Van Vogt, Ray Bradbury, Isaac Asimov, and Philip Farmer wrote in the so-called golden age) were unabashed popular writers with no great pretensions to high culture.

With the dawn of postmodernism, however, certain writers who were generally considered serious artists (e. g., William S. Burroughs and John Barth) began adopting the conventions of sci-fi, first in the form of parody and later in the name of experimentation. The one science fiction writer of the older generation who managed to pass over from pop culture to literary respectability was Kurt Vonnegut, Jr., who began publishing pulp stories in hardcore sci-fi magazines, but ended up producing fantasies for an elite audience. Rather than seeing Vonnegut's success as a vindication of their genre, other members of the older generation looked upon him as a traitor. For Leslie Fiedler, however, Vonnegut represented an interesting test case in the effort to move beyond the strictures of high modernism.

Because he *began* as a pop writer, Vonnegut's early work tended to be mythic rather than mythological, which is to say that he was able to treat the assumptions of the genre with utmost seriousness rather than with ironic condescension. As Fiedler notes in an essay published in the September 1970 issue of *Esquire*, Vonnegut has "written books that are thin and wide, rather than deep and narrow, which open out into fantasy and magic by means of linear narration rather than deep analysis; and so happen on wisdom, fall into it through grace, rather than pursue it doggedly or seek to earn it by hard work. . . . [L]ike all literature which tries to close the gap between the elite and the popular audiences rather than to confirm it, Vonnegut's books tend to temper irony with sentimentality and to dissolve both in wonder."[2]

There is ample precedent in American literature for the assimilation of a popular low-rent genre into the realm of high art. By employing the vernacular of southwestern humor, Mark Twain virtually created American realism in *Huckleberry Finn.* Even if Vonnegut's achievement was not nearly so historic, Fiedler was convinced that it represented an hitherto unnoticed path to an aesthetic beyond modernism. He argues that "art renews itself precisely in the dialectical process of disappearing, reappearing, disappearing. And just as the invisibility of the avant-garde, its unavailability to contemporary criticism at the beginning of the twentieth century, was a source of health and strength for an elitist, neoclassic tradition; so the invisibility of Pop, its immunity to fashionable judgment, seems in mid-twentieth century to have been a source of health and strength to what we now recognize as the New Romanticism: an art which prefers sentimentality to irony, passion to reason, vulgarity to subtlety" (196). The only question was whether Vonnegut's newfound respectability signaled a triumph or an abandonment of popular culture. It was in this environment that Phil Farmer pulled off a literary hoax that everyone but Kurt Vonnegut regarded as hilarious.

In his early books (when he was still in the sci-fi ghetto), Vonnegut created an imaginary science fiction writer named Kilgore Trout. (Using a writer as a fictional alter ego was a favorite device of canonical modernist writers such as James Joyce.) In the early 1970s, after Vonnegut had become a pinup boy for the youth culture and a favorite of establishment critics (and after Kilgore Trout had appeared as a character in *Slaughterhouse-Five*), Farmer conceived of writing a science fiction novel under the pseudonym Kilgore Trout, even

---

2. Leslie Fiedler, "The Divine Stupidity of Kurt Vonnegut," 196. Subsequent references will be cited parenthetically in the text.

going so far as to have a photograph taken of "Trout." Before the whole affair was over, it had developed into a first-class literary feud.

Farmer's publisher (Dell) was enthusiastic about the Trout project but insisted that Phil first get Vonnegut's permission. Initially, Vonnegut appeared quite willing to give it; however, when "Trout's" novel, *Venus on the Half Shell,* actually came out, he was incensed that far too many people assumed he had written it himself. What is not clear is whether Vonnegut was more enraged by readers who thought the book worse than those he had published recently or by those who judged it his best fiction in years. (This affair helped to expose the cleavage between hardcore science fiction fans, who preferred the old Vonnegut, and the more cosmopolitan admirers of his newer "mainstream" work.) Leslie got involved in the whole controversy because he had made some comments about the project and about Vonnegut's abandonment of science fiction on William Buckley's *Firing Line.* In an angry letter to Leslie, dated April 10, 1975, Vonnegut writes, "Your slightly mis-informed glee on the Buckley show was simply the first indication I had that nothing remotely pleasant was going to come from my giving Philip Farmer permission to write under the name of Kilgore Trout with no strings attached."[3] Needless to say, Vonnegut made certain that *Venus on the Half Shell* was "Trout's" only published novel.

Leslie's own efforts at science fiction were considerably more philosophical. Commenting on those efforts he writes, "Imagining the future . . . . is for me finally just another way of discovering or inventing a usable past" (*WWL?* 17). This would certainly seem to be true of *The Messengers Will Come No More.* Like so much science fiction, this book consists of dreams masquerading as extrapolations. Set in the twenty-sixth century, the narrative postulates a future in which the present inchoate feminist revolution has triumphed. With black women at the top of a racist, sexist social hierarchy, we have a variation on one of the hoariest traditions of satire—inversion of the familiar. The matriarchy assigns to men the same role that women have traditionally occupied in fundamentalist Islamic countries, that of sexual slave.

The novel's protagonist—a Jewish archeologist and scribe named Jacob Mindyson—has been the obedient stud of two women in his life. However, both Marcia and Megan have "expelled" (i.e., divorced) him for various reasons—the latter because he surreptitiously had their son circumcised. Jacob is now making time with a young polymorphous nymph named Melissa-Melinda. (Not as high on the social register as Marcia or Megan, Melissa-Melinda resembles a lame-brain hippie of 1960s vintage.) Not only do all the women in Jacob's neck of the woods have names that begin with "M," but

---

3. This and other letters cited in this chapter are in Leslie Fiedler's private papers.

Melissa-Melinda's double "M" may be meant to remind us that a twentieth-century goddess, whom she resembles not at all, was named Marilyn Monroe.

Later in the novel, Fiedler goes so far as to invoke Marilyn's divine name when he describes the final death throes of the Gutenberg culture: "It began with the firing of the Library at the Marilyn Monroe School of Women's Studies (formerly Yale University) by an Assistant Professor of Witchcraft. Refused tenure for her failure to 'publish,' she first kindled the flames, then flung herself into them from the rooftop solarium of the 125-story Parapsychology Building. In the next few days, her example was followed by hundreds, thousands, finally tens of thousands of her colleagues in all lands, who combined book-burning with suicide—not singly, as in the first instance, but in groups of twenty or more."[4]

The usable past that Fiedler derives from this bizarre vision of the future is a radical reinterpretation of the life of Jesus. Because of his arcane knowledge of the long-dead Hebrew language, Jacob is entrusted with the task of translating some ancient scrolls that fit Jesus and the Virgin Mary into a Yin-Yang conflict, which has bedeviled Judaism at least since the power struggle between Mary's namesake Miriam and her brother Moses (the golden calf of the wilderness being only one of many pagan female deities to challenge the patriarchal faith of the Jews). In this rewriting of scripture, Jesus is not divinely conceived by the power of the Holy Ghost, but is the product of the Blessed Virgin's liaison with an extraterrestrial "Messenger." This being later spirits the crucified Lord's soul into the heavens, where it will presumably participate in some intergalactic war of the sexes.

The outer space angle gives something of a new twist to the otherwise conventional motif of the Passover plot. What is unique is Fiedler's demythologizing of the Virgin Mary. In his version, the girl starts out determined to be a prophetess rather than a traditional wife. In order to maintain her virginity, she contracts a nominal marriage with an impotent old carpenter, who has been cuckolded by a succession of previous wives. When she does conceive, with maidenhead intact, she soon becomes the ultimate Jewish mother ("My son, the Messiah"), who raises up a rival to the faith of her fathers. The final irony is that she herself becomes a quasi-goddess figure in the new Christian religion.

It is not difficult to see why *The Messengers Will Come No More* is, as Leslie ruefully admits, "the most unread of all my work" (*WWL?* 16–17). Its theology is probably too abstruse to appeal to hard-core fans of science fiction. Conversely, the ideas in the book seem like nothing so much as themes searching

---

4. Leslie Fiedler, *The Messengers Will Come No More,* 149–50. Subsequent references will be cited parenthetically in the text.

for an audience. Reviewing the novel in the *New York Times Book Review,* the biblical scholar Robert Alter writes that the "fiction as it is concocted seems too often a theological joke without a point, or one that takes itself too seriously, or, still worse, a joke stitched together from threadbare materials, trying to simulate novelty chiefly through the aggressiveness of its bad taste."[5] In a sense, the book is a disguised meditation on a subject that has fascinated Leslie all his life—the question of what it means to be a Jew. (It could hardly be an accident that the ancient prophet who unmasks the Christian Messiah as an extraterrestrial mutant is Eliezar ben Yaakov, a name that can be anglicized as "Leslie son of Jacob," thus identifying him, at least vicariously, with the author of the frame novel.) Unfortunately, the only answer the book offers is that a Jew is one who regards Christianity as a hoax.

One of the most effective scenes in *The Messengers Will Come No More* occurs when Jacob Mindyson—another Fiedler surrogate?—is standing before the ruins of what was once the ancient temple in Jerusalem. (It has been marred by such graffiti as "KILROY WAS HERE," "WE DID SO KILL HIM," "HANDS OFF THE MOON," and—my personal favorite—"MARS SUCKS.") Next to him is "a little man, smaller even than I, with a long, sensitive nose, watery eyes and the faintest suspicion of a hump." Because this obviously devout Jew speaks to him, Jacob assumes that his own visible emotion must have identified him as a coreligionist. But the only word in the man's speech that Jacob can understand suggests otherwise. "And the contempt with which he spoke it would have made it comprehensible to a child of three, whatever his native tongue. '*Goy,*' he said, and moved away through the gawking crowd, in search of a real fellow believer" (94).

I

Nearly a decade after *The Messengers Will Come No More,* Leslie published his only book-length critical study of science fiction—*Olaf Stapeldon: A Man Divided* (1983). This project allowed him to argue for greater recognition and appreciation of a writer he admired and to continue his crusade on behalf of pop literature and pop criticism. Had he discussed such sophisticated stylists as Samuel Delaney, Harlan Ellison, or Ursula Le Guin (or even the transitional Vonnegut), he would have proved only that writers could meet the standards of elite art while laboring at science fiction. If, however, he wished to challenge the assumptions of aesthetic elitism (as practiced by both the high modernists and the parodic postmodernists), it was necessary to champion a writer who

5. Robert Alter, Review of *The Messengers Will Come No More.*

was able to move a mass audience while lacking the craft we normally associate with "serious" literature.[6] Although he could have accomplished this by writing about any of the perennial favorites of hardcore science fiction fans—say, Isaac Asimov, Robert Heinlein, or A. E. Van Vogt—the selection of Stapeldon probably appealed to Leslie because his subject was a refugee from high culture (a professionally trained philosopher), who had embraced popular literature as a matter of choice rather than necessity.

Stapeldon, who was born in 1886 and died in 1950, bridged the late Victorian and modernist eras. His books are not well-made novels or even entertaining potboilers. And his grasp of history and politics was so myopic that the futures he gave us were not nearly as usable as those of George Orwell or Aldous Huxley. (He failed to predict the alliance of the Soviet Union and the Western democracies in the struggle against Hitler, much less the subsequent Cold War between the West and the Soviet bloc.) What redeems Stapeldon in Fiedler's eyes, and makes him a writer worth reading, is a breadth of imaginative vision. In order to appreciate that vision, however, we must set aside certain notions about prose fiction that have prevailed since the time of Samuel Richardson. The realistic or mimetic novel (and this includes such experimental works as the stream-of-consciousness narratives of James Joyce, Marcel Proust, and Virginia Woolf) are concerned with inwardness and portray mental processes quite literally as mental processes.

In contrast, what Fiedler calls the "projective" mode of presentation "appears in fantastic fiction or romance, from the early Gothic tales of M. G. Lewis and Charles Maturin to such contemporary fantasies as the Ring trilogy of J. R. R. Tolkein."[7] It may be that what Stapeldon means "when he warns us that his work though fictional is not fully novelistic is that it is largely projective rather than mimetic: figuring forth in what purports to be apocalyptic cosmic drama, his personal fear of death; and in its accounts of telepathy, group mindedness, and 'possession' by persons from the Far Future, his own ambivalent attitude toward the tyranny of the ego and the reigning theories of his time about what separates sanity from madness" (64–65).

Because most of the books for which he is remembered—when he is remembered at all—were published in the 1930s, it is tempting to think of Stapeldon as a writer of that decade. (The title of Fiedler's second chapter is "Lost in the Thirties.") His disillusionment with capitalism and his flirtation with the Communist Party—which lasted the rest of his life—were certainly characteristic of intellectuals of his time. But even in the 1930s, Stapeldon was an anachronism. At that time, memories of his service as a pacifist and

6. For Fiedler's own discussion of this issue, see his essay "The Criticism of Science Fiction."

7. Leslie Fiedler, *Olaf Stapeldon: A Man Divided*. Subsequent references will be cited parenthetically in the text as *OS*.

ambulance driver in World War I seemed more real to him than the issues surrounding the contemporary Spanish Civil War. Moreover, the way he embodies ideas in fiction resembles the example of modernist writers less than it does the practice of such late Victorian models as George Bernard Shaw and, especially, H. G. Wells.

The subtitle of Fiedler's study is appropriate on several different levels. Not only did Stapeldon call one of his books *A Man Divided,* but that phrase aptly describes the many unresolved contradictions in his own psyche. Although an unequivocal pacifist, he was fascinated by the terrible beauty of war and wrote approvingly of brutality in his fiction. Despite the utopianism implicit in his commitment to Marxism, Stapeldon's truest vision was of apocalyptic nihilism. During the depression, it seemed as if civilization itself was about to fall apart, and Stapeldon could never convince himself that the ultimate disaster was not around the corner—even if that corner was two billion years into an imagined future. By the end, it seemed as if his strongest political conviction was simply a crude and condescending anti-Americanism.

Stapeldon's single most popular book—*Odd John* (1935)—is a celebration of the Nietzschean superman. It is doubtful, however, that Stapeldon had read Nietzsche or that he saw any parallels between his protagonist and the emerging strong men in Germany and Italy. His more likely inspiration was either Shaw's *Man and Superman* (1903) and *Back to Methusaleh* (1921) or Wells's *Food of the Gods* (1904). Stapeldon's view of human nature is perhaps best epitomized in the most frequently quoted passage from *Odd John:* "Homo Sapiens is a spider trying to crawl out of a basin. So long as he's on the bottom he can get along quite nicely, but as soon as he starts climbing he begins to slip" (*OS,* 98). Because Stapeldon's John belongs to a species of supernormal human beings, he has moral license to do what would be considered evil in the behavior of lesser mortals. (This includes deceit, murder, and incest.) In the end, however, he is no match for a hostile universe.

If Stapeldon resembled Wells and Shaw in his ability to imagine macro-history and the continuing evolution of the human species, neither of his predecessors could match the sheer scope of his vision. Fiedler describes Stapeldon's first sci-fi fantasy—*Last and First Men* (1930)—as "a two-billion-year-long mytho-history which imagines eighteen succeeding species of mankind, rising and falling, making and unmaking themselves in an effort to achieve total communion with each other and the indifferent universe before their inevitable end" (50). Unlike Shaw, Stapeldon was not able to envision man as ultimately triumphant. But, unlike Wells, who also saw man as doomed, he did not "regard that prospect with queasiness and terror; finding instead occasions for desperate joy and admiration in its rightness and beauty" (*OS,* 47).

If any of Stapeldon's books achieves mythic resonance, it is probably his penultimate novel, *Sirius* (1944). In this grotesquely compelling tale, superior intelligence is attributed not to an extraterrestrial creature or to a superhuman mutant, but to a dog. To be sure, humanoid animals have always been fixtures of children's books and such outdoor classics as Jack London's *The Call of the Wild,* not to mention countless animated features from Disney and his many imitators. But Stapeldon's novel is at the farthest remove from wholesome family entertainment. For all his intellect and nobility, Sirius is also a convincingly savage canine. Moreover, he is not the faithful companion but the physical lover of his human mistress. Unlike the writers of such fairy tales as *Beauty and the Beast,* Stapeldon refuses to let us imagine his animal groom as a handsome prince under a wicked spell; the situation will not soon give way to perpetual wedded bliss. Not only does Stapeldon's story "end in a premature death rather than a lifelong marriage," Fiedler notes, "but its male protagonist is at the close more rather than less bestial" (201). In that regard, he reminds us less of a fairy-tale prince than of King Kong, whose story dreams the doomed "dream of a love transcending ultimate miscegenation" (202).

Despite Fiedler's advocacy of pop criticism, *Olaf Stapeldon: A Man Divided* is in many ways a conventional work of literary scholarship. Because Stapeldon's novels are largely unknown, Fiedler does not feel obliged to reinterpret them in startling new ways. Unorthodox readings of Shakespeare or the classic American writers inevitably call received wisdom into question. In Stapeldon studies, however, there is no received wisdom outside of a few articles in publications read almost exclusively by passionate devotees of science fiction. It is both reassuring and enlightening to see the work of a "genre writer" such as Stapeldon discussed in terms usually reserved for books aspiring to the status of high art. One of Stapeldon's many celebrated divisions was surely between the philosopher and intellectual he was trained to be and the writer of slightly disreputable pop literature he eventually became. By the time he wrote his study of Olaf Stapeldon, this was a division that had become all too familiar to Leslie himself.

II

One day in the mid-1970s, an ex-Jesuit turned literary entrepreneur with the improbable name of Tom Collins called Leslie out of the blue to try to persuade him to write a book on witchcraft. Although this was a topic that would have appealed to him at one time, that time had passed. Well, Collins asked, was there any other topic with similar popular appeal that Leslie might like to treat? Without really knowing why, he suggested "Freaks." True to his promise, Collins sold the idea to a major trade publisher (Simon and Schuster), who eventually peddled more copies of the book than any other work of Leslie's had ever sold.

The publicity tour for *Freaks* found Leslie on the *Dick Cavett Show, Today, Tomorrow,* and *Donahue,* along with countless lesser known radio and television programs. When he appeared on *Tomorrow,* it was clear that the dimwitted Tom Snyder had no idea who he was or what the book was about. When Leslie mentioned his aversion to seeing his own image on television, Snyder spent much of the interview trying to get him to look at himself in the studio monitor. (The only comparable experience Leslie can recall was the time he spoke to a Montana reading club about *Finnegans Wake,* after which the president of the club said, "Thank you, Mr. Joyce.")[8] Donahue managed to ambush him by bringing some actual freaks—including two black girls joined at the head—onto the show. Apparently, Leslie was being cast as a kind of academic P. T. Barnum, who was making a profit by exploiting and ridiculing the afflictions of those less fortunate than himself.

In addition to the publicity it generated, *Freaks* inspired more personal mail than any of Leslie's other books. While some of the letters raised interesting questions or provided fascinating pieces of information, others were simply weird. One correspondent reported that, after drinking lots of coffee and overdosing on Tylenol for a head cold, he suddenly saw an elf appear at the driver's window of his car. He was convinced that, from that moment on, such supernatural figures were robbing him blind. "One primary object of theirs," he writes, "has been to compromise my keys. Their modus operandi is to steal into a house and hide until the occupants are asleep, then spray anesthetize them, and make impressions of their keys. . . . So far I have foiled it. But I have every confidence that I will not succeed. The result will be that they will in effect say that they can do what they will with me if I don't stay in line."

An even more pathetic communication came from a native of New Zealand. In his late thirties, Leslie's would-be pen pal was a homosexual with a thing for hideously obese males of the circus fat man variety. Because of the rareness of such individuals in his sparsely populated native country, he had emigrated to England. But, even there, he had met with limited success. The few individuals who met his specifications proved not to be willing partners. And he experienced great difficulty in locating proper pornography. (Apparently lean youths were all the rage, even in the disabled gay group he joined in London.) In lieu of filing a civil rights action, he wrote to Leslie for advice. "I was deeply moved by your letter and glad that you could find some psychic satisfaction in my book *Freaks,*" Leslie replied. But he added: "I am afraid I can be of little help to you aside from saying that I sympathise with your plight and hope you can work out a life style compatible with your instincts and taste."

Freaks: Myths and Images of the Secret Self was a book "so equivocally 'interdisciplinary' that library catalogers did not know whether to classify it under

8. Fiedler, interview with author, Nov. 7, 1998.

'psychology,' 'sociology' or 'literary criticism.' " "Actually," Fiedler writes, "my model for it (a secret guessed by one acute reviewer) was [Robert] Burton's *Anatomy of Melancholy,* which would make it, I guess, what used to be called belles lettres; though it has, in fact, intrigued chiefly 'soft' and semi-'soft' scientists, longing to rejoin the humanities" (*WWL?* 34–35). The thesis of the book is that genetic mutants reveal to "normal" people many of their hidden dreams and nightmares. As Fiedler told David Gates, "I'm more interested in defining what's human by the marginal than by the central."[9]

Fiedler begins his discussion by looking at freaks of scale (i.e., dwarfs and giants). These are by far the most common human curiosities and the ones who most frequently inhabit our myths and dreams. Of the two, dwarfs have historically been the most favored. From the time of Knoumhopou, a dwarf who was keeper of the royal wardrobe in ancient Egypt, until well into the eighteenth century, dwarfs were court favorites who served as royal advisers. Fiedler notes that even a few dwarf warriors—Charles III of Naples and Sicily, Ladislas I of Poland, and, according to some accounts, even Attila the Hun— "have proved themselves as capable in battle as any six-foot-tall king."[10] By the late eighteenth century, however, dwarfs had become simply objects of pity and wonder, rather than of veneration. In our own time, they have been exhibited by P. T. Barnum, murdered by Adolf Hitler (who saw them as affronts to the eugenic purity of the master race), and eventually transformed from religious marvel to medical patient to oppressed minority.

If dwarfs—and the host of other little people who have been known by various literary and medical names—are among the most beloved of freaks, giants are among the most feared. The reason for this may be no more sinister than the fact that at one time we were all Gullivers in a world of Brobdingnagians, whereas very few can empathize with the plight of the overgrown. When giants appear in our folklore, whether it be the biblical Goliath or the ogre of *Jack and the Beanstalk,* it is usually as a foil to a smaller but more cunning opponent. In reading these stories, we may simply be indulging fantasies of patricide, an explanation that takes on even more interesting Freudian implications when we consider that the hero is frequently assisted by the giant's treacherous wife.

Although they may not be freaks of scale in quite the same sense as dwarfs and giants, excessively fat and excessively thin people have long been featured in sideshows and celebrated in popular legends. At a deep psychological level, the obese—particularly obese women—represent the dream of eros, while human skeletons signify the fear of thanatos: "All of us have memories of having once been cuddled against the buxom breast and folded into the ample arms of

9. Gates, "Fiedler's Utopian Vision."
10. Leslie Fiedler, *Freaks: Myths and Images of the Secret Self,* 60. Subsequent references will be cited parenthetically in the text.

a warm, soft Giantess, whose bulk—to our 8-pound, 21-inch infant selves—must have seemed as mountainous as any 600-pound Fat Lady to our adult selves" (131). In contrast, the hideously emaciated do not challenge our "conventional notions about growing up or growing down. Rather, they call into question the distinction between the living and the dead" (134).

The distinction called into question by hermaphrodites is, of course, the one between male and female. When the pagan notion of divine androgyny gave way to the patriarchal myths of Judaism and Christianity, the hermaphrodite became a monster to be shunned or an oddity to be exploited. Only in recent years, with the decline of Judaism and Christianity and the rise of a kind of neopaganism, has the situation changed. The unisex look in fashion tends to blur traditional gender identity; radical feminists attack the rigidity of sex roles for political reasons; and transsexuals are increasingly going under the knife to conform their outward appearance to their psychic orientation. The cumulative effect of these developments has been to "normalize" what previous ages either revered or repudiated as abnormal.

For Fiedler, the ultimate freaks are Siamese twins and the even more hideous autosite-parasite linkages. These call into question the distinction between self and other: "Standing before Siamese Twins, the beholder sees them looking not only at each other, but—both at once—at him. And for an instant it may seem to him that he is a third brother, bound to the pair before him by an invisible bond; so that the distinction between audience and exhibit, we and them, normal and Freak, is revealed as an illusion, desperately, perhaps even necessarily, defended, but untenable in the end" (36). (Perhaps thinking of his estrangement from Harold, Leslie dedicated the book "To my brother who has no brother / To all my brothers who have no brother.") Because medical science is making the separation of Siamese twins an increasingly common occurrence, this type of freak is rapidly becoming obsolete. Instead of being of central importance themselves, they "have become supernumeraries in a psychodrama starring the doctors who make normal human beings out of monsters" (199).

Having introduced the reader to an entire gallery of human oddities, Fiedler turns his attention to the image of the freak in modern culture. Although his discussion here leads to the repetition of some points made earlier, it is the most valuable part of his book, elevating the entire study above the level of mere sensationalism. Of particular interest is his suggestive examination of the relationship between freak shows and horror literature. Both are fundamentally forms of pornography designed to excite an uncontrollable reaction, in this case not an erection but a shudder. It is therefore not surprising that from the time of Mary Shelley's *Frankenstein* and Bram Stoker's *Dracula* until the present, the human mutant has become a stock figure of horror literature. How appropriate that a single film director—Tod Browning—should have been responsible for the horror classic *Dracula* (1931) and the hauntingly grotesque *Freaks* (1932).

Although *Dracula* has remained consistently popular, *Freaks* was so far ahead of its time that it was greeted with initially hostile reviews and had to be revived, three decades after its release, as an underground cult film. Browning takes us beyond the exhibitionism of the carnival to show us human oddities as flesh-and-blood people with their own lives and their own sense of community. Indeed, our sympathies are so much with the freaks that they seem more truly human than their "normal" adversaries. An unabashed popularizer, Browning managed to create a mythically resonant work of high art. Unfortunately, as Fiedler points out, a gratuitously "magical" ending partially undercuts the realism upon which the delicate empathy of audience and artifact has been based.

Fiedler's interest in the sort of human deformities exhibited in old-time sideshows is not unrelated to his interest in science fiction. One of the continuing preoccupations of sci-fi writers (of both the old and the new school) has been to imagine new mutations of humanity. The stories in Isaac Asimov's *I Robot,* for example, depict robots striving to be accepted as men, just as Frankenstein's monster had done in Mary Shelley's immortal novel a century before. Even more moving to the counterculture are tales of men mutating rather than manufacturing themselves into metahumans—novels such as A. E. Van Vogt's *Slan,* Arthur C. Clarke's *Childhood's End,* and Robert A. Heinlein's *Stranger in a Strange Land.* These works challenge the boundaries between the human and the nonhuman just as profoundly as the Elephant Man and the Dog-faced Boy once did, stirring "similar feelings of sacrilege and terror" (321).

As engrossing as this book is, it is not without flaws. For one thing, it could have used a more detailed discussion of P. T. Barnum. Fiedler describes Barnum as "a mass educator as well as a mass entertainer, and finally a magician able—long after science thought it had neutralized nature—to remythify it by reviving in adults the awe children feel before its variety and abundance" (279). This interpretation is so much at odds with the standard view of Barnum as merely a cynical bunkum artist that one is left begging for elaboration. Also, for such an abundantly illustrated volume, *Freaks* might have included some discussion of Diane Arbus's photographs of the physically abnormal. Unlike the exhibitions of Barnum, these works belong unambiguously to the canonical world of high culture.

Another surprising omission is Fiedler's failure to mention James Thurber's classic short story "You Could Look It Up" in his discussion of freaks in literature (or even to list that story in his bibliography). This tale of a midget who is sent up to pinch hit in a major league baseball game raises in a humorous context the whole issue of human scale. (Given the proliferation of lowbrow sports literature for boys, there are probably plenty of stories of giants in basketball, as well.) Not only is Thurber's tale a staple of anthologies, but it inspired Bill Veeck—the P. T. Barnum of professional sports—to sign a midget to play with the old St. Louis Browns. When that midget actually did pinch hit and drew a walk (because of his almost invisible strike zone), there was such an outcry that little people were officially banned from the game. This bizarre chain of events raises the specter of life imitating art and also reminds us that there are certain areas of human endeavor where freaks have a natural advantage over their "normal" counterparts.

The most problematic aspect of Fiedler's study is his attempt to draw a connection between the circus freaks of his childhood and the drug freaks of the 1960s. (This connection had first been adumbrated in the lecture he called—appropriately—"The New Mutants.") That the label *freak* was used by the psychedelic young is simply an example of their proudly appropriating a term of derision (like blacks calling themselves "niggers" or homosexuals referring to themselves as "queers"). The main difference between genetic curiosities and hippies, of course, is that the latter have chosen their condition, while the former have not. To be abnormal by choice is, at best, a form of slumming that lacks even the misguided nobility shown by the young upper-class liberal who takes a job as a factory or migrant worker. As we have seen, however, Fiedler was firmly convinced that the counterculture was creating a new (or mutated) form of humanity. Consequently, he took the drug shamans of the era almost as seriously as they took themselves.

As it turned out, the real significance of *Freaks* had less to do with the counterculture of the 1960s than with the emerging field of cultural studies. In 1978, respectable academics were appalled by what they decried as a voyeuristic descent into the world of the circus and the sideshow. Over the next two decades, however, social historians, literary critics, and medical ethicists kept returning to the issues Leslie had raised. Robert Bogdan's *Freak Show: Presenting Human Oddities for Amusement and Profit* (1988) is, in part, a response to *Freaks*. (Bogdan argues that freakishness is a matter of social construction rather than either physiology or myth.) When Brian Rosenberg taught a course on freaks at Allegheny College in Pennsylvania, he was struck by the long tradition of physically mutant characters in literature—including Poe's "Hop-Frog," Wells's *The Island of Dr. Moreau,* Mann's "Little Herr Friedmann," Nabokov's "Scenes from the Life . . . ," Welty's "Petrified Man," O'Connor's "Parker's Back," Beattie's "Dwarf House," and—of course—Browning's *Freaks*. That tradition has continued since 1978 with Bernard Pomerance's *The Elephant Man* (1981) and Katherine Dunn's *Geek Love* (1989).

Perhaps the most compelling testament to the growing respectability of freak studies came in 1996, when New York University Press published Rosemarie Garland Thomson's *Freakery: Cultural Spectacles of the Extraordinary*

Body. This 400-page volume contains essays by twenty-six scholars from various academic disciplines. Among their topics of investigation are "Cuteness and Commodity Aesthetics: Tom Thumb and Shirley Temple," "The Dime Museum Freak Show Reconfigured as Talk Show," "Freaks in Space: 'Extraterrestrialism' and 'Deep-Space Multiculturalism,'" "Being Humaned: Medical Documentaries and the Hyperrealization of Conjoined Twins," "Bodybuilding: A Postmodern Freak Show," and "The Celebrity Freak: Michael Jackson's 'Grotesque Glory.'" It is only appropriate that the foreword to Thompson's book was written by that defiant freak of American criticism—Leslie A. Fiedler.

For Sam and Hattie

BECAUSE OF HIS status as a celebrity nut, Leslie entered his seventh decade with a notoriety enjoyed by few writers and almost no literary critics. "He was," according to Steven G. Kellman, "along with Buckminster Fuller, Che Guevera, Timothy Leary, and Benjamin Spock, one of the very few figures over thirty trusted by the young." (One should add Allen Ginsberg, Norman Mailer, and several aging rock stars to the list.) With his interests growing ever more eclectic, Leslie had also gone for over a decade without writing a book specifically on American literature. In 1969, he published a memoir (*Being Busted*) and a collection of short stories (*Nude Croquet*). Although his mistitled *Collected Essays* did appear in 1971, the two volumes consisted entirely of previously published material. (One essay appeared word for word, under different titles, in both volumes.[1]) In 1972, he gave us *The Stranger in Shakespeare* and a new paperback printing of *Love and Death in the American Novel*—complete with a photograph by Diane Christian, which made the book's author look like Zeus himself. *The Messengers Will Come No More* appeared two years later, followed by the science fiction anthology *In Dreams Awake* in 1975, *A Fiedler Reader* in 1977, and finally, *Freaks* in 1978. More than a dozen years after *The Return of the Vanishing American,* Leslie was beginning to look like the vanishing Americanist.

This hiatus from American studies ended in 1982, when Simon and Schuster (still considering Leslie a valuable commodity on the strength of *Freaks*) published *What Was Literature? Class Culture and Mass Society.* The first half of this book is a breezy and irreverent discussion of the institutions of literary criticism and scholarship. (Here Leslie is extending the argument for pop criticism he originally made in *Cross the Border—Close the Gap.*) Then, the second

---

1. Steven G. Kellman, "The Importance of *Being Busted*," 77. The essay that appears twice is called "Looking Backward: America from Europe" in volume one and "Our Country and Our Culture" in volume two.

half gets down to practical criticism by identifying a tradition in American literature very different from the one Leslie had been examining for over thirty years. Although *What Was Literature?* makes some serious points, it does so with such a mischievous lack of solemnity that Leslie seems to be deliberately baiting elitist critics and scholars. For the most part, they rose to the bait.

Like *Love and Death in the American Novel, What Was Literature?* was a book that everyone seemed to knock. When Hugh Kenner proved too moderate in his estimate of Fiedler's achievement, some editorial factotum at *Harper's* captioned his review: "The battle continues between literature and the man who wants it dead." Kenneth S. Lynn, who reviewed the book for *Commentary,* needed no such help. After spending most of his discussion attacking "Come Back to the Raft Ag'in, Huck Honey!" Lynn writes, "[I]f the New Criticism of the 50's and 60's divorced texts from contexts, and the Post-Structuralism of the 70's and 80's has sought to abolish authors, Fiedler, too, has done his best to impoverish the study of literature by breaking down standards and transforming academic study into a theater of the self."[2]

Writing for the *Atlantic,* Alfred Kazin (whose previous contribution to Fiedler studies was an hilarious parody called "Fucking and Not Fucking Indians in the American Novel"), makes it clear that he is not amused by the notion of pop criticism. "Audience response is never by itself a proof of value," he reminds us; "as Ezra Pound said, literature is news that *stays* news. Much of what Fiedler admires has stayed only with him. The book is full of childhood memories: young Fiedler was allowed to eat his fill of movies and comics, and remembers them as someone on the psychoanalytic couch might remember his mother's breasts."[3]

Although the literary critic is presumed to be someone who loves literature, it has always been considered bad form for him to show too much ardor. In T. S. Eliot's view, the function of the critic is to "correct taste." One must love the right kind of books in the right kind of way. Promiscuity in reading, like promiscuity in sex, is the sign of an undisciplined appetite. If a gentleman slips off to a brothel now and then (in Eliot's case, to a British music hall or a Marx Brothers movie), he at least knows the difference between the whore and the trophy wife. Fiedler commits the unpardonable sin of wanting to bring the whore into the parlor on equal status with the wife. To his mind, elitist criticism is nothing more than the benign face of censorship. Its roots go deep, and limiting its consequences is about as easy as putting the genie back in the bottle.

Fiedler traces the impulse to censorship all the way back to Plato's contention that "art is incitement rather than therapy" (*WWL?* 42). Although

2. Lynn, "Back to the Raft," 68.
3. Alfred Kazin, "Honoring the Dark Impulse."

good liberals tend to scoff at this notion when it is used to suppress erotic literature, they have no compunction about deploring violence in the media. (Comic books were particularly vulnerable because they combined sex *and* violence.) This has led to such absurdities as the bowdlerization of Mother Goose and the Brothers Grimm, as well as attacks on Fiedler's favorite cop shows, *Baretta, Kojak,* and *Starsky and Hutch.* With the dawn of political correctness, various victimized interest groups (blacks, women, Poles, Hispanics, homosexuals, and the handicapped) began to get in on the act. Asserting their sensitivities, they suppressed not only *Amos 'n Andy* and *Little Black Sambo* (regrettable enough in and of itself) but also, at times, Shakespeare's *The Merchant of Venice,* Griffith's *The Birth of a Nation,* and Twain's *Adventures of Huckleberry Finn.* To all book burners with political axes to grind, Fiedler cries, "Enough already!"

But his real targets are those with *cultural* axes to grind. Fiedler's provocative theory is that the elite canon of literature is the special preserve not so much of the old WASP guardians of culture as of the nouveau academics—*arriviste* Jews and East European ethnics whose entire claim to cultural respectability lies in their defense of high literature. In most universities, the study of literature either is or aspires to be an esoteric craft practiced by a cultural elite. One's advancement in academic stature is measured by the extent to which he—or increasingly she—is removed from the task of dealing with ordinary students.

As a graduate student, one is forced to teach freshman composition—not because it is the easiest course to teach but because persons of higher academic rank consider it a burden to be shunned at all costs. Promotion usually carries with it reduced teaching loads and courses consisting largely of upper-division and graduate students, who have been indoctrinated with the tastes and jargon of whatever happens to be the prevailing critical orthodoxy. In other words, we have a kind of self-perpetuating guild system, which is financially supported by the mass of people (taxpayers if it is a public university, donors if it is a private institution) who are outside the guild but who pay it the sort of homage also rendered to opera and ballet.

Those—such as Fiedler—who challenge the elitism of traditional literary study are accused of subverting the standards of high culture, of wanting to "open the gates to the barbarians." To this charge Fiedler simply replies, "I *am* a barbarian, already within the gates" (112). Once the academy allowed courses in living languages (rather than confining literature to a study of the classics), the crucial concession had been made. As more and more recent texts were admitted to the canon, or at least deemed worthy of study, "criticism" replaced "scholarship" as the means for determining literary excellence. Fiedler goes a step further by suggesting that there may be a more adequate standard of criticism than one that would censure technically inept but mythically powerful works of art.

If elitists see this approach as an assault on literature as we know it, Fiedler would argue that such literature is already dead, anyway. It began to die when it was taken out of the court and salon and made available to ordinary people in the eighteenth century. The attempt of Henry James and his followers to redeem the novel for high art, like the attempt of the cineasts to make film into an esoteric medium, did not undo the cultural democratizing and leveling initiated by Samuel Richardson and company. The populace still had its mass-produced body of song and story (the very fact of mass production differentiates popular culture from folk art); the elite had simply laid claim to more rarefied texts within the same genres enjoyed by their less sophisticated brethren.

It might be argued that Fiedler is fighting a battle that has already been partially won. Many universities have courses in American studies and popular culture, and much academic writing is done in these disciplines. However, this represents, at best, a foot in the door. When pop courses are offered, it is frequently a cynical attempt to boost enrollments rather than an admission of the academic legitimacy of such courses. Professors who teach and publish in this area—when they are not certified pedants who are merely slumming—are generally regarded as dilettantes who couldn't make it in the world of "real scholarship." As long as popular literature remains segregated from the rest of the curriculum, it will continue to be stigmatized. It is only when popular culture is integrated with high literature in courses that are organized historically or thematically that we can create what Fiedler calls an "English for everyone: an introduction to works of the imagination over which all humankind can weep, laugh, shudder and be titillated; communal dreams, shared hallucinations, which in a time when everything else tends to divide us from each other join us together, men and women, adults and children, educated and uneducated, black and white, yellow and brown—even, perhaps, teachers and students" (114).

I

Fiedler strenuously protests that, despite his efforts to tear down the walls between elite and popular culture, he is not forsaking the evaluative role of the critic. The fact that some works of art are superior to others is something that he has never doubted. Even the least sophisticated consumers of art express their opinions and preferences, a task for which no arcane critical vocabulary is needed. The responsible critic, however, must offer more than exclamations of approval or distaste—"wow" or "ugh." He must be able to tell us why *Jonathan Livingston Seagull* is "pretentious, banal and essentially stupid," while *Huckleberry Finn* is "subtle and mythically resonant, yet capable of moving a child of ten" (126). To do so, Fiedler believes, requires an appeal to some standard beyond aesthetics and ethics as those terms are commonly understood.

The hazard inherent in traditional aesthetics is that it leads us to the artificial distinction between high and low art. The problem with ethical criticism is that it tends toward propaganda. As Fiedler has amply demonstrated, the temptation to use literature on behalf of noble ideals and to suppress those works that preach an alien gospel is not limited to the "know nothing" fringes of the radical right but also afflicts "enlightened liberals." The Aristotelian notion of catharsis is certainly a clever means of dealing with those Platonists who would impose censorship upon us for our own good, and the Horatian contention that literature instructs as well as delights may even convince some moralists that the poet is a civic asset. In our heart of hearts, however, we know that the glory of literature lies in the fact that it is every bit as dangerous and subversive as its worst enemies claim.

If ethics and aesthetics are somehow inadequate measures of the value of art, perhaps simple popularity would do the trick. Certainly, in a society where the majority is entrusted with crucial political and marketing decisions, there is something to be said for leaving artistic decisions up to a plebiscite. Great literature would, by definition, consist of the novels that stayed longest on the best-sellers list, the songs that were played most often, and the movies with the highest box office gross. Such a position, however, does not close the gap between majority and minority art; but, by opting "for the former rather than the latter, . . . [it simply stands] elitism on its head" (116). (Persons making a claim for such radical populism frequently cite Tolstoy's celebration of folk culture in his essay *What Is Art?*) Fiedler ultimately rejects this stance, just as he does the elitist position, "not only because each in its own way restricts the full freedom of literature, but because each unconsciously *lies* about the works it seeks to defend" (129).

One way out of this impasse is for all critics to become myth critics, that is, to focus on those subconscious and unarticulated sources of appeal that cause certain works of art to move large numbers of people. (How this differs from popularity more crassly conceived, Fiedler does not say.) Because those sources of appeal exist irrespective of the formal excellence of the works in which they are embodied, critics will find themselves "speaking less of theme and purport, structure and texture, signified and signifier, metaphor and metonymy, and more of myth, fable, archetype, fantasy, magic and wonder" (140). What is most important is that the critic not murder to dissect, but maintain and communicate his own sense of excitement in the presence of literature. Longinus referred to this quality as the sublime—or so he has usually been translated. Fiedler prefers the term *ekstasis,* "meaning ecstasy or rapture or transport, a profound alteration of consciousness in which the normal limits of flesh and spirit seem to dissolve" (139).

Phenomenologically, it is perhaps easiest to see how *ekstasis* works if we consider four genres of pop literature where the attempt to evoke a particular audience reaction is most blatant: (1) sentimental tearjerkers, (2) horror stories, (3) hard-core erotica, and (4) low comedy. "There is a real sense in which all four can be regarded as 'pornography,' since they titillate by infringing deeply revered taboos and impel us toward some kind of orgasmic release, ranging from tears to a scream, from uncontrollable laughter to actual ejaculation" (134). Presumably, the same qualities that excite such responses in the buyers of "pornography" operate at a more subtle level in what we have chosen to call "high art."

As refreshing as Fiedler's position might seem, both his theory and methodology present some difficulties. To begin with, the notion of "ecstatics" smacks of the subjectivism touted by Walter Pater and company back during the British fin de siecle. Even though Fiedler leavens his subjectivism with a democratic faith lacking in his British counterparts, it is not clear that he has identified a new set of objective standards to replace the old one he has rejected. I believe Rod McKuen's poetry inferior to Dante's and Erich Segal's fiction less entertaining than Leslie Fiedler's, but the concept of ecstatics gives me no vocabulary with which to convince others that they should share my preferences. When Fiedler pushes beyond ecstatics to the source of literary ecstasy, which he identifies as myth, he suggests a way out of the impasse, but at the expense of limiting the range of his criticism.

At least since the time of Longinus, a substantial number of scholars have asserted that great literature is that which has survived the test of time. What the formalists attempted to do was to articulate critical standards to explain *why* great literature has survived and to identify those contemporary works that have what it takes to make it into the canon. (When Longinus himself sought to differentiate between the true and the false sublime, he did so in rhetorical, which is to say formalistic, terms—without reference to mythopoeic power or communal fantasies.) In practice, however, formalism is less than totally successful. Some works survive that presumably should have died, while others that should have thrived have faded from memory. By suggesting that works of literature either fade or endure because of qualities more deeply interfused than the technical excellence of the language in which they are written, myth critics such as Fiedler are probably closer to the truth than are dogmatic formalists. They are at least not forced to reject certain undeniably great writers (as the neoclassical critics did with Shakespeare and as Yvor Winters did with practically everybody) because they do not measure up to certain prescriptive standards, or else accept them because they can be read ingeniously enough to satisfy those same standards.

If the scholar says that we cannot know ahead of time which works will survive, the myth critic passes judgment by examining current works for the

presence of universal archetypes. It should be obvious, however, that some ren-
derings of myth and fable are more successful than others. Why, for example, has Shakespeare outlasted other playwrights who have dealt with similar
themes? I suspect that Hugh Kenner is close to the answer when he asserts that
"the greatest literary works—the *Iliad, Hamlet,*—owe their distinction to . . .
the union of a powerful myth with expression just as powerfully adequate."[4]
Some works have won academic approval simply because they were well written; others have survived in popular esteem simply because they were mythically potent. Formalists can help us appreciate the former, and myth critics
the latter. No doubt, we should study both. But it may well be that the best
literature is that which unites us at the highest rather than the lowest common
denominator.

II

If *Love and Death in the American Novel* had been criticized as a reductive work, which tried to force too much of American literature onto a Procrustean bed of favored traditions and themes, Fiedler believed the answer to
this charge was not to repudiate the book and its many illuminating insights,
but to explore other traditions and themes, which have also had a role in shap-
ing our literary image of ourselves. *Waiting for the End* and *The Return of the
Vanishing American* were both important steps in that direction, as was Fiedler's
crusade to cross the border and close the gap that separated elite and popular
culture. Properly speaking, however, these efforts either expanded the canon
of works that could be understood in terms of (preferably interethnic) male
bonding or took off in unrelated directions. Not until he began developing the
concept of the "inadvertent epic" in the 1970s did Fiedler begin to appreciate
the power of a mythic vision *diametrically opposed* to the attitudes embodied in
misogynist American fiction. As James Seaton has remarked in another context, "Fiedler's long pursuit of the outrageous has ended in the fostering of two
(contending) academic orthodoxies."[5]

When he began asking himself what differentiated the American novels
admired by academics from such an enduring popular favorite as Harriet
Beecher Stowe's *Uncle Tom's Cabin,* Fiedler discovered that the so-called classic novels "were not only more elegantly structured and textured, more ide-
ologically dense, more overtly subversive—more difficult and challenging, in
short—but they almost invariably celebrated the flight from civilization and

4. Kenner, "Who Was Leslie Fiedler?" 73.
5. Seaton, *Cultural Conservatism,* 105.

the settlement, church and school, from everything which had survived (under female auspices) of Christian humanism in the New World—thus reinforcing the myth of Home as Hell" (*WWL?* 151–52). Having spent the bulk of his career privileging such books, Fiedler turns his attention in the second section of *What Was Literature?* to the largely female countertradition that celebrates Home as Heaven.

Because the reconciliation implicit in interracial male bonding is central to the wilderness myth as Fiedler has long defined it, it is only fitting that the horror of miscegenation (more especially interethnic rape) be a key element of the domestic myth. Not surprisingly, Fiedler finds a series of narratives that exemplify that thesis. This series begins with *Uncle Tom's Cabin* itself (along with the various "Tom plays" into which it has been translated) and continues with Thomas Dixon Jr.'s *The Leopard's Spots* and *The Clansman* (along with their infinitely more famous adaptation as D. W. Griffith's *The Birth of a Nation*), Margaret Mitchell's *Gone with the Wind* (as both novel and movie), and Alex Haley's *Roots* (from *Reader's Digest* condensation through best-selling book to television miniseries). "Read as a single work composed over more than a century, in many media and by many hands," Fiedler argues, "these constitute a hitherto unperceived 'epic,' embodying a myth of our history unequaled in scope and resonance by any work of High Art" (154). Although many might quarrel with this sweeping judgment, the theory of the "inadvertent epic" helps illuminate an intriguing dialogue in American popular culture.

As Fiedler analyzes these works, we see the practical consequences of the myth criticism he has long espoused. None of the narratives in the inadvertent epic would be considered serious art according to the sophisticated standards of high modernism. Only *Uncle Tom's Cabin* has had a significant number of defenders among highbrow critics and scholars. (Fiedler mentions Leo Tolstoy, William Dean Howells, V. L. Parrington, Van Wyck Brooks, Kenneth Lynn, Ellen Moers, and Anthony Burgess.) "But most of them have felt obliged to confess its inadequacy as art" (*WWL?* 149). It seems that only Lynn felt comfortable defending the literary merits of *Uncle Tom's Cabin,* and he was writing as a literary historian rather than as a pure critic. It would be immeasurably more difficult to find respectable enthusiasts for Dixon, Mitchell, or Haley.

Fiedler's case for the works in the inadvertent epic rests in large part on the argument that they have pleased many and pleased long. In the case of *Uncle Tom's Cabin* and *Gone with the Wind,* he is certainly correct. Thomas Dixon, Jr., however, has been forgotten by all but specialists in the pathologies of American racism, while Alex Haley's work is too recent to have passed the test of time. (A quarter century after its original publication, *Roots* seems more like an ephemeral blockbuster than an enduring classic.) But like the more permanent successes achieved by Stowe and Mitchell, the visions of Dixon and Haley have survived in secondary media, which have reached a much larger audience than had ever read the books in which they originated. The authors—or "auteurs"—of the inadvertent epic all possessed an ability to create characters and scenes of truly mythic proportions, "primordial images . . . [that] emerge mysteriously from the collective unconscious and pass, scarcely mediated by [an] almost transparent text, into the public domain, to which, like all authentic popular literature, they properly belong" (161). It is this very transparency that causes Fiedler to break with the New Critics by affirming that the myth, not the medium, is the message.

Readers of *Love and Death in the American Novel* will recognize several of the motifs Fiedler finds in *Uncle Tom's Cabin* as coming straight from the sentimental love religion. To begin with, the Protestant feminization of Christ is everywhere in Stowe's novel. The moral exemplars in *Uncle Tom's Cabin* are almost all women, many of them mothers. Even when we have a bad mother in the person of Marie St. Clare (prototype for a whole succession of spoiled Southern belles, most notably Faulkner's egregious Mrs. Compson), surrogate mothers rush in to fill the void: there is the prim and righteous Miss Ophelia and Little Eva's warmhearted Mammy, not to mention Eva herself, who is something of a mother to both her father and the devilish Topsy. (As Fiedler has suggested in *Love and Death,* Eva and Topsy are pint-sized versions of snowmaiden and dark lady.) There is also the memory of St. Clare's dead mother (who appropriately bears the same name as his daughter), a memory that sustains Augustine—named for the saint who was converted by his mother—as he lies on his deathbed. But perhaps the most important avatar of the maternal Christ is Uncle Tom himself.

Militant blacks are technically correct in asserting that Uncle Tom is a passive figure, who has been robbed of his masculinity (a case made most forcefully by James Baldwin in his anti-Tom essay "Everybody's Protest Novel"). What they neglect to note—or simply dismiss as irrelevant—is the fact that Stowe regards Tom's Christlike suffering as a sign of his moral superiority. The Christ who exhorted his followers to turn the other cheek was arguing for virtues traditionally associated with femininity. Stowe saw negroes as being "naturally patient, timid, and unenterprising." Because they were "home-loving and affectionate," she considered them an essentially feminine, and hence Christlike, people. (Although these views may be judged racist and sexist according to "enlightened" modern standards, they are perfectly consistent with the bourgeois Protestant piety that has helped shape the novel since the time of Samuel Richardson.) It follows that, in *Uncle Tom's Cabin,* the all-important theme of interethnic rape is present exclusively in the violation of black slave women by their white masters. One even suspects that Stowe's strongest objection to slavery was that it offended Puritan notions of sexual propriety. It is no accident that the only character in her novel to manifest overt sexual desire is the diabolical slave owner Simon Legree.

In writing his defense of the South half a century later, Thomas Dixon maintains Stowe's reverence for the home and her revulsion at the thought of interethnic rape. (In his novel *The Leopard's Spots,* he even casts Simon Legree—now a carpetbagger—in the familiar role of villain.) He has simply reversed the racial roles, giving us the nightmare image of the black satyr aflame to ravish the Confederate snowmaiden. The fact that sociologists tell us this image is primarily a Freudian projection of white guilt in no way dissipates the mythic power of the nightmare itself.

In one sense, the American Civil War can be viewed as a battle of the books. Abraham Lincoln claimed that the conflict was started by Harriet Beecher Stowe, while Mark Twain was just as certain that the culprit was Sir Walter Scott. According to Twain's argument, the defeat of the Confederacy did not diminish Scott's influence so much as enhance the South's appetite for romantic self-delusion. Dixon quite explicitly equates the Ku Klux Klan with the heroic highlanders of the Waverley novels. The image of these white knights on horseback, dreamed by Dixon and filmed by Griffith, "has provided the model for a million B-movie rides to the rescue, in which, no matter how stereotyped, it never quite loses its primordial power" (*WWL,* 194).

That this primordial power ultimately transcends ideology and culture is attested to by Fiedler's own observation. He tells us that "I myself once saw . . . the members of a left-wing cine club in Athens, believers all in the equality of the races and the unmitigated evil of the Klan, rise to their feet at ten o'clock in the morning (the year was 1960, two wars and innumerable revolutions after the making of the film) to scream with bloodlust and approval equal to that of the racist first-nighters of 1915 as white womanhood was once more delivered from the threat of black rape" (194).[6]

In recent years, the more conventional attack on high modernism and the old "New Criticism" has come from left-wing zealots. According to their point of view, the attempt to maintain disinterested aesthetic standards is simply a covert strategy for preserving a canon of dead white European male writers. The reactionary social views of T. S. Eliot and the southern Agrarians, not to mention the outright Fascism of Ezra Pound, has lent a superficial credibility to such a charge.[7] In all too many instances, however, the assault on the old canon has simply produced a counter-canon based on standards of ethnic diversity and political correctness. In praising such benighted white males as

6. In "The Pipes at Lucknow," John Greenleaf Whittier, who was certainly one of the staunchest of abolitionists, writes of some Scottish women and children who are threatened by a native (i.e., darkskinned) mutiny in India. Who should come to the rescue but some Scottish clansmen, blowing their bagpipes to signal their advance?

7. On occasion, Fiedler himself has been guilty of such name-calling. In *What Was Literature?,* he refers to the "proto-fascist 'New Critics'" (42). Elsewhere in the same book, he speaks of "the New Criticism with its odd blending of fascist politics and aesthetic formalism" (70).

Dixon and Griffith, Fiedler would appear to be going against this ideological fad just as much as he is challenging the standards of elite criticism.

If Thomas Dixon is among the most aesthetically *and* politically incorrect writers ever to take up a pen, we might ask on what grounds he belongs in even an alternative canon. The answer is his ability to create mythically potent images. In attributing this power exclusively to D. W. Griffith, highbrow film critics simply expose their own ignorance. "When [James] Agee comes to specifying Griffith's tremendous 'magical images,' " Fiedler writes, " . . . two of them turn out to have been borrowed from Dixon: 'the ride of the Clansmen; the rapist and his victim among the dark leaves.' Yet he seems unaware of Dixon's existence and fails, therefore, to understand why Griffith for all his talent never again was able to project archetypes that have refused to fade from the mind of the world" (192–93).

III

The most popular novel ever written in any language comes from a woman who admits to having been raised on Thomas Dixon's books. Over a million copies of Margaret Mitchell's *Gone with the Wind* were sold in the year of its publication (a phenomenal accomplishment when one considers that 1936 was the very depth of the depression). Moreover, the book has rarely sold fewer than forty thousand hardback copies in any subsequent year. It has been translated into at least twenty-seven languages and is as popular in Germany and Japan as it is in Atlanta, Georgia. Although her book had sold over twenty-five million copies by the early 1990s, Mitchell's story is known by an even larger audience through its film version, which has been seen by more people than the total population of the United States. Overseas, the movie has also proved even more popular than the book. Fiedler recalls having once seen it "in a fishing village in Yugoslavia, dubbed into French and subtitled in Croatian—but so immediately apprehensible in terms of its images that no one seemed dismayed even when, from time to time, the sound track sputtered and died" (197).

According to Fiedler, Margaret Mitchell accomplished the "feminization of the anti-Tom novel." Like Stowe, Griffith, and Dixon before her, she valued the domestic life as the locus of meaning and order in an otherwise threatening cosmos. Of the four characters she contributed to our popular mythos, the sole black (Mammy) comes closest to being a moral norm. Like Stowe, Mitchell presents a patronizing image of African Americans as essentially maternal people who rarely aspire to a life beyond the confines of home and hearth. Like Dixon, she believes that blacks are happiest within an hierarchial social order in which they are not encouraged by carpetbaggers and abolitionists to seek elevation from their proper station in life. The black maid in *The Birth of a Nation,* who identifies herself with the South while scorning "free niggers" and "white trash," is a blatant precursor of Mitchell's Mammy. Although a generally passive figure, Uncle Tom is fundamentally different in that his loyalty is to Christianity rather than to the Confederacy. The one thing that Simon Legree can never get him to do is violate his conscience by beating other slaves.

Despite the obvious resemblance between *Gone with the Wind* and the other narratives Fiedler discusses, Mitchell's novel does not seem sufficiently concerned with interethnic rape to fit the pattern of the inadvertent epic. Although Scarlett O'Hara is nearly raped by a black during Reconstruction and is properly avenged by the Klan, that scene is not at the mythic center of the novel. Two other sexual encounters are. In the first of these, Scarlett experiences a kind of erotic ecstasy when she guns down a Yankee attacker who has invaded the sacred turf of Tara. (The first-night movie crowd in Atlanta went wild.) In the second, an inebriated Rhett Butler takes her by force and presumably makes a woman of the coquettish belle. What is most memorable about *Gone with the Wind*—as both novel and movie—is not so much its images of race as its story of intraethnic sex. The three white characters who have made it into the realm of myth—Scarlett, Rhett, and Ashley—constitute an archetypal love triangle.[8] The ineffectually Apollonian Ashley and the vitally Dionysian Rhett are actually male counterparts of the snowmaiden and the dark lady, with Scarlett—a combination Pamela and Lovelace—masquerading as Clarissa.

In Alex Haley's *Roots,* Fiedler finds a book by a black author that is squarely in the tradition defined by Stowe and Dixon. It could even be argued that Haley's moving potboiler is a kind of dialectical synthesis created by the clash of Stowe's thesis and Dixon's antithesis. Fiedler's explanation of why it has taken so long for an African American artist to reach the majority audience with a story as mythically potent as those of Stowe, Dixon, and Mitchell is simple but persuasive. Out of a sense of racial assertiveness, black novelists such as Richard Wright have accepted and glorified the image of the bad—i.e., "uppity"—nigger projected by Dixon. When black rape is justified on sociological grounds, as it is in Wright's *Native Son;* on historical grounds, as it is in William Styron's *The Confessions of Nat Turner* (yes, even white liberals can get in on the act); or on political grounds, as it is in Eldridge Cleaver's *Soul on Ice;* it may go over with the radical chic crowd, but it is not likely to play in Peoria. What was needed was an epic with broad enough appeal to enthrall a biracial middle-class audience.

What Haley has done is to write a socially conservative tale based loosely on the experience of his mother's family. The Gambian society from which his

---

8. We see similar alternatives in *Wuthering Heights* (Linton and Heathcliff), *Tess of the D'Urbervilles* (Angel and Alec), and a host of other tales.

ancestor Kunta Kinte was stolen comes across as an African version of Middle America—more Beaver Cleaver than Eldridge Cleaver. (Kunta's dedication to learning and self-improvement reads like an ad for the United Negro College Fund.) When transplanted to America, Kunta dreams of freedom but finally settles down to a conventionally patriarchal home life. His descendants all harbor bourgeois values and advance themselves through determination and hard work. We are told, on the back-cover blurb of the paperback edition of *Roots,* that the saga "ends . . . at the Arkansas funeral of a black professor whose children are a teacher, a Navy architect, an assistant director of the U.S. Information Agency, and an author. The author is Alex Haley."[9]

Because the middle-class roots of Kunta Kinte's family are posited in Africa, Haley can make his characters "good niggers" without seeming to capitulate to the dominant white culture. Haley also makes a play for the black militant audience by emphasizing Kunta's Islamic faith. (Because that faith is inherited rather than chosen, the white audience is not alienated by a defection from Christianity.) Also, there is sufficient interethnic rape and flagellation— exclusively white on black—to appeal consciously to the righteous indignation of all but the most rabid racist and subconsciously to the prurient curiosity of all but the most confirmed ascetic. As a veteran of the U.S. Coast Guard, a frequent contributor to *Reader's Digest,* and the actual author of *The Autobiography of Malcolm X,* Haley knew how to play both ends against the middle. In Kunta Kinte, he has created a brilliant synthesis of Uncle Tom and Malcolm X.

At first glance, one is tempted to see Stowe and Haley as liberal allies against the neo-Confederate ideology of Dixon, Griffith, and Mitchell. Even if sophisticated blacks cringe at the image of Uncle Tom and smirk at the philistinism of *Roots,* Stowe and Haley at least regarded slavery as an abomination. Thomas Dixon can only be described as a eugenic racist, while D. W. Griffith and Margaret Mitchell could not conceive of a good society that was not founded on class subordination, with white trash being even lower in the hierarchy than faithful darkies.

In the one reference to *Uncle Tom's Cabin* in *Gone with the Wind,* Mitchell shows that she knew and loathed the reputation of Stowe's novel, whether she had actually read the book or not. "Accepting *Uncle Tom's Cabin* as revelation second only to the Bible," Mitchell writes, "the Yankee women all wanted to know about the bloodhounds which every Southerner kept to track down runaway slaves . . . They wanted to know about the dreadful branding irons which planters used to mark the faces of their slaves and the cat-o'-nine-tails with which they beat them to death, and they evidenced what Scarlett felt was a very nasty and ill-bred interest in slave concubinage."[10] Had she lived to

---

9. See the back cover of the 1976 paperback edition of Alex Haley's *Roots.*
10. Margaret Mitchell, *Gone with the Wind,* 662.

read *Roots* (which she might have done had she not been struck by a taxicab while trying to cross a street in 1949), Mitchell surely would have found that book even more offensive. Stowe at least paints sympathetic portraits of several white southerners (particularly George Shelby, Little Eva, and Augustine St. Clare). In *Roots,* there is no such thing as a good white person—northern or southern.

When we get beyond ideology, however, we find that the strongest mythic affinities unite Harriet Beecher Stowe and Margaret Mitchell. Neither Dixon nor Haley could envision a world in which black and white people lived together harmoniously. In contrast, interracial love is at the very heart of the matriarchal world of Stowe and Mitchell. At one point in *Uncle Tom's Cabin,* Little Eva concludes—with no trace of irony—that God must approve of slavery because it gives her more people to love. When the men in her life are gone and Scarlett seems bereft of everything else, she thinks of Tara and remembers one thing above all—"Mammy would be there." (After more than a thousand pages, it is Mammy who endures.) "Suddenly she wanted Mammy desperately, as she had wanted her when she was a little girl, wanted the broad bosom on which to lay her head, the gnarled black hand on her hair. Mammy, the last link with the old days." As Nigger Jim would say, "It's too good for true, honey, it's too good for true."[11]

IV

The final section of *What Was Literature?* completes the foray into literary anthropology that Fiedler had begun over three decades earlier with "Come Back to the Raft Ag'in, Huck Honey!" By exploring the feminine, domestic myth of America (complete with its idealization of the hearth and its obsessive fear of miscegenetic rape), he is not so much repudiating the misogynist tradition of interethnic male bonding as expanding the canon to include an alternative vision to which the Huck-Honey motif stands in dialectical tension. If Fiedler is correct in seeing American literature as fundamentally regional in nature, then the misogynist canon is essentially western, while the domestic tradition is southern. That part of our dream life that lies just over the horizon is by definition incompatible with the social and familial harmony venerated by the South.

As with so much that Fiedler maintains, these regional schematics tell an important but partial truth. Just as the image of the West one finds in *The Return of the Vanishing American* fails to encompass the totality of the West, the

---

11. Ibid., 1024.

South we find in the bulk of the inadvertent epic is only one possible South. In writing what might be regarded as antisoutherns, Harriet Beecher Stowe and Alex Haley have depicted a region obsessed with race. Proceeding from very different motives, Thomas Dixon and D. W. Griffith have done much the same. There is, however, an entire tradition in southern literature in which race is far from the most important concern. On the highbrow level, this tradition is epitomized by the Agrarian movement, in popular culture by *Gone with the Wind.*

Like the Agrarians, Margaret Mitchell was concerned with the assault on tradition and continuity in the South. While Scarlett's response to the situation was more direct and pragmatic than that of the authors of *I'll Take My Stand* (several of whom more closely resembled Ashley Wilkes), Mitchell shared the Agrarians' reverence for the past. (John Crowe Ransom reviewed her book favorably in the *Southern Review.*) While racial subordination was a part of the southern tradition, black people have also fared badly in deracinated, officially egalitarian societies. In contemplating the transition from Old South to New, no less an authority than W. E. B. Du Bois writes that "with all the Bad that fell on one black day, something was vanquished that deserved to live, something killed that in justice did not dare to die; . . . with the Right that triumphed, triumphed something of Wrong, something sordid and mean, something less than the broadest and best."[12]

Fiedler dedicated *What Was Literature?* to "Sam and Hattie." As he argues toward the end of the book, "if Sam Clemens is a literary father to us all, Hattie Stowe is our mother" (243). It is perhaps fitting that, during their later years, Clemens and Stowe lived next door to each other in Hartford, Connecticut, equally rich and famous—she for "celebrating Home and Mother," he "for fantasizing escapes from both" (242). Fiedler suggests that, at certain levels, there are surprising links between the supposedly antithetical worldviews of our literary parents. It is, however, an argument that even Fiedler concedes works better for Clemens than for Stowe. All that really connects Hattie to Sam is the fact that her "characters travel the Mississippi and its tributaries, not merely in quest of a home but in flight from enemies rather like those who beset Huck and Jim" (240).

All of his life Sam Clemens was a mama's boy whose rebellion against home was the ambivalent charade of a Tom Sawyer, and beneath his many descriptions of domestic life—particularly of the Phelps farm, based on the home of his uncle John A. Quarles—runs an undercurrent of affection. At the end of his life, with his wife and daughters dead, Clemens was a lost and pathetic figure:

12. W. E. B. Du Bois, *The Souls of Black Folk,* 47–48.

Hair white, mustache white, clothes white, he must have seemed not, as he liked to boast, the "only clean man in a dirty world," but a ghost reenacting the macho ritual of the mining camp and the saloon, with no woman left to say him nay. All alone, he would smoke, we are told, forty cigars a day, drink God knows how many shots of bourbon, and end playing pool with himself, until he passed out on the billiard table and was carried off to bed by a servant. There doubtless, in intervals between the nightmares of diminution and dissolution recorded in his last unfinished sketches, he must surely have had good dreams, too. But it is hard to say whether he dreamed himself in them as impostor, warmly embraced by Aunt Sally as her own dear sister's son, or a kinless boy forever in flight with an eternally fugitive slave. (245)

CHAPTER TWENTY

Moses in Aspen

AS HE GREW older, a source of continuing sorrow for Leslie was his estrangement from his brother, Harold. One day, when Leslie still lived in Missoula, an adolescent who seemed vaguely familiar appeared at his door. The boy, who looked like a typical college student with long hair and guitar, asked if there were any odd jobs he could perform around the place. It wasn't long before the visitor identified himself as Harold's son, Steve. By now, Harold had completely abandoned his Jewish heritage. Not only were he and his wife (who was also of Jewish origin) devout Lutherans, they lived as purebred goys in rural New Hampshire. Steve and his sister, Carol, had both gone to fancy private schools and were completely unaware of their ancestry. Although Leslie and Steve developed an immediate bond, Harold remained adamantly opposed to reconciliation. When Steve died of cancer at age twenty-three, Leslie's most promising link with his brother's family died with him.

If Harold was downright hostile toward Leslie, he was simply distant toward their mother. He would write her dutifully and send her small sums of money, while avoiding more personal contact. "What have we done that he should treat us this way?" Lillian Fiedler would often ask. (It hadn't helped that she had accused Harold of selling his birthright for a mess of pottage.) When she died in 1985, Harold did call Leslie to settle some financial matters, but he made it clear that the conversation would be confined to business. Not too many years before that, Leslie had called him on his birthday, and Harold had simply hung up.

The only member of Leslie's immediate family to see Harold after his letter breaking off contact in the early 1960s was Leslie's son Eric. Because he was hitchhiking from Athens to Jerusalem, Eric passed through Istanbul, where Harold was still serving as American consul. "I am an American citizen, so he can't refuse to see me," Eric reasoned. With all diplomatic correctness, Harold invited Eric to the embassy for dinner and played the sound track to a currently fashionable musical comedy. Having drowned out any possible conversation,

Harold shook Eric's hand at the end of the evening and said, "We'll never see each other again."[1]

When the respectable Harold severed relations with his family, it fell to the black sheep Leslie to take his mother in during her last days. After her husband had died, when they were both sixty, Lillian Fiedler lived an independent life for as long as she was able to do so. (She got a job with the phone company in Newark by claiming to be younger than she actually was.) But, in her late eighties, she finally moved to Buffalo. Even then, she tried to maintain her own apartment, which was a short drive from Morris Avenue. Unfortunately Buffalo, like Newark, was plagued by urban crime. After her place was broken into for the second time, Leslie moved her into his house, while he looked for a more permanent arrangement. Although Lillian chafed at the thought of going into a nursing home ("Just let me pitch a tent in your backyard," she said), her son found her a place in an elite Jewish facility. One afternoon, after a long visit with Leslie, Sally, and Mimo and her family, Lillian Fiedler settled down with a romance novel and died at the age of ninety-one.

Leslie's own six children have lived varied lives. For years, it seemed as if Kurt was intent on setting a record for the longest adolescent rebellion in history. The trouble began when the family lived in Princeton and continued as he managed to leave or be thrown out of college three different times—Reed College once and Harvard twice. While living as a beachcomber in the Fiji Islands, Kurt finally decided that his vocation was in medicine. He came back to the United States, finished college at the University of New Mexico, and got his medical degree at the University of Utah. He broke up with his first wife and found a second. (At age thirty-three, she was marrying for the seventh time.) Kurt, who now specializes in spinal cord injuries and lives in New Mexico, seems to have found a stability that had eluded him well into his adult years. Leslie is delighted that his son has found a rewarding life. Margaret, however, believes that he shamelessly abandoned his bohemian values. When asked at his second wedding what she thought of Kurt's new life, she replied, "I want to puke."[2]

When Leslie thinks of his sons Eric and Michael, he sees two men with a great capacity for misfortune. Eric has led something of an itinerant existence as a grip in the motion picture industry. (He also spent some time as a secretary and companion to the aged Jeanette Rankin.) He suffered for many troubled years with a woman who had been married to Billy Hutton, who was himself one of the several mentally disturbed individuals to invade 154 Morris Avenue. Not long after he found happiness with a new woman and her two children, Eric was diagnosed with a terminal form of blood cancer.

1. Fiedler, interview with Jackson, June 29, 1989.
2. Fiedler, interview with Jackson, May 7, 1989.

Michael is the only one of Leslie's children to end up back in Missoula. A borderline schizophrenic, Michael lives on Social Security disability insurance. (Much of Leslie's affection for Allen Ginsberg derives from the kindness Allen showed to Michael during earlier days of madness in New York.) During a long-term relationship that has since ended, Michael fathered a daughter, Taira, who is now in college learning how to be a wilderness guide. He also writes poetry, which he reads on the local radio station.

Until recently, it seemed as if Jenny was less capable than Michael of dealing with illness. The most beautiful of Leslie's six children and a talented dancer, Jenny has long been afflicted with a variety of ailments collectively labeled "chronic fatigue syndrome." After fighting these illnesses for years (without the aid of conventional medicine, which she distrusts), Jenny took a turn for the better when her daughter, Posey, announced that she expected to be first in her class and a mother—both in the spring of 1999. The birth of Posey's child, Celia Pearl Arillo Gray, made Leslie a great-grandfather for the first time.

Because of her natural gift for languages, Debbie has made a career for herself teaching English to nonnative speakers in Los Angeles. In an effort to help an immigrant friend remain in this country, she agreed to become his wife. To the surprise of nearly everyone, including Debbie and her husband, Frank Apraku, the marriage has lasted longer than many unions built on more conventional ties. As an African of the Ashanti tribe, Frank shares several customs (including circumcision) with his wife's Jewish ancestors. The couple's two children are named Abraham and Ruth. When their great-grandmother Lillian first saw them, she simply shook her head and said, "Black as the ace of spades." What she would have thought of Leslie's other grandchildren is anybody's guess. Eric's two stepsons (Ivan and Daniel Kim) are half Korean. Jenny's three children (Posey, Eric Sergio, and Wonder Arillo) are half Mexican, while Mimo's son, Thorn, is married to a black woman. As patriarch, Leslie himself is pleased by the diversity of his tribe.

Many of the Fiedler brood now live in and around Atlanta. Mimo's husband, Bob Konrad, works as a nurse at the Emory University Hospital, while Mimo is pursuing a Ph.D. in sociology. The Konrad house, near the Emory University campus, is located strategically close to much of the extended family, including the aging Margaret. Often when Leslie visits Mimo, his former wife will be present. Because he believes in clean and permanent breaks, he instinctively flinches when she tries to smooth out his collar or make some other gesture of wifely affection. Strangely enough, the only person who seems totally comfortable in the situation is Sally. Before she and Leslie have been in town for very long, Sally and Margaret will be washing dishes or straightening up an untidy room.[3]

3. Fiedler, interview with author, Feb. 27, 1999.

I

On June 17, 1994, Leslie and Sally Fiedler were among approximately ninety-five million Americans who watched on their television sets as Los Angeles police pursued a white Bronco across the city's freeways. The Lubavitcher Rebbe had died earlier that week, but his demise had been pushed off the front pages, even in New York, by the discovery of two murder victims a continent away in California. One was Ronald Goldman, a waiter at an upscale Los Angeles restaurant. The other was the former wife of football legend O. J. Simpson. From his days as a Heisman Trophy winner at the University of Southern California to his spectacular seasons with the Buffalo Bills of the NFL, Simpson had been known as one of the greatest running backs of all time. Later, he charmed a nation as a sports analyst for NBC and a movie actor. Now he was the prime suspect in these two murders and the passenger in the sports utility vehicle being watched by an entire nation. Some people sat in lawn chairs to view the "slow-speed chase" as it went by, while others draped banners saying "GO JUICE GO" on freeway overpasses.

Unlike all but a handful of the ninety-five million television viewers, Leslie and Sally had actually met O. J. In the eclectic world inhabited by media celebrities, Simpson and Allen Ginsberg were friends—brought together by their common drug dealer. On December 1, 1975, Allen and Peter Orlovsky had rented a limousine to take them and the Fiedlers from Buffalo to Toronto, where Bob Dylan was appearing as part of his Rolling Thunder Review. Because Allen had an official position with the show, he got backstage passes for himself and his friends. One of the people they ran into backstage was O. J. Leslie remembers him as engaging. Of all the black people Leslie had known, O. J. seemed least likely to be involved in violent crime. Nevertheless, Leslie never harbored any doubt about his guilt. Recalling the many times he had been angry enough to kill Margaret, he knew what an enraged husband was capable of doing.[4]

Although Leslie had no close ties to Buffalo's professional football team, his next-door neighbor, Larry Desautels, did. In addition to teaching with Sally at the Nichols School, Larry ran a program for young people interested in writing. One of the lecturers in this program was Ray Bentley, a player with the Buffalo Bills, who also wrote children's books about a character named Darby the Dinosaur. When the NFL put on a big push to persuade players who had dropped out of school to go back and finish their degrees, Ray was in charge of getting his teammates to comply. One individual, a second-string quarterback named Gail Gilbert, was only one English course shy of finishing his

4. Leslie Fiedler, interview with author, July 10, 1999.

B.A. at Berkeley. In the process of writing a paper for this course, Gilbert ran into problems distinguishing modernism from postmodernism. When Bently called Larry for help, he mentioned the situation to Leslie across the backyard fence. As a result, Ray, Gail, Larry, and Leslie ended up spending an evening talking, eating, and drinking at a sports bar called Billy Ogden's. It turned out to be an unforgettable night for all involved. Leslie had made another foray into the universe of popular culture, and Gail Gilbert got his baccalaureate degree.[5]

Remembering that evening, Larry provided Leslie with another entree into the world of big-time football. Reading Joe Paterno's autobiography, he discovered that the great Penn State coach—he was just an assistant at the time—and his future wife had attended one of Leslie's lectures during the early days of their courtship. "[W]e left together," Paterno recalls, "getting into absorbed discussion of some of the provocative things he'd said. One of us got a little book of Fiedler lectures, and we lent it back and forth, reading one essay after another, and discovered we both enjoyed the competition of disagreement." When Larry informed Paterno's son that he lived next door to Leslie, Joe's wife wrote to ask if Leslie would autograph her old $1.25 paperback copy of *An End to Innocence*. In exchange, Leslie got an autographed picture of Paterno. "To Leslie," it reads. "Some times we never know if somebody is listening. Sue and I listened. Thanks."[6]

Although Leslie was used to getting fan letters from unconventional sources, official recognition was longer in coming. He seemed to have an uncanny knack for currying the disfavor of those in power. Perhaps for that reason, he had been kept out of the American Academy of Arts and Letters, while younger and less distinguished writers were routinely admitted. Because the incumbent members of the academy vote on new admissions, the old guard can effectively blackball anyone they consider particularly objectionable. Leslie is convinced that the old Stalinist Malcolm Cowley blocked his induction because of differences over the Rosenberg case and general animus. (In 1976, Cowley wrote to Kenneth Burke: "Leslie Fiedler likes to flaunt his several children in the faces of the great authors whose work he is discussing, as if to say, 'I am a mature genitally-directed critic and here is my evidence. Whereas you poor bastards are only novelists and poets, orally regressed and fixated in secondary narcissism. You can't get it up.' ")[7] As it turns out, Leslie was finally admitted in 1988, the year before Cowley's death at age ninety.

5. Larry Desautels, interview with author, July 10, 1999.

6. Joe Paterno with Bernard Asbell, *Paterno: By the Book,* 78.

7. Paul Jay, ed., *The Selected Correspondence of Kenneth Burke and Malcolm Cowley, 1915–1981,* 400–401.

It is debatable whether Leslie was more irked by being kept out of or by being voted into the academy. The part of his personality that relished being an outsider told him that accepting membership would be a violation of his populist principles. Better to continue saying "No!" in thunder than learn to say "Thank you for this honor." So, on the day he was to be admitted to the academy, he almost backed out. Sally had to drag him out of the hotel room and practically order him to take his place with the dignitaries on stage. Although the entire affair seemed interminably long, the booze was flowing freely before, during, and after the ceremony. At one point during the preinduction luncheon (complete with a different wine for every course), a prominent American poet introduced himself to Leslie and told him how much he had admired his work over the years. As the man departed, Leslie muttered, "There goes the worst poet in America. Somebody ought to shoot him." It was the sort of display that has earned Leslie his considerable reputation for boorishness, and the main business of the day had yet to be transacted.

Sitting on the stage in a drunken stupor waiting for his name to be called, Leslie could scarcely stay awake. Frantically searching for some sensory stimulation, he began to pick his teeth. He even managed to stand on cue but forgot to sit back down. Sally's guest, a writer of television soap operas, was greatly amused to see the highbrow literary folk engage in such lavish self-congratulation. Sally herself was simply glad when the day came to an end with only minimal embarrassment. For all his protests, Leslie seemed to appreciate the irony of his being admitted to what he regarded as an exclusive WASP men's club. After fifty years, his old Italian teacher had been proven wrong. In spite of himself, Leslie Fiedler was now officially labeled a gentleman and a scholar.[8]

II

A reasonably safe prediction about Leslie's career is that any resolve he makes to stop writing about a particular topic will eventually be broken. When he put together the second volume of his *Collected Essays* in 1971, he was certain that all of the reflections on Jewish themes he would ever wish to preserve were being brought together in "To the Gentiles." By now, the Jews had become so fully assimilated into American life that their time at the center of our literary culture had passed. And yet, twenty years later, he found himself again publishing a book on "literature and Jewish identity," which he whimsically called *Fiedler on the Roof.*

8. Sally Fiedler, interview with author, July 10, 1999.

This collection of essays and talks, dating from 1969 to 1989, begins with a meditation on the long history of anti-Semitism in Western culture. Although he had originally dealt with that topic in "What Can We Do about Fagin?" an essay published in the May 1949 issue of *Commentary,* Leslie was so dissatisfied with this discussion that he has never had it reprinted. Part of the problem may lie in the author's own celebrated ambivalence. As an accomplished critic and aspiring poet, Leslie saw Ezra Pound, T. S. Eliot and other high modernists as aesthetic models. At the same time, he abhorred their politics—which ranged from genteel conservatism to outright Fascism. What was perhaps even more troubling was the fact that Pound and Eliot (along with Hemingway, Fitzgerald, Lawrence, and countless others) were heirs of a centuries old tradition of anti-Semitism in English literature.

In both "What Can We Do about Fagin?" and *Fiedler on the Roof,* Leslie traces this tradition back to the tale told by Chaucer's prioress. Based on the story of Hugh of Lincoln, the tale eulogizes a little boy whose songs of praise to the Virgin so irk the Jews that they hire a murderer to cut the child's throat. This story gives us the image of the predatory Jew with a knife, who appears later in Marlowe's *The Jew of Malta* and, even more memorably, in Shakespeare's *The Merchant of Venice.* This image extrapolates a nightmare vision of castration from the Jew's role as circumcisor. More recent instances of this phenomenon can be found in Dickens's Fagin and in the gangster Colleoni from Graham Greene's *Brighton Rock.*

Neither in 1949 nor later did Leslie favor censoring these images. (As we have seen, writing to T. S. Eliot was not a very effective strategy, either.) If, for the sake of art, we permit the glorification of every other kind of vice, we must also permit anti-Semitism. In banning the poems of Pound or *The Merchant of Venice,* we might lose vile politics, but we would also lose a degree of beauty and true vision. Rather than deny the existence of Fagins and Shylocks (who exist in the Gentile community as well), it is far better to create positive countervailing images of the Jew, as the writers of the postwar Jewish Renaissance would do. In 1949, however, the best examples of favorable Jewish prototypes that Leslie could think of were those of the happy Israeli peasant, the alienated loner (as in Kafka's K), the refined dilettante (as in Proust's Swann), and the citizen-patriarch (as in Joyce's Bloom). To compound the irony of ethnic identity, the last of these figures, who was also the first great Jewish character in twentieth-century literature, was the creation of an apostate Irish Catholic. He is also the subject of two essays in *Fiedler on the Roof.*

As a thoroughly secularized individual who has had three baptisms but no circumcision, Leopold Bloom would appear to be more Irish than Jewish (he even lacks the crucial matrilineal connection); however, he is defined as Jewish by the culture in which he lives. If Stephen Dedalus is what James Joyce once was, Bloom is what he might have become. In fact, in a talk delivered in Dublin in 1969, when he was on his way back from Biafra, Fiedler argues that most of Joyce's corpus is divided between the sensibilities of his two alter egos—Dedalus and Bloom—with the more expansive and life-affirming aspects of his fictional world being associated with the Jew.

Bloom is nevertheless fated to be a perpetual outsider in Catholic Ireland. As such, his most obvious Christian prototype is that of the holy cuckold St. Joseph. (This is surely meant to be taken ironically, in that Bloom's wife, Molly, is no Virgin Mary, while her lover Blazes Boylan has even less in common with the Holy Ghost.) From a classical or pagan standpoint, Bloom is even closer to the thematic center of the novel. He is, according to Fiedler, "Ulysses resurrected and transfigured, not merely recalled or commented on or explained. Bloom is Ulysses rescued from all those others who were neither Jew nor Greek, and who had kidnapped him, held him in alien captivity for too long. Bloom is Ulysses rescued from the great poets as well as the small ones, from Dante and from Tennyson, and—at the other end of the mythological spectrum from James Joyce—from that anti-Semite, Ezra Pound, who liked to think he was the only true Ulysses" (*FOR*, 38).

That Bloom should be dreamed by an Irishman is only fitting when one considers the degree to which the Jew and Irishman are comically linked in popular culture (from Gallagher and Sheen to Burns and Allen). If Joyce could identify himself with both Dedalus and Bloom at various stages of his life, it is no surprise that others—Fiedler included—could do so as well. As Fiedler, the amateur, told his audience of professional Joyce scholars: "I began by thinking that I was Stephen; began by thinking that I was the perpetual victim, perpetually stoned to death by his own infidel kin; began by thinking that I was the high-flying boy doomed to fall in glory and to write the story of my plunge earthward even as I fell. But I ended, as you will end, as Joyce ended, by knowing that I was Bloom, a comic, earthbound father who is also an Apostle to the Gentiles" (45–46).

In "Joyce and Jewish Consciousness," originally delivered as a lecture at the University of Toronto in 1985, Fiedler again stresses Bloom's importance as archetypal Jew. In doing so, he takes direct aim at Hugh Kenner, who minimizes both Joyce's Irishness and Bloom's Jewishness. In Fiedler's judgment, these two identities lurk just beneath the ironic surfaces of the novel. (In the penultimate episode, for example, Bloom and Stephen, "an older Jew and a younger Irishman—spokesmen, respectively, for the middle-aged author who writes and the juvenile self he remembers—converse about their essential Jewishness and Irishness; and attempt to find, not so much in what each remembers, but in what each has forgotten, common ground" [51].) If Stephen—like his creator—has made himself an exile by choice, that role is one that history has chosen for Bloom—and indeed all Jews since the Diaspora. If Bloom and

Stephen become symbolically father and son, it is because both are offspring of Joyce's own sensibility.

One of the ironies inherent in the success of the Jewish American writers of the postwar era was their indebtedness to Christian culture. In an address given at the ultraorthodox Bar-Ilan University in Israel in 1983, Fiedler notes that even the most explicitly Jewish of the postwar fictionists, Bernard Malamud, employed the legend of the Holy Grail in his first novel, *The Natural*. On the surface, this tale may have dealt with the secular game of baseball; however, its symbolic subtext owes much to the influence of T. S. Eliot, who was not only a Christian but an anti-Semite as well. Moreover, the title character of Saul Bellow's *Henderson, the Rain King* is a spiritual anthropologist who obsessively quotes from Eliot's "The Love Song of J. Alfred Prufrock."

Even when we go back to Malamud and Bellow's most important predecessors of the 1930s, Nathanael West and Henry Roth, we find more imagery from the New Testament than the Old. West's final three novels (*Miss Lonelyhearts, A Cool Million,* and *The Day of the Locust*) are permeated by crucifixes and Christ figures. Roth's *Call It Sleep,* which is set in the Jewish community and populated by Jewish characters, also owes much to the Christian Eliot. Moreover, when the novel's protagonist quotes the prophet Isaiah, he instinctively chooses a verse that Christians believe foretells the coming of Christ and renders it in the English of King James. Perhaps such appropriation of the Christian ethos was inevitable in a society that tried to teach Jews to pass and rewarded them greatly for doing so.

If there is one essay in this collection that is likely to stand the test of time, it would be "Why Is the Grail Knight Jewish?: A Passover Meditation." Here again, Fiedler's approach to myth contrasts sharply with the methods of more conventional literary anthropologists. He takes particular issue with Jessie Weston's attempt to turn the Grail legend into an upbeat tale, in which the impotent ruler is cured and his land restored. Even a child reading a picture-book account of the exploits of King Arthur's knights can sense that the Grail quest is far more problematic. It involves vision, not repossession. And the cost of that vision would seem to be the destruction of a pagan glory.

In order for the Grail knight—who is called Perceval or Galahad at different times—even to be conceived, Lancelot must betray his true love, Guinevere, for whom he has already betrayed his true king, Arthur. After he is seduced and betrayed by a Jewish woman, the child they conceive in passion becomes an ethereal, sexless being, whose accomplished quest brings the ideal of the Round Table to an end. Although Fiedler could not know it as a boy, the final encounter of Galahad and his father Lancelot "represented in allegory or projection the troubled nightmares occasioned by the transmission into Britain, the ultimate West, of a strange new morality and an even stranger messianic myth by way of [Joseph of Arimethea,] the first Jew who ever landed on its shores" (94).

Despite the attempts of later apologists to make the knights of the Round Table into a kind of Christian commune, the ideals of chivalry and secular honor embodied in Camelot stand in opposition to the ethics of Christian charity and forgiveness embodied in the Grail. One could be an admirer of the Round Table or a Christian, but there seemed no way that one could be both at the same time. The utility and scandal of the Grail legend was that it obscured this crucial choice by making the Grail knight Jewish. One could lament the passing of Camelot and all it represented by blaming it on the Jews. It was bad enough that they killed Christ; now they were destroying a great Celtic society by searching for his cup. Thus, an ostensibly Christian pursuit becomes just another pretext for anti-Semitism, which is itself a virulent denial of Christian charity. Speaking of the rendering of the Grail legend in the famous poem by Chretein de Troyes, Fiedler writes:

> But it is fitting, after all, that a work which ended by denying a charity it had begun by evoking, denying it specifically to God's Chosen People, and thus contributing in its own small way to the centuries of persecution that lay ahead for the Jews of Europe, should, at its most memorable moments, be a poem about failure: the tragicomic failure of the goyim to live by the code they had learned first from Israel, and with which, to speak the truth, they have not yet come to terms. (102)

III

The one major figure of the American Jewish Renaissance to maintain a significant presence in *Fiedler on the Roof* is Bernard Malamud. What intrigues Fiedler most about Malamud, however, are aspects of his writing that are only peripherally Jewish. Not only is his use of the Grail legend in *The Natural* mentioned in two different essays, the one selection that is devoted exclusively to his work discusses him as a writer of the American West. Fiedler is particularly struck by a characteristic he and his friend shared as residents of the West—their identity as displaced easterners. (One can't help noticing the degree to which Fiedler's comments on Malamud's western fiction can be applied to his own efforts in *The Last Jew in America*.) What Malamud has written is actually an easterner's book—or a metawestern. In a sense, the Jew in the West is as out of place as a Jew in Ireland. According to Fiedler, "the very notion of the Western Jew is like that of the Irish Jew a joke in itself." He goes on to ask us to "reflect on the fact that any traditional catch-phrase out of Western literature becomes hilariously funny the minute it is spoken with a Yiddish accent: 'Smile ven you say dot, strrengerr!' " (134).

In his next essay, Fiedler considers another figure whose ethnic identity is debatable. Although the Book of Job has long been a part of the Hebrew tradition, there is some question whether Job was meant to be a Jew at all and whether his story is sacred scripture or merely a great secular poem. For Fiedler, however, these questions are finally less interesting than the great philosophical and theological issues raised by Job's story. These are questions that have had a different meaning for him at different stages in his life. At fourteen, when he was convinced that he did not believe in God, Leslie was nevertheless capable of raging, like Job, against "the palpable injustice of the world," while dreaming—in spite of his non-belief—that "A Voice from Somewhere would somehow declare that I had spoken the thing which was right" (145).

Ironically, it was the very injustice of the universe and the pervasiveness of evil (the Holocaust, World War II, etc.) that finally convinced Leslie there must be a god. "Such suffering 'for nothing' only a God of the Cosmos, omniscient, omnipotent, but vindictive or indifferent, a Hangman God, could have, *must* have—for reasons unknowable and unthinkable to mere humans—instigated or, in any case, permitted' (145–46). When he proposed to wrestle publicly with the Book of Job, it was in an introductory humanities course at Montana State University. Although the course was audited by local clergy, suspicious of both eastern Jews and the humanities, Leslie's erudition soon sent them away in bored confusion.

In systematic fashion, he demonstrated that many religious and philosophical traditions would not have had as much difficulty as Job does with the problem of evil. The avowed atheist would not expect anything resembling divine justice; the ancient Greek would blame it all on fate; the Manichee would simply say that Good never had better than a 50–50 chance of triumphing; and the Hindu would say that karma and reincarnation will eventually settle accounts. Even the orthodox Christian would find a way out by believing in Jesus Christ and reward in the hereafter. Job, however, is reluctant to accept a God of all power and no justice, and he gives no indication of believing in an afterlife— particularly not in one that seems contrived to take our mind off of terrestrial inequities. The answer that the Book of Job seems to offer is that mere human understanding will never be able to fathom the inscrutable purposes of an omnipotent God. Only when he sees God in the whirlwind does Job realize (and accept) the proposition that there is no answer.

Even if such a solution may seem plausible to Job, it fails to take into account the frame story of which Job is apparently unaware. Why would God allow a righteous man to be the unwitting subject of a cruel experiment? Why would God allow himself to be so manipulated by Satan? The answer that makes most sense to Fiedler is that the frame story, which depicts a wager between God and His adversary, is simply an allegorical rendering of doubts that the Almighty Himself entertains about human virtue. If the notion of a self-doubting deity raises theological difficulties, the answer is that this story tells us more about ourselves than it does about the nature of God. Fiedler puts the matter as follows:

> It is with Himself that God is betting: with His own "Other Side," from which He cannot otherwise exorcise the suspicion that no man, not even Job, His "perfect" servant, does good "for nothing." It is this nagging doubt that entices Him into making the cruel test, whose outcome, we tell ourselves, He surely knows from the start. But then, like Him perhaps, we remember how Adam, similarly tempted, fell. Certainly, ever since that mythological event, which is to say, since mankind first knew Good from Evil, we have been haunted by doubts about our own virtue, which we project in fear and trembling upon our Maker. (156–57)

In the concluding essay in this book on Jewish identity ("In Every Generation: A Meditation on the Two Holocausts"), Fiedler concedes that he is not only a minimal Jew but "a terminal one as well" (179). As a youth, he had considered himself a Communist rather than a Jew. Part of the ideal of the classless society lay in sacrificing old tribal loyalties for the sake of universal human brotherhood. Such a society would not know the anti-Semitism that had threatened Jews in every generation in memory. But, in exchange, Jews would have to give up any sense of their separate identity as a people. As Henry Roth put it: "I feel that to the great boons Jews have already conferred on humanity, Jews in America might add this last and greatest one: of orienting themselves toward ceasing to be Jews" (164). Fiedler has no doubt that one of the boons to which Roth was referring was Marxism.

When the dream of Marxism died, many Jews of Fiedler's generation began to reassert their ethnic identity. In only a few instances, however, did this result in religious observance. More often, American Jews became passionate Zionists and dedicated themselves to promoting the interests of Israel. Although Leslie has been to Israel more than half a dozen times, he has felt himself more a stranger there than in America. On one of his more recent visits, he was heckled by a group of ultraorthodox zealots for smoking a cigar outside his hotel on the Sabbath. On an even earlier visit, Prime Minister David Ben-Gurion urged him to give up his unauthentic life of exile in America and move to Israel. " '[U]nless more Jews like you return,' he went on to explain, '*they* will eventually outnumber *us.*' It was clear that by *they* he meant the Sephardim, the 'black Jews,' and by *us,* the Ashkenazim, the 'white' ones." "Never in my life," Leslie concludes, "have I felt less like a Jew, black or white" (176).

Hitler's unsuccessful attempt to destroy the Jews may actually have strengthened the sense of Jewish identity. It is doubtful that the state of Israel would have come into existence had it not been for the Holocaust. At a more mundane level, marginal Jews have reaped benefits from the sense of collective guilt that swept through Western society in the wake of World War II. Leslie candidly confesses to having "profited from a philo-Semitism as undiscriminating as the anti-Semitism in reaction to which it originated, . . . [to having] shamelessly played the role in which I have been cast, becoming a literary Fiedler on the roof of academe" (177).

What could not be effected by the dream of a Communist utopia or the horror of the Nazi death camps may finally be accomplished by the Jews themselves. Throughout the United States, Europe, Russia, and the British Commonwealth, intermarriage and other acts of assimilation are fast destroying the last vestiges of Jewish identity. (Observant Jews refer to this phenomenon as the "Silent Holocaust.") Although Leslie does not celebrate this development, he realizes that he and millions like him have helped to bring it about. The best that he can say about this second Holocaust—this truly final solution—is that "we unreconstructed assimilationists, unlike the Nazis, seek not to obliterate along with their bodies the very memory of the Jews, but rather to memorialize in honor the last choice of the Chosen People: their decision to cease to exist in their chosenness for the sake of a united mankind" (180). Nevertheless, like Lot's wife, Leslie cannot avoid the backward glance. If one were to ask him why such a minimal Jew has written so obsessively about Jewishness, all that he could do would be to quote his grandfather Rosenstruach: "Not because I believe but so you should remember" (181).

IV

In 1989, Leslie celebrated his fiftieth anniversary as a college teacher. Even at seventy-two he was not ready to retire from the profession he loved. Instead, he stopped teaching conventional classes and began giving nothing but tutorials. In many ways, it was an ideal situation, because he ended up working only with those students who sought him out with a project that interested both of them. Even as his health began to deteriorate in the next decade, he kept coming to campus three mornings a week. When the department moved from its quonset huts on Main Street to its new campus in the suburbs, the English department was housed in a building called Clemens Hall.

Since its golden days in the late 1960s and early '70s, the Buffalo English department has experienced mostly lean times. As many of the stars brought in by Al Cook either retired or moved on to other jobs, their positions were allowed to go vacant or were filled by entry-level appointments. When hiring once again picked up in the mid-1990s, there seemed to be a generation gap between the old holdovers and the newcomers. In his own words, Leslie had gone from "the status of *enfant terrible* to that of 'dirty old man' without passing through a decent maturity" (*WWL?* 19). The newer critical theorists regarded his myth criticism as hopelessly outdated, and he managed to outrage the rising generation of ideologues with his political incorrectness. At the same time, hardcore elitists would not forgive him for his continuing assault on highbrow "standards."

If American trendsetters believed that Leslie had ceased to be avant-garde without ever having entered the mainstream, he continued to be venerated overseas. Foreign students who came to Buffalo especially wanted to work with him, and once a visiting scholar from India crawled under his desk to kiss his feet. Often the American students who sought him out were on the margins of society. One entire class consisted of disabled persons, who studied the treatment of physical abnormalities in literature. As one might expect, this was not a class of meek-spirited Tiny Tims. "We're not 'handicapped' or 'disabled,'" they would say. "Goddamit, we're cripples and proud of it." By the end of the semester, a dwarf anarchist had given a huge engagement ring to a girl with flipper arms.

Leslie himself encountered physical setbacks in the 1990s. Like many men past middle age, he developed prostate cancer. Upon being wheeled into recovery after surgery to remove his prostate gland in 1991, he observed of Sally: "What a fine figure of a woman. And such a well-turned ankle." Thanks to excellent health insurance, he can afford the pills and shots necessary to keep his testosterone low and the cancer at bay. Although the disease briefly spread to other parts of his body, it appears to be in remission. Knowing that cancer runs in his family and that his father died from it at age sixty, Leslie feels lucky to be alive.

With his cancer seemingly vanquished, Leslie developed a tremor in his hand and began to lose his balance. He had to stop taking his habitual long walks when he started to feel as if he were pitching forward. After a couple of falls, he was diagnosed with Parkinson's disease in January 1996. This ailment causes a deterioration of brain cells and a gradual loss of coordination. In a major concession to reality, Leslie gave up driving in 1998. For a couple of years thereafter, a driver would appear at his door at 8:30 on Monday, Wednesday, and Friday mornings, and again in front of Clemens Hall just before noon. (For him, riding in the back of a chauffeur-driven Lincoln Town Car was more a necessity than a luxury, the cost of which he bore because he could not stand to see the word *emeritus* attached to his name.) By 2001, Leslie's disease had progressed to the point that he was forced to rely increasingly on a wheelchair, a walker, and physical therapy. Nevertheless, he still received students in his home.

In addition to the ravages visited upon his body, Leslie suffered a major loss of property in the mid-1990s. About four o'clock on the morning of December 14, 1995, Sally was awakened by the sound of the second-floor smoke detector. Three hours earlier, a neighbor from across the street had smelled smoke but gone back to bed when he looked out his window and saw no flames. (His wife, who remained asleep, dreamed of a fire.) An exposed wire in an extension cord under a rug in Leslie's study had ignited a small fire some time that night. Had it been caught in the first hour or so, no great damage would have been done. But, with the first-floor smoke detector broken, the fire continued to smolder unnoticed until the study was in flames.

Rather than feeling the bedroom door (as she had been taught to do), Sally instinctively threw it open. When she saw the smoke, she had sense enough to know that she and Leslie would have to leave by the second floor if they hoped to make it out alive. She awakened Leslie and managed to get both him and herself through a bathroom window and onto a balcony outside the house. By this time, a neighbor had arrived with a ladder that was far too short, as potentially lethal smoke kept billowing out of the house. Within a matter of minutes firetrucks arrived at Morris Avenue. The firefighters cradled Leslie and Sally in their arms and brought them down to safety in the bitter cold. Larry Desautels was waiting next door with blankets. As he saw Leslie coming through the drifted snow and falling sleet with nothing but a bathrobe on his body and sandals on his feet, he thought, *Moses in Aspen.*

The fire damage to the first floor was extensive, and the entire house was permeated by smoke. It would be some time before anyone could tell how many valuable papers and books had been lost. (The casualties eventually included bound galleys of *Catch-22,* numerous first editions, and much of Leslie's collection of nineteenth-century American literature.) After the fire was extinguished, Leslie and Sally were able to enter the house to get medicine and a few belongings. But then, when the heat came back on, the trapped fumes began to circulate, and it was impossible for anyone to remain in the house for very long without a special mask.

After spending the first night with Larry and Lucy Desautels, Leslie and Sally moved in with Bruce Jackson and Diane Christian. Then, after a month, they rented a small furnished house from a music teacher at the Buffalo Seminary (an exclusive girls' school where Sally taught after leaving the Nichols School). Having lived for so many years in the house on Morris Avenue, they felt as if they had moved into a cottage. But it was a comfortable and charming place in which to regain their privacy and start putting their lives back together. Although much in the old house was gone, other items could be partially restored. It would just take time and patience and plenty of insurance money.

As traumatic as the fire itself had been, the aftermath was in some ways worse. Leslie and Sally spent month after month haggling with their insurance company over virtually every expense. Trying to prove that a particular repair was required by the fire rather than by other causes was often difficult. When they did get a check, it was frequently late and from a distant bank, so that it would take longer for the check to clear and the company could collect more interest on its deposit. When the parties went to what was supposed to be binding arbitration and the company didn't like the findings, it simply refused to comply. Finally, after nearly four years of bickering, Leslie settled with the "good-hands" people for far less than the replacement value he thought he had purchased with nearly forty years of insurance premiums.[9]

Larry Desautels is convinced that, on the morning after the fire, his neighbor's long-repressed knowledge of Japanese had surfaced. Although Leslie himself has no recollection of having done so, Larry heard him say something that sounded like *"Fukochu no saiwai,"* which means "fortune in the midst of misfortune." Leslie kept consoling Sally by telling her that what they had lost was "only stuff." In the end we leave the world with no more than what we brought with us. But for Leslie that time had not yet come. Because no one would be writing his obituary that day, it was not yet necessary to say anything good about him.[10]

9. Leslie and Sally Fiedler, interviews with author, Feb. 27, 1999.

10. Larry Desautels, interview with author, July 10, 1999. Also, see Desautels's story "Upon the Burning of His House."

CHAPTER TWENTY-ONE

The Sorcerer's Apprentice

EVEN AS HE experienced physical setbacks in the 1990s, Leslie remained intellectually active. In 1999, for example, he published *A New Fiedler Reader.* The earlier version of this anthology had appeared in 1977, when Leslie was still riding high as a celebrity nut. Perhaps for that reason, the jacket photograph made him look like a longshoreman. On the cover of the later book, he seems a patriarchal—almost rabbinical—figure, holding his glasses and a manuscript, while sitting in a straightback chair. (Leslie himself calls the picture "Whistler's Father.") In addition to the entire contents of the first reader, Leslie has included a narrative poem ("Momotaro, or the Peachboy: A Japanese Fairy Tale"), a short story ("What Used to Be Called Dead"), and recent essays on the gun in American culture and Jack London's much-neglected science fiction novel, *The Star Rover.* He has also preserved chapters from two earlier books—*Fiedler on the Roof* and a remarkable collection of essays called *Tyranny of the Normal.*

In the years after *Freaks* came out, Leslie was frequently invited to speak before professional medical groups "about gerontology, child abuse, euthanasia, cosmetic surgery, and organ transplants, as well as the images of doctors and nurses in literature and the popular arts" (*TON,* xv). Like the genetic curiosities who appeared in the sideshows and carnivals of a bygone era, recent advances in medical technology were raising questions about the definition of humanity, which physicians alone were not capable of answering. In one of the signal ironies of his career, the inquiries that had once made Leslie seem like a crass popularizer were now earning him a distinguished reputation in an entirely unfamiliar field. Subtitled "Essays on Bioethics, Theology and Myth," *Tyranny of the Normal* was published in 1996.

The first predominantly "medical" essay in this book deals with images of the disabled in literature and the popular arts. By calling his ruminations "Pity and Fear," Fiedler suggests that our response to the handicapped is not that far removed from what Aristotle postulated as the normal human response to tragedy. No amount of propaganda designed to convince us that the disabled are nothing more than physically challenged versions of ourselves can quite dispel the notion that they are like us only in being projections of our nightmares. Sensitive gimps, such as the paraplegic Vietnam veteran played by Jon Voight in the movie *Coming Home,* or noble freaks, such as the protagonist of Bernard Pomerance's play *The Elephant Man,* seem more products of political correctness than genuine myth. When we think of the disabled in literature, we are more likely to remember villains such as Shakespeare's deformed Richard III; Dickens's monstrous dwarf Quilp, who pursues Little Nell in *The Old Curiosity Shop;* Melville's one-legged Captain Ahab from *Moby-Dick,* or his counterpart from Stevenson's *Treasure Island,* the smiling murderer Long John Silver. Even a character as virtuous as Hugo's Quasimodo in *The Hunchback of Notre Dame* fills us with a kind of primordial revulsion.

Another stock literary figure who challenges conventional notions of normality is the dirty old man. In the new comic fable of Chaucer and Boccaccio, any older man foolish enough to lust for a younger woman is deemed fit for whatever grief can be visited upon him. In our deepest imagination, we associate old age with thanatos, not eros. If the old man thinks it his duty to cheat death by getting it up just one more time, we affirm our youth by laughing at his efforts. But it is a nervous laughter, designed to conceal the realization that we too may grow old some day. Beginning with certain popular movies made between the two world wars (e.g., *The Blue Angel*) the dirty old man has increasingly become less a predator than a victim of the female coquette. (In Vladimir Nabokov's *Lolita,* the temptress is a mere thirteen, thus putting an entirely new spin on the nightmare of child rape.) If the myths embodied in narratives of the vamp and gold digger can displace the guilt felt by elderly lovers, the shame nevertheless remains. Perhaps this is because the image of an older man with a younger woman calls to mind the even greater horror of father-daughter incest. Although Fiedler does not mention Roman Polanski's *Chinatown,* that film ends with an absolutely chilling image of the dirty old man, when Noah Cross (played by John Huston) wraps his comforting arms around the young girl he has produced through incest with his own daughter.

Our conflicting social constructions of old age can be inferred from the fact that, when he became a senior citizen, Leslie began to get two kinds of unsolicited mailings. One type was for funerals and burial plots. The other was for medical aids to restore sexual potency and vigor. The choice seems to be clear—either go gentle into that good night by "prearranging" the formalities of your going forth or recapture the magical elixir of youth. "I am 76," one testimonial proclaims. "After the first 30 capsules, my penis became firm. I am proud of it and when I urinate I think I am holding someone else's" (71).

At the other end of the life span, one might think that the most familiar figure in society is the child. If the majority population cannot, except in nightmare, see itself in cripples and freaks and can regard old age only as a future burden it best not think about, we have all passed through childhood. But the very familiarity of that experience is itself deceptive. In growing up, we have betrayed the Peter Pan impulse. The adult must finally view the child, including the child he himself once was, as a stranger. The variety of attitudes adults have taken toward children can be seen in the changing image of the child in literature. (This is evident to anyone who has read "The Eye of Innocence.") One index of the duplicity and ambivalence in our view of children is the depiction of what we have come to call child abuse in novels written from the Victorian period on. The mixed reactions of righteous indignation and sadomasochistic fantasy produced by such depictions allow us, morally speaking, to have it both ways.

Psychic discrepancies also characterize the way in which our culture views physicians. Today medical dramas seem ubiquitous on the tube. From *General Hospital* in the daytime to *E. R.* at night, the doctor appears to have replaced the cowboy and challenged the lawyer and the cop as the most popular figure on television. Nevertheless, the good doctor we see in our living rooms several times a week also has his dark twin. Whether he be Roger Chillingworth, Dr. Rappacinni, Dr. Grimshawe, or Aylmer in Hawthorne's fiction; or, moving more fully into popular culture, a doctor named Frankenstein, Jekyll, Moreau, Caligari, Fu Manchu, Strangelove, No, or Hannibal Lecter, he is finally indistinguishable from the mad scientist of horror literature. The prototype for all such figures is Dr. Faustus. (Even though he is a professor rather than a physician, Faust seems more magician than scholar.) The futuristic dystopias of twentieth-century science fiction (e.g., Huxley's *Brave New World* and Burgess's *A Clockwork Orange*) are often presided over by bad doctors, who seek to remake humanity out of some Faustian lust for power and knowledge. The importance of physicians in our lives breeds both dependency and apprehension. Thus, at the deepest levels of imagination, we are never quite certain whether the truest image of the doctor is that of Albert Schweitzer or Joseph Mengele.

If the physician can be viewed as anything from a god to a devil, a similar ambivalence informs our view of nurses. Despite the increasing number of female doctors and male nurses, our imagination enforces the traditional sexual division of labor. In fact, our view of the nurse is in certain ways mixed up with the confusion with which we view our own mothers. (One definition of the verb "to nurse" is for the mother to suckle the child at her breast.) Historically, the image of the nurse as a ministering angel is relatively recent. (Prior to Florence Nightingale, the prototypical nurse more closely resembled Dickens's Sairey Gamp—an ignorant lowlife, who often did more harm than good.)

Even the erotic dream of the nurse as an easy lay (e.g., Catherine Barkley in Hemingway's *A Farewell to Arms*) is short-lived, "since nurses, once they are promoted from neophytes to Head Nurses, are no longer imagined as sexually vulnerable sisters but rather as equivocal, asexual mothers. Sometimes they are conceived as Good Mamas, but more often as bad ones: bullying, blustering, or condescending to the full-grown men helpless in their hands" (123). In our own time, Ken Kesey's Nurse Ratched is not only the mythic nurse par excellence, but also the symbol of hated matriarchy, of all that Huck Finn meant by the term "sivilization."

Fiedler concludes his book by examining two bioethical issues, which is to say dilemmas raised by advances in medical science. The first of these is organ transplants. How do we account for the relative paucity of organ donors when surveys indicate widespread support for the concept of transplantation? One can only imagine that, beneath the enlightened view that we should all be willing to give the gift of life, there is some deep archetypal hesitancy to do so. If we turn to popular literature, we find a possible explanation for this conundrum. When Mary Shelley's Dr. Frankenstein sought to create life from an assemblage of spare body parts, the result was a monster who ultimately destroyed his creator. Although Bram Stoker's Count Dracula is no physician, his horrors are motivated by the benign desire to make "undead." Other pop versions of Faust (H. G. Wells's Dr. Moreau and Robert Louis Stevenson's Dr. Jekyll) also wreak havoc when they try, with the best of possible intentions, to extend the boundaries of nature. What such cautionary tales suggest is that the quest for everlasting physical life is doomed from the start. At some point, we must heed the words of Shakespeare and "endure our going hence even as our coming hither."

Although organ transplants raise some troubling metaphysical questions, the aim of the procedure is ostensibly noble. The same cannot be said of the mind-set that Fiedler discusses in his concluding essay. He first became aware of what he calls "the tyranny of the normal" when he discovered that more imperfect newborns were "allowed to die" in modern hospitals than had been deliberately killed in the "Bad Old Days when they were exposed and left to perish by their fathers" (148). Medical technology has even enabled us to identify abnormal children in the womb and to destroy them through legalized abortion. It is one thing to use medical science to repair abnormalities (e.g., to separate Siamese twins); it is something else to say that a life is worth living only to the extent that it approximates some ideal physical norm. In researching his book on freaks, Leslie became convinced that many physically abnormal people lived happy and productive lives. Surveys indicate that even the vast majority of babies deformed by Thalidomide were later glad to have escaped the abortionist's knife.

Once we surrender to the eugenic tyranny of the normal, we may well be on a slippery slope. Hitler tried to create a master race by eliminating anyone who did not fit his ideal human norm. In America, and the rest of the "advanced" world, it is possible to move toward a similar goal through more innocuous means. Genetic engineering, which was once the stuff of science fiction, has become a medical reality. In less sophisticated times, it was common to see black people purchasing skin bleaches and hair straighteners and Jewish women turning to cosmetic surgeons for nose jobs. With breast implants, liposuction, and face-lifts, we can now remake our recalcitrant flesh into a caricature of perpetual youth. Provided we can afford to do so. Fiedler can imagine a future "in which the rich and privileged will have as one more, ultimate privilege the hope of a surgically, chemically, hormonally induced and preserved normality—with the promise of immortality by organ transplant just over the horizon. And the poor (who, we are assured on good authority, we always have with us) will be our sole remaining Freaks" (155).

I

As the millennium drew to a close, Leslie's work was winning belated appreciation from a variety of unexpected sources. Perhaps he had simply been around long enough that even those guardians of taste who used to denounce him had to concede his importance. (One is reminded of Ezra Pound writing of Walt Whitman: "I have detested you long enough.") The battle lines in academia are now drawn differently than they used to be. Like any other kind of politics, literary politics makes strange bedfellows. As Leslie has continued to avoid following the herd, he has sometimes found himself in company with those whom the latest herd has left behind.

The ascendancy of poststructuralist critical theory since Jacques Derrida gave his first lectures in America in the late 1960s has tended to minimize the differences among the various critical approaches that did battle in an earlier generation. When the American literature section of the MLA chose to give Leslie its Jay B. Hubbell Award for lifetime achievement in 1994, it wasn't because the old establishment had come around to his way of thinking and certainly not because he had joined them. It was simply the case that both parties shared a belief in the central importance of literature to life, and they were able to converse with each other in a common language.

In his acceptance speech (which failing health prevented him from delivering in person), Leslie felt compelled to remind his more conventional colleagues how much of a rebel he had been and still was. As with so much else, he felt ambivalent about his newfound "respectability." "I must confess to being pleased a little," he says, "but even more I am dismayed—wanting to cry out against all such misapprehensions, to protest that I have remained a jack of all fields and master of none, continuing to write and speak as I have from the first, about whatever moves me at the moment."[1]

If Leslie and the old establishment have not come closer to each other, the world around them has shifted to the point where those issues that used to divide them have come to seem less important than the common love of literature that unites them. In his speech accepting the Hubbell Award, he noted how disturbed he was to find that "I am now routinely quoted in jargon-ridden, reader-unfriendly works I cannot bring myself to read, and am listed honorifically in the kind of footnotes and bibliographies I have always eschewed" (24). The worst thing that Leslie can say about a fellow critic is not that he is wrong but that he does not enjoy literature. Since first encountering the newer critical theorists, he has believed that to be their primary failing. (In 1982, he told Patricia Ward Biederman, "I want to write as differently as possible from structuralist, poststructuralist, deconstructionist critics who write a private jargon, a secret language, hermetic code that's only available to the initiated."[2]) Many of the professional Americanists listening to his speech would have agreed.

Leslie's reaction was much less ambivalent when he was feted in a more personal way the following spring. For several years, Bruce Jackson and Diane Christian had wanted to organize a special tribute for their friend, but the grandiose plans urged on them by other members of the department never seemed to get off the ground. Finally, they secured funding from the university president's office and asked Leslie for the names of three people he would like to have speak on his behalf. The individuals he chose were Allen Ginsberg, Ishmael Reed, and Camille Paglia. As old friends, Ginsberg and Reed were obvious choices. Camille Paglia, however, was only a casual acquaintance at the time. She had first heard Leslie when he spoke at Yale during her undergraduate years. (As she recalls, no one from the English department was in attendance.) She later went on to become a controversial cultural critic—an independent feminist capable of stirring the wrath of the organized sisterhood. At the height of her celebrity in April 1995, she came to Buffalo to honor one of the seminal influences on her career. In a blurb for a paperback reprint of *Love and Death in the American Novel*—published three years earlier—she had said: "Fiedler created an American intellectual style that was truncated by the invasion of faddish French theory in the '70s and '80s. Let's turn back to Fiedler and begin again."

1. Leslie Fiedler, "Hubbell Acceptance Speech," 24. Subsequent references will be cited parenthetically in the text.
2. Patricia Ward Biederman, "The Critic as Outlaw," 11.

Three years after the Buffalo "Fiedlerfest," the National Book Critics Circle gave Leslie its Ivan Sandorf Award for lifetime achievement in a public ceremony at the NYU Law School on March 23, 1998. (This was sixty years after his unheralded graduation from a much less distinguished branch of NYU.) The following year, he received a similar career award from PEN West, a regional branch of the famed international association of writers. The judges cited Leslie's "fierceness as a critic and . . . his belief that culture speaks to an entire populace, a belief borne out by his own engaged prose style." While gratefully accepting all of these awards, Leslie couldn't help noticing that these organizations were "giving a prize for a whole body of work, of which no single essay ever received such a prize or even very high praise."[3]

Unfortunately, this overdue appreciation from certain segments of the literary establishment has coincided with Leslie's virtual disappearance from the canon of modern criticism as it is represented by standard textbooks in the field. When I entered the "profession" as an undergraduate English major in the early 1970s, anthologies of criticism typically included either "Come Back to the Raft Ag'in, Huck Honey!" or "Archetype and Signature." This is no longer the case. More recent anthologies tend to focus on structuralism, deconstruction, feminism, new historicism, ethnic studies, and reader-response theory. Usually, there is an historical section or two, featuring old-timers from Aristotle to the New Critics. When myth criticism is included at all, Northrop Frye is invariably the representative figure. It is not just that Leslie Fiedler is not fashionable these days, the standard texts seem intent on denying that he was ever of importance.[4]

The irony of the situation is that Fiedler's influence on much of contemporary criticism has been so fully absorbed that it tends to be invisible. In a discerning tribute to him, Susan Gubar suggests that feminist criticism, queer theory, African American Studies, Native American Studies, and Jewish Studies (to name only five fields) would be much poorer had he never written. "Yet probably many of the practitioners in these fields would not feel the need to name Fiedler as a progenitor or adopt him as a precursor." If anything, he might seem to them, not so much a father as "a vaguely embarrassing because unpredictable, irreverent, irascible second cousin twice removed." As he was

---

3. Letter from Leslie Fiedler to Mark Royden Winchell, June 14, 2000.

4. When I took a course in twentieth-century literary criticism in the spring of 1970, Fiedler was present in all three textbooks we used. "Archetype and Signature" was reprinted in Walter K. Gordon's *Literature in Critical Perspective: An Anthology* (New York: Appleton-Century-Crofts, 1968). In Wilbur S. Scott's *Five Approaches of Literary Criticism* (New York: Collier, 1962), he was represented by "Come Back to the Raft Ag'in, Huck Honey!" Even Walter Sutton's historical text *Modern American Criticism* (Englewood Cliffs, N.J.: Prentice Hall, 1963) devotes four pages to a discussion of *Love and Death in the American Novel*. In contrast, Fiedler is completely absent from the several more-recent texts available for teaching such a course.

preparing to review Fiedler's *Collected Essays* in 1971, Charles R. Larson had occasion to read several M.A. exams in American literature. It came as no surprise to him that the critic most frequently cited was Leslie Fiedler. Perhaps just as predictable was the fact that the one paper that did not mention him directly simply cribbed his ideas without attribution.[5]

I suspect that the scholars who owe most to Fiedler's groundbreaking work are feminist critics of American literature. With a few honorable exceptions (principally Susan Gubar and Ann Douglas), they have been reticent about admitting their debt. Such critics will typically mention Fiedler's name in an essay and then proceed to ignore or distort the arguments he makes about the very issues they are discussing. A prime example is Carolyn Heilbrun's "The Masculine Wilderness of the American Novel." Published in the January 29, 1972, issue of the *Saturday Review,* this essay begins with a discussion of James Dickey's novel *Deliverance.* "Whatever Dickey's intention," Heilbrun writes, "his achievement is one more version—dare we hope it is the last?—of what Leslie Fiedler identified for us more than a decade ago in *Death and Love in the American Novel* [*sic*]: the woman-despising American dream."[6]

One who relied solely on Heilbrun's essay would have no way of knowing what Fiedler thought about this American dream. In his book, however, he makes clear his belief that the failure of the American novel to deal with mature heterosexual love is one of its major limitations. Heilbrun obviously agrees. She writes, for example, that "American novels are not in the mainstream; they are outside it; turning away from fully human women whom the great non-American novels have seen as a redeeming force. . . . —Becky Sharpe, Jane Eyre, Madame Bovary, Anna Karenina." Unfortunately, this is presented as an original insight on Heilbrun's part. Obviously, she has misremembered more than the title of Fiedler's book, because later she writes, "No one, certainly no American critic, has noticed that . . . the novel is the great androgynous form, the embodiment of the peculiar human need to join the sexes in a shared destiny, whether through passion or work or conversation." Heilbrun does make an exception for Hawthorne's *The Scarlet Letter.* According to her, in "the America James fled," that book "stands isolated as the one classic American novel that is not a fantasy of two or more men fleeing women, borne by natural forces down some river toward deliverance."[7]

At this point, the astute reader might wonder: where have I heard all this before? Try the first chapter of *Love and Death in the American Novel:*

5. Susan Gubar, "A Fiedler Brood," 169. Charles R. Larson, "The Good Bad Boy and Guru of American Letters."

6. Carolyn Heilbrun, "The Masculine Wilderness of the American Novel," 41.

7. Ibid., 44, 41–42.

Where is our *Madame Bovary,* our *Anna Karenina,* our *Pride and Prejudice* or *Vanity Fair?* Among our classic novels, at least those before Henry
James, who stands so oddly between our own traditions and the European
ones we rejected or recast, the best attempt at dealing with love is *The Scarlet Letter,* in which the physical consummation of adultery has occurred
and all passion burned away before the novel proper begins. For the rest,
there are *Moby-Dick* and *Huckleberry Finn, The Last of the Mohicans, The
Red Badge of Courage,* the stories of Edgar Allan Poe—books that turn
from society to nature or nightmare out of a desperate need to avoid the
facts of wooing, marriage, and child-bearing. (25)

Ever since its publication in 1978, Judith Fetterley's *The Resisting Reader*
has been considered a watershed in feminist criticism of American fiction.
Although some of her readings seem tendentious and wrongheaded, she has
many perceptive things to say about Washington Irving's "Rip Van Winkle." Fetterley begins her discussion of Irving's story with epigraphs from
Philip Young and Leslie Fiedler. This makes sense, in that Young and Fiedler
were the two critics who had previously had the most to say about "Rip Van
Winkle."[8] Although both dealt with the story in terms of myth, the difference
in their perspectives was more important than the similarity. Young operated
as a conventional anthropologist, cataloging various sources of the Rip myth.
While paying due homage to Young, Fiedler contends that "what is remarkable and significant . . . is not the European past, but the American future of
the tale: the differences of Irving's version from its presumed original and the
surmised antecedents of that" (*RVA,* 56).

Fetterley obviously agrees with Fiedler's emphasis because, like him, she
focuses on Irving's original contribution to the tale of the enchanted sleeper—
the battle of the sexes. As she points out, "the German tale on which he based
'Rip' has no equivalent for Dame Van Winkle; she is Irving's creation and addition. . . . What drives Rip away from the village and up into the mountains
and what makes him a likely partaker of the sleep-inducing liquor is his wife;
all the ills from which Rip seeks escape are symbolically located in the person
of the offending Dame Van Winkle."[9] Ten years earlier, in *The Return of the
Vanishing American,* Fiedler had made essentially the same observation: "It is
Irving who invents the character of Rip's wife and his difficult relationship
with her, Irving who first portrays Dame Van Winkle as an intolerably effi-
cient and shrewish wife" (56).

Fetterley also recognizes the durability of Irving's prototype in American
culture. "Like his more famous successor, Huckleberry Finn," she writes, "Rip

8. For Young's essay, see Philip Young, *Three Bags Full,* 204–31.
9. Judith Fetterley, *The Resisting Reader: A Feminist Approach to American Fiction,* 3.

wages a subterranean and passive revolt against the superego and its impera-
tives." The image of the woman-persecuted male has even survived into the
late twentieth century: "It is not hard—there are lots of pointers along the
way—to get from Irving's Dame to Ken Kesey's Big Nurse, who is bad because she represents a system whose illegitimacy is underscored by the fact
that *she,* a woman, represents it."[10] Again, we find Fiedler having said much
the same things a decade earlier: "Rip . . . is the first of those escapees from
what women call responsibility, the first American character shiftless enough
to be loved by the audience which loves Cooper's Natty Bumppo, Melville's
Ishmael, and Mark Twain's Huck Finn, as well as Saul Bellow's Henderson
the Rain King and the hero of Ken Kesey's *One Flew over the Cuckoo's Nest"*
(*RVA,* 60).

Inattentive readers—as well as those who know Fiedler's views only at second hand—often assume that he is celebrating the motifs that he identifies
in American fiction. Such an inference simply ignores the critic's essential ambivalence. Although he is capable of being moved by our "boys' books," Fiedler
also knows where they fall short of full maturity. (Remember, many of the
early reviewers of *Love and Death in the American Novel* thought that he was
trashing his own tradition, fouling his own nest.) Ironically, when feminist
critics such as Carolyn Heilbrun and Judith Fetterley set Fiedler up as the
patriarchal straw man against whom they are doing battle, their arguments
invariably echo points that he himself had made with greater subtlety and nu-
ance.

When the feminist critics go on the affirmative and try to promote a female
countertradition, Fiedler is no longer necessary as a straw man. It is, therefore,
all too easy to forget how much of *Love and Death in the American Novel* is devoted to reviving the reputations of nineteenth-century women writers, who
are as reviled in our own time as they were lauded in their own. Although
Fiedler can see their shortcomings as well as he can the limitations of the
canonical male novelists he discusses, he treats both categories of writers with
respect. To her credit, Susan Gubar acknowledges that Fiedler's "treatment
of *Uncle Tom's Cabin* helped put Harriet Beecher Stowe's name back into the
principal position in twentieth-century literary history that reflects her central-
ity in the nineteenth-century literary scene."[11] Unfortunately, not all of Stowe's
defenders have been so ready to acknowledge Fiedler's efforts on her behalf.

Although a committed minority of critics have always been willing to defend *Uncle Tom's Cabin,* its place of honor in the feminist canon probably
dates from 1978, when Jane P. Tompkins published her much-heralded essay

10. Ibid., 6.
11. Gubar, "Fiedler Brood," 167.

"Sentimental Power: *Uncle Tom's Cabin* and the Politics of Literary History." Tompkins begins by decrying the patriarchal view of American fiction she herself had accepted unquestioningly as a graduate student. Now she asks us to view the popular female novelists of nineteenth-century America as not just a "damned mob of scribbling women," as Hawthorne had resentfully called them, but as exemplars of an entirely different approach to literature. Although some observers might argue that it was the hegemony of modernism and New Criticism that doomed Stowe and her sisters to excommunication from the High Church of literature, Tompkins is convinced that it was all a male plot. She is even willing to name names, arguing that "the tradition of Perry Miller, F. O. Matthiessen, Harry Levin, Richard Chase, R. W. B. Lewis, Yvor Winters, and Henry Nash Smith has prevented even committed feminists from recognizing and asserting the *value* of a powerful and specifically female novelistic tradition."[12]

Is it mere oversight that the one major Americanist whose name is conspicuously absent from Tompkins's list is that of Leslie Fiedler? To have included him would have been to admit that there was one male critic who took the women seriously. Although Tompkins seems to owe very little to what Fiedler said about *Uncle Tom's Cabin* in *Love and Death in the American Novel,* her views on Stowe and the American canon are remarkably similar to those he would publish in monograph form as *The Inadvertent Epic* in 1980. One might even suspect Fiedler of having been influenced by Tompkins, if it were not for the fact that he had been voicing his most recent assessment of *Uncle Tom's Cabin* in lectures and television appearances since at least the mid-1970s. What we have is "confluence" rather than influence, but one that Tompkins is loath to admit. In twenty-two pages of text and over thirty footnotes, she does not even mention Fiedler's name.[13]

Not only does Fiedler elevate Harriet Beecher Stowe to parity with Mark Twain, his view of the politics of canon formation would seem to put him in the feminist camp. In *What Was Literature?* he looks back with a skeptical eye on some of the critical assumptions underlying even so radical a book as *Love and Death.* Although he had written about the women novelists his fellow male critics tended to ignore, he had been too much the prisoner of elitist assumptions about them. He had, for example, faulted Harriet Beecher Stowe for a lack of tragic ambivalence and radical protest, without ever questioning the

12. Jane P. Tompkins, "Sentimental Power: *Uncle Tom's Cabin* and the Politics of Literary History," 502–3.

13. Elizabeth Ammons, who edited the Norton critical edition of *Uncle Tom's Cabin,* which includes Tompkins's essay, publishes nothing by Fiedler. Although this particular volume appeared in 1994, the only reference to Fiedler in Ammons's "selected bibliography" is to the rather minor essay "New England and the Invention of the South." Fiedler's more significant statements in *Love and Death in the American Novel* and *What Was Literature?* remain essentially invisible.

supreme importance of these qualities. One might even imagine Jane Tomp-kins applauding what he has to say about the guardians of high culture. "These guardians have traditionally been white Anglo-Saxon Protestants," he writes, "more often than not genteel, almost invariably straight males or closet gays. Even when vulgarians of lesser breeds or women have more recently begun to make it into the Old Boys Club, they have done so by introjecting the values of their predecessors, proving, therefore, quite as incapable of judging fairly works produced by and for culturally marginal groups in our society, including those to which they themselves belong" (156).

Having made such an observation, Fiedler does not feel compelled to right the balance with reverse discrimination. To replace the old canon with an op-posite one that is just as rigid would simply promote ideology at the expense of art. The myth criticism that Fiedler advocates is a boon not just to previously excluded women and minorities but also to those straight WASP males who managed to write memorable works of literature while shunning the strictures of modernism. Whatever the merits or limitations of his approach to criticism, Fiedler does not seem to be motivated by political ideology or tribal loyalty. If he is preaching a party line, it is a party of one.

II

To be sure, it took no great courage or originality to attack modernism in the 1960s. By then, most observers realized that the literary revolution of the early twentieth century had simply run out of steam. Even if it had been a victim of its own success, it had no more battles left to win. Certainly, part of the problem lay with the inherent obsolescence of the term itself. The concept of modernism had existed in the English tradition at least since Swift's "The Battle of the Books." What made the modernism of the early twentieth cen-tury different was that, in addition to mere novelty, it introduced the notion of apocalypse. Not only was the contemporary epoch different from anything that went before, it was also the end of the road. If the Renaissance saw civiliza-tion emerge from the Dark Ages, we seemed to be headed into another dark age—one characterized by despair not faith. This was the thematic statement made by much modernist literature, but, even more important, it was also the testimony of the experimental and discontinuous approach to literary form one found in modernist fiction and poetry.

Of course, no literature that is predicated on the expectation of apocalypse can last indefinitely. Being a remarkably resilient people, the consumers of highbrow literature took the decline of Christian humanism in stride, much as if they were witnessing the cancellation of a popular sitcom or the demise of a sports dynasty. After awhile, even the stylistic innovations of modernism (distorted chronology, unreliable narration, fragmented language) were accepted as conventions or—worse yet—clichés.

The term *postmodernism* was simple enough to coin. It was somewhat more difficult to figure out what it ought to refer to. One trend—influenced by such older writers as Beckett, Kafka, Hesse, and Borges—led toward neofabulism. Fiedler initially endorsed this trend with his early support for the work of John Barth and John Hawkes. It soon became apparent, however, that this variety of postmodernism was, at bottom, a desperate parody of modernism. (Barth himself characterized his fiction as "novels which imitate the form of the Novel, by an author who imitates the role of Author."[14]) If the early modernists undermined epistemological certitude, they were at least attacking the concept of an existent truth; having discarded that concept from the outset, the neofabulists were content to play word games. It soon became an open question as to which would wear out first—the genre itself or the reading public's patience with it.

If the central works of modernism had the advantage of representing a genuine revolution of consciousness (rather than exhaustion with a past revolution), they were also blessed with a generation of critics who made these difficult texts more reader-friendly. I am referring not so much to a critical system or methodology as to a kind of voice and sensibility. From the New York intellectuals to the southern New Critics, the interpreters of modernism made their subject matter accessible to the intelligent general reader. (That is perhaps why the southerners and the New Yorkers could publish so easily in each other's magazines.) In contrast, the critical interpreters of postmodernism are all too often more unreadable than even the primary works they are discussing. Professional academics can get tenure and promotion by mastering the code, but they seem frequently to be speaking only to each other. Now, as never before, our culture needs a talented amateur critic with no ideological turf to defend.

In trying to identify a literature appropriate to our age, Fiedler has had the good sense to realize that you can't go beyond modernism. (That road disappears into a black hole.) In fact, much of the literature he extols (true popular literature, not just high-camp parodies of pop) is decidedly *premodernist* in its approach to literary form. From the beginning of time, the general public has preferred stories with a plot and songs with a tune. If anything, it is a conservative—even counterrevolutionary—position to argue that such artifacts, when they have pleased many and pleased long, merit the critic's attention. This insight has allowed Fiedler to champion works that have never

14. John Barth, "The Literature of Exhaustion," 33.

been in the canon of high art (*Gone with the Wind, Dracula,* the classic works of science fiction). But it has also allowed him to argue for the recanonization of writers whom the modernists toppled from their pedestals. Anyone can be an iconoclast these days; it takes a true original to restore a fallen icon to his place of former glory. This is what Fiedler has done for Henry Wadsworth Longfellow and a host of other writers who once crossed the border and closed the gap between elite and popular culture.[15]

In the days before "critical theory" and "cultural studies," the public intellectual was a recognizable presence in American life. Leslie Fiedler may have been a bit wilder and more provocative than the rest of the breed, but he was not an unfamiliar character type. Writing in one of Leslie's old publication venues, *Commentary,* Joseph Epstein describes such a figure: "Unlike the scholar . . . , the intellectual did not work with primary sources, . . . did not feel the need to back up his assertions with footnotes, did not seek out new factual material that might change the shape of a subject. . . . The natural penchant of the intellectual was not to go deeper but wider—to turn the criticism of literature or art or the movies or politics into broader statements about culture."[16] As his body of work (up through and including *Tyranny of the Normal*) amply demonstrates, Leslie is among the few active writers whom this description still seems to fit.

Leslie's characterization of himself as "a teacher who writes" is not a description of two discrete activities. On the page, he has a presence not unlike that of a great performer. It should come as no surprise that he spent his adolescence speaking on street corners as well as hanging around libraries. If so much current critical discourse sounds as if it exists only on the page, there is an unmistakably human voice behind Leslie's utterances. We may have reached a point in literary studies when the rare pleasure of hearing such a voice makes it finally unimportant whether we agree with what it has to say.

In one of her more perceptive essays, Joan Didion has said, "Certain places seem to exist because someone has written about them. . . . A place belongs forever to whoever claims it hardest, remembers it most obsessively, wrenches it from itself, shapes it, renders it, loves it so radically that he remakes it in his image."[17] Ever since Aristotle wrote about *Oedipus Rex,* it seems that certain realms of literature also belong to certain critics. In our own time, the metaphysical poets have become the property of T. S. Eliot. Yoknapatawpha County belongs not just to William Faulkner but to Cleanth Brooks. At

---

15. See Leslie Fiedler, "The Children's Hour: or, The Return of the Vanishing Longfellow: Some Reflections on the Future of Poetry."

16. Joseph Epstein, "Intellectuals—Public and Otherwise," 48.

17. Joan Didion, *The White Album,* 146.

least one generation of readers first saw the early modernist writers through the eyes of Edmund Wilson. And for more than half a century now, the archetypes of American literature have borne the signature of a runaway boy from Newark—dreaming dreams too good to be true.

BIBLIOGRAPHY

Primary Works

BOOKS

Back to China. New York: Stein & Day, 1965.

Being Busted. New York: Stein & Day, 1969.

The Collected Essays of Leslie Fiedler. 2 vols. New York: Stein & Day, 1971.

The Continuing Debate: Essays on Education. With Jacob Vinocur. New York: St. Martin's, 1964.

Fiedler on the Roof: Essays on Literature and Jewish Identity. Boston: David R. Godine, 1991.

A Fiedler Reader. New York: Stein & Day, 1977.

Freaks: Myths and Images of the Secret Self. New York: Simon & Schuster, 1978.

The Inadvertent Epic: From "Uncle Tom's Cabin" to "Roots." New York: Simon & Schuster, 1980.

In Dreams Awake: A Historical-Critical Anthology of Science Fiction. New York: Dell, 1975.

"John Donne's *Songs and Sonnets:* A Reinterpretation in Light of Their Traditional Backgrounds." Ph.D. diss., University of Wisconsin, 1941.

The Last Jew in America. New York: Stein & Day, 1966.

Love and Death in the American Novel. Rev. ed. New York: Stein & Day, 1966. Reprint, New York: Anchor, 1992.

The Messengers Will Come No More. New York: Stein & Day, 1974.

A New Fiedler Reader. Amherst, N.Y.: Prometheus Books, 1999.

Nude Croquet: The Stories of Leslie A. Fiedler. New York: Stein & Day, 1969.

Olaf Stapeldon: A Man Divided. New York: Oxford University Press, 1983.

The Return of the Vanishing American. New York: Stein & Day, 1968.

The Second Stone: A Love Story. New York: Stein & Day, 1963.

The Stranger in Shakespeare. New York: Stein & Day, 1972.

Tyranny of the Normal: Essays on Bioethics, Theology and Myth. Boston: David R. Godine, 1996.

Waiting for the End: The Crisis in American Culture and a Report on Twentieth-Century American Literature. New York: Dell, 1965.

What Was Literature? Class Culture and Mass Society. New York: Simon & Schuster, 1982.

343

ESSAYS, STORIES, DRAMA

"The Bearded Virgin and the Blind God." *Kenyon Review* 5 (summer 1953): 540–51.

"The Children's Hour: or, The Return of the Vanishing Longfellow: Some Reflections on the Future of Poetry." In *Liberations: New Essays on the Humanities in Revolution,* edited by Ihab Hassan. Middletown, Conn.: Wesleyan University Press, 1971.

"The Criticism of Science Fiction." In *Coordinates: Placing Science Fiction and Fantasy,* edited by George E. Slusser, Eric S. Rabkin, and Robert Scholes. Carbondale: Southern Illinois University Press, 1983.

"The Divine Stupidity of Kurt Vonnegut." *Esquire,* September 1970.

"Fulbright I: Italy 1952." In *The Fulbright Difference,* edited by Richard T. Arndt and David Lee Rubin. New Brunswick, N.J.: Transaction, 1993.

"Getting It Right: The Flag Raisings at Iwo Jima." Typescript in the author's possession.

"Hubbell Acceptance Speech." In *Leslie Fiedler and American Culture,* edited by Steven G. Kellman and Irving Malin.

"Literature as an Institution: The View from 1980." In *English Literature: Opening up the Canon,* edited by Leslie A. Fiedler and Houston A. Baker. Baltimore: Johns Hopkins University Press, 1981.

"New England and the Invention of the South." In *American Literature and the New England Heritage,* edited by James Nagel and Richard Astro. New York: Garland, 1981.

"Remembering Iwo Jima: A Trip through Time." Typescript in the author's possession.

"Second Thoughts on *Love and Death in the American Novel:* My First Gothic Novel." *Novel: A Forum on Fiction* 1 (fall 1967): 8–11.

"Toward an Amateur Criticism." *Kenyon Review* 2 (autumn 1950): 561–74.

"What Can We Do about Fagin? The Jew-Villain in Western Tradition." *Commentary,* May 1949, 411–18.

Secondary Sources

Aldridge, John W. *The Party at Cranton.* New York: David McKay, 1960.

Alter, Robert. Review of *The Messengers Will Come No More. New York Times Book Review,* September 29, 1974, 5–6.

Appleton, Wanda H. *When I Am King.* Los Angeles: Appleton Films, 1982.

Atlas, James. *Bellow: A Biography.* New York: Random House, 2000.

Barth, John. "The Accidental Mentor." In *Leslie Fiedler and American Culture,* edited by Steven G. Kellman and Irving Malin.

———. "The Literature of Exhaustion." *Atlantic Monthly,* August 1967, 29–34.

"Being Unbusted." *Time,* July 17, 1972, 50.

Bellman, Samuel Irving. "The American Artist as European Frontiersman: Leslie Fiedler's *The Second Stone.*" *Critique: Studies in Modern Fiction* (winter 1963): 131–43.

Biederman, Patricia Ward. "Leslie Fiedler: The Critic as Outlaw." *Buffalo Courier-Express,* March 7, 1982, 9–11, 13–15.

Bloom, Alexander. *Prodigal Sons: The New York Intellectuals and Their World.* New York: Oxford University Press, 1986.

Brooks, Cleanth. "A Note on the Limits of 'History' and the Limits of 'Criticism.'" In *Seventeenth-Century English Poetry,* edited by William R. Keast. New York: Oxford University Press, 1962.

———. *The Well Wrought Urn: Studies in the Structure of Poetry.* New York: Reynall & Hitchcock, 1947.

Bryden, Ronald. *The Unfinished Hero and Other Essays.* London: Faber & Faber, 1969.

Campbell, Joseph. *The Hero with a Thousand Faces.* Princeton: Princeton University Press, 1949.

Chase, Richard. "Leslie Fiedler and American Culture." *Chicago Review* 4 (autumn–winter 1960): 8–18.

Clark, Tom. *Charles Olson: The Allegories of a Poet's Life.* New York: Norton, 1991.

Clausen, Christopher. "Reading Closely Again." *Commentary,* February 1997, 54–57.

Cowley, Malcolm. "Exploring a World of Nightmares." *New York Times Book Review,* March 27, 1960.

Cox, James M. "Celebrating Leslie Fiedler." In *Leslie Fiedler and American Culture,* edited by Steven G. Kellman and Irving Malin.

Crane, R. S. "The Critical Monism of Cleanth Brooks." In *Critics and Criticism,* edited by R. S. Crane et al. Chicago: University of Chicago Press, 1952.

Daniels, Guy. "The Sorrows of Baro Finkelstone." *New Republic,* May 22, 1965, 25–27.

DeMott, Benjamin. "The Negative American." In *Hells and Benefits: A Report on American Minds, Matters, and Possibilities.* New York: Basic Books, 1962.

———. "A Talk with Leslie Fiedler." *New York Times Book Review,* March 5, 1978.

Desautels, L. C. "Upon the Burning of His House." *Plaza* 4 (autumn 1998): 22.

Dickstein, Morris. *Gates of Eden: American Culture in the Sixties.* New York: Basic Books, 1977.

Didion, Joan. *The White Album.* New York: Simon & Schuster, 1979.

Dorrien, Gary. *The Neoconservative Mind: Politics, Culture, and the War of Ideology.* Philadelphia: Temple University Press, 1993.

Du Bois, W. E. B. *The Souls of Black Folk.* 1903. Reprint, New York: Dover, 1994.

Dunne, John Gregory. *True Confessions.* New York: Dutton, 1978.

Epstein, Joseph. "Intellectuals—Public and Otherwise." *Commentary,* May 2000, 46–51.

Fahringer, Herald Price. "Appellants' Brief in the *People of the State of New York vs. Leslie A. Fiedler and Margaret Fiedler.*"

Fetterley, Judith. *The Resisting Reader: A Feminist Approach to American Fiction.* Bloomington: Indiana University Press, 1978.

Fiedler, Sally A. *Eleanor Mooseheart.* Buffalo: Weird Sister Press, 1992.

Fitzgerald, F. Scott. *The Great Gatsby.* 1925. Reprint, New York: Scribner's, 1995.

Fitzgerald, Robert. "A Place of Refreshment." In *Randall Jarrell: 1914–1965,* edited by Robert Lowell, Peter Taylor, and Robert Penn Warren. New York: Farrar, Straus & Giroux, 1967.

Frye, Northrop. *Anatomy of Criticism: Four Essays.* Princeton: Princeton University Press, 1957.

Gates, David. "Fiedler's Utopian Vision." *Newsweek,* January 9, 1984, 11.

Gilbert, Sandra M. "An Interview with Ruth Stone, 1973." In *The House Is Made of Poetry: The Art of Ruth Stone,* edited by Wendy Barker and Sandra M. Gilbert. Carbondale: Southern Illinois University Press, 1996.

Gioia, Dana. "Longfellow in the Aftermath of Modernism." In *The Columbia History of American Poetry,* edited by Jay Parini and Brett C. Miller. New York: Columbia University Press, 1993.

Gubar, Susan. "A Fiedler Brood." In *Leslie Fiedler and American Culture,* edited by Steven G. Kellman and Irving Malin.

Haley, Alex. *Roots: The Saga of an American Family.* New York: Dell, 1976.

Heilbrun, Carolyn. "The Masculine Wilderness of the American Novel." *Saturday Review,* January 29, 1972, 41–44.

Jackson, Bruce. "Buffalo English: Literary Glory Days at UB." *Buffalo Beat,* March 4, 1999.

Janssen, Marian. *The Kenyon Review, 1939–1970: A Critical History.* Baton Rouge: Louisiana State University Press, 1990.

Jarrell, Mary, ed. *Randall Jarrell's Letters: An Autobiographical and Literary Selection.* Boston: Houghton Mifflin, 1985.

Jay, Paul, ed. *The Selected Correspondence of Kenneth Burke and Malcolm Cowley, 1915–1981.* New York: Viking, 1988.

Jorgenson, Chester E. "William Ellery Leonard: An Appraisal." In *Studies in Honor of John Wilcox,* edited by A. Dayle Wallace and Woodbrun O. Ross. Detroit: Wayne State University Press, 1958.

Kazin, Alfred. "Honoring the Dark Impulse." *Atlantic,* January 1983, 92–93, 96.

Kellman, Steven G. "The Importance of *Being Busted.*" In *Leslie Fiedler and American Culture,* edited by Steven G. Kellman and Irving Malin. Newark: University of Delaware Press, 1999.

Kenner, Hugh. "Who Was Leslie Fiedler?" *Harper's,* November 1982, 69–73.

Kristol, Irving. *Neoconservatism: The Autobiography of an Idea: Selected Essays 1949–1995.* New York: Free Press, 1995.

———. "A Traitor to His Class?" *Kenyon Review* 2 (summer 1960): 505–9.

Larson, Charles R. "The Good Bad Boy of American Letters." *Saturday Review,* December 25, 1971, 27–28, 35.

———. "Leslie Fiedler: The Critic and the Myth, the Critic as Myth." *Literary Review* 4 (winter 1970–1971): 133–43.

Leitch, Vincent B. *American Literary Criticism from the Thirties to the Eighties.* New York: Columbia University Press, 1988.

Leonard, William Ellery. *The Locomotive God.* New York: Century, 1927.

LeSeuer, Joseph. "Theatre: *My Faust.*" *Village Voice,* February 16, 1967, 20.

Lewis, R. W. B. *The American Adam: Innocence, Tragedy and Tradition in the Nineteenth Century.* Chicago: University of Chicago Press, 1955.

Looby, Christopher. " 'Innocent Homosexuality': The Fiedler Thesis in Retrospect." In *"Adventures of Huckleberry Finn": A Case Study in Critical Controversy,* edited by Gerald Graff and James Phelan. Boston: St. Martin's, 1995.

Lynn, Kenneth S. *The Air-Line to Seattle: Studies in Literary and Historical Writing about America.* Chicago: University of Chicago Press, 1983.

———. "Back to the Raft." *Commentary,* January 1983, 66, 68.

Mailer, Norman. *The Armies of the Night: History as a Novel/The Novel as History.* New York: New American Library, 1968.

Marx, Leo. *The Machine in the Garden: Technology and the Pastoral Ideal in America.* New York: Oxford University Press, 1964.

Mitchell, Margaret. *Gone with the Wind.* 1936. Reprint, New York: Avon, 1973.

Nuhn, Ferner. "Teaching American Literature in American Colleges." *American Mercury* 3 (1928): 328–31.

O'Faolain, Nuala. *Are You Somebody? The Accidental Memoir of a Dublin Woman.* New York: Holt, 1996.

Paterno, Joe, with Bernard Asbell. *Paterno: By the Book.* New York: Random House, 1989.

Podhoretz, Norman. *Doings and Undoings: The Fifties and after in American Writing.* New York: Farrar, Straus & Giroux, 1964.

"Potted Ivy." *Time,* May 19, 1967, 98, 100.

Radosh, Ronald, and Joyce Milton. *The Rosenberg File.* 2d ed. New Haven: Yale University Press, 1997.

Raine, Kathleen. "Extracts from Unpublished Memoirs." In *William Empson: The Man and His Work,* edited by Roma Gill. London: Routledge and Kegan Paul, 1974.

Rexroth, Kenneth. "Ids and Animuses." *New York Times Book Review,* March 17, 1968, 4, 47.

Rosenberg, Harold. "Couch Liberalism and the Guilty Past." In *The Tradition of the New.* New York: Horizon Press, 1959.

Seaton, James. *Cultural Conservatism, Political Liberalism: From Criticism to Cultural Studies.* Ann Arbor: University of Michigan Press, 1996.

Spears, Monroe K. *American Ambitions: Essays on Literary and Cultural Themes.* Baltimore: Johns Hopkins University Press, 1987.

Stone, Ruth. "Turn Your Eyes Away." In *New American Poets of the '90s,* edited by Jack Myers and Roger Weingarten. Boston: David R. Godine, 1991.

Thomson, Rosemarie Garland, ed. *Freakery: Cultural Spectacles of the Extraordinary Body.* New York: New York University Press, 1996.

Tompkins, Jane P. "Sentimental Power: *Uncle Tom's Cabin* and the Politics of Literary History." In *Uncle Tom's Cabin.* Norton Critical Edition, edited by Elizabeth Ammons. New York: Norton, 1994.

Twain, Mark. *Adventures of Huckleberry Finn.* 1884. Reprint, New York: St. Martin's, 1995.

Viereck, Peter. *The Shame and Glory of the Intellectuals.* Boston: Houghton Mifflin, 1953.

Wald, Alan. *The New York Intellectuals: The Rise and Decline of the Anti-Stalinist Left from the 1930s to the 1980s.* Chapel Hill: University of North Carolina Press, 1987.

Watt, Ian. *The Rise of the Novel.* Berkeley: University of California Press, 1967.

Webster, Grant. "Leslie Fiedler: Adolescent and Jew as Critic." *Denver Quarterly* (winter 1967): 44–53.

Weinstein, Allen. *Perjury: The Hiss-Chambers Case.* New York: Knopf, 1978.

Whittemore, Reed. "Tough Martyr." *New Republic,* April 18, 1970, 27–28.

Williams, Tennessee. *Cat on a Hot Tin Roof.* In *The Theatre of Tennessee Williams.* Vol. 3. New York: New Directions, 1971.

Wilson, Edmund. *To the Finland Station: A Study in the Writing and Acting of History.* New York: Harcourt, Brace, 1940.

Wimsatt, W. K. "Northrop Frye: Criticism as Myth." In *Northrop Frye in Modern Criticism: Selected Papers from the English Institute,* edited by Murray Krieger. New York: Columbia University Press, 1966.

Wimsatt, W. K., with Monroe C. Beardsley. *The Verbal Icon: Studies in the Meaning of Poetry.* Lexington: University Press of Kentucky, 1954.

Wimsatt, W. K., and Cleanth Brooks. *Literary Criticism: A Short History*. New York: Knopf, 1957.

Young, Philip. "Fallen from Time: Rip Van Winkle." In *Three Bags Full: Essays in American Fiction*. New York: Harcourt, Brace, 1967.